EDIE CAY

Edie Cay [signature]

A LADY'S FINDER

To all the people who live somewhere in between

CAST OF CHARACTERS

Lord Lorian, earl, father of Lady Lydia and Lady Agnes

Lady Lorian, countess, mother of Lady Lydia and Lady Agnes

Lady Agnes Somerset, youngest daughter of the earl of Lorian

Lady Lydia/Mrs. Arthur, eldest daughter of the earl of Lorian, married to the stockbroker and champion prizefighter John Arthur

Vasily, driver and friend to Lord Lorian from their war days.

Mary Franklin, upper class miss and close friend of Agnes. Long-lost half-sister of Os Worley.

James Wallingford, Lord Andrepont, viscount, nephew of Lady Lorian, cousin to Lydia and Agnes

Lady Andrepont, viscountess, mother of Lord Andrepont, sister to Lady Lorian

Lord Andrepont (deceased), father of the current viscount, husband to Lady Andrepont.

Margaret Miller, half-sister to James Wallingford, daughter of the deceased Lord Andrepont and a maid. Taken in by Lady Andrepont, married to Lord Elshire.

Lord Elshire, earl, married to Margaret Miller, half-sister to James Wallingford, cousin by marriage to Ladies Lydia and Agnes

Henry Parks, Lord Kinsley, marquis, known as "Bill" in some circles, good friend of Andrepont and Jack About Town. Married to Rose, Lady Kinsley

Lord Hackett, an old title that has lost a great deal

of money, an old friend of Lord Denby and the deceased Lord Andrepont

Lord Denby, a deceased viscount widower with no children. Former patron of Miss Bess Abbott, and friend of the deceased Lord Andrepont.

Jack About Town/Jack Townsend, the best finder of lost things in London, former student of Bess Abbott, works at the Cock and Prance Inn.

Miss Persephone, a female impersonator who lives at the Cock and Prance Inn.

Mrs. Bettleton, the owner and purveyor at the Cock and Prance Inn.

Lord Haverformore/Mr. Wycliff, a gentleman of London who frequents the Inn.

Mrs. Lacey, a patron of the Inn, who lives with the other Mrs. Lacey

Mrs. Lacey, a patron of the Inn, who lives with the other Mrs. Lacey

Mrs. Townsend, Jack's mother, an avid letter-writer

Captain Townsend, a sea captain, father to Roland and Jack.

Roland Townsend, Jack's brother, who works at the highly regarded Drummond's bank

Mrs. McKenzie, proprietress of the Women's Home on Hog Lane.

Mr. John Arthur/Corinthian John, a prizefighter who has become a successful stockbroker. Continues to box for the joy of the sweet science. Husband to Lady Lydia, father of her child. Friend of Andrepont and Bess Abbott.

Miss Pearl Arthur, younger sister of John Arthur, lives with John and Lydia, had previously boarded at Mrs. Tyler's Boardingschool for Ladies.

Miss Mathilda Perry, friend of Pearl, boards at Mrs. Tyler's Boardingschool for Ladies.

Mrs. Tyler, owner and chaperone for Mrs. Tyler's Boardingschool for Ladies.

Bess Abbott, a female prizefighter, acknowledged to be the best in London, John Arthur's best friend.

Os Worley, blacksmith and soon-to-be husband of Bess Abbott. Son of Mrs. Thomasina Franklin, and half-brother to Miss Mary Franklin.

Violet Jeffers, a boxing student, whose father is a drunk, has been taken in by Bess and Os.

Jean Fabron, the blacksmith's apprentice.

Basil, boxing announcer.

❦ I ❧

LONDON, 1818

If Agnes were a man, a befrilled and lace-capped aunt would sit in the corner of the Franklins' artfully curated drawing room to monitor every exchange. As it stood, with Agnes being another unmarried miss from the *ton*, she was considered as dangerous as a titmouse. And in this, somewhat disappointingly, Society was absolutely correct.

But she felt comfortable here, in Miss Mary Franklin's drawing room, almost as comfortable as she felt in her own. So when she bustled in, her mind sparkling with the anticipation of the visit, the arrangements for her women's charity collection, she didn't notice Mary Franklin's troubled expression.

Had she been more aware, less comfortable on the new sofa with its beautiful silk pillows in a shade so new that half the *ton* was tearing its collective hair out trying to obtain it, Agnes would have noticed that Mary Franklin couldn't even look at her.

And after a year, wasn't that something?

A year of correspondence and outings, of teas, of traipsing unnoticed through ballrooms and afternoon garden parties. A year of hand-holding and stolen kisses. A year of passionate words that no one ever bothered to peruse or steal or notice. Because how much trouble could Lady Agnes be? Even at her impressive height, it was hard to remember she was in the room.

But Mary—Mary was her North. It was hard not to point towards her, focus on her, with the sprinkle of dark freckles on her dark skin. The hair that curled and curled and curled, endlessly, around Agnes's fingers. Skin that took on the delicate soaps her mother bought, filled with cloves and lavender and scents that seemed as heady as goblets of ruby red port. Not that Agnes would know.

While even Agnes wasn't quite sure what to call their *close friendship*, which was more potent than any *friendship* she'd ever experienced, it didn't have the gravitas of an engagement. It didn't have the urgency of John Arthur's courtship of her sister. It was rather comfortable, actually, which is why Agnes held the belief that this plump and easy love between them would last until her dying breath.

"Just a reminder," Agnes started, as she started most visits with everyone, "I will be by in the morning to pick up this week's linens for the Women's Home. Unless you think your household will not produce any more, in which case, I can take them with me today."

"They're ready in a hamper by the door," Mary said, facing the window, her back to Agnes. Odd to have such a cold reception. Mary typically greeted her with an embrace, or at least a smile that could warm Siberia.

"Excellent. Then, shall we discuss the Royal Academy Exhibition? I can't believe it's been a year already. We've already missed the opening days, which is a shame. It can be a bit of a crush, but sometimes that's the fun of it, to be in and amongst so many people, seeing all of the paintings for the first time, together."

"Agnes."

"This week, then?" Agnes's gloves looked a bit dirty. Were they truly dirty, or was she being particular? Sometimes she could be particular, which not everyone appreciated. It was challenging to overlook things like these, even as her mother advised her to allow trivial items to pass through her notice, saving energy for bigger projects.

"I cannot go with you." Mary's voice sounded dull, like a chafing dish with a gleam of fat hardened and cooled in the bottom.

Agnes looked up, finally noting Mary's posture. Her voice. The coolness of the room. "Oh." There was no tea tray laid out with tidbits and a steaming pot. There were no baskets of embroidery at the ready, or even a book chosen carefully for their appointment.

Every bit of closeness they'd stolen over the last year was erased from the scene.

"Mary?" A deep pit formed in her stomach. Dread filled her so completely that she wasn't sure it hadn't sprung out of her fingertips.

"I have good news." Mary's voice was still flat.

"Must be quite the thing," Agnes quipped, still cataloguing the absence of creature comforts. Mary did not appear to be "in" today to receive visitors.

"I wanted to be the first to let you know that I am engaged." Mary turned finally, her face drawn but her eyes set and cold.

"I beg your pardon?" Agnes's mouth dried. Upon closer inspection, Agnes could detect a distinct puffiness around Mary's eyes. She had cried.

"I'm quite overjoyed at my luck."

"Engaged to be married?"

"Yes, what other kind of engagement would there be?" Mary twisted a handkerchief in her hands before stuffing it up her sleeve. Her jaw flexed before she pulled herself up.

"One might engage in all sorts of behavior. For instance—"

Mary's shoulders slumped again. "Agnes, please don't make this harder."

"I'm sure I don't know what you are talking about." The pit was replaced with stone, pinning Agnes to the fashionable sofa. The clock on the mantel ticked away. Her eyes began to blink in time with the second hand. The silence was horrid. Did Agnes prefer to escape or did she prefer to stay? It didn't matter. Her feet were leaden.

"His name is Sir James Carraway. He's from Hampshire. And he's a nice man." Mary took on a false lightness. She'd been practicing. Practicing lines to seem excited about her betrothed.

Once, Agnes had taken exercise with her sister and Miss Abbott, the lady boxer. She'd watched as Lydia struck Miss Abbott as directed. When it came time for Agnes to do the same, she couldn't bring herself to even try to throw a punch. All she could think of was how it felt to be hit. To want to be hit. And in this moment, she felt as if Mary had hit her square in the chest.

"Oh," was all Agnes could bring herself to say. Sir James Carraway was a man. A man who could marry a woman and call her his own. Make her take his name. Erase her. Erase the Mary Franklin who sighed Agnes's name as if calling out to a saint.

"It will be announced at the Reedleys' ball tomorrow night. I wanted to tell you myself." Mary didn't cross the room. Mary didn't take her hands or plead for understanding.

All Agnes could think of was the feel of Mary's hair tangled in her fingers. Or what the freckles on her nose looked like close up. They were the most perfect and particular arrangement of beauty marks. She regularly told Mary that she was lucky to have so many. A lump stuck in Agnes's throat. What would John Arthur have done, had Lydia announced such a thing? He would have struck on, confident. "And how will this affect me, exactly?"

Mary stared at her, and had she had an hour less of finishing instruction, her mouth would have been hanging open. But Mary Franklin was her mother's daughter—refined, beautiful, graceful at all costs. The kind of woman that any man would want. Any man. Any woman.

Agnes charged on, suddenly feeling determined. "Because I fail to see why our friendship must change. Surely, your address will, and thus you will not be so convenient to visit as you have been. But our—" It was here that Agnes faltered. For what to call their time together?

Mary shook her head slowly, as if trying to wake herself from a nightmare. "Agnes, I cannot go forward with this when I am married. I cannot."

"Why not?" Agnes asked. Her mouth took control, leaving her heart weeping and her brain stopped in its tracks. And her mouth was quite sick of euphemisms and half-truths. "For it isn't as if *I* can make you pregnant."

Now Mary's mouth did hang open. Her cheeks darkened—a blush that Agnes had never seen before. Mary's dark complexion kept her seeming more constant than Agnes, whose fair skin had a propensity to flush with every eyeblink. But now Mary's eyes filled with tears and she sank into a chair near the window. "Agnes."

"That was perhaps the most vulgar thing I have ever said aloud," Agnes said, her mind catching up to her mouth. It was hard to feel more of an oaf than she did almost every day of her life, being taller than most and clumsy to top it all, but she had managed to outdo even herself. "I do apologize."

Mary didn't respond. The dampness threatened her eyelashes but didn't spill. Of course it wouldn't, because Mary could hold herself together. Instead of sobbing, which is something Agnes would likely do, Mary pulled out the handkerchief in her sleeve and stoppered her tears before they ever spilled down her cheeks. Agnes sat in abject misery.

"This isn't how I wanted this to go," Mary whispered.

"Then let's change it," Agnes insisted. It was all she could do not to spring to her feet and throw herself at Mary and grovel. "Why can we not stay together? Two spinsters. We'll get a house together—my father has already committed to me that I may have my dowry as a stipend, and my sister's husband has quite a head for money. He's assured me he can keep my investments safe. We'll be fine together. Always."

"But I want children, Agnes. I *want* the life you were born into. I *want* a family and I *want*—"

"We'll adopt orphans," Agnes said, although she had no idea how one went about adopting orphans. Or where one found the orphans that needed two spinsters looking after them. Nor did she have any inclinations towards children and babies, orphaned or otherwise, but other people clearly had very strong feelings, which she could imitate.

"No, Agnes." Mary raised her head. She was so very regal when she delivered crushing blows. "I want to feel it. I want to feel the quickening in my belly. I want a child of my blood. I want *more*."

It was a bewildering statement. And it struck such a blow to their differences that Agnes finally realized that Mary was severing their friendship.

Forever. She sagged back against the sofa in a most unladylike fashion.

"But." Agnes stared at the corner of the drawing room.

Mary was on her feet now, emboldened perhaps by her ambitions or perhaps by Agnes's capitulation. "There is power in having a husband, Agnes. Through him you can do things, change the world in a way that a single woman cannot. I have things I want to do."

"But we could be happy," Agnes insisted, quietly, knowing she had already lost.

"Happy isn't enough," Mary said. "I need more. Why must you insist on living so small?"

"I don't live small," Agnes said, righting herself on the sofa. "Nothing about me is small." Her feet, for instance, were far more comfortable in men's work boots than in dancing slippers.

Mary's eyes narrowed as she went in for the kill. "But you *are* small, Agnes. Otherwise you would mind that people forget you're in the room. They don't see you sitting there, or standing in the corner. You have the opinions and stature of a potted fern."

Agnes's mouth opened and then closed. Mary had taken all the air in the room, leaving none for her. She wasn't wrong. And that was precisely what hurt. Was this the kindness in Mary? To hurt her so badly that forgetting her would be easier? Perhaps. Agnes stood, pretending to press wrinkles out of her heavy brown skirt. The hot lump in her throat wouldn't go away. Why wouldn't it go away?

"I'm sorry Agnes. I'll be married in two months' time. We will marry at his estate in Hampshire, where we will live. It's expected." The clock continued to tick, despite the fact that the laws of physics should have ceased to function a full minute ago.

Agnes licked her lips, the stone in her belly

wanting disgorgement and the hot lump forcing tears that she didn't wish to shed.

"May I please have a moment before I go?" Agnes asked with all the dignity she could muster.

"Of course." Mary left the room, holding onto her grace as any graduate of the best finishing schools. Sir James Carraway was getting an excellent lady for his estate.

When the door shut behind her and Agnes was alone, she wept. Even though it wasn't her drawing room. Even though those windows looked out over gardens that weren't hers. Even though this was the last time she would be in that house. She cried, something that Agnes did not do often. She was a woman of standards and amiability, even-temperedness, and levelheaded practicality. Crying was not her milieu.

She cleared her throat and straightened her dress, standing and pulling herself up to her full, surprising height. If she were her sister, how would Lydia handle this? Had Lydia ever been heartbroken? Truly cut to the quick?

Yes, there was that time in the country where she had thought John was pursuing Mary Franklin, but it was merely a massive misunderstanding. Not the same as your love standing next to a window declaring her engagement to someone else. Perhaps her cousin James would be a better person to commiserate with—he knew all about unrequited love.

Quite devastating, this love business. Which Agnes promised herself she would continue to feel miserable about, in full force, in the comfort of her own chambers, preferably with two pots of chocolate and whatever other indulgences she might dream up on the walk home. She pulled out her handkerchief and sniveled into it.

The walk home.

She was to go to her sister's after this visit, as Lydia only lived a few streets over. Agnes did not want to see her demanding, exacting, severe sister. Lydia viewed the world in either-or terms. There was never a soft finesse or a curving bend, or a sentence that might trail off and leave ambiguity. Lydia was yes-or-no, black-or-white.

And Agnes traded in ambiguities as Lydia's husband traded in stocks. Agnes lived in ambiguity. She adored it, relied upon it. And today, she absolutely did not want Lydia to know she had suffered a blow so severe that she might actually tell another soul she was in love with Mary Franklin.

Because that kind of love was the kind that required ambiguity and finesse. Because it didn't produce heirs or transfer fortunes. There was no money to be made or found in that sort of love. So it was quiet, which was something Agnes rather preferred.

But Lydia would be far more suspicious if Agnes didn't show. So, she pulled herself together and stepped out of the Franklin townhouse into a very incongruous and mild sort of day. An errand boy sat across the street, waiting, no doubt, for his errand. Whenever she saw him outside the Franklins' townhome, he mostly slumped down and looked the other way. But today, he looked her square in the eye and Agnes knew that he really saw her. She saw pity in the young man's dark eyes. It made her look away. Mary was right—she was small.

⚜

JACK WAS WEARING A DRESS THAT WAS A SHADE somewhere between light brown and yellow. Likely it had once been yellow and had only turned brown through scrubbings—it was threadbare despite Lady Agnes's mending. Either way, Lady Agnes had personally donated it to the Women's Home, and therefore, the dress belonged to Jack.

Fact: Lady Agnes put a signature yellow stitch in all of her tasks, hidden in a tidy row of *X*'s.

Why: No idea why, but she did, and it only contributed to the mystery of her in Jack's mind.

Whenever Jack and Miss Persephone trekked to the Women's Home over on Hog Lane, Mrs. McKenzie made sure the linens were sorted before they arrived, with the understanding that all the ones containing a yellow stitch went home with them.

Miss Persephone tried to mock him for it once, but the dark look that Jack gave made it clear this was not a matter for mockery. Yellow stitches went to Jack, no questions asked, or your drinks were likely contaminated with a gob of spit at the very least. Never mind all the other dangerous bits and bobs Jack knew.

Today, however, was not a day to think on the lovely, meticulous Lady Agnes, but rather a market day. Jack liked to be in the market, to keep up with the gossip and people, to learn what needed to be learned from the housekeepers of fancy houses and the ladies of lesser ones. A body could learn more than expected by having available ears in the right place.

The previous week had been dismal with gray skies and a thick yellow miasma from the Thames, despite the calendar showing summer months, but today was approaching sunny. Jack turned his face to the sky to enjoy the unexpected warmth. Times like this, it was hard to stand like a girl, to take away the wide stance, the confident set of shoulders, the playful but unyielding gaze. Playful gazes whilst wearing a dress invited trouble. But Jack's straw bonnet was ribboned with blue and yellow and pink, and a few silk flowers—the best of the lot.

Across the way, a thin matchgirl accepted a bit of moldy bread. The ragman took his rounds, and the milkmaid set down her half-full pails of fresh milk. It was early, the bells had just rung eight, and people were still collecting amongst the stalls. The housekeepers and mistresses were out in the early hours, ready to catch the best available, whether it was cheese or fish. They were the ones with large bonnets and lists, moving from stall to stall, weaving between enterprises that didn't appeal.

Jack watched with amusement as a young dairymaid tried to catch the attention of the curly-headed blacksmith's apprentice. But the young man was on a mission and could not be dissuaded from his vigorous pace. And she had a cow and wasn't as agile in a crowd.

"You—" a voice spat, pulling Jack out of his reverie.

Bewildered, Jack spun, searching for the owner of that familiar voice, though the tone was unfamiliar.

Lady Agnes stood there, her color high in her cheeks, looking—quite significantly—marvelous. She was commanding her body the way her sister did in the ring. Her eyes flashed and she bore down on Jack, who was at once grateful and terrified.

Instinctively, to preserve his role of Innocent-Flower-Girl-Don't-Mind-Me-A-Bit, Jack dipped into a curtsy. "My lady."

It caused Lady Agnes to pull up short and blink. Jack's heart pounded.

Fact: She recognized him. She had seen through not only today's ribboned bonnet and faded gown, but also the tailored waistcoat and ragged cap Jack wore when he worked as an errand boy. She had seen Jack. Not Jack's clothes or personas, but Jack.

Shit on toast. How? Jack's own mother couldn't do that.

Lady Agnes blinked and stared. "You," she repeated.

Jack gave her a modest smile, the kind a lower-class girl might give to a gently bred lady. Not the grin that might dazzle her, might draw her in, ask for more—the kind Jack wanted to give her. By all the gods of his mother's homeland, this was an incredible woman and he hated squandering the opportunity to flirt.

"I beg your pardon," she said, the words saying one thing but the tone another. Lady Agnes narrowed her eyes, assessing, evaluating.

Jack held his breath. Fact: Clothes made the flower girl.

Her mouth pinched. "Might you have a brother?"

"Yes, m'lady." Fact: Jack indeed had a brother, Roland, who was ever so proud of his job at Drummonds bank. Roland was also a pompous arse and they had not spoken in almost a decade.

Fact: An errand boy had followed Lady Agnes from the Franklin household to the Arthur household the previous week.

Fact: Lady Agnes had sped up when she noticed the errand boy behind her.

Also Fact: That errand boy had been Jack.

Her eyes flashed with a sudden indignant anger. "You ought to tell him to mind his own affairs, then."

The comment stung. Jack didn't know much, but heartbreak was the same across all streets, rich or poor.

He'd followed her to make sure no footpads took advantage of her flustered and bereaved state, to make sure she wouldn't accidentally step in front of a horse. His intentions were pure, even if he hadn't been as careful as he could have been to make sure the lady didn't notice. "My brother is a nice lad. Whatever it is that he did, I'm sure he meant you no harm."

Lady Agnes bristled, and a stray lock of mahogany hair fell out of her bonnet. Distracted, indeed. Lady Agnes was never careless like this. She was practically shaking with rage. "Mockery isn't harmless."

"Mockery?" Fact: There had never been any mockery.

"What is his name?" she demanded.

"Whose name," another young woman asked as she approached. She was genteel, well-dressed in a gown that belonged on a watercolor of flowers. "Why, Lady Agnes, is this a potential protégé?"

Jack squinted into the sun as the woman grew closer. When her image cleared, she appeared to be a young miss at the height of fashion in pastel blues and yellows. Whether she was pretty would have to depend on the beholder.

Lady Agnes seemed to fold her anger inwards. It astonished Jack to witness it—as if all that emotion, those flashing eyes, the errant hair was tucked into a tidy envelope and put into a secret pocket. Goodbye anger, hello manners.

Fact: Lady Agnes was extraordinary.

"Miss Perry. How lovely to see you. And unexpected." Lady Agnes folded her hands in front of her as the other young woman sank into a light curtsy.

"I am delighted to see you here. We thought to meet up with you at the Women's Home to donate all of our linens. You really are the most thoughtful of creatures, spending your time on charities." The pastel Miss Perry glanced over at Jack, making it clear exactly what she thought of him.

It was Jack's turn to bristle.

Fact: It was easier to pry open secrets than an

oyster, and all Jack needed was a name as a place to start. If this rude miss was going to malign him or Lady Agnes any further, then a first name was all he needed.

"I am here to buy another round of rags, see what we can salvage. It's a good cause, and well needed." Lady Agnes was the picture of demurity now. Her hands were clasped in front of her as if she were an old maid already. Miss Perry clearly disdained her, obvious on her face, it was.

"This gown here is one of my lady's mends." Jack held out the skirt for inspection.

Lady Agnes glanced over sharply while the other woman pretended to inspect it with a sniff.

"How can you be sure?" Miss Perry challenged.

It was stupid to say it, but sometimes pride took hold of the reins. Jack gave her a sideways glance that was not entirely without menace. "Because I learn everyone's secrets."

There was a silence as Lady Agnes stared and Miss Perry shifted uncomfortably. Then Miss Perry tittered as if Jack had made an incredible joke.

"Nay, all of my lady's gowns hold a yellow stitch as a signature." Jack held out his arm so that the yellow X was visible upon close inspection.

"What a remarkable find you are, miss. Will you be accompanying us to the Women's Home then? Since you seem to know so much about your patroness?" The woman glanced at Lady Agnes, her eyes full of questions.

"We had been discussing that very matter," Lady Agnes said through gritted teeth. "But—"

Fact: Sometimes the mouth started speaking before the brain started thinking.

"Yes, I will be. I'm an excellent judge of the cloth here for sale in Covent Garden. Lady Agnes couldn't do it without me." Jack gave a winning smile.

"I'm sure," murmured the other woman. "Mrs. Tyler herself is chaperoning me today—just there." She pointed out a stout woman bartering at a lace stall. "So we have a carriage, if not some cotton to stuff in our ears when Mrs. Tyler decides to start lecturing. Why don't you come with us? Are you in a phaeton with your, your—"

"Yes, I am. Thank you. What a generous offer. I'm sure Vasily will be fine if I am in your company."

"And you as well, Miss—?"

"Miss Town—Townsend." Shit on toast, there was his mother, approaching.

His mother looked well, as she always did. She had stopped turning heads, but her beauty was still incontrovertible as she grew mildly thicker with age, a fullness that made him happy to see. Her voluminous dark hair was twirled and pinned underneath a simple bonnet that was accented in a striking red. Her dark eyes flitted across the other two women, and she looked to Jack with questions.

Fact: Even a chance meeting between his mother and Lady Agnes made his whole body pulse like it was its very own frog heart.

"Good morning, miss. I beg your pardon, ladies. If the flowers are not spoken for, I am interested." The slight accent Jack remembered from childhood was gone. But she had sounded more and more English every day for years. She was being kind to not out him.

"Thank you for the courtesy, but no, the flowers are not spoken for," Lady Agnes said.

Jack stood frozen, waiting for one of the threads to unravel.

Fact: He and his mother could communicate without words. It had driven Roland to the absolute brink. His brother's jealousy of their relationship was only part of their personal discord. The larger bit of their friction had to do with Jack's refusal to believe that it mattered if a person wore trousers or skirts. Fact: That was an unpopular opinion, but Jack had experience in both skirts and trousers, and it had yet to make much difference to how he felt. Rather, it changed how *other* people felt about him, and that seemed downright silly.

"The flowers look fresh today," his mother continued. *Are you safe?*

Lady Agnes flicked her eyes from Jack's face to his mother's. She figured it out. She knew. Jack had his mother's eyes, the cupid bow of her lips, and the thickness of that black hair. Oh, by the holy devil himself, no one else knew. How was it that this woman could figure him out in an eyeblink?

Fact: No one could ever truly know what another person was thinking.

Probably.

Miss Perry, on the other hand, was gazing around at the stalls in Covent Garden, shopping with her eyes. No trouble there.

Jack cleared his throat. "Yes, ma'am. Very fresh. Excellent for any arrangement." *Everything is fine.*

"We will be hosting a dinner party this evening, and I'm thankful we can have such a stunning display." *When will you come see me?*

"An asset to any occasion. Do you need more flowers?" *I'll come soon, I promise.*

"This will be enough, thank you, if I may buy the whole lot?" His mother glanced to the other women, cutting short their conversation. *You should be with young ladies like this.*

"Oh, marvelous," Miss Perry said. "So Miss Townsend may come to the Women's Home after all, now that she has sold all of her wares. What luck!"

His mother cut a strange look at Miss Perry and then back to Jack.

"Yes, quite, thank you." Jack waited for his mother to draw out her coin purse, but she didn't. She waited for an explanation, which any mother would do.

Fact: His mother would never understand how guileful Jack was, and how very innocent these women were. To his mother, Jack was still the scrawny girl out in the yard, throwing dirt at the neighbor boys and stealing their breeches. Even when Jack was that little girl, it had never felt real. Nothing felt real when you were treated by the sum of your clothing.

Explanations then. "This gracious lady," Jack gestured at Lady Agnes. "Has agreed to take me under her wing. I help her with her charity work, and she, er, she, well—"

Lady Agnes did not come to his aid. No, Miss Perry jumped in, explaining as if everyone standing there was the dumbest fool in all of the Empire.

"Lady Agnes will help Miss Townsend with her finishing. Help her meet and marry a fine man and provide security."

Jack's mother's eyes lit up at that. Marriage.

"I don't—" Jack began to protest. Lady Agnes shot daggers at Miss Perry, who was already bored again.

"That sounds like a very lovely opportunity for you, miss." Jack's mother bustled, drawing out her purse. She snatched up the flowers. "I wouldn't want to hold you fine ladies up when there is work to be done. Your charitable efforts shall surely be rewarded, my lady."

"But—" Jack protested again, accepting the coins and handing over the flowers.

"Go on, now," Jack's mother shooed them all with her hands.

"Yes, come. I see Mrs. Tyler is ready to be off. Did

you need to visit the ragman?" Miss Perry prompted, turning away.

Lady Agnes was still evaluating. "I don't believe that will be necessary this morning after all. We can signal Vasily to bring the mended linens to your carriage."

Miss Perry ushered them along, clearly ready to be done with this portion of her morning.

Jack stowed the coins and picked up the basket, trailing after the other two women. Lady Agnes was the one who looked back. Jack knew she was watching how he walked. It made him feel like he was tripping over his feet to suddenly have that much attention.

Fact: Well-bred girls walked in short steps.

There was a lump in Jack's throat. He had a life, obligations, friends. There wasn't room for a side job moonlighting as a young miss in need of charitable deeds. And for what gain? To spend more time with Lady Agnes?

Well, yes. But Jack was far more comfortable as an errand boy around her, where he could give roguish winks and gallant bows. He couldn't flirt in a carriage as Miss Townsend, Innocent-Flower-Girl-Don't-Mind-Me-A-Bit.

Shit on toast. Jack clambered up into a carriage.

Fact: This was a terrible idea.

Agnes eyed Miss Townsend as the footman opened the carriage door. The girl looked so much like that errand boy, the one who had frightened her until she realized his true intent must be mockery. Leaving Mary Franklin's house had been a painful trudge. It had taken every ounce of decorum to not sob the entire way to Lydia's, and Agnes had not appreciated the audience.

In a way, the errand boy had done her a favor in scaring her so badly that she couldn't cry. Believing that rocks would be thrown at any moment, she'd shown up breathless on the Arthurs' doorstep, shaking. At least her heartbreak could pass easily as terror—her sister then promptly scolded her for not engaging with Miss Abbott and pugilistic pursuits.

Agnes, given her rank, was the first handed up to the carriage. Habit made her take the less desirable seat of facing backward, giving Mrs. Tyler the opportunity to take the best seat, facing forward. The woman settled in, and Miss Perry followed after some indecision on whether or not to sit next to Agnes or her chaperone. Finally Miss Townsend was handed in, and given no other option, settled in next to Agnes.

Miss Townsend and the errand boy both

possessed dark eyes, high cheekbones, and a sleekness of movement that seemed unlike anything Agnes had seen before. No, not quite. Miss Abbott had that same economy, as did John Arthur. Was Miss Townsend a pugilist? She knew for a fact that women engaged in the sport, given Miss Abbott's profession and her sister's amateur interest. But the girl's nose was unbroken, and her teeth surprisingly white and straight.

Miss Townsend gave a small but still surprisingly engaging smile. How did she do that? It was the same confidence that Lydia sometimes exuded, except Lydia was all dark choler and challenge. But Miss Townsend was different, more ordered, more sure. Where Lydia was a jagged tear in a piece of fabric, Miss Townsend was the neat X of a mended stitch.

The carriage lurched into motion and Mrs. Tyler started engaging Miss Perry in a recounting of the purchases made for the boarding house. There was no room for discussion outside of it, given the small space they were squeezed into. Miss Townsend's sleeve settled next to Agnes's, and Agnes spotted the yellow thread.

Agnes had started the yellow stitch as a way to track how many garments she had personally mended. The number of women who had benefited from rags remade into respectable wear. It was pride, no mistaking it, though small and quiet. Evidence that she was there, in the world. Her mark was made.

And Miss Townsend noticed.

The carriage jostled over a bump, pushing Miss Townsend flush against Agnes. The warmth of the girl's body surprised her. She smelled of her fresh flowers and something else—a scent Agnes couldn't place, almost familiar and assuredly pleasant. Miss Townsend murmured polite excuses and pushed herself away, a brief touch on Agnes's forearm. The heat was bubbling, like a kettle starting to boil. Agnes stared at her arm. The pressure and shape from Miss Townsend lingered through layers of fabric. She glanced up at the girl in surprise.

Miss Townsend met her gaze, calm but knowing. She knew exactly what Agnes felt. Did that mean she felt it too? The girl bit her bottom lip, as if wrestling with questions unknown. Looking at those lips, Agnes felt desire start to pool.

No.

Agnes cleared her throat and shifted, ensuring no contact could be made with the mysterious Miss Townsend.

"Pardon me, Lady Agnes," Mrs. Tyler said, booming now towards her. Agnes had to fight an urge to cover her ears. "I am quite intrigued about your taking on this young miss. Can you tell me more of your plans? How do you hope to lift her circumstances?"

Miss Perry rolled her eyes in a manner only those so familiar with the stout woman would dare to do. If this was the volume of conversation, what would her angry lecture sound like?

"Well, ma'am," Agnes searched for a way to not be so impolite as to bluntly reveal that Miss Perry had invented the whole circumstance and passed it off as truth. "As you are the expert in etiquette and young ladies, I'm sure you have much advice to impart."

The flattery plumped Mrs. Tyler up even further. "I do. And many success stories. I hope to hear fine things for my former pupil, Miss Arthur, given her connection to you."

Pearl Arthur, John's younger sister, had moved from Mrs. Tyler's Boarding House for Young Ladies into John and Lydia's home in Marylebone. It was a queer position—according to the aristocracy, Pearl was decidedly unmarriageable, given the perceived grasping nature of her brother and Lydia's odd behavior in marrying him. But to the lower orders, Pearl's position was enviable—living in an expensive house in a rapidly rising and developing neighborhood with titled nobles for in-laws. Perspective, Agnes reminded herself.

"Yes. Miss Arthur is a fine young lady. I have no doubt that your skills have aided her."

Miss Perry's expression bordered on insolence.

Miss Townsend kept a neutral gaze even though they spoke as if she weren't present.

"I do try my best," Mrs. Tyler said. "Of course, it is all dependent on the young lady." The matron shot a disparaging look at Miss Perry.

"I have no doubt that once Lady Agnes is finished with Miss Townsend, she will be polished into a fine gem," Miss Perry declared.

"I'll get you an invitation to the Houghtons' ball—it's the biggest event of the Season. There's always a write-up in the papers about it. That can be the crowning moment of your achievement: to see Miss Townsend triumph at a ball!" Mrs. Tyler clapped her hands.

Agnes was unsettled about every bit of this conversation. She had no desire to attend any balls. She knew of the Houghtons' soiree, and Mrs. Tyler was correct that there would be a mention in a few papers. A few minor nobility attended, but it was mostly the picking grounds of third and fourth sons, men who wouldn't inherit, and the upwardly aspiring commoners who hoped for untimely deaths of potential brothers-in-law. Agnes had never been to it.

Also, Agnes was not a person who enjoyed balls. Or the gowns. Or, for that matter, the gawking. She needed to dispel this notion before it got out of hand.

"Unfortunately, Mrs. Tyler—"

"That would be most generous of you," breathed

Miss Townsend. "I can only hope to prove worthy of the faith and effort from both you and my lady."

Agnes cut her eyes over to the girl. That tone was new. Obsequious, even. Agnes had a sneaking suspicion that there was more to Miss Townsend than Innocent Flower Girl. And her brother, the mocking footpad.

"There's been a slight misunderstanding," Lady Agnes cut in.

The carriage lurched to stop, and Agnes threw her hand out to keep from launching into Mrs. Tyler's ample lap. The errant hand landed on Miss Townsend's solid, strong thigh. A firm, muscular kind that one saw on a person who knew physical labor. Or someone who ran. Perhaps Miss Townsend was a thief. Either way, the firm thigh gave Agnes pictures that were wholly undeserving of either of their stations.

"I've got you," Miss Townsend murmured, placing a steadying hand on top of Agnes's. The low promise of the girl's voice made Agnes's stomach drop and the air grow thin. Could the other women feel this? Could they see it? Agnes fought a blush.

"I'm quite capable—" Agnes couldn't even finish her thought, trying to catch her breath.

"We're here!" Miss Perry practically threw open the carriage door herself.

"We wait for the footman, Miss Perry," Mrs. Tyler chided.

But it was hard to pay attention to the other two women in the carriage.

"I'm quite—" Agnes couldn't even finish her thought, trying to catch her breath.

"You needn't do everything alone," Miss Townsend said, dark eyes boring into Agnes's, seeing far more than what was comfortable.

Alone. No, she hadn't been alone until Mary

Franklin decided to become Lady Carraway. Why did this girl care? Unless she and the errand boy were up to no good.

❦

THE PASSEL OF SKIRTS UNLOADED IN FRONT OF THE Women's Home. The building itself was grand but dirty—left by a benefactor worried about "fallen women." Poor women, unwed mothers, and reformed prostitutes lived here, worked here, subsisted here, until they left or died, either option aided by the help of some new man.

Fact: Jack himself had sought refuge here the first night he'd run away from home.

Lady Agnes managed to be first up the steps, as Mrs. McKenzie her own self appeared at the top of the stair, surprise registering in her deep brown eyes at the sight of Jack cavorting with the likes of Lady Agnes.

The footman unloaded trunks of linens from the back of the carriage. "Inside, thank you," Mrs. McKenzie murmured to him as he entered the building. She opened her wide, fleshy arms to the women traipsing at a much more regal pace up the stairs.

"Mrs. McKenzie," Lady Agnes acknowledged her while Mrs. Tyler came puffing up behind, more red-faced than the others.

Lady Agnes really knew how to lay on the aristocratic benefactor routine. Jack hadn't seen her perform like this, but she was elegance to behold. Her posture was perfect, her height seemed to stretch to grandiose heights, and her head tilt was spot-on. Jack wanted to learn that affectation. The genial acknowledgement by your betters. That'd be a trick.

"Miss Townsend, that's quite a grin on your face,"

Mrs. McKenzie acknowledged, which, of course, made Lady Agnes send another sharp look in Jack's direction.

Jack curtsied in deference. "It's a fine day for a smile."

"And for such exalted company. I admit that I'm surprised about your companions," Mrs. McKenzie said, ushering them up the stairs, letting Lady Agnes go first.

Miss Jane, a girl of about sixteen who had been raised at the Women's Home before she started working there, stood at the door, fidgeting. Her mouth gaped open as Lady Agnes passed. Jack knew her thoughts, written plain on her sleeve. *Real nobility!*

"Is there something amiss with Miss Townsend in our company?" Lady Agnes called back to Mrs. McKenzie. Her tone sounded probing, not defending.

Fact: Lady Agnes was suspicious. It thrilled a bit. Not that Lady Agnes might think ill of Jack, but that she was curious about him at all.

"No, no, not a'tall," Mrs. McKenzie said. "Miss Townsend is a fine lass, very helpful to us when it comes to the mends you bring us. Picks the best out for our girls and hers."

"Hers?" Lady Agnes questioned as they entered the building.

Inside, it smelled of damp wool, old sweat, and the animal smell of tallow and warm bodies.

"Surely, why—Miss Townsend, you haven't told these fine ladies about your brood?"

Oh, that was a fine way to put it. Made it sound like Jack had a harem lurking about. Hens in a coop. "It isn't a brood, ma'am."

"I don't know quite know what you would call it, but a fine group of ladies under the auspices of a respectable matron," assured Mrs. McKenzie.

"A boarding house!" Mrs. Tyler said now that she had regained her breath.

"No, not precisely that," Jack said, desperate now to avoid explaining.

Fact: Jack picked up loads of dresses in all sorts of styles.

Fact: All of those dresses were worn by people. Perhaps not precisely the group he had described to Mrs. McKenzie.

Miss Jane approached and whispered something to Mrs. McKenzie. "Pardon me, my lady, ladies, I do have a small matter to attend to. Then I can get that accounting ledger for you, Lady Agnes."

Jack wanted to disappear. Skip ahead to when the other ladies once again forgot to include him in their banter.

"You have quite the protégé, Lady Agnes," Mrs. Tyler announced. "Running a boarding house at the tender age of, what? Eighteen?"

Jack stumped a quick curtsy. Try twenty-five, but then Jack's short stature and slim build often made it far easier to pass as a youth.

"Yes, Miss Townsend cuts quite the figure," Lady Agnes said, the sharpness in her tone all the sharper given her accent.

Miss Perry was clearly bored. "Are we not touring the workshop?"

"Ah, yes, of course," Mrs. Tyler said. "We've a notion to create our own such space, either for our own girls or to offer employment for girls who may not be able to pay up front."

Jack had to commend the woman for an expanding business model. Unless it was a way to find free labor, in which case, she was a horrid woman and could be eaten by rats.

As the other two women shuffled towards the workroom, noted by a sign that read *Work Room,* which hung from the doorknob, Lady Agnes stepped closer to Jack.

Her dark eyes glittered. Jack knew he should feel like he was in trouble.

Fact: It was hard to feel bad about something he'd pictured a thousand times. To be sure, it was a different reason to have her eyes glittering with interest, but, well, Jack knew how to take what he was given.

"Miss Townsend. You are quite the puzzle."

"Thank you, my lady. Means a lot coming from you."

"I'm not sure it is a compliment."

"And I take everything as one so's I never hear an unkind word." Jack tried very hard to keep Innocent-Flower-Girl-Don't-Mind-Me's gutter accent, but when talking to Lady Agnes, he wanted to fall into his own speech so very badly. To speak to her as himself.

Lady Agnes sat back on that one. "You are very clever."

Jack dropped Miss Townsend's guard an inch. "That sounded less like a compliment in tone, even if it did in words."

"When the other ladies return, I will announce that you have decided to not accept my tutelage due to your other commitments—to your brood, as it were." She pulled at her gloves, tightening her grip.

"No need for that." It was hard to remember he was Miss Townsend right now. He wanted to be Jack with her. He blinked up at her through lashes, willing Lady Agnes to fall down the well of his eyes. "I would welcome any opportunity to learn whatever you are willing to teach."

A small flame appeared in her cheeks and she licked her lips before catching herself. "I'm not sure what you are after, Miss Townsend. But I do know that you are more than what you seem."

"Both statements seem true," Jack agreed.

"Why should I spend my time with a liar?" Lady Agnes challenged, her tone suddenly imperious.

"I haven't lied." Some truths a bit stretched, perhaps, yes.

Fact: Jack didn't believe in lies. Truth was hard enough, both to recognize and to practice. Roland had never understood that Jack was being more truthful by not being Gwen. It wasn't right. It wasn't all of him. To be Gwen was like only using one arm and one leg. Ridiculous, silly, nonsensical, especially when he could be Jack. Jack could be man or woman, moving freely through social spheres and strata in a way that Gwen never could.

"So if I ask you a question, you'll answer me truthfully?" Lady Agnes said. "It will be a condition of our association. I cannot be friends with a liar. I won't."

Jack gingerly lifted Lady Agnes's hand, turning it palm up. He pushed down the glove, exposing the fleshy bottom of her palm. Looking up into her eyes, he raised her hand to his mouth, pressing a kiss gently, reverently there. She smelled like rose and vanilla soap, her skin so soft and delicate. He had to keep himself from pushing back more cloth, kissing more bare flesh. Tamp down the compulsion to make her moan.

Fact: She tasted better than he'd dreamed.

"I swear to always tell you the truth."

Lady Agnes's breath hitched. Mrs. McKenzie bustled down the hallway, breaking Jack's spell completely. Of all the timing.

"Lady Agnes, do forgive the interruption. Follow me to my office and we can get our accounting straight. I want to be sure that you and your family understand the depth of our gratitude to you." Mrs.

McKenzie ushered Lady Agnes of the blazing eyes—such restraint!—down the hallway.

Jack took the opportunity to slip out unnoticed.

Fact: The best performances left the audience wanting more.

PEARL ARTHUR SAT IN THE PARLOR WITH AGNES and her sister, which was a nice change. Lydia's one-sided discussion with her infant was, frankly, disturbing. The baby's arms flailed periodically, and she gurgled and sighed as Lydia murmured at her. But Lydia didn't seem happy. Certainly not like what had been depicted in pamphlets and books about the blossoming of motherhood. Quite the opposite. Lydia was still swollen, not only the weight from her pregnancy, but swollen with fatigue and an almost curdled milk pallor.

Lydia seemed as if she were putting on a show, a different kind than she used to perform in ballrooms as she at once entranced the *ton* and pumped them for information, but a show nonetheless. Agnes honestly could not remember what her sister was really like between those performances. She had only come alive during training sessions with Miss Abbott in their parents' ballroom, which Agnes had been happy to attend though not participate in.

"May I pour?" Pearl asked.

Agnes nodded, admiring how Pearl executed the maneuver with the genteel style Agnes struggled to master. "Your good manners are wasted on us."

"Nothing is wasted on me." Lydia sniffed.

Pearl gave Lydia a knowing smile—an intimacy that pricked at Agnes. Of course they knew each other well, living in the same house, caring for the same child, even if there was a nursemaid.

29

"Pearl, if I may, I have a few questions that I hoped you may be able to help me with," Agnes started.

"Of course," Pearl said, sitting back down in her chair, perched on the edge, spine straight. She had all the qualifications for a spectacular marriage if she could shake the shadow of Lydia's scandal. Well. And the circumstances of her birth. "Is this what Miss Perry mentioned?"

Ugh, Miss Mathilda Perry. Agnes really did not care for the girl, but she tried very hard not to speak ill of anyone. "Likely. What did she say?"

"That you were taking on a charity case to help with marriage prospects."

Lydia burst out laughing, startling the baby. Pearl glanced over, alarmed as well.

Agnes's sincere disinterest in marriage was not a secret. But since Miss Perry and Miss Arthur had never been in Society, they didn't know. Surely, didn't Agnes's wardrobe of serviceable round gowns in shades of browns, greens, and grays signify?

Lydia's laughter continued, color returning to her cheeks. She jostled the baby to stop its crying.

The door opened and Mr. Arthur appeared. "Do I hear my lady love laughing?"

Lydia sighed, trying to contain her amusement. Mr. Arthur glanced between Agnes and Pearl, a hopeful look on his face. Pearl shrugged and Agnes shook her head.

"Agnes...is going to help young girls..." Lydia gasped. "Get married!" She launched into another peal of laughter.

"It honestly isn't that funny," Agnes grumbled.

Mr. Arthur gave her an indulgent smile. "Whatever it takes for her to find a moment of amusement."

New creases had appeared on Mr. Arthur's

square-jawed face. Was it sleepless nights with a newborn? Or was it something else? "Since you're here, Mr. Arthur," Agnes said, "might I trouble you with a query?"

"Agnes, he's *family*. You may use his Christian name," Lydia admonished, wiping her eyes with a sigh.

Agnes shifted in her seat. But he wasn't family to her. He was, yes, married to her sister, and that made sense, but he hadn't been there for all those years of planning and scheming. All the nightmares, all the times Agnes had climbed into Lydia's bed while her sister cried in her sleep. Agnes had been there. James had been there. Margaret had been there. But this man, well, he was new. Lydia might have told him her secrets, but he couldn't know the visceral reality of their *life*.

"Yes, well," Agnes stammered.

"John," he supplied, taking a seat. Pearl poured him a cup of tea, which he accepted with surprising grace. They both had worked on their etiquette.

"I know. John," Agnes allowed. "I was curious if you were aware of a particular young woman who engages in pugilism. Perhaps in connection with Miss Abbott?"

"Of course," he said. "Bess teaches in the back of the Pig and Thistle every week. There's a group of young girls, roughly six or eight any given week. We sponsor them with a bit of food to make sure they get something in their bellies."

"Would a Miss Townsend be among them?"

"Oh, I don't know last names. Most of the chickabiddies don't talk much."

"Chickabiddies? Oh, no, Miss Townsend is likely eighteen, or perhaps twenty?" Truthfully, Agnes thought Miss Townsend was older than that—but Mrs. Tyler's observation had made Agnes question her own assessment. It was in Miss Townsend's eyes that her age showed. The confidence, the assurance— it wasn't the arrogance of youth, but something else. Independence, perhaps. The intoxicating idea that one could take care of oneself.

John's eyebrows raised in surprise as he sipped his tea. "No, I don't believe Bess is working with someone that age. She doesn't have many older students who are interested in pugilism." He gestured to his face, intimating that the sport didn't help a person's features. Though even Agnes had to admit that there was something charming about John Arthur's slightly broken nose.

"Oh, well, thank you."

"May I ask why you are inquiring?" John's tone gentled. Clearly, he didn't want to seem prying.

"I have a new acquaintance, and it may sound silly, but there is something about the way she moves—" Agnes glanced over at her sister, whose eyebrows raised. "It is reminiscent of an athlete. The way both you and Miss Abbott move."

"Not me?" Lydia challenged.

"Well, no," Agnes faltered. "You are too burdened with lady's dance steps to move like them."

Lydia snorted in a most unladylike fashion. Why was it that Lydia had always acted a boor and everyone found her charming? Her entire life, Agnes had followed the rules, held her tongue, and she was still derided. With Mary Franklin's rejection and the mystery of Miss Townsend, Agnes had finally found wit's end with her sister's unrelenting rudeness. But still she found she could not open her mouth.

The tension between sisters was palpable, like a length of fabric stretched between them, straining before it tore completely.

"May I take the baby?" Pearl asked, reaching out.

Lydia handed over the infant, eyes still locked in challenge with Agnes.

"The nurse has the afternoon off today," Pearl explained. "But I'm all too happy to hold this precious bundle. John, we should go to the kitchens to find a bit of goat's milk to tide over the child."

"But Nurse Perkins said—"

"John," Pearl said in a low voice, then ushered him with a swift kick to the ankle. He set his teacup down and they beat a hasty retreat.

As soon as the door closed, Agnes exhaled her anger.

Lydia stood. "Can't you even say it?" Her gown shifted, and Agnes could see the weight she still wore, her ankles still swollen. She looked miserable.

"Say what, Lydia?" Agnes mirrored her sister, standing, towering over her. Agnes was the thin one now, though it didn't give her any pleasure to realize it.

"Whatever it is that's bothering you. The bee in your ridiculous, proper little bonnet," Lydia snarled.

"I'm sure I don't know why you must take out your anger on me," Agnes said.

"I'm not taking anything out on you, Agnes. Not everything is about you."

That shook her to the core, the idea that Agnes was the self-centered one. "Me? Me?" Agnes sputtered. "I've spent my entire life in your shadow. We made a ridiculous pact not to marry because of you. Your pain. Your revenge, your hurt. The rest of us skipping through meadows of wildflowers, the way you see it."

Lydia scoffed. "I did all that for you. For the other girls out there. To keep you safe, to give you good marriage prospects. I had every intention of finding some dusty old duke and marrying up so you could have a decent life!"

"Ah, such altruism. When I sat and watched you with Miss Abbott day after day for how many years? Waited with the other wallflowers at the balls, seeing you dancing and simpering to get whatever *information* you thought you needed."

"Thought I needed? I did what I needed." Lydia positively shook, incandescent with her rage.

Agnes knew the signs of Lydia's temper well—it was as familiar as the flower-papered walls of their nursery when they were growing up. They were all a hostage to it, never able to speak out of line for fear it would upset Lydia, and hadn't she suffered enough?

Keep placid, keep small, and Lydia would feel better. But Agnes was sick of it. Was that what Mary Franklin meant? Was this why Mary Franklin had chosen Sir Carraway over her?

"Look at the time. Mama expects me home soon." Agnes swooped out of the room before Lydia could explode.

The butler had Agnes's gloves and hat collected and handed them off as she swept out. His expression was one of pity, but Agnes didn't care. Vasily came tearing around from the mews in the phaeton. The whole house likely had heard the altercation. Vasily eyed her with concern as he helped her up, but wisely said nothing. A dark, unfamiliar pit settled into her stomach.

Jack scooted out of the carriage and onto Drury Lane. He had taken the longest route possible, despite the midsummer evening mist, through mews and shortcuts, busy roads and crowded taverns. Then Jack finally got to the Inn. Home.

He slipped in the back door, stomping the mud from his boots. It was nearing sundown, and the footmen and maids would arrive soon. He needed to get ready for the evening crush.

"Jack, that you?" Mrs. Bettleton called from the kitchens.

"I'll be down soon." He thundered up the stairs.

Jack's room was sparse but comfortable. An attic room meant for servants, but that's not what he was at the Inn. He was more, but like everyone, there was no title to describe him. Sliding under the bed, he retrieved the purse that hung from the ropework. He added tonight's coins to the bounty and retied the purse. It was a fair sum—not enough to lease an office or a home, but a nice buffer should the worst come. The Inn needed him so he wasn't about to leave Mrs. Bettleton or Miss Persephone, but if nothing else, life had taught him that choices were everything.

He yanked off his cap and jacket and stowed them in the box that served as his bureau. The boots, hose, and short breeches came off, too. Clad only in the long linen shirt, Jack poured fresh water from the ewer into the basin and gave a quick wash with a rag. His chest bindings were starting to smell of sweat, but he figured he could manage tonight in them still.

Jack rubbed some orange-scented parfum to cover the aroma, then donned the white hose, satin breeches, and matching satin waistcoat. He outlined his eyes with kohl, powdered his face as pale as he could stand, and added some rouge and a beauty mark. With the light powder on his skin, no dark contours to bring out the squareness of a jaw or outline a broad forehead, Jack looked more girlish than he cared to appear. A wave of fear swept through him, but he tamped it down. This was the Inn. No one would ask, and fewer would care.

"Jack!" Heavy, heeled steps thudded down the hallway. His door flung open. "I hope you're decent."

Jack whirled around, ready to put on his own heeled shoes with shiny brass buckles. "As decent as I can be."

Miss Persephone gave an amused harrumph. "I have your wig whenever you are finished with your toilette." Miss Persephone had been an apprentice butcher from St. Albans before coming to work at the Inn. She loved showing off her well-developed back and arms in sleeveless evening gowns. Tonight she was still in her underthings as the wide skirts alone would cram the hallways. "You're late, by the by," she tossed over her shoulder.

"Couldn't be helped," Jack said, slipping into the shoes. They were a bit large, but considering the price he'd found them at, it was worth stuffing the toes. He clomped down the hallway to Miss Persephone's room.

Whereas Jack's room was comfortable and well-appointed, Miss Persephone's was stuffed as full as a holiday goose. Fabrics, rags, ribbons, silk flowers in every shade from new mauve to deep indigo, bits of woven straw, and scraps of lace all hung in an incomparable rainbow mosaic that made Jack almost dizzy to behold.

The two wigs could not have been more different. Miss Persephone's wig was almost the height of Jack in stockinged feet. Powdered white, it had intricate braids and bits of gold and lace woven in.

"Is that a boat?" Jack asked, spying a small but very clear mast and sail peeking from the far side of the wig.

Miss Persephone laughed—her real laugh, deep and throaty, not the amusing titter she used during the evening parties. "Yes," she purred. "Isn't it wonderful? I couldn't help myself. It was mine as a boy."

"You'll be Marie Antoinette tonight?" Jack asked, spying his wig there next to hers. It looked so puny in comparison: a perfectly respectable powdered queue, held together by a blue satin ribbon that matched his coat and breeches.

"Who else would I be?" Miss Persephone asked, her whole body tightening in response.

Fact: The rivalry between Miss Persephone and Lady Godiva was intense and deep, and both had declared themselves Marie Antoinette for tonight's gaiety. Jack didn't know the origin of their spat, but he knew it spilled out of the Inn and into the lives of everyone who interacted with Lady Godiva when she wasn't Lady Godiva.

Miss Persephone, on the other hand, was more often than not Miss Persephone. Living at the Inn, like Jack and Mrs. Bettleton, gave her a space to be who she was all the time. If only Jack could feel the same.

Of all the places he'd ever lived, who he was at the Inn was the closest he'd ever felt to being himself. Yet even here was another stage where he was living the happiest of all faces, not acknowledging a lonely night that could not—or would not—be assuaged by a one-night bedding. This was a communal boarding house where they all pitched in: Jack ran the errands, went to market, helped with the cleaning and the gardening. Mrs. Bettleton cooked and tended the wash, and Miss Persephone did the house cleaning and the water hauling. It was a tight ship, and they hired in extra hands when needed, especially on days of a costume ball, but they managed, all in all. It gave them all a roof over their heads, food in their bellies, a bit of blunt in their pockets, and nightly laughs to fill the whole of England.

Fact: The Inn was the best, most elegant molly-house in town, and everyone knew it. There were some private homes that invited guests and were also mollies, but those were not open to the public and therefore could not be counted in a survey of most elegant establishments. Most places wouldn't admit women, either. It seemed funny to Jack that a molly-house would limit its clientele in such a way, given that women could wear trousers and attend if no one was the wiser, or that the men, once there at the molly-house, might don a dress. But either way, Jack was proud that the Inn made no such distinctions. All were welcome at their place, as long as they behaved.

"Who will be your King?" Jack asked, letting Miss Persephone comb back his black hair with her fingers. Her hands were wide and strong from her days as a butcher, but also from the work here at the Inn. But she was surprisingly gentle and Jack wanted to lean back into her hands and rest. Instead, she fitted the wig on, tugging here and there. "Miss Persephone?"

She shrugged, grabbing a dish of powder to give one last retouching. Jack grabbed the cone to hold over his face before she afflicted the area.

Fact: No one wanted to inhale powder.

"You can put the face guard down now," she said.

"Tonight is going to put me through my paces, is that what you're telling me?" Part of Jack's job at the Inn was smoothing its patrons' rough edges. Keeping troublemakers apart, refilling wine glasses, and watching for potential raids. Normally Jack enjoyed his job—always one step ahead of everyone, reading the room, anticipating the responses of others before they acted.

39

"There may be several Kings tonight," Miss Persephone allowed. "Can you hold the door? My gown is too wide to dress up here."

Fact: With two possible Marie Antoinettes and a multitude of Louises, this could either be a smashing success or a party that ended with two amateur pugilists and a flurry of white powder.

Jack helped with wig transport and then checked in with Mrs. Bettleton. The kitchen was stocked with food, ready to be laid out in the dining hall—not that anyone would sit to eat supper. It wasn't that type of crowd on these nights. Not to mention, wearing pre-Revolutionary French court dress made sitting in a chair a nightmare for half the attendees.

The three of them scuttled about when the first guests began arriving. They'd hired on two footmen and two maids for the evening, but a costume ball was pure chaos. Jack played butler, gravely opening the door, giving a deep and elaborate bow, and accepting the ribboned tokens required for entry.

Powdered wig after powdered wig dropped the wooden tokens, tied with different colored ribbons, into the glass bowl. Blue was an invitation from Jack, yellow from Miss Persephone, and black from Mrs. Bettleton. They were open about the meaning of the ribbons, but it was also a small security measure to ensure the Inn's safety. Raids were not unheard of, and while it had been years since the last time molly-house patrons were hung for indiscretions, it still draped their activities with a shrouded threat.

Fact: A raid could be costly, but salvageable. An arson after a raid would be devastating, but survivable. But what they might do to Miss Persephone, Mrs. Bettleton, and Jack? Fatal.

And it all hinged on politics. Which was Jack's job.

"Mr. About Town!" roared Lord Haverformore in

greeting. He was an older fellow, dressed in red silk breeches with a red embroidered dressing gown over them. His shoes were the appropriate style, with massive buckles that were hastily decorated in paste jewels. The night was young, but if the ruddy hue of his cheeks was any evidence, he'd started drinking long before.

As the last guest to arrive in this set, Jack grudgingly accepted Lord Haverformore's beefy embrace and guided him into the ballroom. Decorated with panels of white fabric and chandeliers draped in greenery, with pots and vases of rainbow-colored flowers edging the floor at varying heights, the Inn looked like an ethereal wonderland. Chairs were set at one end for those who didn't wish to dance. Through the back was another sitting room with the usual furniture ready for use: a few settees and divans, tea tables, and a small setup of chess in the corner.

"How do you fare on an evening such as this?" Lord Haverformore demanded.

"Quite well, my lord," Jack answered.

"Good, good." The man stared off at the growing mass of guests. Lady Godiva had not yet made her entrance, so all was well. "I have a job for you, utmost importance."

Jack did his best not to flinch. Known in many circles as London's best finder of obscure objects, Jack had no doubt about his abilities. His last big job became Town gossip, driving more clients his way. The specifics weren't known, of course, but the idea that Jack had essentially conjured up Mr. Worley's mother with so little information made Jack seem magical in his skills. London did not know that it was luck and his admiration for Lady Agnes that had put the pieces together. Stroke of luck, that was. If Lady Agnes hadn't mended dresses with yellow X's, then

Mr. Worley would have never met his mother. Strange how the world worked sometimes.

"It's a ball, my lord. Save business for another time." Jack gave his best smile, hoping that the man would forget. Jack couldn't put his finger on it, but he disliked Lord Haverformore. Partly his chosen name, partly the assessing way he dealt with other people—that even here, at the Inn, every person was a transaction. Even Miss Persephone avoided him, and her threshold for moral ambiguity was remarkably lower than Jack's.

"Of course, you're right. Who can think of business when faced with this bounty?" Lord Haverformore gestured to the dance floor, where Miss Persephone was being promenaded by the first of several King Louises in attendance. In the corner, the quartet of their usual musicians was shabbily costumed, but they kept the dances lively.

Fact: It wasn't the first Marie Antoinette ball they'd given. Recycled costumes were a given. They even had some upstairs in case guests wanted to accent their attire.

"Excuse me, my lord, I must attend my duties," Jack said, giving another deep, gracious courtly bow. On nights like these, his manners were exaggerated, overly polite. It was fun to an extent, but exhausting as well. Jack took his leave of Lord Haverformore and found a familiar, handsome face.

A man with hair the color of gold, tied back in an elegant ribboned queue, stood in the corner, watching the dancefloor antics with amusement.

"Bill," Jack greeted.

Fact: His name was *not* Bill.

Most chose aspirational names, or mythological names, or bawdy names to conceal their identities. The outside world was a bother, fake, and here, a body could be anything. But *Bill?* As if this man could ever be *Bill*. Outside these walls, *Bill* was an influential recently-inherited Peer whose title was synonymous with progressive politics, money, and all the power that came with those burdens.

"Mr. About Town," *Bill* said with a shallow bow, prompting Jack to return it. His bright blue eyes seemed haggard, but in the process of rejuvenating due to the amusement found here at the Inn. That was the point of the Inn. To refresh them all, to help them get through the drudgery of the days, whatever the substance of drudgery might be.

"Have you just returned home? You were gone for a long sojourn with your wife, were you not?" Jack knew full well when they had returned. Any literate citizen of London could keep tabs on this man as he was mentioned in every Society paper and gossip rag for miles.

"Indeed," *Bill* said, sipping his smuggled champagne. French wine for a French Queen.

"Was it not the relaxation you had hoped for?" Jack knew this was prying. This was too far. But here, at the Inn, rules were different. He spoke to *Bill* as a man he might meet at the tavern.

"There were complications. My wife is—" Bill thought to himself for a moment. He was a kind man, at least Jack had always thought so. "She is still learning about the world. Doesn't understand the limitations she must inhabit. The woman has no fear. It's bloody unnerving." He finished with a shaky laugh that seemed to cross into admiration.

"Is she here tonight?" Jack scanned the crowd for a new face, knowing he wouldn't find one.

"Dear God, no." Bill sighed. "She'd probably love it. She's surprisingly and refreshingly...uncomplicated about our marriage."

"Sounds like a delightful lady."

Bill gave him a winning smile full of straight,

white teeth that had Jack near weak at the knees. He normally didn't pay much heed to male beauty, but this man was practically blinding.

Fact: Some beauty was empirical and did not need to have an eye to behold it.

"Go on now, Mr. About Town. I know you have your tasks on these nights."

"Much obliged." Jack gave a deep bow, which Bill echoed.

No sooner had he left Bill than he ran into Mrs. and Mrs. Proctor. "Ladies," he greeted, his arms wide. Neither of them had much in the way of height, making up for it entirely in width. They were two plump cakes in their courtly skirts, festooned with ribbons. It couldn't possibly make Jack happier to see them.

Fact: If becoming like either of the Mrs. Proctors was his fate, he'd gladly consign himself to it.

"Oh my, Jack, aren't you a picture in your French breeches," said Mrs. May Proctor. She was slightly older than the other Mrs. Proctor and the more salacious of the two.

"May," the other admonished, smacking her erstwhile wife with her fan. "Leave the boy alone."

Jack spun in a lazy circle, daring them. "I don't charge for looking."

They tittered in response. "It's not that we don't appreciate you, Jack. We don't want to be impolite," Mrs. Lacey Proctor said.

"Of course," May agreed. "Because here at the Inn is where we must mind our manners."

"Manners are appreciated in every arena," Jack said, taking Mrs. Lacey Proctor's hand and dabbing a quick kiss across her gloved knuckles.

"You see?" Mrs. Lacey Proctor said to her wife.

"When will we see you here with someone, Jack?" Mrs. May Proctor challenged. "You work too hard."

"When I can find someone who lives up to your ineffable standards," Jack replied with a flirtatious grin.

The two ladies cackled and shuffled off to find a place to hold court, but before they got too far, Mrs. Lacey Proctor turned around and laid a hand on Jack's arm. "We mean it, Jack. You're a fine person, and you deserve to have a love that lasts."

If that wasn't one for the heartstrings, Jack didn't know what was.

The door opened, Mrs. Bettleton playing butler for the moment, and in walked Lady Godiva, dressed as Marie Antoinette with skirts as wide as the Thames. The whole of the Inn gathered their collective breath and waited.

Fact: Lady Godiva had added paste jewels to encrust her gown. Miss Persephone would not be pleased. Shit on toast.

"You look in a foul mood," Agnes's mother said, pulling on her gloves.

Agnes glanced up from the book she was reading in the drawing room, waiting for her parents to dress. "I'm not." She snapped the book closed and launched to her feet.

"Oh, are you looking forward to this evening?" Her mother asked, hope glimmering in her voice.

She hated to disappoint her mother, but honestly, when had she ever been truly excited for a ball? A rout? An assembly? Wastes. Of. Time. She'd only ever gone for her sister, and now, well, now. Now Lydia had gotten exactly what she wanted and was still a whinging mess over it all. "Not particularly," Agnes said, doing her best to mitigate her tone and failing miserably. Why was she feeling so petulant?

"Ah," her mother said, returning to her above-the-elbow white gloves, acting as though Agnes was still as sweet as sugar. But that was her mother—no matter the situation, gloss it over, smooth the rough edges, pretend all was well, fit in with the crush.

How horrible it must be to have two daughters who couldn't fit in no matter how hard they tried.

"Shall we go down?" Her father appeared in the doorway. They made an elegant couple, the Lord and Lady Lorian. They lived the dream of every person in London—wealthy, elegant, well-mannered, and beautiful—both of them. And then, there was Agnes. Brown like an oversized grouse, waddling behind them.

"Shall we, dear?" Her mother's dark hair was glossy in its coif, dotted with white feathers and gold thread.

Agnes's lady's maid had wanted to do her hair in a similar fashion, but Agnes brushed off the suggestion. The less comparison drawn to her mother, the better.

"The sooner we go, the sooner we come home." Agnes wore dancing slippers, which she hated. She could feel the cold floor seeping up through the thin soles. And her long, wide feet never looked delicate when she danced, so why pretend with the fabric slippers? She much preferred boots.

But, no boots at a ball. If it were true for men, then it was doubly true for Agnes.

"Not exactly an auspicious start to the evening," Papa said.

Agnes caught her mama giving him a pointed look, which caused him to silence himself. All for the best. Her parents chattered all the way there, ignoring Agnes as she stared at her hands, replaying the argument with her sister, wishing she could have said something—anything.

As they arrived, her father exited the carriage

first, and her mother put a hand on Agnes's arm. "Whatever it is, let it go for the evening. Drop it from your thoughts and think of the last thing that made you smile."

Alone for the briefest moment in the carriage, an image of Miss Townsend, pressing a kiss to the fleshy root of her palm, came to Agnes. The glimmer in her eyes, the heat of her lips, a promise somewhere in the riddle of her statement, *I would not lie to you.*

A smile tugged at her lips for the first time, and Agnes held the image in front of her like a nosegay all evening.

"GIVEN THAT THERE ARE AT LEAST SEVEN KING Louises here, I can't see why two Marie Antoinettes would be out of the question," Jack reasoned with Miss Persephone.

The air was thick from the crush of people and massive swishes of hooped skirts. The sound of glass breaking and a peal of high-pitched laughter made Jack wince. He needed to grab a broom and clean that up.

Fact: The footmen they'd hired were nearly drunk and would not think to grab a broom.

"I think it's in poor taste, is all," Miss Persephone said, blinking rapidly. Sweat ran from her hairline under the wig, leaving flesh-colored trails along her powdered cheeks. In another hour, she would have to run upstairs for a quick shave and reapplication. It would be a good time to try to let Lady Godiva shine and then hustle her out the door before Miss Persephone came back down.

"And it is in poor taste," Jack assured her, backing away from where they stood near the fireplace in the back room. "Let me go clean up the broken glass from a moment ago, and I will bring you some cool champagne. Do you want me to send in Roderigo? He's the Spanish King Louis."

Miss Persephone brightened at the mention of Roderigo coming to pay his respects. Roderigo, to be fair, was a stunningly beautiful man. With dark hair and dark eyes, he moved through a crowd like silk. He was not a terribly good conversationalist, and often a bit of a misanthrope, but he was beautiful, so on a night like this, he was perfect company.

"I'll send him in and return with cold champagne for you both." Jack turned back to the ballroom, where most of the vases along the floor had been kicked over despite their best efforts. What they did for the aesthetic. More than anything, he wanted to be back in that carriage with Lady Agnes, her long thigh resting against his, her eyes darting over as if she hadn't been noticing his nearness. Even the remembrance of the moment thrilled him, made him feel powerful and successful. It was enough to keep him going through the night. He'd have to see her again soon, somehow.

Roderigo was swinging around another King Louis, already a bit tipsy. They were both laughing. Jack caught them and sent them both to attend Miss Persephone, promising wine.

Pushing through the crowd, Jack finally got to the servants' door, hoping to run down and retrieve a broom.

"I am not for sale," a low voice said, anger barely contained.

There was more murmuring as Jack descended the narrow staircase. By the time he hit the landing, he heard the wet smack of flesh on flesh. Rounding the corner, Lady Godiva pushed past Jack, makeup smeared, small tears in her skirts.

"Fucking unbelievable," Lady Godiva muttered in

her natural baritone, then she stared right at Jack with a blind rage of fury. In her Lady Godiva voice, she said, "Get him out of here. Now."

"I, uh—" Jack stammered.

"Throw him out on his arse. I want to watch it happen so I can cheer." Lady Godiva squeezed up the narrow staircase, her skirts pinching and hitching higher as she climbed.

Lord Haverformore emerged from the shadows, one hand over his eye. "Can I trouble you for a bit of something for my eye?"

Jack sighed and turned toward the kitchen. Finding Mrs. Bettleton scurrying about and producing more puddings, Jack gestured at Lord Haverformore, who followed in behind him like a naughty schoolboy. Stains were showing down the front of Haverformore's white linen shirt, and there was dirt on the hem of his caftan.

Mrs. Bettleton pursed her lips, causing more wrinkles to show. Then she gestured for Jack to go out to the cellar. He grabbed a lantern.

Fact: They were not about to waste their hard-won ice on that dirty cully's blackened peeper.

The night air was cool, and it didn't take Jack long to find a potato large enough to do the job. He hurried back up, returned the lantern to the hook, and handed the root vegetable to Mrs. Bettleton.

"Waste of a good potato," she muttered, chopping it in half with a loud whack of her kitchen knife and then slicing a thick round from the middle to cover Lord Haverformore's eye socket. "Watch him," she said, handing Jack the slice.

"I'll get him out of here through the back after we get him settled." Jack took the man to the small pallet off to the side of the kitchen, where a kitchen boy would sleep if they had one.

Fact: The Inn required far more people living in it

49

than it currently housed. Mrs. Bettleton wanted more hands.

"Sorry about the ruckus, and all that," Lord Haverformore said, stumbling as Jack guided him.

"Put this on your eye," Jack said, handing him the potato slice. The man followed directions, for once.

"Thank you. Really, even if they aren't women, their uncanny ability to behave like them is remarkable!"

Jack leaned against the wall and closed his eyes, willing himself not to kick the man while he was down. Haverformore was lucky Mrs. Bettleton hadn't heard that comment, because she would kick anyone who said such a thing, lying down or not.

"Don't you think? Why, a simple proposition is not untoward in a place like this. Opera dancers don't sit so high on the horse as these types."

Jack tried to think of something else. Something far away. Something perfectly untouched by the likes of Lord Haverformore.

"Which brings me to our business. You have the reputation of being quite the locator of treasures, Jack, my boy. Ha! My boy! The only real one here, I'd say."

Jack said nothing. It was dangerous to say what he felt: that it didn't matter if a body was a boy or a girl. A body was a body—a vehicle for running, jumping, fighting, laughing, kissing. Did it really matter which variety it came in? Seed cake or oat cake, they were both good.

Fact: The world did not believe what Jack believed. The world believed it *meant* something to be a man, like it *meant* suffering to be a woman. Both ideas were equally ridiculous.

"I have something I'd like retrieved. I believe I know where it is—or at least, where it was around fifteen years ago or so. I can pay handsomely."

"Half upfront, half at time of delivery," Jack said in a monotone.

"It's the art portfolio of a dear friend of mine. Sketches. Dear friend, now passed. I'd be most obliged to find it."

Jack made a noncommittal noise.

"Name your price. That's how much I want it back."

At least the smells from the kitchen were worth standing here, listening to this right prick spout his mouth off. Mrs. Bettleton could cook any dish, any style. Everything from roasted grouse to curry to cakes. She was a marvel. Jack's stomach growled. He remembered the champagne. And the broken glass. Shit on toast, this night was never-ending.

"I'm busy at the moment," Jack said. "Booked full."

"I'm a patient man," Lord Haverformore said, squirming to turn round and look at Jack. "Name your price."

To get the wanker to shut up, Jack said, "Right, then. Twenty pounds."

Fact: Twenty pounds was a ridiculous sum. More than most saw in a year's worth of wages. Ten years, even. Jack could bribe every magistrate from here to Newcastle with such a princely sum. It would keep Mrs. Bettleton and Miss Persephone safe forever.

Lord Haverformore choked. "You can't be serious."

Jack shrugged as Lord Haverformore sat up, clearly sobering up. "The best is expensive. I'm the best."

The other man hoisted himself to his feet. "I'm not feeling well. Would you be so kind as to order my carriage around?"

"Why don't we exit it through the back? That way, you don't have to climb the servants' stair again."

The man lurched and clamped his meaty hand onto Jack's arm for balance, groaning. He dropped the potato slice to the floor and balanced himself.

Hating himself for his own compassion, Jack steadied the man and guided him outside through the kitchen gardens. Late champagne was the least of his worries. It was already a long night.

Fact: Jack did not want to work for Lord Haverformore, but if he was willing to cough up twenty pounds, Jack would run through the streets naked for it.

❦ 4 ❧

"I hope you don't mind me calling on you, Lady Agnes," Miss Perry gushed, taking in the Lorian drawing room.

"Not at all." Agnes rang for tea. Hardly anyone visited during her at-home days, especially since Mary Franklin—well. Not since Mary Franklin.

"My curiosity is positively boiling over. Have you taken steps with Miss Townsend? Is she still selling flowers? Or have you managed to already find her a match? Is he an honourable?"

Agnes held her hand out as if to steady the spill of wild speculation from Miss Perry. Her ridiculous assumptions were what put Miss Townsend in that carriage with them. Which also led to the most stimulating kiss on the hand that Agnes had ever experienced, so there was some credence to be given to Miss Perry's meddling.

"To be quite frank with you, Miss Perry, I haven't seen Miss Townsend since we visited the Women's Home."

Miss Perry visibly deflated. A footman brought in tea, which seemed to bolster her guest. Though Miss Perry did not know it, this tea set, with its serviceable black lacquerware and gold accents, was the lesser of the tea services. Agnes didn't know if it was a comment towards her or towards Miss Perry.

"May I?" Agnes asked, gesturing to the cups.

"Please," Miss Perry said. "Cream and sugar."

Agnes poured. They both sipped for a moment, enjoying the warm brew. It was Agnes's favorite blend, a bold-flavored restorative even on the most lethargic of days.

Miss Perry put down her cup, still mostly full despite the cream and sugar that had gone into it. She arranged her hands, clearly building up to a request. "May I say that while I am very impressed with—"

"Pardon me, Lady Agnes. You have another caller. A Miss Townsend," the butler announced, stepping into the drawing room and revealing Miss Townsend behind him.

She was dressed in a pale pink gown—another mending that Agnes had herself done not too long ago. The round gown was simple, but with an added yellow ribbon that made Miss Townsend look all the more innocent and unworldly. Agnes suspected this was the case, but rather that Miss Townsend was dressing for a role.

Miss Perry gasped. "Why! Miss Townsend, we were only now speaking of you! How uncanny." Miss Perry glanced over at Agnes for reassurance of her use of the word *we*.

Clearly, Miss Perry was desperate for a *we*. While Agnes didn't necessarily care for the company of the feather-brained girl, she at least understood the loneliness of not having a *we*.

"Thank you, Robling. Can you ring for another cup? Come have a seat, Miss Townsend." Agnes had never had this happen—unconnected callers. She wasn't the sort of young miss who had friends to stop by, other than Mary Franklin, really. When Lydia was here, there were callers, and ostensibly they were for

Agnes as well, but not really. It was hard to compete with the pull Lydia held over a crowd.

Miss Townsend crossed the room and curtsied in front of Agnes, a deferential nod for Miss Perry, who returned the acknowledgement, clearly pleased to be a social superior. "Thank you, my lady."

"You must be positively thrilled," Miss Perry gushed at Miss Townsend, who smiled demurely as she sat on the sofa next to Agnes while Miss Perry sat in the blue silk chair across from them.

"The attentions of Lady Agnes are beyond my wildest dreams," Miss Townsend said, giving Agnes a confident glance that sent a shiver up her spine.

I'll never lie to you. The flesh of Agnes's palm tingled suddenly, remembering the sensation of being pressed to Miss Townsend's lips. It made her want to leap up and pace the room, but Miss Townsend's inky stare kept her seated.

"Most generous," Miss Perry agreed.

A footman entered with another cup and saucer for Miss Townsend. There was silence as it was deposited, and when Agnes gestured at it, the girl nodded her acceptance, not bothering to ask for cream or sugar.

"Well. May I ask what the plan is?" Miss Perry prompted in the silence.

But Agnes was too busy watching Miss Townsend bring the gold-rimmed teacup to her pink mouth. Watching her large, dark eyes close with appreciation as she inhaled the strong brew and then tipped the cup edge slightly more, washing tea between her lips. Agnes's fingers twitched, wanting to brush over the sooty fringe of Miss Townsend's eyelashes, test the smooth slope of her profile.

Miss Townsend's eyes opened, gleaming with satisfaction. It was then that she caught Agnes staring at her. Agnes looked away.

"There isn't much of a plan," Miss Townsend said, lowering her cup without letting it clatter against the saucer. She'd had some etiquette training—unexpected, and interesting.

"Well, I am so pleased you are here then, because," Miss Perry was flush with excitement, her voice pitching higher and higher as she spoke, "I managed invitations for you *both* to a ball next week!"

She waited for a squealing response but only received polite smiles. Miss Perry was clearly put out.

"That's very generous of you, Miss Perry," Lady Agnes said, finally recovering her voice.

"Darling?" the door swung open to reveal Agnes's mama, beautiful and soft in a mint green day dress. When she saw Agnes's company, the dimple in her cheek showed as she bit back a smile. "Oh, I didn't realize you had company."

"Mama, these are two new friends," Agnes said, standing, as the other women did as well. Miss Perry's mouth was dangerously slack in the face of a countess. "Miss Mathilda Perry and Miss er—"

"Guinevere," Miss Townsend supplied in a low voice, pitched only for Agnes's ears. It made her name feel like a secret even though Agnes was about to announce it to everyone. Still. Agnes wanted to hear more words, pitched in that quiet voice, for her alone.

"Miss Guinevere Townsend," Agnes continued. "This is my mother, Lady Lorian."

They curtsied, and her mama was very gracious with a charming smile and nod. It was all the manners one could hope to find in a countess. Miss Perry was surely near to faint.

"Might I join you, then?" her mama asked, and she rang for another cup.

Miss Perry squeaked in delight as another chair was brought, and Lady Lorian settled between Miss

Perry's seat and Miss Townsend, who sat on the couch next to Agnes.

Another cup was brought, along with a fresh pot of tea, a few sandwiches, and apricot scones. It was lovely, really. Agnes poured for her mother. Everyone took a scone, even Miss Townsend, who looked suddenly and surprisingly hesitant.

"May I ask what you were discussing before I entered?" her mama asked. Miss Perry, agog with her proximity to actual aristocracy, looked as though she were speaking with the Almighty Himself.

"A ball," gushed Miss Perry. "I was telling them that I had secured invitations for them both at the Cuttingsworth ball."

Agnes's mama raised her delicate brow, doing her best to hide her expression. She glanced over to meet Agnes's eye. Agnes tried to give a very subtle message back, hoping to psychically let her know that this was the first Agnes had heard of it. And no, she did not know who the Cuttingsworths were, or anything about their ball.

"How exciting," her mama said.

"Mrs. Tyler—she runs the finishing school—she'll be with us as chaperone, of course," Miss Perry assured them.

"I have not been introduced to the Cuttingsworths," Agnes said.

"Oh, when I told Lady Cuttingsworth about you, she knew right who you were, of course," Miss Perry said. "And when I told her you had taken on Miss Townsend as a project, she couldn't wait to issue the invitations."

"Project?" her mama asked.

"Oh, yes," Miss Perry cut in. "Has Lady Agnes not told you?"

"It's been a very busy time in our household," Agnes bit out.

Miss Townsend placed her empty cup on the table so Agnes refilled it, wishing that Miss Perry would vanish, along with her chatter.

"Please tell me more about this project, Miss Townsend." Agnes's mama turned to face Miss Townsend across the table.

"My lady." Miss Townsend kept her eyes pitched at the rugs. "It wasn't my idea."

Agnes hated Miss Townsend looking so abject. So like...like a maid believing herself to be fired in the next moment.

"No, it wasn't," Agnes confirmed. Truthfully, it was Miss Perry's idea, and they were both innocent enough to be bowled over by the young woman's verbosity.

"And what, precisely, is the project, if I may further pry?"

"Marriage!" Miss Perry gushed, immediately downing the rest of her teacup in her excitement.

Now both of those perfectly groomed eyebrows went up, and Agnes's mama's gaze shot back to her daughter. "For whom? Does this have to do with Miss Franklin's engagement?"

Agnes winced at the reference to Mary Franklin and caught that Miss Townsend did the same. Odd. Did Miss Townsend somehow know Mary Franklin? Pieces of a puzzle shuffled in Agnes's head: her brother no doubt engaged as an errand boy for the household, hence following her and scaring her out of her wits the day Mary Franklin broke off their friendship. Not an emotion she wished to recall here, in present company.

"No, it doesn't," Agnes choked out.

"Miss Townsend is in need of introductions to a better set. For opportunities to make a good match. And Lady Agnes, of course, is so generous with her time."

"Not a match for Lady Agnes then," her mother questioned.

Miss Perry stammered, blushing for the first time that Agnes had ever seen. "We hadn't discussed that, exactly. I'm sure she would want better prospects than would be found at the Cuttingsworth ball, but they are fine gentlemen. Mostly honourables, baronets, and sons of well-to-do tradesmen."

Lady Lorian looked scandalized.

"Which is why it is so generous that Lady Agnes would deign to come, a way to give Miss Townsend here an opportunity."

At this point, Agnes was surprised that her mother would not be thrilled to hand her over to the second son of a wealthy merchant if it meant Agnes would be taken care of. It's not that they lacked money to provide for her, and the estate had long ago been settled on a nephew of her father's they'd never met. But her parents believed Agnes needed a partner in life, someone that would allow Agnes to fulfill her duty as a "helpmeet." They said it as though they were Quakers themselves, that happiness could be found in the simple work of a simple wife. As if they were simple.

Agnes had thought she had found that simple life with Mary Franklin. When they turned twenty-five, they would be old enough for the shelf, spinsters in the making, and could excuse themselves from Society, rent a lovely townhome in some less expensive district, and live happily ever after, reading books and mending garments for charity. A quiet life, filled with sunshine and humble pursuits.

Which, Mary Franklin would now be spending in the country with a man. And eventually, their babies. While Agnes sat in the steam of London's refuse alone and unwanted. On account of her being so small. Or thought small, anyway, given that her stature was not now, nor ever had been, small.

Her limbs suddenly felt heavy. Low and leaden with the hurtful words that still echoed from Mary Franklin's mouth to what felt like the rooftops of London. Miss Townsend was at least a distraction. If she followed Miss Perry's lead into this bizarre scenario, she could at least expect that Miss Townsend would find a man to marry, and in the meantime forge a friendship.

It was something. A small something. Like her.

⚜

FACT: JACK DID NOT LIKE BEING IN LADY LORIAN'S presence. Not that he didn't appreciate Lady Agnes's mother. Lady Lorian was beautiful, keen, and possibly able to see right through Jack. Younger people—especially those like Miss Perry—were so self-obsessed that Jack could strip down naked and Miss Perry might not even notice.

To be polite, Jack took a scone, but he nibbled carefully. Jack had the teeth of a merchant's daughter—naturally straight and white—not the kind that would belong to a poor girl who lived in low circumstances with her brother.

Fact: Jack had all of his teeth. And decent tooth powder. Lady Lorian might even notice the fake hair clipped onto the back of Jack's head, despite Miss Persephone's assurance that it looked natural and wouldn't be ruined by wearing a bonnet.

"To take a young woman under her wing is very generous of my daughter," Lady Lorian said, giving Jack the eye. "Especially for a social event like a ball. That certainly calls for new dresses, does it not?"

Miss Perry was all aflutter, like a fly on horseshit.

"Mama—" Agnes protested, putting her arm out, and in the process, brushing across Jack's.

Jack's stomach somersaulted. It was a poor idea to come to call. He hadn't expected Miss Perry, and certainly not this turn of events. He'd actually come to tell Lady Agnes the truth—that he was both the errand boy and the flower girl. That he'd only meant to keep her safe on that walk, and it wasn't pity that had urged him to do it. He'd never pitied her; but rather envied Miss Franklin, the person who held such sway over Lady Agnes.

It was a gambit, in some ways, to see if she could see Jack for who he really was—see the jumble of inside bits that didn't have names or shapes. The parts that were squishy and imperfect, the ones that made Jack's brother Roland hurl insults that echoed in his bones.

But instead, Miss Perry's charade hurtled forward, and Jack didn't know how to stop it. Or rather, he did, but not at the risk of alienating Lady Agnes entirely. There was still hope. Maybe Lady Agnes would deign to see the real him, the one that didn't care which wrapping it came with. She had in that first moment, eyes flashing with anger.

"Nonsense," Lady Lorian said. "It isn't much time, but I'm sure that we can find appropriate frocks for everyone. Miss Perry, have you time this afternoon to go to Bond Street? Miss Townsend?"

Shit on toast. No. No Bond Street, no fittings, no clothing. This was too far. He couldn't possibly accept new clothes, despite how much Miss Persephone would love it.

"I couldn't possibly accept such generosity, my lady," he managed, his eyes downcast again.

"Don't think of it as generosity. My daughter has been in a bit of a choler of late, and if you can cheer her up with your marriage prospects, then by all means. I would love to help." Lady Lorian gave them all a firm smile, the kind that let them know that no argument would be tolerated.

Jack's mother also had the same expression. It was not the first time that Jack had wondered if one had to give birth to a child to learn the expression, or did some people naturally have that in their emotional quiver?

"Will we be going now, my lady?" Miss Perry asked, eyes wild with anticipation.

"Why not? Agnes, are you expecting any more callers today?"

"No," Lady Agnes replied, her tone surprisingly sedate. She replaced her teacup on the table, next to the rest of the service. "We are at your disposal."

"I must humbly apologize, my lady. I cannot go, I am expected—" Jack's mind blanked. Shit on toast. "Elsewhere."

"That's a pity, but we shan't force the point." Lady Lorian stood. "We can send a bolt of quality fabric to you, nonetheless." She was of an impressive height. Not as tall as Lady Agnes, but still. It was the straightness of her back and the relentless hold of her gaze that made her seem more than she was. Lady Lydia held that same proud gaze, but Lady Agnes was different. Softer, somehow. Sweeter. Jack wanted to gather Lady Agnes up like a feather pillow and hug her as hard as he could, and never let her go.

"My thanks for your generosity, my lady," Jack said, scrambling to his feet. "Lady Agnes, I trust you."

Lady Agnes blinked rapidly, as if she'd heard his remark as he had intended. He did trust her, not only for fabric but also to keep him safe. She was a good person. Jack could only hope she knew it.

THE NEXT DAY, AGNES AND HER MOTHER ARRIVED at Lydia's Marylebone ostentatious townhome, a grand affair for this newer neighborhood. Of course, Lydia was not one for subtlety, and John Arthur had grown up in the mud puddles of London and couldn't be expected to have good taste.

Even after they had been announced and ushered into the lavish spectacle of a drawing room, Lydia refused to acknowledge either Agnes or their mama, staring out the window as Mary Franklin had stared out the window of her drawing room. Mary Franklin's drawing room was the ideal of the *ton:* light and pastel colored, with paintings of well-heeled ancestors and idyllic landscapes hung cheek-to-jowl along all four walls. Lydia's drawing room was wallpapered in dark blue and bright gold. The paintings on the walls were large in scale, landscapes of the ocean on one side and landscapes of foreign mountainsides on the other. Nothing of a pastoral English countryside.

Not that it should be too surprising.

Lydia's pointed silence was obvious. A pit sat in Agnes's stomach. Another rejection from her sister. Another time of being too little, too small, too ineffectual, too boring.

Their mama accepted the tea tray with grace. Her sister's butler seemed awed by their mother. Of course. Lady Lorian cleared her throat, trying to get Lydia's attention. Being hostess, Lydia ought to be sitting, pouring, engaging her guests with witty and appropriate banter. But Lydia was silent. Haggard and puffy in her dark round gown. Lydia hated that style —Agnes's favorite style—as the gowns were simple, form-concealing, and practical.

Even Lydia's hair—typically coiffed with curls and added pins and feathers and bits and bobs—was pulled back with a simple ribbon. Small hairs escaped from its hold, creating an effect of slovenly indifference.

But Lydia didn't come over to sit at her mother's prompting. With a raised brow, their mama poured three cups of tea. A little sugar for Agnes and two large lumps for Lydia, which Agnes recognized as the childish enticement it was meant to be.

"Come over and have a cup, Lydia. You'll feel better once you do."

Lydia floated over, not making eye contact, a dull version of the normally vivid sister. Odd for Agnes to be the lively one. Such a strange turn from the argumentative, loud Lydia of last week.

"I've noticed some tension between you two of late, and I'd like to clear it up. Now, who would like to start?" Their mama glanced between them.

"No more than usual," Lydia said.

Agnes startled. That was entirely an untrue assessment. While Lydia yelled regularly, Agnes had never let on that she disliked it. From her point of view, this was a new development for their sisterly relationship. She was simply tired of being belittled.

"That's not true," Agnes finally protested.

Lydia turned her wide, dulled gaze to her sister. "Really? I'm self-absorbed, you have no interest in what I'm doing, and I have no interest in what you're doing because you're boring. Is that not it?"

Agnes huffed. "More or less."

"I would think you would be interested in Agnes's new pursuits of the marriage mart," their mama prompted. "I've met the young girl in question. She is in need of some charity. Though I am concerned we know nothing of her family."

"Truly, Mama? Agnes helping a young girl get married? I have my doubts." Lydia's eyes sparked a tiny flare of life.

"You're always so suspicious of people," Agnes complained.

"Because people are terrible. So, tell me, Agnes, if you are so concerned about this girl from nowhere getting married, what about you? Do you have prospects you are currently hunting? What are your criteria for a husband?"

Agnes's cheeks burned with embarrassment.

"These are important questions, Agnes. Have you thought about them at all?" Her mother was using that reconciliatory tone that Agnes recognized from servants' disputes. She and Lydia had always been invited to watch her mother deal with servants' complaints as a training course for when they would run their own households. Lydia never showed to a single one. Agnes went to them all.

Her mind went blank. A good mistress of the house was kind. Shouldn't that extend to its master? "I would want a partner who was...kind?"

Lydia snorted.

"Lydia, please. That is a good and reasonable answer. Thank you, Agnes."

"How kind, Agnes?" Lydia spat, leaning over the chair's spindly arm, dangerously close to Agnes's face. "Kind enough that he won't beat you? Or your children? But what about the servants? The dogs? The horses? Where will you allow him to put all of his entitled rage?"

Agnes shrank away from her sister and squeezed her eyes shut. This was why she couldn't be around Lydia. There was so much bleak anger that made her uncomfortable. She didn't understand it, and she didn't like it.

"Lydia, enough!" their mama admonished.

Her sister settled back in her chair. The vivid light from her anger died away, replaced with the dullness again.

Glancing back at the door, ensuring that it was closed, her mother said in a whisper, "Is this about your marriage? Is this about Mr. Arthur?"

Lydia laughed that horrible, brittle laugh. "Not at all. John would never hurt me or the babe. Or a stray dog, let alone a horse."

"Then where is this coming from?"

"Agnes needs to understand what men are. She has no idea. It isn't fair to shove her out there and shackle her to one that she can't fathom. Be specific about what you want, because goodness knows, whichever man it is will be specific in the marriage contract."

"Agnes," her mama said, pointedly catching her eye. "Not all men are as beastly as your sister seems to believe."

"But some are, and that's my point. Sometimes you don't even know it until your sister marries him and then the whole family is saddled with a monster."

Oh.

Her mother sighed and put her hand over her eyes. "We don't need to discuss that man."

Her mother's sister, now the Viscountess Andrepont, had married young. They'd had one son, Agnes and Lydia's cousin James, the current Viscount Andrepont. But before the former viscount died, he had inflicted terror upon more than one woman, in more than one station. Including Lydia. When she was a child.

"We don't need to discuss that man? We should *always* be discussing him," Lydia contradicted. "Now that I have a child, I can't imagine how you allowed him—"

"I allowed nothing," her mama hissed, a look on her face so dark that Agnes could see Lydia's expression in it.

Agnes looked at her mother in shock. She had

never seen the Lady Lorian in anything but a pleasant mood. Lady Lorian did not hiss or argue.

Her mama cleared her throat. "Lydia. You must not invite the bad into your house with this kind of behavior. You are a mother now and have a family to look after, not the other way around."

Lydia looked like she'd been slapped. Agnes surprised herself by feeling sorry for her sister.

"Now, come over here and have a cup. You'll feel better," their mama instructed.

Agnes and Lydia locked eyes as Lydia meekly followed instructions, and for a moment, Agnes saw Lydia's lip twitch—not a smile, not an apology, but recognition of them being daughters of the same mother. It wasn't much, but Agnes would take what she could get.

JACK WHISTLED AS HE STRUTTED UP TO THE Mayfair residence. He ought to go round to the back kitchen entrance, which is where he would go as an errand boy. But today he was Miss Townsend's brother, Jack, picking up a bolt of fabric that had been delivered to the Lorian estate, given Miss Townsend's reluctance to give out their meager address.

The day was overcast but warm, and walking up those front steps in Mayfair, wearing his best pair of breeches and fine linen shirt, gave Jack a trembly sort of euphoria. Like he was getting away with something, or rather, that everyone knew what the game was and they wanted him to play anyway.

Instead, when he arrived, the butler solemnly ushered him in and up the stairs to the drawing room, where Lady Agnes worked on a basket of mending.

Probably more for the Women's Home. She was industrious, she was.

He thought he'd pick up fabric, haul it back to the Inn, and call it a successful visit. Instead, he was granted an audience. It took everything he could to not grin like a fox in a henhouse.

The butler announced his presence: "A Mr. Jack Townsend."

Fact: The only thing better about playing at being Miss Townsend was that it was easier to take a piss in skirts. If he could be treated the same as Jack and still wear a skirt, he wouldn't mind at all.

Jack bowed low to Lady Agnes, who was watching him closely. Odd that this room had felt different when he was dressed as an Innocent. The light was still pretty, streaming in through the window. The butler returned with a tea tray, giving Jack the eyeball as he placed it on the table in front of Lady Agnes.

"Mr. Townsend." Lady Agnes acknowledged him.

Her demeanor changed toward him completely now that she believed him to be the brother of Miss Townsend. With Miss Townsend, she was not warm, exactly, but open to possibilities. Not unguarded, exactly, but less chilly than she behaved now.

"Do sit down." Lady Agnes gestured to the blue silk chair across from her, where Miss Perry had sat a few days ago.

"Thank you, my lady," Jack murmured, taking a seat, trying for all the world to remember to walk like an errand boy since he'd given his cap to the butler when he'd entered the house. The room was bedeviling him. Or maybe Lady Agnes's piercing gaze was. Whatever it was, the confidence he'd had standing on her stoop had shaken away like dust from a rug, disappearing into the fresh air.

"Tea?" Lady Agnes offered, the teapot poised.

"Please—and thank you, my lady." Jack wiped his sweaty palms along his knees.

She handed the teacup across the table to him, watching every gesture and eyeblink. No one had ever scrutinized him this closely. Not even the first time his mother had caught him in Roland's old breeches.

"I thought we might take this moment to talk."

The smell of the tea, so strong, so dark and potent, made Jack close his eyes as he inhaled. It had bordered on magical the last time he was here. A savor, something his mother taught him, took a small moment from your day to enjoy life. To enjoy the second that is spending itself in front of you. He tipped the cup slightly and heard Lady Agnes's sharp intake of breath.

"Something wrong?" Jack asked, returning the cup to the saucer with a clatter that he associated with men's overshooting of delicate objects.

Lady Agnes's eyes narrowed. "No," she said, in a tone that did not convince Jack in the least that nothing was wrong.

"What would you like to talk about?" Jack ran through the different ways he could have said that.

Question: Would Mr. Townsend say *talk* or *chat* or *converse*? Talk. Errand boy. It was disorienting to be here with Lady Agnes.

Her dark hair was swept up, glossy strands falling artfully. More adorned than normally. Was that for him? Her dress was the color of an evergreen, and if one didn't look too closely, one would dismiss it as boring. But she had embroidered leaves on it, in the same shade of thread. The pattern washed over the bodice—fitted, which was an unusual choice for Lady Agnes—descending across the skirts. Jack couldn't see her hem, but if he had to guess, there would be a subtle pattern there, as well.

Fact: She was adorable. And talented.

"I wanted to reassure you of my good intentions towards your sister. And in a show of good faith, I've obtained an invitation to the Cuttingsworth ball for you, as chaperone to your sister."

She gestured to an envelope on the table, addressed to Mr. Jack Townsend.

Oh, that's a sticky bit.

Fact: As good as he was, Jack couldn't be in two places at once. Would she expect both Jack and Miss Townsend to show up? Sweat erupted on his palms again. He rubbed them on his trousers.

"Is there a problem?" Lady Agnes asked.

Jack shook his head no, and when he looked up at her, with that imperious look on her face, he wanted to come clean. He wanted the burgeoning friendship she allowed Miss Townsend, but he wanted it for himself, as Jack. But if he told her the truth of himself, she wouldn't give that to either Jack or Miss Townsend. Would she?

"You've a very pretty gown," Jack said, instead. "I've heard that your embroidery skills are very fine."

An arched brow was all he got in response. But it didn't make him panic in the way she probably meant it to. The arched brow made him want to misbehave.

"Have I wronged you somehow, Lady Agnes?" Jack knew the answer, but he shouldn't know the answer.

"When was the last time you saw me, Mr. Townsend?" Agnes asked.

Shit on toast. "Er, well, hm—"

"It was two weeks ago, outside of the Franklin townhouse in Marylebone. Where you are oft employed as an errand boy, so I understand."

"Oft might not be the right word." Jack had made himself useful for a few weeks when investigating the Worley case, becoming a right regular in the kitchens.

When Jack reunited the mistress with her long-lost son, he'd felt good about it, thank you very much.

After delivering the information to Mr. Worley about his mother's identity, Jack couldn't help but stand outside and wait for the day when Mr. Worley knocked on that door. So he stayed, finding a comfortable place to lean. Day after day Jack returned, counting himself lucky the times when Lady Agnes would come and go. That is, until the moment Lady Agnes exited shaky and bewildered.

"And then you followed me. What were you planning on doing, exactly? Throwing rocks? Petty theft?"

Jack flushed with embarrassment. "Nothing like that," he blurted. "You were upset, and you weren't watching where you were going! I couldn't let you get run over by a carriage or kicked by a horse because of heartbreak."

"Heartbreak?" Lady Agnes echoed, a dangerous tone creeping into her voice.

Fact: Jack worked very hard to keep secrets hidden. "I heard every rumor in those kitchens, Lady Agnes. I mean no offense, and I offer no judgement. But when a dear friend," Jack had to clear his throat. "When a dear friend leaves, no matter the reason, a body can become distraught."

"And you believed me to be distraught."

"Yes, my lady." Jack wanted to take her hand. Wanted to lean in close to her, whisper reassurances until she melted against him and rested her head on his shoulder. But none of those things were possible when he was Jack. Even as Miss Townsend, it wasn't feasible. Agnes was a proper lady.

"Then..."

Jack could stand the charade no longer. "I only wanted to keep you safe."

Color appeared on her cheeks. "I didn't realize." Her eyes dropped to her lap.

Fact: Jack had surprised her. He wasn't sure if he was pleased or ashamed that she hadn't been able to tell before.

"Perhaps I've been unfair to you, then."

Oh, of all things. She'd never been unfair to him. He was being unfair to her by not showing her the whole of who he was. But how to explain a thing like that? It's not a thing a body drops in during polite conversation. *Oh yes, one lump please, no cream. By the way, I dress in both boy's and girl's clothing because having only one path is silly rubbish. Also of interest, I can speak French and English, and I can make a grown man blush in Russian, German, and Hindi.*

"I think mayhap we've been unfair all the way around," Jack suggested gently.

Fact: An idea was forming. It wasn't a good idea. It wasn't even a sound idea. But his gut was telling him that this was a way to show Lady Agnes who he was. A gift, of sorts. In a way, it was politicking, which he was very good at. Just ask Lady Godiva.

"What do you mean?" Lady Agnes asked.

She was so innocent, Jack felt almost bad. She was so easy to maneuver. "The whole mentoring my sister for a good marriage. We all know that's a farce. You got caught out by Miss Perry and didn't contradict her."

The noblewoman looked down at her hands, swallowing hard. Oh, fer crying out loud, now Jack did feel like a proper rogue.

"But understandably so, and my sister was flattered by your attentions. Really."

The swiftness of her raising her head caught Jack off guard. Oh, she did prefer the company of Miss Townsend to himself. His heart beat faster. Maybe his plan wasn't so foolish after all. As his father would say, it might catch wind.

"My sister isn't really interested in going to the ball, exactly. It makes her nervous to be in a crowd such as that, to be looked at and scrutinized."

A series of expressions fluttered through Lady Agnes's face, becoming clear to Jack what he'd already thought: she didn't like those kinds of balls, either. Everyone eyeing young people like prize thoroughbreds.

"But I wouldn't mind making an appearance at least, since you've already gone to the trouble to get me an invitation."

"Thank you for telling me, Mr. Townsend. I'd feel terrible if Miss Townsend were uncomfortable."

"Then I will tell my sister that she can stay home the night of the ball if she so desires. But I assure you that I will attend. Perhaps I can be so bold as to ask you to reserve a dance?"

Her eyes fluttered, blinking rapidly. "Oh."

Question: Did Jack misread her? Was this not appropriate? He thought through every bit of etiquette he could remember from the years he'd had a governess.

"I can reserve a dance for you. Thank you for asking."

Jack managed to excuse himself quickly after that, wanting to escape before the awkwardness overtook both of them. He collected the bolt of fabric at the door. Miss Persephone would love it.

"**D**arling, your hair!" Lady Lorian's face lit up like someone had presented her with a pearl the size of an orange. She wore her blandest evening wear, which would still outshine even the most fashionable matron at the Cuttingsworths' ball.

"I let Miss Elise do what she wished." Agnes prodded at her coif, her hair ornamented with extra twists and dotted with a small peacock feather that was woven into the strands so as not to be garish. It wasn't for Agnes to question the aesthetics of hairdressing—it was her job to fit in, be polite, and hold her head high. And dance with Mr. Townsend. Would he understand the irony of a subtle peacock feather? Miss Townsend certainly would. Agnes's cheeks heated.

Well. Her new gown was lovely. Her mother did have something of an eye for color, and she had not steered Agnes wrong with the jewel tones of emerald and sapphire, giving her complexion added depth and her hair extra luster.

"Perhaps I ought to go as well, in case I need to field any sudden proposals," her papa quipped, rounding the corner into the drawing room. He was wearing his silk banyan, a note that he would be staying at home, warm by the fire in his library, enjoying himself with a book and a snifter of brandy. If only Agnes could join him.

He meant well, her papa. He couldn't possibly imagine what it was like for Agnes. That's all. So she smiled at him indulgently, as he used to do to her when he slipped her an extra lemon candy.

"I wish you'd managed to be this amenable earlier in the Season," her mama said. "Think of the missed opportunities."

"Not missed," Agnes returned with a note of finality. Opportunities she did not want were like roads that disappeared into a river. The roads were there, all fine and well, but it didn't do anyone any good unless they were willing to swim. "Shall we?"

Now that it was the three of them—no Lydia to cater to—her parents had relaxed into less formality when Agnes was in the room. They joked and flirted and played, all things they kept quiet while Lydia was here. Her papa actually kissed her mama on her cheek—a subtle endearment that never would have occurred if they were attending a ball with Lydia. Agnes didn't know if it was because Lydia was gone or if it was because they forgot Agnes was still in the room.

Lord Lorian walked them to the hallway before veering off to his study, bidding them good luck and good night. The warmth and ease of his study beckoned, but Agnes set her jaw. Tonight she would do it. Tonight she would be the aristocratic miss that the other young ladies wanted to be. Like Miss Townsend. No. Not like Miss Townsend. Like Mary Franklin? No, not like her either. Best to put comparisons away.

Her mother chatted the entire way to the address in some unfamiliar neighborhood. Agnes was suddenly struck by the thought that she and her mother would be overdressed. Would they embarrass everyone else who was there by having such fine gowns? Or would it be as she had read in the newspapers, where the nouveaux riches and Americans wore their finest jewels to the park in a bid to look richer than they were?

"Is everything all right?" her mama interrupted her mental fretting.

"Why wouldn't it be?" Agnes was reasonably sure her feet were sweating. Also her palms underneath her new sapphire blue gloves. Oh, she should have worn something more subtle. Something in brown. Blue and green was like wearing the entire bird, not only the feathers. And the neckline was far too low to be something any reasonable woman would wear. Her mama should have noticed something like that. Isn't that what marriage-minded mamas were all about? Unless they were trying to shove the last chick out the door.

"Here," her mother said, pulling something out of her reticule. She gestured towards her own upper lip. "Blotting paper."

Agnes took it and did what she was told, tucking it into a deep pocket that was the only concession she achieved for the night's attire.

"Is it what Lydia said?" her mama asked.

Oh goodness. What had Lydia *not* said over the years? "Which part? She can be opinionated."

Lady Lorian gave an uncharacteristic chuckle. "I will give you that point. What Lydia said about husbands. Is that why you are reluctant to dance at balls? Men scare you?"

Agnes did her best not to laugh in her mother's very classically beautiful face. How to explain that men were the furthest thing from her mind? That she had no desire to interact with them, dance with them, smell them, listen to them opine, or accept glasses of overly sweet ratafia punch from them? Let alone marry them, spend a wedding night with one, and then procure squalling babies for them. That wasn't a life. That wasn't even a decent hobby.

"I think I'm not ready." Thinking of Mr. Townsend, whom she'd promised a dance, Agnes said, "But I'm willing to try tonight. We won't know many people, and I think that might help."

Her mama nodded. "You've never liked having people watch you, have you? But I will warn you that as a titled lady, you will always have eyes on you."

"That may be," Agnes conceded. "But with Mr. Townsend by my side, I think I will manage."

"Mister Townsend? What happened to Miss Townsend?"

"It was brought to my attention that she finds balls uncomfortable, and I had no wish to push a new friend into such a situation. However, her brother, Mr. Townsend, has agreed to come in her stead."

Her mother's lips thinned. "I will only say this once, and then I will say no more. I know that your sister managed to marry a man from a different station in life than us, but it isn't always the answer. In fact, it is rarely the answer." She held up her gloved hand as if to stop any would-be protest from Agnes. "Our lives are different, our concerns more rarefied. It isn't that those without titles are worse or bad, they are merely different. And those differences can be more challenging to overcome than you might think."

Agnes's cheeks flared. "I have only agreed to dance with Mr. Townsend, not to marry him." Though, given his resemblance to the haunting Miss Townsend, would it be all that bad? Better than some of the other prospects that had drifted her way in the past.

Lady Lorian dropped her gloved hand. "I'll say no more."

They arrived at the surprisingly large home. When they were announced into the ballroom, a crush far more crowded and far better dressed than Agnes had anticipated was in full sway. Fears were all for naught, apparently. A cursory glance didn't reveal Mr. Townsend, but then, it was a large ballroom, and there were likely other chambers full of card games and such.

Pushing through the crowd, Miss Perry found her. Gripping her arm, the girl practically panted with excitement as she pulled Agnes through the crowd.

"I must introduce you to some young ladies," Miss Perry said over her shoulder. "They didn't believe that I got you here, but if you'll greet them, then we can put that whole rumor to bed."

"What rumor?" Agnes asked, a stab of fear running through her. There were so many terrible rumors, rumors that were true and others not, rumors that could hurt both her and people she loved. Doing her best not to stumble on the men and women that Miss Perry pulled her through, Agnes excused herself where she could, but her path was not making a decent impression on anyone.

Miss Perry huffed, as if Agnes was horribly daft. "The rumor that I made up our association."

Never underestimate the power of self-obsession, Lydia had once told her as she was about to embark on discovering exactly in which companies the odious Lord Hackett owned majority shares. At the time, Agnes had thought Lydia's efforts were ridiculous, childish even. But she was right. A few easy questions and Lord Hackett had boasted about all of his financials, never once suspecting Lydia's revenge.

The world was bizarre. None so bizarre as being presented to a group of young ladies, two of whom were rouged and powdered—her mother would be scandalized—all wearing white dresses with an infinite number of flounces about the hem.

"May I present," Miss Perry announced, her nose high in the air and her voice louder than it needed to be, "Lady Agnes Somerset, daughter of Lord and Lady Lorian, seventh earl—"

"Eighth," Agnes whispered the correction.

Miss Perry colored, but continued. The other girls stared at Agnes in awe. It made her dreadfully uncomfortable. Especially because she was wearing a sapphire and emerald gown while these ladies stuck with the Almack's-approved white. But it was a private ball, wasn't it? Agnes glanced around quickly. None of these people were part of the *ton*. Why were they mimicking the most boring aspects of it?

The girls curtsied at the end of the introduction, and Miss Perry went through, naming each. Agnes couldn't remember any of them within seconds of meeting them. They all smelled like cheap imitation rosewater. And her mother would be livid if Agnes were caught chumming around with the two wearing rouge.

If only Miss Townsend were here to offset this bevy of curious social climbers. Or at least Mister Townsend. She couldn't pretend she hadn't been looking for him. He was short, yes, and there was such a crush, it would be easy to lose him. Men all dressed so similarly. Surely, Mr. Townsend's presence wasn't what she was hoping for, was it? It was easy to admit she was intrigued by Miss Townsend, but her mother had a point about mixing stations in life.

It wouldn't be fair to Miss Townsend to pursue more than personal friendship when Miss Townsend had so little and Agnes had so much. It had been easier with Mary Franklin because they were both young ladies of a certain wealth—no. No thinking of

Mary Franklin. Not tonight. The pang at the thought of those dark curls springing at her touch bounced from her head to her toes and back again.

She felt a presence at her elbow, and there was a familiar scent that she still could not place.

"Pardon me, Lady Agnes," Mr. Townsend said, bowing. "I do not mean to interrupt."

Relief washed over her. Her rescue had come. "Not at all," Agnes said, trying to keep her tone even. "I'm glad you made your presence known."

The social climbers all focused on him now. And he cut quite the figure. Smaller than her, yes, and slight. But his dark hair was tousled in the way that was in fashion, curling at the high white starched collar. His cravat was tied in an intricate knot, held in place by a bright red enameled pin. His waistcoat was fitted tightly, showing off a slim torso, and as Agnes was admiring that, she realized that he had dressed to match her. The waistcoat was in the same jeweled blue and green as her gown, brilliantly offset by the red pin and a subtle red stitching and gold buttons. It was an elegant piece of finery, and no doubt cost him a year's income. Unless Miss Townsend was also a master seamstress. No, surely not.

He wore trousers, as most of the men here did, even though most of the *ton* still wore breeches to these affairs. But they weren't the baggy sort that the ladies of Almack's bemoaned. Mr. Townsend's were tight like the Beau Brummel illustrations, showing off shapely calves and muscular thighs. Agnes colored at her own delight of his details. She should not be looking at such things, but then, judging by the looks of the other women, they, too, noticed the fit of Mr. Townsend's trousers.

"Ladies, I would like to introduce an acquaintance of mine, Mr. Jack Townsend."

He performed a sweeping bow, which elicited a

gasp of appreciation from the young ladies. He cut a dashing figure, even she had to admit that.

"I hate to take you away from such delicate company, but you have promised me a dance," Mr. Townsend said with a smile, showing off a mouthful of straight, white teeth. Something felt out of place, but she couldn't figure it.

Perhaps it was that he looked so much like Miss Townsend. The smile could be a family trait, true. The way they both reacted to her tea—eyes closed, those beautiful, long, dark, lashes on display, as if trying to savor the moment in their minds. Agnes put it out of her mind, as she was determined to enjoy her dance if she could.

Mr. Townsend offered his hand, eliciting sighs from the other young ladies. His hands felt surprisingly soft. As if he wore gloves regularly, or was a gentleman. Agnes took his arm, and there was something about it that felt comfortable. More comfortable than any other man's arm that she knew. Not like taking her father's arm, but different somehow. Safer? No, not that. Like she wanted to sink into him, the way she had felt when pushed up against Miss Townsend in the carriage. What was it about this family?

Agnes looked around for her mother and nodded for permission. Her mother smiled, gracious as always, standing next to Mrs. Tyler of the boarding house, likely already bored silly. Perhaps this would drive her to cards and gambling. The thought made Agnes giggle, which earned her a curious glance from Mr. Townsend.

The dancefloor shifted, the musicians readying the next piece and the dancers rearranging themselves accordingly.

Agnes was a proficient dancer but not particularly enchanting, she knew. Lessons had been part of her education, as had French, pianoforte, and her embroidery. But with large, wide feet, dancing made her feel far more like a duck than a swan.

"Are you well this evening, my lady?" Mr. Townsend asked.

There was a glimmer in his eyes, as if he were expecting a gift at any moment. What could he possibly be gloating about? Well, dancing with the daughter of an earl was a coup at this sort of event, surely. Even one with duck feet.

Her slipper chose that moment to dislodge. This was yet another reason why she preferred to wear men's work shoes. They didn't pop off her feet at the worst moments. If she didn't stop soon, she would lose the slipper entirely.

"Oh, pardon me," she said, wincing. Was it better to fix the slipper here or limp to the corner? Limp to the corner and try to see if she could fix her wardrobe without the scrutiny of an entire ballroom. "My slipper seems to have a problem. Would you mind dreadfully escorting me to the side? I'm so sorry."

"Not at all. Your company is enchanting regardless of the musical accompaniment." Mr. Townsend deftly guided her out of the crowd of dancers and to a chair against a wall. "And if I may, we didn't even start dancing. I still believe you are obligated to fulfill your promise later."

Agnes hung on to him as if he were rescuing her from drowning. He still seemed pleased with himself. She took a seat and adjusted her slipper with a quick and hardly noticeable motion. Her cheeks heated. All of this for her feet. Not exactly the picture of grace she was supposed to be as the daughter of an earl.

"Would you like me to get you some ratafia? Or perhaps you'd prefer to take some air on the veranda?"

The veranda? He couldn't possibly be offering an

assignation? Not that she would engage in such, but still. Very surprising. But there were unscrupulous young men who wanted to climb the social ladder and thought an earl's daughter was the best stepping stone.

That glint was there again. Not avarice, but something entirely different—childlike almost, like inviting her to play a game of chase.

"Thank you, yes. Some air would be lovely." Agnes stood. She didn't want to gag down another cup of ratafia in her life.

Mr. Townsend smiled and slipped out the doors with her. The night was cool, but welcome after the heat of the ballroom. She shivered as a breeze prickled the skin of her bare arms and low neckline.

"My apologies, I should have realized—" Mr. Townsend was babbling an apology as he catalogued the bumps on her skin. But he swallowed hard, drifting his gaze up her arm.

Agnes felt curiously warm. She'd never been on the receiving end of a glance like that. Not even Mary Franklin looked at her like Mr. Townsend did, as if every inch of her revealed skin was a temptation. Perhaps she did need the cool air. She was quite light-headed suddenly.

Agnes waved him off. "It isn't your fault. It's the fashion of women's dresses. Men have the opportunity to wear layers to keep warm. All of my layers are—are—" Was she really talking about her underthings to a man? Oh, bloody hell, her mother would have her head.

And then, suddenly, a thought occurred to her. When she and Lydia shared parfum, they smelled entirely different despite the fact that they were sisters.

JACK ALMOST CHOKED AT THE OBLIQUE MENTION OF Agnes's clothing and the layers it did or did not have. There would be a shift, of course, thin fabric, something beautiful and soft, most likely. Silk stockings on those long, long legs. What color ribbon would they be tied with? Blue like the ocean? Green like a meadow? Deep brown, the color of tree bark in the darkest of enchanted forests? She always wore such serviceable colors, but what was the color she wore to make herself happy?

Fact: Thinking of a woman's underthings was not a way to carry on a conversation. Focus. Jack blinked away the visions of Agnes's long legs, ribbons tied around supple thighs to hold up silk stockings.

He tried to concentrate on their similarities. His waistcoat was of the same fabric as Lady Agnes's dress. Miss Persephone had gushed at the quality of it, paired it with red thread and gold buttons, despite Jack insisting he wanted something more sedate. Miss Persephone had huffed about men's fashion for a good quarter of an hour, blaming Beau Brummel for taking the bright colors from men's palette, and cursing him into oblivion. "If a peacock has all the praise in the world for its tailfeathers, shouldn't the male breeds be given the same God-given rights? Where are the Americans on about that, I ask you?" Miss Persephone said before giving up her rant and concentrating on the fine red stitching.

Fact: Jack had planned something big, which was why he wanted a sedate costume. Something to blend in and fade away, but matching Lady Agnes, implying they were of a pair, was too much of a temptation. Miss Persephone had won, and the waistcoat was a triumph. The way the other young ladies gawked was not lost on him.

Tonight he had a plan. He did not know how it would play, but he wanted to try all the same. If Lady

Agnes got angry, he could skip out over the garden wall. But if she agreed, oh, the night they could have together.

"Lady Agnes," he said, drawing her gaze. His mouth went dry and his heart skipped a beat. Could he do this? "There is a certain freedom in men's clothing."

She looked bewildered. "I'm sure there is."

How to bring this deftly around to his offer? "Being a man gives allowances, permissions, if you will—"

Her expression changed to horror.

Oh, shit on toast. She thought he was trying to proposition her. He stumbled over his words, trying to get them out fast enough. "I would never suggest anything dishonorable. Rather, I want to share with you a freedom."

An arched brow. Pursed lips. And then widened eyes. Well, he deserved her skepticism. Wait—the way she was looking at him was one of realization. Ah, fuck.

Fact: One cannot hide forever.

"Do you wear any scent?"

"Pardon?" He waited for the blow of her anger, but a question on hygiene was not what he expected.

"Or perhaps it is a soap. It's very distinctive. Where did you get it?"

"I don't see what my soap has to do with anything."

"Do you share your soap?"

"No, of course not. My soap is my own."

A satisfied wisp of a smirk flitted across her face.

Fact: Lady Agnes's smirk was something he would desperately like to see again, despite his sinking feeling that he was the victim of it and not sharing in it.

"Which one are you, really?"

Fact: He wanted to kiss that smirk off her smug, beautiful face, leave her panting, which was not helping a conversation that was very likely fraught. This was not at all how Jack had imagined this conversation going.

"It has been hard for me to tell. You seem so comfortable in both a gown and in the breeches. And your mannerisms are impeccable."

Lady Agnes assessed him up and down. It was damned unnerving, and all it served was to make his tongue stick to the roof of his mouth.

"But it was your tea drinking that gave it away. Good tea, after all, is a great equalizer. Not to mention the orange scent. I can wear a perfume and lend it to my sister, and we smell entirely different. Yet Mr. Townsend and Miss Townsend smell oddly identical."

"Now, I—" Wait. His mind took in all the information, chewing it thoughtfully, like an already full dog. His mouth struggled to hurry along his brain. Her gaze made him want to both strut and hide.

"Personally, I believe you to be Miss Townsend because no man would be insane enough to ever want to live life as a flower girl, selling blooms in Covent Garden."

Fact: *No one* recognized him as he shifted between his identities. His mind flipped over itself like a freshly caught fish. "I'm not really a flower girl," was all he could manage.

She raised an eyebrow at him. She was a right goddess, there was no doubt about it. Instead of making him feel like a lowly insect creeping in front of her, he adored her even more as his mind flopped this way and that.

She didn't appear to want to call the constables on him. He loved that she wasn't going to call constables on him. He loved that she seemed to enjoy finding him out.

Fact: None of this was helpful.

It was more mess than helpful. While Lady Agnes clearly preferred feminine assignations, she did not prefer Jack. But she didn't really know who he was, did she?

"Are you—"

Dear God, what was she asking? He nearly blushed. If it was too much to discuss the weight of a chemise in polite company, how was it polite to discuss what lay beneath his trousers?

He knew she would eventually ask this question. Because the world looked clean and clear to most people. A or B. This or that. Black or White. Brit or Foreigner. What about if the world was A *and* B? Why did wanting A preclude B? And particularly unpopular, why did being either boy or girl preclude being the other? Why could people not see that the whole idea of it was a bit silly in the first place?

"Neither. I'm neither. Both." Jack shook his head. He relaxed into his normal voice, a bit higher than Mr. Townsend's, a bit lower than Miss Townsend's. "You've got me all addled, that's true." There was no way to give her an easy answer. Because her whole world would have to change in order for her to understand.

Her gaze softened, so at least there was some progress. "There now, there you are. Enough games." She held out her hand. "Hello. A pleasure to finally meet you." She looked at him expectantly.

He reached out to her as if she were a man, like they were somehow equals. But weren't they, though? In some glorious worldly view of the entire bloody earth that he hoped she could see? He felt wild and short of breath and exploding all at once. "Jack. I'm just Jack."

"Jack." Her hand snaked out, unsure, grasping his. "Lady Agnes Somerset, daughter of the eighth earl of Lorian."

"Jack About Town," he answered, still wanting to hold something back from her. He didn't want to lay himself completely bare—he had to protect himself somehow. "Of less illustrious parentage."

"I'm surprised," she admitted. Her eyes flitted over him, assessing and measuring again. She seemed disappointed somehow. "I truly thought you were Miss Townsend."

Jack met her eyes, bold as anything. He was a greedy fiend, to be sure. "Nothing I said was untrue."

Fact: He wanted everything she would give him. Every glance, every syllable from her beautiful mouth. She made his heart pound, and he was addicted to the nervous clutch she caused.

"Well," she said, clapping her gloved hands together. "At least that settles it. I no longer have to scheme to find you a husband, do I? And if there is nothing else I can do for you, sir, I shall be on my way."

Jack caught her hand, the satin of her glove so smooth and cool. This was his chance. "Perhaps there is something I can do for you."

Disdain flashed across her features. "Offer me a no-strings-attached marriage, yes? Snag an earl's daughter, acquire her dowry, and shunt her off to some decrepit country house once you get your hands on the family fortune? I thought you had more imagination than that."

Jack barked out a laugh and shook his head. "I promise that I'll never offer to marry you, my lady."

For a moment, her face seemed to crease with displeasure. Her voice was low with hostility. "Then what are you offering?"

Jack let go of her hand, retreating. She was like a

cat: the animal will disdain being coveted but can't stand to be ignored. Lady Agnes would have to come to him. "Freedom. Real freedom."

Lady Agnes stared at him a moment, her expression unreadable. Then, she rolled her eyes. "I don't know what kind of charlatan you are, but I promise you, I'm not one to fall for these types of schemes. I recommend a boat to America. Plenty of wide-open spaces and gullible bores."

"I want to show you a different path. One that you've likely never seen and possibly have never heard of."

She snorted. "That won't take much. Have you no knowledge of the coddled state of young ladies like myself?"

Jack inclined his head, trying to give respect, but also hint at his own past. "Perhaps more than you'd expect."

"Then what do you propose?" She crossed her arms and set her jaw, clearly not ready to believe anything he had to say.

"Back in this garden—"

She snorted again. "I'm not going into that garden with you. I'm not a fool."

"I didn't say I would go in there with you," Jack corrected. Finally, he was feeling one step ahead of her. He gave her his best grin, the kind full of invitation and mischief—or at least as much as he could muster since she was making him pant with nerves. "I left a pile of men's clothing. Change, snip snap, it's an easy step up to the garden wall, and from the garden wall to the roof."

"You must be joking."

If he were to draw her in that moment, she would be all scowls and crossed arms, and thin, humorless lines.

Fact: Jack was surprised.

Very few people reacted to him so poorly, which made it hard to know what to do next. He couldn't believe she wouldn't jump at the chance to run through the streets whooping like an unruly hooligan. "Don't you want freedom? A small taste of it?"

"Who doesn't?" She jabbed back, but nothing in her posture was relaxing.

"I'm offering to be your guide. I'll meet you on the rooftop."

Her eyes narrowed. "What do you gain in this bargain?"

"The pleasure of your company."

She snorted in disbelief, which was not terribly ladylike, but at least she was being authentic. "No. See, that's the bit so many don't understand. I have to cultivate a number of different skills as the daughter of an earl, and one of those is to know where I don't belong. I don't belong with you, sir, and I don't belong on a rooftop. I'll bid you a good evening. *My regards to your sister.*" She spat the last sentence at him like it was poison and left him alone on the veranda, heart pounding and gasping for breath.

❧ 6 ❧

Agnes stomped through the ballroom, wishing once again for her boots. She'd stomp every hem and dainty slipper in sight. Her mother was doing her best to not look bored by two matrons who had cornered her.

"Pardon me," Agnes said, not bothering to wait for a pause in the conversation. "Mama, I have a terrible pain in my—head. May we please go?"

Her mother eyed her, wordlessly calling out Agnes's extremely poor lying skills, but accepting the situation.

"My apologies ladies, I must go. You know how it is with our delicate daughters." Her mama gave the women a smile that would alleviate any rudeness and accompanied Agnes out. "Do we need to make your excuses to Miss Perry or our hostess?"

"There's plenty of people here. We won't be missed," Agnes groused as they weaved around guests.

"You know there are greater expectations on us than on others," her mama reminded her, deftly sidestepping ratafia cups and fielding apologies with a gracious smile.

"I'll pen a note in the morning to both of them, explaining my stomachache."

"I thought it was your head, darling," she murmured.

They gathered their cloaks and the footman called for their carriage. As they waited, her mother watched as Agnes fidgeted and stamped and huffed in a small circle. Agnes had never been so grateful as to sink into those seats.

Her mother picked at her gown as the carriage lurched into motion. "Would you mind telling me the source of your head and or stomach pains?"

Agnes bit her lip, contemplating not revealing anything but also realizing that would never work, and she was an atrocious liar. She must give her mother credit. "You were correct about Mr. Townsend."

Her mama gave her a sympathetic smile. "Better to know now."

"Of course." And then the carriage was silent the rest of the ride home, allowing Agnes to sulk quietly to herself. The audacity of Mr. Townsend made her skin positively itch. How dare he proposition her? What man would stoop so low? And how would he know she preferred the company of other young ladies? The last thought worried her. It wasn't unusual for a young woman such as herself to have the preference, given how sheltered they were from young men, but she didn't like the idea of someone *noticing*. Elegance, after all, was the art of being gracefully invisible.

MRS. BETTLETON WAS IN THE KITCHEN WHEN JACK arrived home. The ten o'clock tidbits were ready to be served. "What're you doing back so early?" The woman didn't look up from her stacking of food on the tray.

"Just finished, that's all." Jack rounded the kitchen workspace where Mrs. Bettleton stood and snatched up a confusing mess of bread and spread.

"Oi now, leave that for company."

"It's my night off," Jack said between chews. It wasn't bad, sort of wet. Good thing most of the guests were likely already pissed. "I am a guest."

"Take that tray up to the rest of 'em and I'll consider it even."

Jack nodded and hoisted the large platter. The narrow stairs up to the main floor were challenging with this tray, but he'd done it many times before. He tried to feel insulted that he was working on his day off, but he was grateful to not go sulk in his room.

Fact: He'd made the effort and extended the offer, and Lady Agnes said no. Ladies did not go off cavorting with the likes of Jack. Even ladies like her— the kind who wore men's boots.

But those things that caught his attention, well, they had made him think Lady Agnes was like him and was in need of freeing. And that was his mistake.

Fact: She wasn't like him, and she wasn't for a person who lived like him, in a molly-house, combing through the secrets of London to find the best bits like a mud larker of Society. It was a reminder that even he was so selfish that he couldn't see past what was right in front of him. They were not the same, no matter how much he wished it.

As Jack opened the door from the servants' stair, a drunken guest whirled in an unstable circle. "Is this the pâté? At last!"

"Yes sir," Jack answered, unsure and not caring if he was right. He bustled over to the empty table in the corner, clearing glasses with one hand to make way for the tray of whatever this was. If Miss

Persephone was doing her job, she should be here in a moment to help with the tray.

"Hold still, little pip!" the drunken patron cried, trying to grab a morsel from Jack's tray. His face was puffy with drink, cheeks rosy and eyes glassy. His clothes were finely tailored, and the trousers fit so closely to his calves that Jack could see the ribbons from where he tied the padding.

"Let me put it down first," Jack growled, trying to balance the tray against the attacks.

"If you'd stop swaying so much, I could get my fill," the patron whined.

"Give me but a minute and you'll have your way. You can feed like a donkey at a trough."

"Are you calling me an ass?" The patron drew back as if thoroughly affronted. He suddenly reminded Jack of a squirrel in Hyde Park.

"Your words, sir, not mine." Jack cleared the last of the wine glasses and set down the heavy tray.

"And here I believed this to be a place of manners —I'll not darken these doors again!" The patron wobbled on his heeled shoes as he made his way to the door.

This was Jack's job: to smooth over ruffled feathers. The insurance that they'd not get reported to the constable, not be subjected to a raid. "Fuck me running," Jack mumbled and clomped after the man.

"Ho there, friend," Jack said, putting a hand on the man's shoulder. Unfortunately, the man was drunker than even Jack had perceived, and the weight of one hand brought the patron to the ground.

"I've broken my ankle! Help!" the patron writhed on the floor, his eyes squeezed shut.

"Now, now," Jack said, trying to smile at the other guests, hoping that the man wouldn't make the scene he was already clearly making by shaking his presumably hurt foot in the air. "It can't be as bad as all that."

The patron pried one eye open. "You! Donkey Boy! Away from me! Get your hands off of me. I cannot, cannot——"

Miss Persephone sauntered over, powdered and rouged, kohled and bedecked. "Must be a good night. You're home early *and* you've upset the clientele."

"Not in the mood," Jack ground out.

"Want me to handle this one, Donkey Boy?" Miss Persephone cooed, making sympathetic faces at the patron who was still ranting on the floor.

"Fine." Jack wanted wine. Or ale. Or gin. Or whatever it took to make this night end.

"Say thank you and you get the door." Miss Persephone was already bending down, reaching to scoop up the miserable drunk patron like a baby. "Do you need another glass of wine? Or ale? What can I get for you, *ma chérie?*"

Jack grumbled and went to the post by the door. It wasn't a formal night so there were no tokens being dropped in a bowl, or even a stool set aside to collect them. Instead, it was a small table and chair nearest the door. Which, at least, Miss Persephone still had a carafe of wine at the ready. Jack poured himself a cup —Miss Persephone kept an extra one on the table should she find a new guest particularly charming.

He smoothed his embroidered waistcoat and took a sip. The clothes, at least, had been well-received. Lady Agnes had eyeballed them, her expression surprise and pleasure. The admiration of the other ladies was a lovely bonus, but it was her he'd wanted to impress.

The Inn was fairly crowded for it being so early. They were more of a late-night establishment—the after-party for a certain set.

There was no reason Jack was any different than

the other guests. He could be a patron tonight, dressed as he was, drinking wine as he was. And didn't he deserve time off?

The musicians returned from a break and began to play a country dance. A cheer went up and couples crowded the floor. A circle formed, widening as each person joined. Jack cradled his cup of wine and sat back to watch. This, at least, should take the edge off his dark mood.

"Hullo, Jack." Familiar faces ambled through the door. Jack raised his hand to return the greeting. He could be politic if he could shake the refusal from Lady Agnes.

He should get up and circulate. He could keep an eye on the door, and Miss Persephone should be done with that drunken baby soon. As he stood, the circle of dancers wobbled and split. A rogue stepper careened into Jack, spilling claret down his embroidered finery.

"Oh my, I do apologize," the rogue said, fingers scrabbling at the embroidery, catching on the thread, pulling and yanking. The peacock waistcoat, the pair to Lady Agnes's gown, was ruined.

Fact: Jack never lost his temper.

The music stopped. The dancers all stared.

"Oh dear," the rogue repeated, snagging another thread with an errant fingernail, brushing at the claret-soaked fabric.

"Stop!" Jack snatched the rogue's hand, crushing it without thought.

Regular patrons knew this wasn't his usual behavior. He was smooth like French cream. The air grew thick with tension.

"I beg your pardon," the rogue said, wrenching his hand free.

"By your leave," Jack said through clenched teeth,

trying to sidestep the man, who seemed to be in the way at every turn.

"Please, send me the bill," the rogue said. "Your clothing—the wine—it—"

"I am aware." Jack skirted the rogue and the circle of dancers. The music started up again and the room tore away their collective gaze.

This night was the worst he'd had in a long while. He spotted another familiar face, this one clomping towards him with a determined look. Shit on toast.

Lord Haverformore waddled up. "Jack. We need to discuss terms."

"Terms of what?" Jack demanded. The claret was soaking to his skin. Not only did he not get to drink it, he was basting in it.

"Your fee! I have it, so you'll have it. Come to my house tomorrow eve. I can fill in the details and get you the first portion of your payment."

"Fine," Jack said, wanting to hide upstairs before he did something foolish.

"Grand! Come by way of the servants' entrance, if you would. Discretion, and all that."

"Yes, my lord," Jack mumbled, edging away.

"Deuces," the lord mumbled to his companion as Jack left. "That was easier than I thought."

The drunken baby blocked Jack's access to the servants' stair. "You! I demand an apology!"

Jack groaned. "Leave me be."

"No, you twisted my ankle, and—"

"What, not broken anymore?" Jack said, crossing his arms, squeezing the wetness even closer in. The shirt beneath was already ruined. He might as well settle in with the claret soak.

"You little—" the drunk hissed.

Miss Persephone came up behind him and shrugged her shoulders, as if to say there was nothing else to be done. In that brief moment when Jack's attention was elsewhere—that's all it took—the drunk took a swing at Jack.

Fortunately, the training Jack had undergone with Miss Bess Abbott—London's Boxing Championess—was thorough. He easily sidestepped the sloppy fist and let the drunken baby fall onto his face. But perhaps that was worse, because for the second time that evening, the drunken baby was wailing on the floor.

"I'm going to bed," Jack grumbled to Miss Persephone, who only nodded, looking in dismay at the damage the claret had done to Jack's clothing.

He slipped into the servants' stairwell, heading up to his room. He stripped off his coat, whipping it to let fly any more droplets of wine. He'd soak it in the cold water he kept in the ewer and deal with it in the morning.

It wasn't late—the clock hadn't even struck eleven yet. But here he was, alone, stripping off wine-ruined clothes that were too fine for him to wear. He knew that. He *knew* it. But he had taken the risk anyway because that's who he was. And he knew that you couldn't ignore who you were, because of all the people in the world, you couldn't escape yourself. That person never went away. And you'd best reconcile yourself because you couldn't fight forever.

As the waistcoat soaked in the washing basin, he shucked off the black low-heeled dancing shoes. He'd liked those—gave him some height. Then Jack stripped off his trousers and stockings. And finally, he pulled off the long linen shirt, pink with touches of claret soaked through. He stuffed the shirt in the basin along with the waistcoat, hoping to get some magical result by tomorrow morning.

He pulled off the chest bindings, easing off the wide linen bandaging. His breasts puckered in the cool air.

He poured cold water into his hands and scrubbed his face with a rag. The powder came off, the dark and the light that Miss Persephone helped him apply to make his jaw seem squarer and his cheekbones sharper. This life. He liked the shifting of identities, the dodging of answers that kept him safe.

Except tonight. With Lady Agnes. When he'd tried to give her the answers, tried to show her his path and invited her along. She'd refused. She wasn't even tempted.

He slipped on a nightshirt before clambering into bed, trying to settle on the well-padded mattress, the ropes creaking underneath as he shifted.

All he wanted were simple things: a job, some friends, someone to love who might smile at his jokes. Simple things. So why did everything have to be so complex and convoluted? He was not a person bent towards melancholia, or even towards dark comedy. Yet, here he was: wine-soaked in the most literal and unsatisfying way, feeling more alone than he had in years.

He snuffed the candle and willed his mind blank.

❦

THE NEXT MORNING, AGNES PENNED APPROPRIATE excuses to both Miss Perry and Lady Cuttingsworth, citing vague ailments that alluded to unexpected menses, which ought to curtail further discussion or visits.

Despite the polite words and excellent penmanship, Agnes was furious. She hadn't been this furious in—well, perhaps never. Was this how Lydia felt every day? There was something curiously energizing about the experience, though she also felt feather-brained at the same time.

When she arrived in the upstairs drawing room

with her embroidery, she found her mother already there with a novel. After Lydia moved out, her mother had taken back the room that Lydia had dominated since her debut.

"Aren't you ill?" her mother asked, lowering the book only slightly.

"Never felt better," Agnes said, hearing the thin, sharp tone that screeched from her mouth.

Her mother raised a delicate brow and returned to reading.

Agnes set up her embroidery hoop, starting a new abstract pattern that she had sketched onto the linen a few days ago. Not at all fashionable, with the exception, perhaps, of her color scheme, the geometric figures were intertwined, creating a diagonally radiating design. Not something to be displayed in a public room, perhaps, but gratifying nonetheless. While threading her first needle, she pricked her finger—an unusual occurrence, but hardly noteworthy. As soon as she got the vermilion threaded, the light shifted. She sighed and chased the light to another seat nearer to the window. Before she could get much accomplished, the light changed again. She picked up her basket to move.

"Agnes!" Her mother said sharply. "Why don't you go take some exercise?"

"Pardon?" Agnes stopped in mid-stride.

"You are clearly out of sorts. Might you take a walk? Or visit your sister?" Her mother's normally genial face was lined with frustration.

"Of course." Agnes blinked. The changing clouds might signal rain, so a walk in the park was an unappealing prospect, but visiting Lydia might help Agnes figure out her sudden anger.

Her mother nodded in approval, watching Agnes leave the room as if she were a sheepdog bounding about with muddy paws.

Thus, Agnes found her way to Marylebone, driven by Vasily.

Parsons escorted her to the drawing room, told her he'd ring for tea and let Lydia know she had an early caller. They were sisters. Was it truly too early to visit her *sister*?

Suddenly, the visit felt odd. She wasn't some stranger. She'd witnessed Lydia's change as a child—from flirtatious and bold to sullen and melancholy. And of course, she'd kept company while Lydia trained with Miss Abbott, week after week, year after year. Had even heard an ungraceful pop the first time Lydia had not adequately defended herself against Miss Abbott's attacks. Had handed over her own handkerchief to staunch the blood.

So why was she sitting in the formal drawing room, waiting to be received?

A maid brought in a tray of refreshments. At least tea would occupy her. She poured the hot, dark brew —it appeared that Agnes's note to Pearl had done the trick. In fact, the tea appeared very similar to the kind they served at Agnes's house. Or her mother's house. Her father's house? Whose house was it, exactly?

Agnes shook her head. She was definitely out of sorts today.

Picking up the lightly painted white teacup full of hot tea, she remembered Mr. Townsend's—no, Jack About Town's—reaction to it. The closed eyes, the dreamy appreciation evident on his beautiful face. Those high cheekbones and long, dark lashes, the indent of the cupid's bow of his upper lip. She felt a stirring in her belly before remembering the events at the ball last night. His scrambling, grasping trick to compromise an earl's daughter.

The fury sped through her again. She set the teacup down as her hands began to shake. The idea that she would be so stupid as to run off with some duplicitous street hoodlum! It was positively insulting. Demeaning, really. As if she would go *remove her clothing* in a garden at someone else's ball? Really. How idiotic would a person have to be to fall for such a ruse?

She stood and paced the room. Where was Lydia? Is this why she had begged for a boxing instructor? Because pacing was not at all restorative.

The door swung open, admitting not Lydia but Pearl Arthur.

"Lady Agnes," Pearl said, a soft, glimmering smile on her elven face. She was like her namesake, somehow otherworldly in her grace and luminous eyes. How she and the hard, raw-boned prizefighter John were of the same parentage, Agnes would never know. There was something about the pair that confirmed their connection, but for the life of her, Agnes couldn't figure it out.

"If you use my title, I will have to return the formality," Agnes warned. She tried out a smile. Yes, Pearl could soothe this monster inside of her.

Agnes was granted a swift curtsy. "As you wish, Agnes. So good of you to call." Pearl made her way over to the sitting area, which made Agnes return to the upholstered chairs as well.

"I see the tea has already been made available. Excellent." Pearl poured herself a cup.

There was a silence, which was where Agnes expected to hear why her sister was not here. But Pearl said nothing.

"This is lovely tea," Agnes said. "Very similar to what we serve."

"How was the Cuttingsworth ball? Miss Perry wrote me that she was very pleased you would be attending."

The feeling of Mr. Townsend's arm, the flutter of

excitement she had felt, bubbled to the surface, only to be replaced by the shame of being fooled by his flattery. "It was a fine ball. More guests than I'd believed possible. We didn't stay late, however."

"Oh?" Pearl asked, her polite question making it clear that her mind was elsewhere.

Not surprising, considering Agnes's mind was also elsewhere. Whose wouldn't be during a conversation this vapid? Where was Lydia? "I do hope Miss Perry managed without my company. She seemed to have many friends."

"Yes, a personality like Miss Perry's guarantees many friends." Pearl's light blue eyes settled on Agnes's, as if focusing on her for the first time.

"Yes."

"Mm." Pearl sipped at her tea.

Agnes copied the same motion. "Well."

"Yes." Pearl's eyes unfocused again, looking past Agnes out to the garden window behind her.

The whole thing was about to drive Agnes mad. Finally, the door opened again, and this time Lydia appeared.

She looked terrible.

Her pallor was off, and her normally smooth skin looked puffy, almost doughy. Her eyes were rimmed in red, and her face was flushed.

Agnes stood. She couldn't help it—the alarm of seeing Lydia look so...human...was shocking.

"Good morning, Agnes," Lydia said as if nothing in the world was wrong. "I didn't realize you were visiting today. And so early, too."

"I know it isn't visiting hours yet." Agnes glanced at the clock on the mantel. It was nearly noon. Not a terribly early hour, and certainly not an early hour for a family that didn't attend social events. "But since we are sisters, I didn't think it an imposition to call. Mother suggested it."

Lydia should have snorted—but she didn't. Instead, she slowly and gracefully sank into the seat next to Pearl.

"May I pour?" Pearl asked Lydia, as if there was formality between two women who lived together.

"Please," Lydia said.

The whole thing was enough to make the hair on the back of Agnes's neck stand on end. She wanted to throw Pearl out of the room and shake Lydia by the arms. But of course, she wouldn't.

"How have you been?" Agnes asked.

"Since our last visit?" Lydia questioned, her eyes flicking up from the teacup, the familiar challenge of her gaze muted but present. This wasn't Lydia. This wasn't her fire-breathing sister.

It was like Lydia was there, buried deep beneath layers of flesh and burden. And Agnes had no idea how one went about excavating a sister.

7

Jack hated himself as he dragged his feet to the servants' entrance at Lord Haverformore's home.

Fact: Haverformore's real-world identity was Mr. Wycliff, the second son of a second son. The man had worked—briefly—until he made some lucky investments and wealthy acquaintances, which allowed him to take on the life of a gentleman.

Fact: When wanting to know the wealth of a man, it was helpful to maintain friendships with both members and staff of gentlemen's clubs.

Mr. Wycliff styled himself a collector. And, according to the staff at his club, Mr. Wycliff preferred objets d'art that were of a more scandalous nature, bragging about them to other club members. Jack assumed that meant pornography of some kind, and each person had their own flavor of preference, not that Jack cared who liked what, as long as no one got hurt.

Jack knocked on the kitchen door. A large man with a barrel chest and a salt-and-pepper mustache greeted him. The man had clearly been waiting for his arrival.

"Mr. About Town?"

"Pleased to meet you," Jack said, reaching out his hand, but it was ignored. The man towered over him, and Jack was reminded again that superior strength was not his skill; his skills were confidence and information.

Fact: Some people mistook this as cleverness because they didn't understand the difference between that and being well-prepared.

Jack followed the bull-like figure up through the servants' stair and into the public rooms of the modest home. The location may have been Mayfair, an enviable address, but the house itself was nothing of note. In fact, even Jack and Miss Persephone kept the Inn cleaner than this home. Obviously, Mr. Wycliff, née Lord Haverformore, spent his money on things other than staff.

The mountainous butler knocked on a door.

"Yes," called Mr. Wycliff from inside, prompting the butler to swing wide the door.

It was a small room made all the smaller by being crammed full of books and curio cabinets. A gas lamp was lit on the small desk where Wycliff sat, and a low fire was going in the far side of the room, necessary even in June in this sort of drafty room.

The low light cast the features of Haverformore, or rather Wycliff, in a craggy light. At the Inn, he used paint and powder on his face to cover the pockmarks, but here, in his own domain, his natural state seemed more ominous.

"Ah, Jack, so good of you to come." The words were thick, as if he may have already been indulging too much before Jack's arrival.

"Mr. Wycliff," Jack acknowledged. He noted that the butler had left, and the door clicked shut behind him. There was nothing truly imposing about the room, but still, Jack felt ill at ease. Like he needed to be ready to run.

The man grunted in surprise. "You know my name."

"May I sit?" Jack asked, gesturing to the rickety-looking chair in front of the desk.

Wycliff gestured for him to sit. "Business, then?"

Jack nodded, noting the man's furtive glances as he shuffled papers while trying to hide their contents.

"Here is the banknote." Wycliff looked at it longingly for a second before pushing it across the desk. "All in order."

"Many thanks," Jack said, not glancing at it, merely folding it and tucking it into a concealing pocket he'd sewn into the inside of his waistcoat. He preferred keeping money close to his body. Pickpocketing was an art, and the best of them could steal your smallclothes without you noticing.

"To tell you the import of this item, I'd like to tell you a bit of my history, if you will indulge me. Brandy, first?"

Jack shook his head no but gestured for him to continue, very curious to hear what the man might say.

Fact: Some secrets people outright told you. But you had to listen.

"As one garners years and friends, they both accumulate, until sadly, the former continues to ascend and the latter declines." Wycliff did look a bit dismayed at that, looking into the fire across the room.

Jack wondered if that distracted stare was for his benefit or if it was a true longing. He had his doubts.

"I had the unfortunate distinction of losing a very dear friend early on. Quite a mind. Fiercely intelligent, accomplished artist—all in all, quite a man."

"Sounds like it." Jack reserved judgement on those mentioned in a eulogy.

"His sketches were of great import to me, as you can imagine. Sketches of us, our wild youth, that sort of thing." Wycliff made a flopping motion with his hand, as if this explained or excused whatever he meant by *wild*. "More than anything, I desire to see those sketches again. Relive our *bonhomie*, if only through his long-crumbled pencil. It's been many years since I last saw them. I want you to find them."

Those sketches were likely not profiles or landscapes. Jack's shoulders relaxed. He hadn't any idea why the task was worth the exorbitant fee he'd named, but it didn't matter. Sketches were innocuous and not something he had to bend his feelings around. So find he would. This time, for loads and loads of money. They could fix up the Inn. He could buy a share off Mrs. Bettleton, make the Inn permanent in his life. Make it his.

"Where was the last place you knew the sketches to be?" Jack pulled out a small book to write down any information Wycliff might give.

The man looked surprised. "I didn't realize you would record any of this information."

Fact: A mind could only retain so much before the waters muddied. Given what had happened with Lady Agnes, Jack didn't trust his mind at the moment. "I record things like account numbers or addresses, things that must be precise."

"Of course." Wycliff took a swallow from his brandy snifter. "The last time I saw the contents were when the man in question slid his portfolio into his private safe in his study."

Jack blinked at the man across from him. He closed his book. Shit on toast. "You want me to break into a safe in a private home."

Wycliff shifted in his chair, his expression like a guilty child's. "Well, if it remains there, then yes."

"And how long ago was this?"

"Perhaps about fifteen years?" Wycliff levered himself out of the chair and took to pacing the small rug in front of the fireplace.

"That's *very* illegal."

"And your prices are *very* high," Wycliff retorted.

Jack set his jaw. Wycliff had a point. The portfolio might not be in the safe anymore. The man in question—yet to be named, Jack noted with some concern—had died. His effects may have been transferred elsewhere. He could at least research heirs and estates before breaking into someone's home. Jack sighed. "It's only one portfolio?"

"The one."

"No other *while-you're-there* requests?"

Fact: Clients always had a *while-you're-there* list that often was the real reason they wanted him to find things in the first place.

"None."

"Fine. Terms accepted. Full payment upon delivery."

Wycliff harrumphed. "As long as you give me the information you've found along the way."

"Denied." Jack stood. "Before I go, I need to know the name of this esteemed gentleman who drew these priceless works of art."

Wycliff looked him in the eye, his expression cleared of doubt and shame. Suddenly, his eyes glittered with greed instead. Jack doubted they'd been anything more than passing acquaintances. Likely, Wycliff had a buyer in mind for whatever these sketches were and needed the money for this Mayfair address. "His name was John Wallingford, the fifth Viscount Andrepont."

The name took the breath out of Jack's lungs. He was no esteemed gentleman. There were stories about him stretching the length of England, and none of them good. He had been a demon shoved into the body of an angel. And he was Lady Agnes's uncle.

⚜

AGNES WAS NOT A BOLD PERSON. OR TERRIBLY clever. She was an average person in roundabout ways. But she did have one trait that she took pride in, the one that allowed her to spend weeks on a single intricate embroidery design, and that was persistence. Agnes could be persistent, pressing even, at the best of times.

Her new goal, since there was absolutely not a single thing to do, was to find her sister again. The one that was buried beneath red-rimmed eyes, doughy skin, and blank politeness. Especially that last bit. It was *disturbing* to hear Lydia's genteel responses murmured over a teacup, with no caustic inference underlying the words. She was merely polite.

It wasn't natural and Agnes didn't like it.

Their mother had never really gotten along with Lydia—or perhaps had never understood her—and so it was only reasonable to include repairing the mother/daughter relationship as part of her mission.

Since there had been few invitations to dinners and even fewer invitations to balls after her abrupt exit from the Cuttingsworth ball, even the less socially important had stopped inviting her to grace their ballrooms. She hadn't even managed to dance the once, anyway.

Mary Franklin had accused her of being small, and here she was, being exactly that. Living small, with little Society and fewer friends. She continued mending dresses for the Women's Home, but it wasn't exactly a thrilling outing to drop off the garments. Was this what she wanted? To become a shut-in old maid before she reached the age of majority at twenty-five?

Her mind drifted to Jack's hopeful expression out on the veranda at the Cuttingsworth ball. Where he'd given her the option to dress in men's clothing and go explore London. Lydia would have done it.

Agnes shook her head. No, she'd made the correct decision. A lady does *not* change clothing in a garden. What if she'd been caught? Or what if it was a kidnapping ploy? Certainly possible.

But Jack had said that he would never lie to her. On the other hand, what sort of person claims to be his own sister? That was not a lie—it was a bizarre scheme, which perhaps he had good reason to engage, but even so.

On the other hand, Jack had known her signature yellow stitches even though Agnes purposefully hid them. How could he have noticed? She'd never told anyone, and even her family had never noticed. How had he seen her through all those dresses, all that fabric?

◌◌

FACT: THE HARDEST PART ABOUT FINDING WAS knowing where to start. Finding wasn't groping about blindly, hoping for good results. Finding was collecting information and then homing in on the path that would lead a body to the object in question while drawing the least amount of attention. Sometimes, a body wouldn't even know what information to collect until it was already in front of a person's nose.

Of course, a body couldn't go knock on the door of Lord Andrepont and ask to see the contents of a safe, even if that was the quickest and most direct route. Finding required finesse.

In an effort to start collecting information, Jack made his way to the butcher. There was already quite a crowd streaming in from all quarters, and the hour was early—they'd still be in the midst of the amateur fights. Jack elbowed his way in front of some toffs, paid his shilling, and disappeared into the basement. It smelled like blood—from the beasts, as the people had yet to begin to bleed.

It was convoluted logic, but he'd spent the last few weeks poking gently at the edges of the previous Lord Andrepont, and it wasn't pretty.

Everyone from friend to servant had roundly agreed upon the former Andrepont as being a handsome man—his son, the current Lord Andrepont, being the very living image of him—and he was also intelligent. Yet he was not well liked by gentlemen as he preferred to outwit and talk his way out of every bargain, finding loopholes and excuses. Typically, not only to weasel out of paying his debts but also to belittle and demean his opponents. The report of the gentleman's club was terse, to say the least. His title meant he kept his membership, though he was often asked to leave for the sake of other members.

As Jack found his way into the butcher's basement, lit by tallow lamps and reeking of rendered animal fat and human sweat, he recognized some of the crowd. But, given as to how most people knew him—as the resident voice of the Inn—he waited until the others acknowledged him before giving a nod back.

Fact: Friends at the Inn were friends on only one side of the door.

The stories of the previous Lord Andrepont coming from the downstairs of the houses were equally unflattering. Many housemaids had refused to work for the Andrepont household, and those that did were no longer in service. Jack tracked the few to brothels where they worked or, in one case, owned. Every single woman said that cruelty was Andrepont's aim. One, a woman working at a specialty brothel, told Jack that Andrepont never violated her, but he had beaten her and exposed her. That he would stop sooner if she cried.

There was a story of a mistress, mother to the bastard that the current Lord Andrepont had financed until a socially advantageous marriage took her out of London. Jack had a mind to go ask her about the sketches, but she lived rather far out of Town and he'd have to take the mail coach to get there.

Jack had little faith that he might uncover these priceless works of art and didn't want to spend the first installment if he didn't have to. This job was going to take some time.

The crowd was already anxious and frenzied, like a stray dog that's suddenly been tethered. Jack pushed his way through the sea of elbows to better see the ring.

"Oi! Wot's this?" A man screamed at the ring. "You can't do that! Them's just girls!"

"Shut yer gob! A fight's a fight!" Another man yelled. Betting was frenzied, a mad froth of gambling afoot.

Sure enough, two girls, about ten or twelve years of age, all pony-legged and straggling hair, faced off in the ring. Both girls were tall—as tall as Jack at least— and had a determined set of their jaw. A look Jack knew well. Based on the stance of one of the girls, the coach could only be one person. Jack elbowed through the crowd again, hoping for a glimpse of the kneeman and bottleman in the corner, and sure enough, there stood Bess Abbott, towering above the spectators.

Jack grinned. He loved Miss Abbott. She'd given him a chance when most wouldn't. Accepted him as he was without questions. Trained him but never pushed. She never judged, never asked, never suggested. Handed him a pasty regardless of whether or not he was hungry. So when Mr. Worley had left a message at the White Hart asking to see him, saying that Miss Abbott had sent him, Jack knew he'd take on whatever Mr. Worley required.

And now look at them: Mr. Worley wearing a smart beaver skin hat and Miss Abbott in a dress without rips or frayed hems. There was a healthy glow about her—the kind that only happiness and ample food can bring. Jack hung back and watched for a moment. Miss Abbott touched the little girl on her side of the ring, gentle pats on the back, reassurances on the arm. The girl turned and looked up into Miss Abbott's face, and while there was uncertainty and fear, there was also love and trust in her wide, plain eyes. The girl fiercely wanted to do Miss Abbott proud. Who wouldn't?

The betting ceased and the skeletal master of ceremonies Basil announced the fight, telling the crowd that the girls wouldn't peel—the prefight ritual where fighters removed clothing until they were in nothing but their breeches, or in this case, their thin shifts—as per decency, which earned a few boos from the crowd. The girls toed the line in the center, staring at each other with an intensity that any fighter would recognize, and the bell rang.

Miss Abbott's girl was fast, ducking a first swipe and delivering a stunning blow. The other girl shook it off, but Miss Abbott's girl was back on her, showering her with face shots until the girl went down.

Mr. Worley was yelling for her, and the pride was unmistakable. That was family, there. That's what it looked like. While Mr. Worley was effusive, his arms pumping in the air for her swift victory, Miss Abbott was calm, her arms folded, her fingers kneading the fabric and flesh of her upper arms. Her expression was the same as Mr. Worley's, and her eyes were glassy.

Their girl looked over in shock as Basil motioned to her opponent's kneeman, hoping he could rouse her. But the two men who ambled over, a father and brother, most likely, given the looks of them, couldn't wake the girl. They dragged her back to the corner, and after inspection, conceded the fight.

"Violet Worley is the winner in a one-round knockout!" Basil crowed.

Jack smiled at that. Names meant a lot. Names connected people, held sentiment and bloodlines. The fact that the girl used Mr. Worley's name meant that's where she belonged. And belonging was an important thing. It's what Jack had been looking for his whole life.

It's one of the reasons why Jack had left home. Names.

Miss Abbott enveloped Violet in a massive hug only to have Mr. Worley wrap his arms around both of them. Jack made his way over but politely kept his distance until the family moment had passed.

"Mr. About Town!" Mr. Worley rumbled, seeing him first.

Jack couldn't help but grin. The man was nothing but himself a crackling hearth fire—warmth and tenderness wrapped in a massive package. Mr. Worley held out a hand, and when Jack put his own hand in to shake it, it was as if his hand disappeared. "Mr. Worley. Wonderful to see you again."

"And you." The man wasted no words, but that meant his sentiments were all the more genuine.

"Jack," Miss Abbott greeted him, a slight smile the only indication of her pleasure at seeing him.

"Miss Abbott," Jack said, giving a gallant bow. She snorted in amusement.

"This here's Violet," Miss Abbott said, hooking the sweating girl closer. With brownish hair and the long-limbed look of a person still growing—and growing fast—she didn't have the look of either Miss Abbott or Mr. Worley. Violet nodded but didn't speak.

"Congratulations on your triumph, Miss Violet. Knockout in one round is quite the achievement for any fighter." Jack swept another bow, not quite so gallant as the first.

"Damn right," Miss Abbott growled, pride barely contained.

"Os, Os—" A young man with curly hair and surprisingly broad shoulders came skidding up, holding a wad of papers. "You'll never believe how much money I won. Oh, Violet, I could kiss you!"

Violet blushed a deep red in response, but her childish desire was clear—if this young man wanted to kiss her, she would gladly receive it.

"Pardon, Miss Abbott," Jack said. "I don't want to take you away from your success, but I was hoping to have a word." He used his fanciest accent and his fanciest words, hoping that it would let Miss Abbott know he respected her and her time.

In response, the fighter shouldered around her family and took a few steps away to gain the privacy Jack craved for their conversation.

"Jack. Wot you using that tone with me fer?"

He dropped the pretense. "Bess. I'm on a job. I need information."

"I don't know what I know, but I'll share if I can." She continued to scan the crowd. Fact: Old habits die hard.

He took a steadying breath. "It's about Lord Denby—"

Miss Abbott grunted and looked away. Sore spot, then.

"And his predeceased associates."

Miss Abbott eyed him. "And who in particular?"

"Lord Andrepont."

She shook her head. "That's trouble, and you know it."

"The money makes it worth it," Jack said, knowing she would respect that. She knew as he did how dangerous it was to be without blunt, to be in the cold. And how a body might do anything to prevent those days again.

The fighter hadn't stopped shaking her head. "Can you talk to young Lord Andrepont? He's not likely to want to discuss his father. Bad terms, and all that."

Jack inclined his head. "I could, but I'm not ready yet."

"This is a job, right?" She narrowed her eyes. "Ain't something else you got in mind?"

"No, not at all." Panic scratched at his throat. She couldn't possibly know about his interest—former interest—in Lady Agnes. About how she still haunted his dreams, both when he was asleep and when awake.

"Right." She sucked at her teeth, clearly not believing him. "Wot you need to know about Denby?"

She detailed her relationship to the man—who didn't sound all that terrible. He was impotent and looking to a female fighter for something novel, but that didn't turn into what he'd hoped, so he treated her like a regular fighter: sponsored her, made sure she ate well, bought her clothes, showed her off to his friends for pocket money. Treated her like the Fancy treated champions.

"Listen, not saying the man was all tea and cakes. He'd done some bad turns afore I knew him, and the mouth on that gent would make my own da's toes curl. There was something amiss with my Lady Lydia and him, but not sure what exactly..." She trailed off, glancing around.

It didn't escape Jack that she'd said *my Lady Lydia*, which is precisely how Jack felt about Lady Agnes, but probably for different reasons.

"Oi! John!" She yelled into the crowd. Turning back to Jack she said, "The other pisser is Lord Hackett. Look into him as well. Let me introduce you to John Arthur—he knows him. That's Lady Lydia's husband, you know."

She said the last bit with pride, as if she were bragging. Maybe she was.

A man shouldered his way through the people and made his way over to them. His shirt hung loose on his frame, but it didn't hide the muscled breadth of his shoulders and arms. As the crowd cleared, Jack recognized him as Corinthian John, the prizefighter. His reddish-gold hair was cropped short, and already his ruddy complexion was rosy. He'd fought for years —and fought well.

"Oi! Bess!" he said back at her with a grin.

"This here's Jack About Town. He's got questions, and they're for a good reason. I trust him. You should, too." Miss Abbott clapped Corinthian John on the shoulder and left, leaving Jack to convince this man of his worthiness.

Jack swept a bow to the man. "Jack About Town, at your service."

"John Arthur," he said, giving an incline that at least showed some respect. "You look familiar. We met before?"

Jack shook his head, heart pounding. He'd played the errand boy outside of Mr. Arthur's house before, and of course knew it from Lady Agnes's visits. But had they met? Fact: They'd not been properly introduced, so no, they had not met. Not a lie.

Corinthian John sighed. "If Bess trusts you, I trust you. What do you need?"

"Answers, mostly. I have questions about Lords Denby and Hackett." Jack left out Andrepont on purpose. He wasn't ready to talk freely of his actual target.

Mr. Arthur's expression darkened instantly. "What do you need to know about them?"

Another wave of uncertainty rose. This was not a man to anger, and clearly, those names did not sit well with him. "I have a client looking for an object, and those men may know about it."

"What's the object?" he demanded.

"I'd prefer not to say in this company," Jack said, partly because it was true, but also because he'd rather discuss the matter when Mr. Arthur wasn't ready to fight. Emotions clouded memories, created false ones, obscured long-buried ones.

"Corinthian John! Get your arse in line, man! Time to warm up!" A man bellowed through the crowd.

Mr. Arthur ignored the call and took a good long look at Jack. Another thorough inspection. "How old are you, really?"

Ah. The short pants didn't fool this one. Jack dressed as a boy to explain his smooth chin, to elicit trust and kindness. Better that than to dress as a man and become a target for other men who want someone to steal from or beat on to vent some long-lost rage. Still. Jack hesitated. Miss Abbott said that Mr. Arthur could trust him, but could Jack trust Mr. Arthur?

"I've a fight in a few rounds here." Mr. Arthur

shifted, impatient and losing interest fast. The prizefighter glanced over his shoulder.

"Twenty-five," Jack blurted. Truth would out, wasn't that the saying?

Mr. Arthur's blue eyes were back on him, piercing through the layers of horseshit that Jack put on every morning. "Come by my house tomorrow. We can talk." Mr. Arthur made his way to depart, but Jack laid his hand on his arm, surprising them both.

"Of course. Er, do you have a preferred time? And perhaps you might tell me where?" Jack was suddenly aware that he was much shorter than Mr. Arthur. Much, much shorter. He did not want Corinthian John thinking he'd already been to the man's house under different pretenses.

"Evenings. A bloke has to work, after all. Bess'll tell you where. Marylebone—I'm coming! Keep yer britches on, you old cheeser." Mr. Arthur picked through the crowd, leaving Jack alone.

Always tomorrow, always more information later. It was frustrating and alarming that tomorrow would find him once again closer to Lady Agnes. He would be visiting her brother-in-law, in her sister's family home. Would Lady Agnes be there? Probably not. But maybe yes?

A knot formed in Jack's stomach—unexpectedly so. He hadn't had many paramours, but many flirtations. They were pleasant, with a stolen kiss here, a shady corner there. In one comical circumstance, a hedge. He wasn't entirely inexperienced. But none of that mattered when it came to a woman like Lady Agnes.

For shit's sake, why would he even think that? No, Lady Agnes was too far above him, even with his education and upbringing. And even with that which made both her and Jack different. Even still. She was a lady, and, well, he wasn't.

The crowd surged as the next fight began. He'd paid his shilling, might as well stay and watch the rounds, especially if he could see what kind of destruction Corinthian John might deliver. He elbowed over closer to the ring to get a better look, the smell of blood and sweat and fat and salt filling his nose. Didn't help that he was the height of some of these blokes' armpits.

Once he was ringside, he watched two young men, neither of them filled out to their full potential, take a crack at each other. Lots of false swings, and the crowd began to boo. Violet and her opponent were faster than these two. Finally one of them connected, sending the other to the ground, ending the round. They retreated to their corners. Across the ring, Mr. Arthur spoke in close quarters with a lean, dark-haired man. When the bell rang for the fight to resume, Mr. Arthur went back to shadowboxing and the dark-haired man turned, finding Jack in the crowd.

Jack exhaled slowly, trying to prevent his whole body from shaking. The dark-haired man was the current Lord Andrepont, with his glossy crow's wing hair, square jaw, and cheekbones that could cut glass. Everyone said he was the very image of his father— the man whose art Jack sought. Something in the set of that face—handsome though it was—chilled him. Impossible to know if it was a cool demeanor or cruelty itself.

8

This time, Agnes was ready. Armed with her embroidery basket, she'd made a date with Pearl to mend shirts and darn socks. In reality, it was an excuse to be near Lydia, to see if she could excavate her sister from somewhere under the layers of motherly fog and artifice. Vasily drove her in the phaeton—it was a bit far to walk with a full embroidery basket, and while many ladies drove their own phaetons, Agnes had never quite trusted her skill with horses. Honestly, she didn't care for horses and preferred the reliability of her own two feet, thank you.

During the slow prance from Mayfair to Marylebone, where she nodded to a few ladies on the street with whom she had the pleasure of acquaintance, she had half a mind to chatter away to Vasily of her sister's strange behavior because he might take it upon himself to ask questions in the kitchen regarding Lydia. But in the end, Agnes kept silent. Instead, she watched the grand houses change to the crowded thoroughfare, covering her nose when they stopped fully, stuck behind a particularly large carriage whose team of horses refused to cooperate.

"A team of horses must be all of the same

personality," Vasily grumbled to her, his own odd way of imparting knowledge.

"Yes," Agnes agreed automatically, a good student in whatever subject was at hand.

"These are things you must know if you become a great lady," he insisted. "Horses must cooperate to work, must be trained for carriage work. A plough horse doesn't know how to drive a carriage and a carriage horse would be lost in a field."

"So true," Agnes added, wondering if there wasn't anything more obvious he could have said. But then he gave her a cold, lidded look, and she instantly realized he was using a metaphor and she had been too stupid to grasp it.

She'd always suspected that Vasily preferred Lydia —she was prettier, more exciting, dared to do illicit and dangerous things—all of which Vasily seemed to condone if not enjoy. Lydia loved horses, knew all about them, was an accomplished horsewoman, and of course, gave sincere advice to many a person over a dinner table on the purchase of racehorses. Agnes was able to listen attentively and agree well, which assured her invitations as long as more lively conversationalists would be present.

Vasily had put on weight since Lydia had left the house. He wore it well, but it was a sign that he was growing complacent as he looked after Agnes. She wished she weren't such a bore.

The butler ushered her up to the drawing room. Pearl was already at work with a pillow cushion, no doubt ready to start in on mending and darning when necessary. Her stitches were a bit wide and clumsy to Agnes's eye, but nothing a few small directives couldn't help. It was a relief. Finally, something Agnes understood and knew about.

"Good afternoon, Lady Agnes," Pearl stood and bobbed a quick curtsy.

Agnes inclined her head, wishing Pearl wouldn't address her so formally but not daring to contradict the girl. Hadn't they already established first names? They were, after all, sisters-in-law. "Miss Arthur," Agnes returned in greeting.

The girl gave an elfin smile, the sun highlighting the pale red hair that brought the resemblance to her brother into focus. "Pearl. Yes, I know. I find it challenging to drop the honorifics. Please." She motioned to another chair, which she dragged over to the window with better light.

"Thank you," Agnes acknowledged, setting down her basket and taking up the chair. As she sat, she realized she was a great deal taller than Pearl. A great deal. It made her feel a bit like a hulking giantess, but well. That's the card she had been dealt, as her cousin James might say.

A pang of loneliness assailed her. Since Margaret had married and Lydia had married, she hadn't seen much of James lately. Their gang, Margaret, James, Lydia, even Sebastian! They'd all but disappeared.

"And how is my sister faring today?" Agnes asked, unpacking her basket as if it were the most casual question in the world. Why shouldn't she ask after the health of her only sibling?

"I have not seen her yet this morning," Pearl confessed. Her hands stilled in her lap, and she took a long look at Agnes. "May I confide in you?"

At last. Relief flooded her. "Of course."

"I am worried for her. Ever since the baby came, she's been...not herself."

Agnes looked up at Pearl, holding her breath.

"I know it's unseemly for an unmarried woman to speak of such things, but..." she trailed off.

Was Pearl worried that Agnes would judge her harshly? Did Pearl believe all the nonsense that Miss Perry spouted about Agnes's paragon of maidenly decency? Had everyone assumed that Agnes's disinterest in marriage and children sprang from modesty and not from sincere apathy? Inwardly, Agnes sputtered in fury. Outwardly, Agnes folded her hands in demure interest. "Go on."

"I...I take care of our womanly things in the household. You know, obtaining more...*rags*." She whispered the word, looking towards the drawing room door in horror lest someone walk in. "And, well, your sister has bled for a very long time. A long, long time. More than what is normal." Pearl's face froze in horror. "I mean, that is to say, growing up, I helped many a mother. I don't mean that *I* know personally what it is to have a child, I—"

Agnes held up a hand, feeling so much like a fraud. "It's perfectly reasonable, Pearl, to know about such things when living in closer quarters with married women. I wouldn't presume to judge you on such knowledge."

Yet another thing that Agnes knew nothing about. It was ridiculous how ignorant she was about her own body and the processes of which she was expected to participate in. Another flare of anger surged through her. Did Lydia know what was normal? Did Lydia know that she suffered more than other mothers? They'd been kept so ignorant. Especially Lydia, as they'd assumed she'd never have children because of—because of—Agnes couldn't even bear to think it.

Shame washed through her, familiar and deep. Lydia suffered. That's what she did. While Agnes was there to witness, be good, let everyone focus on how Lydia needed more. How selfish it was to want more. Agnes dropped her head, willing herself to accept her old role. This was the way it had always been, and with Margaret, James, and Sebastian scattered, it was even more her responsibility to take care of Lydia. But she was so ill-prepared.

"Pearl, I don't wish to offend delicate sensibilities, but what would you do if you knew a young mother in other parts of London that might be afflicted like my sister? Would you fetch a surgeon or a physician?"

Pearl's face turned pink. "Never!" she breathed. "Not that those mothers had the money for one, either. No, a midwife was who we called. An herbwoman who knew how these sorts of things happened. Surgeons, physicians, apothecaries—they think they know a woman's business, but their specialty is telling other men a woman's business." Pearl's accent began to slide down into the Irish-inflected houses she must have been raised in. "You want a mother's help, and if you can, a mother who has many daughters."

Agnes nodded. That made sense, in its own way. She was raised to trust a physician or a surgeon, knowing that those were the men who were called for her family. But yes, women's business was a different subject, and Agnes had hated how she'd seen the family physician talk down to her mother—her *ladyship*—in the hallways after seeing to Lydia. Her mother would ask questions about Lydia's welfare, and the physician would pull himself up and give pronouncements, scoffing at her mother's concerns. "Where do we find such a woman?"

Pearl shook her head. "I'm not entirely certain anymore. It's been so long since I was in the old neighborhood—"

The door swung open, causing both of them to jump a mile.

"My maid told me you'd arrived," Lydia said as she entered. Her hair was pinned up in a hasty manner, and the simple dark round gown didn't flatter. Her complexion was pale—and not in the luminous shell sort of way that Pearl had, but a rather disheartening pallor of illness. Dark circles pulled at her eyes, and the normal spark and flash that entranced so many in ballrooms was thoroughly extinguished.

Agnes stood, throwing her mending aside. "Lydia." She gave a short bob of a curtsy, the kind that would appall their mother, but Agnes hoped would make Lydia feel at home—even if it was her home. Make her think that Agnes was familiar and welcoming.

Lydia noted the bob and nodded her acknowledgement in return. "Agnes. Thank you for calling on us. During proper visiting hours and everything. Shall we ring for tea?"

Agnes ignored the cut. "Please. Your house tea is quite invigorating."

That finally put a small spark in her sister's eye. Lydia rang for tea, asked the maid for a more elaborate setting than was truly necessary, and then proceeded to inform Agnes all about the local teahouse that Mr. Arthur had found and the master tea blender who made them their own exclusive personalized tea.

While Lydia talked and poured, Agnes pulled out the ragged dresses and handed a pile to Pearl. Between sips and explanations, Agnes gently directed Pearl on her stitches, showing her how to hide the patching up work so that a young woman might feel more herself when wearing a charity dress. Agnes wanted the dresses to not *feel* like charity dresses. She wanted women to put them on and feel right at home, capable, worthy, ready for whatever may come.

It felt so terribly normal, and Agnes loved it. Even Lydia seemed energized by it. Color returned to her cheeks and she sat on the edge of her seat as she chatted through minute details of the household that Agnes didn't always follow.

The door opened again, and this time Mr. Arthur entered. He looked imminently pleased to see his wife chattering away—uncharacteristic even before the baby. He crossed the room in two strides, coming to sit next to his wife and taking her hand. She startled at his attention but seemed pleased by it. When he kissed her hand, Agnes turned away, suddenly embarrassed.

She knew they kissed. Their love was clear. It was only—just—*must* they? When Agnes would never inspire that kind of ardor? When she could hope only for tolerance and pleasantness like she'd had with Mary Franklin? Which she had been quite comfortable with, thank you. Not everyone needed or wanted such inflamed passions. Because Agnes wasn't ridiculous. She knew she was not such a person that induced it.

"Lady Agnes, what a pleasure it is that we've been able to enjoy your company this afternoon." Mr. Arthur's accent was spot-on, a mimic of her own. Pearl's was not quite as accurate, but she did well.

"The pleasure was all mine. I do apologize for overstaying my welcome." Agnes smiled and held her place in the mending with a simple stitch. She'd stow her goods, ask them to fetch Vasily, and return home.

"Not at all. I wanted to check with my darling wife, of course, but I have some company in my study, and I thought that we might all dine together. A little liveliness in the house? What do you say?"

"Who is the company?" Lydia asked, a note of apprehension clear.

"A new acquaintance and—"

James appeared in the doorway, leaning against it as if the weight of his good looks and charm were too heavy to bear for one more instant. "And your favorite relative."

Relief was palpable in the room. Agnes stood,

barely catching herself from rushing over and throwing herself into his arms.

Lydia rose, too, Mr. Arthur subtly helping her to her feet. Pearl's advice echoed in Agnes's mind. A midwife. She'd find one.

"A sight for sore eyes. You've been missing for too long," Lydia scolded.

James pushed himself off the door jamb. "I've had other matters to attend to. Namely, myself."

"Selfish bastard, wot," Mr. Arthur said, his accent back to the gutter.

"John!" Pearl gasped. "Ladies are present!"

"You might be the only one," Lydia said, her familiar dark humor surfacing.

James crossed the room to hold Lydia's hands in greeting, then Agnes's. Over James's shoulder, a shorter figure appeared in the doorway.

"I shouldn't want to intrude," said the man as he came into view.

Agnes audibly gasped.

James looked at her oddly, a small smile forming as he glanced back at Jack Townsend. Agnes tried to cover her faux pas with a cough, but even Lydia wasn't fooled. They all looked at her with curiosity.

"Are you already acquainted?" Mr. Arthur questioned her, an eyebrow raised.

It was as if Agnes could see him thinking, running through possibilities and questions. Safe Agnes didn't want to be known as a young lady who associated with people of such unusual circumstances as Jack, but despite Jack's very lewd bid to ruin her—if that indeed had really been what it was—she genuinely enjoyed his presence. Or perhaps it was the presence of him pretending to be his own sister.

I never lied to you. It was as if he was trying to speak it into her mind as he stared at her. Clearly, he was waiting for her cue. Was he here because of her?

"Yes," Agnes affirmed for the room. "We are acquainted."

"I believe Lady Agnes still owes me a dance," Jack said, entering the room with small steps. Not so much an intrusion as an inclusion. Joining. How did he do that?

Pearl tittered in her corner.

"It's true. There was an issue with my slipper."

"When is there not an issue with your slipper?" Lydia sniped.

"Faulty slippers are a well-known menace in London. My condolences will forever be yours, Lady Agnes." Jack swept into a gallant bow that had James and Mr. Arthur very amused, but Agnes had a hard time tearing her eyes from him.

He looked dashing in his breeches, fitted tightly to his form. His waistcoat was a simple gray with gold buttons. But it wasn't his clothes that enthralled her. It was the way he looked at her. As if she could inspire ardor. The way John looked at Lydia.

Jack turned to Lydia. "I'm afraid I'm not dressed for dinner, my lady. I humbly ask that you overlook my breach of etiquette. The invitation was quite sudden."

"Truly," Mr. Arthur told Lydia. "My fault entirely. Mr. Townsend and Andrepont are quite the conversationalists and I would hate for you to miss out."

"No apologies needed," Lydia said, gracefully. "Our table is open to anyone of wit."

Agnes was thrilled that Jack would be included, but doubt pinched at her. She was not known as a person of wit, but her good breeding and sisterly relationship earned her a place at the table. Nepotism wasn't exactly something to be proud of.

But perhaps she could become someone of wit. Someone who could gain the knowledge to help. And she could start by helping her sister. Her mind sparked. And perhaps Jack could help.

JACK'S HEART POUNDED. THE SMALL PARTY CHATTED in the drawing room with the ladies for a time, and all the while, he tried unsuccessfully to unstick his tongue from the roof of his mouth. Lady Agnes kept stealing glances at him, and dear snotty devil below, it gave Jack hope. Maybe she didn't think ill of him and instead felt the draw between them—the invisible tether that he hadn't been able to release, no matter how hard he'd tried.

Then suddenly they separated again, the ladies and the gents, and Jack trudged behind Corinthian John and Andrepont back down to the study. He hadn't managed a single intelligible word during the entire conversation.

The whole visit was a damned turn. First, Jack showed up as instructed only to find Andrepont elegantly draped in a chair in Corinthian John's study. Those green eyes—the color of fresh spring peas—followed him, not questioning but tracking him like a cat, curious if he were prey.

Jack managed to ask some questions about Hackett and Denby, wanting to be upfront with Corinthian John as a sign of respect for him and for Bess, but under the eye of Andrepont, Jack found he couldn't say anything.

Andrepont didn't trust him, didn't like him—that was clear. But why? He'd never done the viscount a bad turn. Well, not yet anyhow.

Fact: If he tipped his hand too early, Andrepont would never allow him to get close enough to find his quarry, this mysterious and suddenly profitable art portfolio. It was best to go slow, keep with his strategy to ask around what he wanted.

"Claret?" Corinthian John offered, ensconced in the study once more.

"Anything stronger?" Andrepont asked.

Jack stayed quiet, watching. So much to glean.

"I have some Irish whisky and some daffy so strong you'll forget you have eyes."

"How appealing." Andrepont made his way over to the sideboard. "But a viscount couldn't be caught drinking gin. What would people say?" He eyed Jack, challenging him to admit that he would sell a story to the papers about the evening.

Fact: Gossip rags didn't pay near well enough to spill Jack's secrets.

The study was a modest room, large in size but not opulent in furnishing. Clearly to Arthur's taste. No need for showing off, just efficient. But then again, was that not a prizefighter's life? Corinthian John was renowned as the master of the peel. But while his peel was outlandish and flashy, his fighting style was condensed and minimal. He didn't move much, preferring quick strikes and waiting for his opponent to tire. The same could be said for his house. The front was opulent and luxurious. The study, where his real work was done, was simple. Comfortable chairs, plain tables, bookcases that were meant for references and not for show.

Jack wondered what Andrepont's house looked like. He couldn't even begin to guess.

"Jack? Are you a fan of frog's wine?" Andrepont turned those green eyes on him, pinning him. Jack suddenly felt possessive of his preferences. He didn't want to tell Andrepont anything, including his drink of choice.

"Jack?" Corinthian John prompted. "Daffy or whisky or claret?"

He preferred nothing, wanting to keep a clear head. Fact: Drunk men talked too much. "Claret would be fine."

Andrepont scoffed. "Since I quite like my eyes, I'll take the Irish whisky. I'm surprised you have any. I didn't think you were willing to pay the tariffs."

Corinthian John raised his eyebrows. "Who said anything about paying tariffs?"

Andrepont shot Jack a knowing look. Did the viscount not know that *most* of London engaged in smuggled goods? Especially the rich? It was hardly noteworthy. But that in of itself was news: Andrepont found amusement in the transgressions of others. Or perhaps this viscount was trying so hard to be the opposite of his father that he himself would never engage in vices such as smuggling.

"It's early," Corinthian John declared. "I'll join Jack with the claret. We are about to have dinner, after all."

"And leave me looking the sod with the whisky," Andrepont muttered, accepting a glass.

"Worried about your reputation?" Corinthian John shot back, handing a glass of claret to Jack.

"More like I don't want to offend your sister's delicate sensibilities," Andrepont said with a leer insinuating he was interested in precisely that.

"Don't," Corinthian John growled. His jovial demeanor suddenly vanished.

Andrepont shrugged at their host and turned to Jack. "So, tell me, Jack. To change the subject from the lovely Miss Arthur, what really brings you here?"

Jack knew what the viscount meant. Not *here*, as in the questions about Hackett and Denby, gossip he had gleaned weeks ago. Rather, why did he go all flustered in the drawing room, and why did the normally staid Lady Agnes get fluttery? And the other unspoken question, *How did they know each other?* Those green eyes shot through him like an arrow. There was no getting out of this one.

"Lady Agnes mends clothing for the Women's Home over on Hog Street. We've run into each other there." Which was true.

Andrepont's green eyes narrowed, and that same protective instinct that had roared in Corinthian John simmered to the surface in Andrepont. The room was suffused with the scent of ruffled feathers. "Funny. You don't seem the type to help with a Women's charity."

If they were at the Inn, Jack would pet and soothe and ply the irritated with drink. But here? Jack braced himself and straightened his spine, ready to do battle himself. "Mysteries abound."

They stared at each other, Jack a full head shorter but with as much mettle as the viscount. Corinthian John cleared his throat and pushed off the desk where he'd been reclining. "Shall we sit instead? Talk of the fights, perhaps? Or did you have more questions, Jack?"

Jack allowed himself to be handled and ushered over to the sitting area in front of the fireplace. It was rare that Jack allowed himself the luxury of being angry. But Andrepont had found a sore spot—Lady Agnes—and the worst of it was that not only did Andrepont do it on purpose, Jack had let him see his success. If he was smart, he'd tell Corinthian John he'd come back later when Andrepont wasn't there. Instead, he let the man needle him.

"I do have a few more questions." Well, no one had ever accused Jack of being smart. And he couldn't let Andrepont win. "Everyone says you are the spitting image of your father, my lord."

"That isn't a question." Andrepont's voice was cold and even.

"Have you ever been tempted to take your seat in Parliament, as your father before you?"

"I don't see what that has to do with anything," he growled.

Jack ignored the warning. "As I understand it, the former viscount was also a dear friend of Lords Denby and Hackett. Did you also take up the acquaintance?"

The current viscount's face went cold and detached. "I'm sure you've heard plenty, but make no assumptions on me."

The two of them sat, Andrepont and Jack in the cushioned chairs in front of the fireplace, while Corinthian John hauled over an extra chair from the side of the room. The prizefighter paused, letting the insinuations settle over them, before continuing to draw up a chair.

Jack feigned disinterest with a shrug but felt the surge of power nonetheless. "There were plenty of conversations where your father's name came up. The Andrepont name is well known in certain circles."

Calling the dead viscount *father* was a low blow and Jack knew it. But he was angry, and that made him reckless. How dare this man imply that Lady Agnes was naïve or uninformed? Lady Agnes knew herself and knew Society, and that was a hell of a lot more than Jack could say for most people.

Corinthian John stiffened. "Gentlemen, perhaps we ought to stick to the fights, or even theatre?"

Andrepont growled. "If you have a specific question, *Jack*, I beg you to ask." As if emphasizing a name could put Jack in his place. Because he wasn't a person with a title. Or anything.

Oh, he had plenty of questions. But none he wanted to ask yet. Mostly, *Where is your father's art portfolio*, and *What sort of disgusting sketches might I find in it?* As much as he'd like to set the viscount back on his arse, he couldn't compromise himself. He'd like the money, because who wouldn't? And now he'd like to snag the portfolio just to shove it in Andrepont's smug face.

"Perhaps Corinthian John is right. We should address a less sensitive topic." Jack sipped his claret, wishing the dinner gong would ring. There was only so much good luck he could get in one day.

"Quite right," the host said. "Speaking of the sweet science, how do you know Bess?"

"Took her classes," Jack said, without thinking.

Corinthian John sat back, and Jack realized what he'd revealed. *Fuck me running.* Bess Abbott only ever taught young girls.

Shit on toast. He had to be more careful. Andrepont brought out the worst in him.

AGNES WAS IMPRESSED BY JACK'S TABLE MANNERS. It wasn't that they were spectacular, it was merely that they existed. But then she caught her own snobbery—had she expected him to eat with hands, shoveling food in hand over fist? *Well.*

They were a small table, interspersed gentleman and lady, as one might find at a proper meal. It had been a few months since the last dinner party, before the baby was born, and this felt almost normal. Lydia looked tired, seated between their cousin James and the mysterious Jack.

Pearl sat across from James, next to her brother John, who sat next to Agnes. So Agnes was across from Jack, which would assuredly weaken her resolve to not stare at him all evening. His long, dark lashes fluttered against his cheek as he inspected the soup. Agnes tried very hard to ignore it.

Agnes didn't understand it. She'd found men

beautiful before but had never felt anything more. They took up too much space, demanded things, smelled unappealing, ignored her, or said awful things and expected to be congratulated. But now here was Jack, who presented himself as both a man and a woman to her—or neither? Jack *smelled* right somehow, and the awareness of him lit up her skin like a gas lamp turned on high.

Not that Agnes smelled him. Because she wasn't the sort of woman who went around sniffing people, no. It was merely a figure of speech for the way she was having a hard time not watching the way he put the spoon in his mouth, his lips pursed as he withdrew it. His tongue darted to the corner of his mouth to catch an errant drop. It was enough to fill her mind with the darkest thoughts she'd ever conjured.

Jack glanced up, catching her out.

If a person could trip over themselves while sitting down, Agnes would have done it. The heat of a furious blush spread throughout her body and she stared down at her own untouched soup.

At least she was the person no one noticed and she could curl up and die without anyone the wiser. The heat slowly abated as conversation swirled around her.

"Agnes?" prompted her sister.

Cooled somewhat, Agnes looked over at Lydia. "Hmm?"

"James asked if you were quite all right. Are you?" Lydia prompted, her gaze clear and somewhat stern. Like she'd always been.

Oh. She'd been so busy tamping down her unmaidenly lust that she hadn't noticed conversation directed at her. And now five pairs of eyes stared at her, including Jack's.

"Perfectly well, thank you." Agnes feigned a smile,

and all eyes returned to their own business, with the exception of James's and Jack's. James looked between her and Jack, and Jack stared back at her, his expression unreadable.

She took up her spoon, giving a bright, polite smile that she didn't feel in the least. It was an expression to brush a person away, but Jack still watched her as she fumbled with her soup spoon.

It wasn't proper for her to want to be alone with Jack. After all, he had been very clear about wanting to compromise her for his own gain. Even so, she wanted to ask for his help in finding a midwife for her sister—who else but someone who could be discreet? And there was never a time when one shouldn't help one's sister. That was some kind of moral constant that could not be ignored.

She sipped at her soup but didn't taste it. Jack had long since gone back to his. She felt confused. And hot. And like her skin was somehow too tight. She was beginning to believe this was all Jack's fault, and she liked that even less.

WHEN LADY AGNES FLUSHED, SHE EITHER WENT red as a beet everywhere or, as now, her cheeks pinked up enough to make her look as fine as any English rose. Jack's poor heart creaked and jumped, and he cast his eyes back down at his now empty soup bowl. A footman cleared his dish. Jack tossed back the rest of the white wine. It was better than he'd thought it would be. Crisp and light, like the broth.

"My compliments, Mrs. Arthur," Jack said, doing his best to summon his politic self—the self that charmed the drunks at the Inn. He was capable of being the best friend of every stranger he met. Even with Lady Agnes present, distracting him.

"Thank you," the hostess said, eyeing him with what Jack would describe as extreme interest.

Was it because Lady Agnes had shown him special interest herself? Must be, since he'd already gotten the once-over from the viscount. *Again.* "Do you employ one of those French man-cooks?" He already knew the answer was "no" because he'd looked into the downstairs of every prominent house when looking for Mr. Worley's mother. It was the best place to look for someone, either because the person worked as a servant or a servant worked for them. Over a third of London was in service, so it had been a game of odds.

"No." Mrs. Arthur's tone was polite and cool, crisp and clean and distant, so unlike her sister's. "But our cook came highly recommended. It is a matter of pride."

Pride. As if Jack didn't know about that, for himself and for his family. Mrs. Arthur seemed proud as well. And the stories about her—well. She was popular with the Fancy for her courage and popular with the regular folk for how happy she made the captured Corinthian John.

But what kind of woman would sacrifice her position to be with a bruiser? A proud one. And that sort of thing might run in the family. Jack stole another glance at Lady Agnes, who was doing her best to find her soup fascinating.

Hope swelled, which Jack couldn't tamp down. He would get her alone to ask her questions about her uncle and then perhaps try to explain that he wasn't trying to take advantage of her. But, wasn't interrogating her about a relation already taking advantage of her?

As the next course was delivered, Jack did his best

to push away any qualms he might have about pursuing a conversation with Lady Agnes. And so it went throughout dinner, with Jack eating everything and barely tasting it as he tried to engage in polite conversation with Mrs. Arthur and Miss Arthur.

But it was no use. As the ladies adjourned to the drawing room, all Jack could remember from the meal was Lady Agnes and the searching looks she had stolen across the dinner table. It was going to be agony to sit at the table and pretend to drink and smoke with Corinthian John and Andrepont. The men stared at each other.

"You're intriguing company and all that—" Andrepont started.

"Absolutely titillating—" Corinthian John added.

Jack grinned at the good-natured ribbing. He couldn't resist this kind of camaraderie. He'd always craved it. "You lot are most fascinating."

The men swiveled to look at him, both amused that he'd been bold enough to join in.

"Excellent. May we go, then?" Andrepont asked.

"No post-dinner daffy?" Corinthian John teased.

"After all that wine? You must be mad, sir. Or else you wish to drive me mad." Andrepont said.

Corinthian John stood. "How could I possibly add to a situation that is already so well advanced?"

"Polite way to say it," Andrepont said.

"Aren't you supposed to be polite when you deliver insults, or did my upbringing steer me wrong?" Jack added.

Corinthian John clapped him on the back. "Let's go find the ladies."

Jack had no idea how he would manage a moment alone with Lady Agnes, but by all that was holy, he was glad he had the opportunity to try.

SIPPING TEA WITH PEARL AND LYDIA WAS SHEER torture at this particular moment. Neither had much to say, and both watched Agnes over the edges of their teacups as if she were about to break into a bawdy rendition of "The Plenipotentiary."

"That's the most interesting dinner we've had in months," Lydia said, a spark in her eye. "Since the baby, anyway."

"Very diverting," Pearl agreed, looking to Agnes.

"Yes," was all Agnes could bring herself to say. Instead, her brain ran away with scenarios where she could get Jack alone. To talk, of course—not to promise he would never lie to her, not to kiss her hand in such a way that heat pooled in unmentionable places and the promise sounded too much like something else entirely.

The men entered the room and palpable relief pervaded the air. Pearl finished her tea in one herculean gulp and excused herself. She and Lydia communicated somehow without speaking, which irritated Agnes since Agnes and Lydia were actual sisters but had never been able to communicate in such an intimate manner.

The men arranged themselves, everyone giving Jack the opportunity to sit nearest to Agnes. While they were happy to give them the physical space, the others clearly hung on every word exchanged between Agnes and Jack.

"Did you enjoy your meal?" Agnes finally managed, feeling completely at odds with her family for putting her into such an uncomfortable position as to be on after-dinner exhibition.

"Very much so. My compliments to Mrs. Arthur for her planning. And the cook is excellent."

Polite smiles all around. Yes, nodding heads, very agreeable. More staring over teacups.

Jack stood, bowing to Lydia first. "This has been

most delightful. Thank you, Mrs. Arthur, for allowing me to join your table. Lady Agnes, your company is always most stimulating. Lord Andrepont, I consider your acquaintance most valuable, and Mr. Arthur, I do hope we can maintain our friendship."

"It's very good to see you again," Agnes said, offering her hand to him, an extreme courtesy that wasn't warranted but gave her an excuse to whisper, "I'm going to market to buy flowers."

Understanding flared in Jack's eyes, along with something that she might have called interest, but now, if he at all mirrored her feelings, might be labeled as longing. "My lady," he murmured before taking his leave.

Her heart pounded with her indiscretion, anticipation chugging through her veins like a locomotive with an unending supply of coal.

9

T his was the hour when the lowliest of servants awoke. When fires were lit, water was drawn, and inky purple skies turned pinkish yellow. For Jack, he had not yet gone to bed.

It had been a quiet night at the Inn, with regulars and musicians. They drank, they danced, and they laughed, but the reputed raucous flash of mollyhouses was nowhere to be seen. Jack had sat by the door nursing a single glass of claret for the entire night, prompting Miss Persephone to check on him. She knew his moods. Knew he would talk when he was ready.

Usually Jack did talk to her, but now, after coming face to face with the owner of the object he had to steal, he needed more clarity. He'd watched the woman who made his very belly lining ache with need stare at him with unasked questions. Suddenly Lady Agnes *wanted* to meet him. But it couldn't be about the job, could it? She couldn't know that he was poised to steal from her cousin, could she?

The air was still cool as he skirted through neighborhoods, hoping the footpads that he didn't see were already drunkenly snoring in a ditch. The paths through the neighborhoods, if a body bothered to know them, were obvious. He finally got to Bloomsbury in time to witness the first lamp lighting in his mother's room.

But in that room, it wasn't a lowly scullery maid coming to light the fires, it was his mother. She rose first, lit a fire in her private room on the second floor to begin her letter writing. She wrote letters to relatives who had flung out to the furthest reaches of the globe, and she was determined to not lose touch with anyone—not the fur trapper uncle in the remote wilds of Canada, not her mother in India, not the brother trading lacquerware from Japan. She never forgot an acquaintance and never let a friendship wither from inattention. She was a social butterfly in ink, if nothing else.

Soon, the scullery maid would bring up a pot of water and the missus's own tea blend—spiced like one might find in those far-flung places—to help fuel her pen.

Jack scaled the tree and knocked on the glass pane. His mother looked up sharply. Her long, dark hair was in a thick braid over her shoulder, and she wore her dressing gown and slippers. Her large, dark eyes, like Jack's, were already alert for the day. Fact: His mother was objectively very beautiful, with high cheekbones and a firm jawline that had enough roundness to seem feminine. Jack knew there must have been a scattering of broken hearts all over the Indian subcontinent before she married his English sea captain father. Not that she would admit to such a thing.

"Good morning," she greeted as she slid up the window to let him in.

The smell of his parents' house wafted out. Lemon oil and furniture polish, tallow and clove, the smells of his parents: warm and salty and human. Jack could even discern the smell of the two parakeets they kept in the other room, blankets still covering their cages.

"Good morning, Mama." Jack slipped in, thankful again for being slightly built, able to navigate these places with ease.

"Shall I have Annie bring up another cup?"

"What happened to Ruth?" Jack took stock of the room. Nothing else had changed. The rug was still frayed in the same corner and the chair was still covered with the same wool blanket that she kept handy in case she ever got cold. Had it been so long since his last visit? The writing desk was stacked with paper and foolscap, ink, quill, and penknife, and as-yet unanswered letters stacked according to the day on which they were received. His mother was a creature of habit, which he loved. She was predictable, happy in the small bits of her life that she had perfected. She used ink whose smell wasn't quite so pungent, quality paper practically the thickness of bedding, a custom-made penknife gifted from an admiring dinner guest, a supply of goose quills cut and ready, and even a tea blend that she had perfected herself. She knew her own mind and executed it with satisfaction.

"Ruth married. Annie is her younger sister. A cup, then?" His mother went to the door and, upon opening it, found young Annie walking up the stairs with a tray in hand. She had barely cleared the door when she came to a sudden stop and stared. The shock on the girl's already pale face was clear.

"Annie, this is my son Jack. He visits at peculiar hours because he was always a peculiar child. Pay him no mind. And would you please fetch us another cup? Thank you, dear."

The girl glanced at her mistress and then wordlessly set the tray down on the small table next to the chair. She wandered back to the door, almost dazed in her confusion, before nodding and leaving to fetch the cup.

His mother gave Jack a look that concealed her laughter.

"Poor girl," Jack clucked. "When you answer all of her questions, she's got nothing to gossip about."

His mother shrugged her shoulders and patted the seat next to the fire, the more comfortable of the two places to sit in the room. While she poured the hot water into the tea to steep, she assessed him.

"You're more Jack every day," she said, taking the seat in front of her writing desk.

He smiled. "I noticed you introduced me as your son." Son, daughter, it made Jack no nevermind. He was both, he was either, anyone could call him what they wished.

"I couldn't possibly confuse the poor girl." She leaned forward and whispered, "She isn't as sharp as her sister."

Jack laughed, and his mother joined in. She always made him feel like they shared a confidence that no one else could break. They were too alike, Jack's brother had always complained. *You could make friends with a lamppost,* he'd said to their mother. *How do you know I haven't already?* It was in the before times. When they could laugh together. Before Jack left.

But that was what Jack's brother, Roland, didn't understand. They weren't shutting him out, they were only being themselves. Roland, in a move that perfectly imitated their father, chose to not speak and instead shut Jack out forever, choosing to act as if he had never existed at all, which was somewhat more insulting than pretending he was dead.

Jack believed that Roland was relieved to act as an only child, as if the privileged seat of Eldest Son hadn't been enough for him. When Jack left, Roland remained. Where Jack changed, Roland remained. For all he knew, Roland was sleeping under this very roof still.

The situation taught Jack an important rule for any decent finder of lost items: don't ask questions you don't want answers to. Not only could it tie a body up for hours learning about great-aunt Felicity's long-lost cat, but it could also lead to sticky moral implications that were better left unexplored. So Jack didn't ask after Roland, and his mother never mentioned him. An easy, quiet arrangement that left everyone with more peace. Or at least left the wound to scab over.

Annie appeared with the cup, staring at Jack the entire time. He nodded at the girl pleasantly, trying to reassure her that he did in fact belong here, but she backed out of the room. His mama flipped the long, heavy snake of her braid over her shoulder and stood to pour another cup. She prepared his tea on the tray, adding extra sugar and milk, as if he were still a child.

She settled back down in her chair to watch him take his first sip. He closed his eyes and inhaled the familiar scent. It was an indulgence, a flavor that he would only associate with her. The chai always tasted like home because it was hers.

"So," she said, satisfied that he'd had his first taste. "To what do I owe this early morning visit?" She didn't have to say what he knew already lurked in her heart. *What about your association with a lady? Will you finally go back to being a girl? Will you finally be the daughter I believed I had?*

Jack swallowed hard. "Are you sure you don't want to wait until your tea is ready?"

She waved her hand at him. "I'd rather know what has you climbing in my window this morning."

"I've met someone," Jack started. He immediately wished he could take it back. He wanted to start with the job, not with Lady Agnes, but of course his mouth didn't cooperate.

His mother lit up like a lighthouse. "An acquaintance through the young lady at the market? She was from a good family, wasn't she? I knew it. Her shoes were odd, but I could see all that aristocratic blood in her. Did she introduce you around?"

Jack set his jaw. He knew his mother would love him no matter what. She'd proven that. It was only her dogged belief that his world—his life—was a passing fashion that hurt. As if dressing like a twelve-year-old boy one minute and a twenty-year-old girl the next was something he was choosing to do out of boredom. She didn't understand how the life she led as a sea captain's wife chafed at Jack. How stays and a corset could chafe. How trousers could end up chafing. How Jack existed somewhere in a middle that didn't make sense, and he wished it would.

"It isn't anyone she introduced," Jack said, inhaling the spices of the tea in front of him.

His mother's expression softened and she nodded, but Jack could still read the disappointment on her face. "Her, then? A lady, yes?"

Jack nodded. "But I don't think she will like me in that way."

"What way?"

"The way I want to be with her."

She stretched to touch Jack's hand.

He swallowed a lump in his throat. There was so much that his mother saw even when Jack didn't want to share it. So much he wanted her to see but was afraid she couldn't. And Lady Agnes, he wanted her to see him that way too—what he was on the inside, not the decoration on the outside. "Yes," he whispered.

"My darling chicken," she said, smiling at him. "I don't know this lady, but if she has any ounce of sense, she'll know how special you are."

A blind platitude if there ever was one, but still nice to hear it. Nice to have his mother in his corner regardless. It made the world a bit bearable knowing it.

"Besides, I know that once you make your mind up about something, you will work until it happens."

He flashed her one of his rakish, flirtatious grins and shook off the uncertainty that had shrouded him since he'd left Mr. Arthur's house, flushed and miserable, ready to crawl out of his own skin. He would meet Lady Agnes at the market and think about the ethics of his work later. He was having morning tea with his mother, and he wanted to soak up the warmth of her love like an Arctic explorer.

"By the way," his mother said as she fixed her tea, keeping her gaze firmly on the teacup. "Your brother's wife has had a child. The christening is this week."

The news hit Jack like a fist to his chest.

"I know I've promised not to talk about Roland. But, it is my first grandchild." The tremor of love and need in her voice broke his heart.

Jack was the one that had left. He was the branch that couldn't bend in his family tree. His mother's desolation was his fault. She wanted to rejoice in the expansion of their family, the birth of a new love, and here was Jack limiting her, creating a problem when there should only be joy.

The spoon tinked in the cup as she stirred in a small amount of sugar. She only took sugar when she felt like indulging. Was it in celebration of her grandchild? Jack's own nephew or niece? Or was it to console over the fracture of her children?

Jack took the coward's way out. "Tell me, how is the fur-trapping in Canada? Have you heard back from Uncle Rafe lately? I've been imagining the wilds of North America for so long."

঩঵ঌ

VASILY TRAILED BEHIND AGNES, WHICH WAS ALL well and good, but she needed more room today at market. She had informed him that she wouldn't have any packages to hand off, but the man insisted on staying close to her all the same. It was unfortunate. How was she supposed to have a sensitive discussion with Jack if Vasily was standing there? How to talk about Lydia's *motherhood issues* while he stood there like a giant brooding tree?

It was thoroughly impossible. The idea that anyone would ever trifle with Lady Agnes was laughable. On the best of days, she was invisible. For instance, today, as she took a second lap around the market hoping to spot Jack, people literally stepped *on* her.

But Jack had never said he'd meet her. She wracked her brain. Did she even say which day she would come? Or what time? Oh, she was such a fool. Perhaps she expected too much. She had rebuffed him, after all. He had no reason to help her, no reason to want to be near her. Instead of healing from Mary Franklin's severed friendship, she pined after the only person she'd ever met who made her feel seen.

She was not only foolish, she was childish. Lydia would have never made this sort of mistake. Agnes had lost her chance to be bigger than she was, to be daring, to do more than sit at home and mend dresses for women who would actually live their lives.

The lacemaker eyed her as she made her second perusal of her wares. The lace was decent, nothing exceptional, but a fine thing to add to a bonnet or a bit of trim elsewhere. Agnes fingered a bit, as if to test it while she scanned the marketplace again. The lacemaker cleared her throat as she looked at Agnes sharply.

Ah, yes. In an effort to be even more invisible than usual, Agnes had worn her most drab brown round gown. She could be a governess or a down-on-her-heels lady, but she was not mistaken for what she actually was. So that was a success of a sort. Agnes gave the lacemaker a polite smile and moved on.

"You dropped this, miss," a voice said from behind.

Agnes turned and there he was, looking more of a grown man than he had at dinner the other night. His shoulders seemed broader, the cut of his waistcoat more sophisticated. He held a coin out to her.

"Thank you, sir," she said, trying to act as if he were any other person in the world and not the only one who sent her heart rioting out of her chest. Even Mary Franklin hadn't accomplished that feeling. With Mary, she'd felt warm and happy, as if Mary were a candle that helped her see in a dark hallway. Jack was a bonfire, ripping through logs and popping embers, loud and chaotic. A heat that could singe.

Or illuminate.

Jack stared at her with those large, dark eyes, fringed with thick lashes. He really had the most remarkable eyes. He cleared his throat at her.

Oh, the coin. Yes. Agnes graciously took the coin from his outstretched hand, concentrating so that her hands wouldn't shake. Was she supposed to pretend this was hers? Or was she to return it? She wasn't sure how this kind of game was played.

"How kind you are," she remarked. How was she supposed to engage him to walk with her in this ruse?

"Perhaps you would treat me to a cider or some such as a reward," he whispered.

"Perhaps I could treat you to a cider or some such as a reward for such gallant honesty," Agnes repeated, rather proud of herself for adding that bit at the end.

Vasily harrumphed from afar. Agnes couldn't tell if he wasn't fooled or wasn't amused.

"Come, sir," Agnes announced, perhaps a touch too loud, but she'd never been one for acting.

"Why thank you," Jack said through gritted teeth and came to her side to walk.

She hadn't the faintest why he might be so put out —they were walking together in public, weren't they? "Thank you," she said, hoping that would at least soften that handsome clenched jaw. It seemed sharp enough to cut paper.

"What did you need, my lady?" Jack asked, his voice pitched for her ears only.

"I have a bit of a problem," she confessed. "But it's very private. I can't let it be widely known."

Jack looked at her in alarm. She could feel his sudden tension radiating through the air. "What do you need?"

"It isn't for me. It's for my sister."

Visible relief washed over his face. "Of course. I'm happy to oblige."

"It isn't something that one speaks about in polite company."

Jack looked over his shoulder. "I think we're safely away from that."

"It's, well...I mean...I know nothing of these things, but I was wondering if perhaps you might know of someone—through your circles of acquaintances, I mean, not that you yourself would know, of course."

Suppressing a smile caused Jack's cheek to dimple, and it had to be the most adorable thing Agnes had ever seen, which only caused her to stammer harder and blush from the bottoms of her feet to the ends of her hair.

"What I mean to ask, that is, is would you perhaps be able to procure an appointment?"

"After all that, I still don't know an appointment with whom exactly." The grin on his face was maddening. "Perhaps. Who does she need to meet? The mayor? Old Boney? Prinny?"

Agnes blushed harder, which she didn't think was possible, her cheeks throbbing red. "Oh, please don't make fun of me even further. I know I positively resemble a garden vegetable." Agnes hated to look a fool, especially in front of someone like Jack. It made her feel so ignorant. And she knew she *was* ignorant in many areas, but couldn't he be kind to those who didn't know?

"My apologies. I am particular toward garden vegetables, so you'll have to pardon my goading."

Agnes moaned in frustration and tried to get a handle on herself. She should have never asked to see him. This wasn't her business. She wanted to be useful, to help her sister. Which, in all likelihood, Lydia wouldn't even appreciate.

"In all seriousness, my lady. I will do whatever you desire."

The words left his mouth in all innocence, she knew that. But she couldn't help glancing up, her heart stopping as he'd said them. Her tongue was thick, unable to speak. Even he seemed shocked by what he'd said.

"Oh look," he said, in a far too casual tone. "Cider."

She pulled her gaze in front of her, once again struggling with the war inside her body that made no sense whatsoever. She'd never had this reaction to anyone before. Never. Not once. Not even the fantasy husbands she'd constructed in her mind in an effort to make the whole practice of the marriage mart seem appealing. But Jack. Jack was doing something to her that confused her.

"Oh, cider," she echoed.

They ordered the cold pressed apple cider and stood drinking in wooden mugs near the stand so that they might return the mugs once they were finished. It felt companionable, easy. Not the way things felt when she was in the presence of a man.

"Very refreshing," Agnes said.

Jack made a noise in agreement as a couple passed them by. Once no one was in earshot, he asked, "So what kind of appointment is needed for your sister?"

Agnes gritted her teeth. If her sister could fight in a boxing ring, or even go through the humiliation of her childhood, then Agnes could manage to say to this, this, this—this veritable street urchin—that her sister needed a midwife of a sort.

Jack wasn't a street urchin. Agnes didn't know what it was, but she hated that she'd even thought it.

"My sister had a child not long ago, and I don't think she's healing properly. And it isn't only that her color is off, but also her humor. Even her husband is worried. Oh, I can't believe I'm saying this." Agnes pinched at her wrist to keep herself talking. "And the physician that sees her doesn't seem to be helping. Do you know of a midwife or herb woman that might be willing to come visit?"

The expression on Jack's face changed as Agnes recited Lydia's problems. He looked positively understanding.

"And discreetly!" Agnes added. "Of course."

"Of course," Jack echoed. "Any particular day or time?"

Agnes shook her head. "Whenever one can be available."

"I'll send a note when I find someone to visit your sister's bedside. Should I send it to you or to Mrs. Arthur?"

"To me, please. I'll let Lydia know. It's, well, it's embarrassing."

Jack gave her a soft smile, one without bravado or artifice. "It's the business of life. It cannot be embarrassing."

The bonfire that was Jack lit inside of her chest. "Thank you."

"My pleasure. Now. May I ask something of you?"

"Of course. After that, I feel like nothing ought to shock me."

Jack laughed, and it felt like there was finally sunshine on this overcast and yellowish morning. "Careful of what you say, my lady. You know I like beets."

Agnes knitted her eyebrows. "What on earth could you say?"

"Don't challenge me," he purred.

Agnes's tongue went thick again, and the odd tumbles and bits that she'd imagined in her bed on those lonely nights came to mind, finally with a face attached to a body. A *person* attached.

"I would be honored if you would consider—" Jack glanced back at Vasily, who stood a respectful distance away. "Running away with me. Only for a day."

Agnes couldn't help but eye him. The same suspicions ran through her as had the night of the ball. A bubble of excitement rose in her chest. Even her toes seemed to tingle. Could she? Would she? She glanced back at Vasily. He wouldn't mind being alleviated of his responsibilities for a day, would he?

She could still be ruined, of course. But it was

daylight. And, well, she didn't want to marry anyone anyway, so what was the harm?

Her whole body vibrated as she leaned forward and whispered, "Yes." It felt like drinking champagne to say yes to Jack. Heady and sweet and wonderful.

The reward was a slow smile from Jack, his dark eyes searching her face. "Then we start slow. We'll walk to the crowded end of the market and disappear down an alleyway. Are you ready?"

Agnes glanced back again.

"Don't look at him. Look at the shops. The sky. Me."

Jack was easy to look at. His tight vest, the shaggy, inky fringe of hair visible from his hat, it all made Agnes feel somehow...fizzy. He proffered his arm, like a gentleman, and Agnes took it, despite the fact that she stood taller than him by a good four inches.

"My goodness, are we really running away?" Agnes asked, surprising even herself that she sounded so breathless. So carried away.

That sultry grin split his face again, making her mouth go dry. "Oh no, my lady. I'm not running away. I'm going about my business. *You* are running away."

For a moment, Agnes wanted to tell Mary Franklin. To throw it in like a tasty piece of gossip. *You'll never believe what I did the other day.* Her own way to say, *I'm not so small now, am I?*

But when Jack was around, Mary Franklin seemed so dull. Utterly ordinary. Why would she have water when she could have whisky? Not that in this analogy, water was even offered anymore. And the pang she expected to receive with that thought didn't come. It had been a few months, but could it be that she was over Mary Franklin? How truly odd.

Agnes's hand was threaded through Jack's elbow, and he put his hand over hers, signaling to sidestep down an alleyway. Agnes turned to glance back at Vasily.

"No, not at him. Watch me," Jack said.

So she did. He became her whole world.

And sometimes, she thought dimly as she quickened her steps, that's all it takes.

❦

JACK PUT EVERYTHING BUT AGNES OUT OF HIS mind. He wanted today to be about them and the brilliant opportunities London had to offer. They ditched the giant first by walking through the crowded market stalls of Covent Garden and then by entering the Panorama. Jack gladly paid the sixpence that admitted them to see the life-size depiction of the Battle of Waterloo. Neither of them wanted to gaze on that mass of destruction, however, and very soon, they made their way out of the Panorama, finding themselves without the oversized chaperone.

"Are you well?" Jack had heard some people complain that panoramas made them dizzy. But Lady Agnes's cheeks were flushed and her eyes were bright.

"Very well. And you?"

He couldn't help but grin. "Also very well. Come with me." They doubled back through the market and Jack bought cherries from a young maid. He took Lady Agnes's hand and led her down away from the Strand, through the warrens and narrow back streets.

"Oh, books!" She exclaimed.

"These are the secondhand books," Jack explained, slowing to let Agnes see the cart piled high. Her serviceable day gown made her look less aristocratic and more ordinary, so it wasn't such an odd pairing for them to be walking together.

A hawkish woman came down the street. "Are you looking for something more exciting?"

"No, thank you," Jack said, gripping Lady Agnes's hand once more. But it was easy to forget how a woman's dress made her a target for all things. How much easier it was to navigate as a man.

"Why not look for something exciting?" Lady Agnes asked, looking at the woman.

The woman cackled. "Yes, why not more excitement, eh lad?"

"Come on," Jack said, pulling Lady Agnes along.

"What's wrong with more excitement?" Agnes asked. "I thought we were having a day of new things?"

Jack squeezed her hand. "I don't think you were quite ready for that kind of excitement, my lady."

He could practically see her mind churning with possibilities.

"The woman sells pornography," Jack admitted. "She thought we might need some, um, inspiration." It was Jack's turn to blush. It was a rare event and he didn't like it.

"*Oh,*" Agnes said softly, before she noticed Jack's rosy cheeks. "You know, I rather like vegetable gardens myself."

He gave her a stern look, but he still thrilled at her comment. She was letting formality slip away— she was being herself. She was *teasing* him. He led her on through the narrow streets until they crossed down to the river, where they encountered more street vendors.

More people pushed up against them, and Lady Agnes pulled herself towards him, which he couldn't have felt more gratified by.

"Do you like oysters?" He couldn't help but feel pride in his chest, puffing out like some damn songbird as her eyes goggled in delight at the newfound aspects of her hometown.

"Of course," she answered, still breathy and wide-eyed.

He loved watching her like that. Exposed, vulnerable, one might say, but also wondrous, luminous, exploratory.

Down here at the docks, ships lurched and gulls squawked. The smell of rot, the refuse of the Thames, but also salt and fish and people. There were sailors from all over the world, women from all over the world, children scampering to deliver messages and invoices, large men hauling large cargo into warehouses. Nets swinging from ship to dry land, and most importantly for Jack and Lady Agnes, the oyster mongers.

"Oysters for ye, then?" a wrinkled woman asked as they approached. Her skin was thin from age and roughened by the days spent out of doors.

Agnes nodded, instinctively knowing she shouldn't use her toff accent here. Jack burnished his own a bit for good measure. "Two, if you please, missus."

The old woman reached a gnarled hand into a bucket, pulled out two large oysters, and cracked them open with the large knife she carried in the other hand. She handed both to Jack, who gave one to Agnes. They took a step to the side of the oyster monger.

"Yes?" Jack asked, his oyster poised.

Lady Agnes lifted her oddly beautifully sculpted eyebrow—how did a woman possess such a beautiful eyebrow?—and made as if to toast her oyster to his. And then she tossed it down, practiced as anyone. It thrilled Jack to his toes and he did the same, letting the cool, wet saltiness slide down his throat.

He took the empty half shell from her and tossed both his and hers into the bucket of empties left from previous customers. Her eyes were shining like a cat's.

"Another," she insisted.

"As you wish." He returned to the oyster monger for two more, and the smug look on the lined face told him that she'd expected him to return. He laid another coin on her stool. Silly perhaps, but he couldn't quite place why he was so absolutely chuffed to provide something that Lady Agnes asked for. She wanted something, and he could give it to her.

Fact: Being able to provide for her felt like a greater accomplishment than ejecting a belligerent drunk from the Inn without a fuss.

"You know, a woman is always happy to know her fella likes oysters," the old woman cackled as she handed over two more opened shells.

Jack winked at her. "And if she's lucky, she'll know exactly how much."

The old woman threw her head back and cackled. As he strutted back to Lady Agnes, Jack was glad she hadn't overheard the exchange. She would have been mortified.

"Quite friendly, isn't she?"

"She's a dream."

"Well then," Lady Agnes murmured, taking her half shell and slurping it back. Jack did the same. She said, "What next?"

"Would you like a surprise, or would you like to guide the tour yourself?" There were so many places to show her, so many places to see.

Agnes shook her head. "I haven't the faintest. I don't know what I don't know."

He proffered his arm again, which she took. "Those are the words of a very wise woman." She snugged right up to him, even with a crowd pushing her, and it made him feel *right*. Correct in a way that he couldn't define. As if an itch had finally been scratched. This was how he was meant to be—and the person he wanted to be with.

He could show her the dirtiest corner of Seven Dials and she'd *ooh* and *aah* over it. It was a lovely thing to have someone so unimpeachable, so clean. So perfect.

Instead, he brandished the bag of cherries that he'd shoved in his pocket. Jack led her over a few streets and encountered a gang of children betting over a beetle race. He and Agnes joined in, throwing a ha'penny in to enrich the pot. They cheered their beetle, jumping and stamping with the children, egging on the scurrying bugs. When their beetle lost, they left the children the ha'penny with good cheer.

"I have a spot I like," Jack said, climbing up the wall near the river steps. "It isn't clean, and it isn't comfortable, but it has a lovely view." He helped her up and they sat on the wall, the bag of cherries between them. They spit the seeds down below into the mud of the Thames.

They spoke of nothing important. Jack told jokes and Agnes laughed. Agnes did impressions of her sister and told Jack stories of mishaps at balls. It was nothing and everything all at once. The sum of dozens of days, a smattering of years, the ways in which they moved in their respective worlds.

Once the cherries were gone, they sat, hands creeping closer together. Jack was aware of her nearness down to the tips of his arm hairs.

"You are like none other, Mr. Townsend," Lady Agnes said, giving him a wistful smile. The sun was setting, giving a golden gleam to the sky and making her skin seem all the more porcelain in its light. "And I mean that as a compliment."

"Taken as one," he said. How could he not study her? The slope of her nose, the easy, changeable flush of her cheeks, the call of her lips as she chewed on the bottom one.

"You speak as someone who is widely read. Educated, even."

Fact: People didn't like to come right out and ask questions. They danced and feinted, trying to wheedle information. And most people were shite at it.

"If you'd like to ask me questions, I'd be happy to answer you. Even if I have to swear you to secrecy." His heart thumped hard in his chest and his hands sweated. He wiped his palm on his trouser leg. He would tell her anything. He promised he'd never lie to her, and he meant to keep that promise.

"It seems like such an imbalance. You know quite a bit about me, but I know nothing of you. Have you a family? Siblings—real ones? Where are they? Why do you never speak of them?" Here she seemed quiet and almost sad. Oh, dear salty devil below, did he make her sad?

He stared out at a ship moving slowly downriver. "I have a family. My parents are both alive and well. A brother, as well, who doesn't approve of me. And a large extended family that is flung all over the world. Without my mother, we'd fall apart, but she is the great letter writer who never lets a single acquaintance wither away."

"How admirable. And how time-consuming. I admit that I would find it tedious," Lady Agnes's shoulders seemed to have come down from around her ears. She really did want to know about his real life. She was *interested*. The idea of it seemed beyond hope.

"My mama is the best person I've ever met. She and I are very much alike."

"You are also a prolific correspondent? I find that

hard to believe," Lady Agnes said, her smile signaling that she was teasing him again.

"We both love people. I like to talk. And I like to listen. You never know what you might learn."

"Ah yes, for *finding* things. Since that is what you do."

Jack shook his head. "It didn't start out as a job. It was something I was good at. I'm good at helping people." He shrugged. That sounded too much like bragging, and it made him want to shrink back down.

"How did it start?" she asked, looking down at her ungloved hands. She'd taken them off to eat cherries, not wanting to stain them. But now, by the looks of it, she was thinking about putting them back on. Gloves on meant going home. Gloves on meant a return to their different stations in life. Gloves on meant they ended.

Shit on toast, *someone* had to make a move. He grabbed her hand in his, the red stains on his fingertips matching hers. She didn't try to tug her hand away, not even in surprise. Her face remained implacable, polite, interested, not giving any emotion away other than friendship. But her fingers wove into his, and she settled her palm against his, supple and warm. He prayed he wouldn't sweat on her. He stared at their intertwined fingers. They looked perfect, natural, right.

"How did it start?" She nudged him again.

He tore his eyes from their connection and looked up at her, getting lost once again. "It started with a baby."

"Your baby?"

"Oh, dear God, no," Jack said, watching her flinch. "My apologies for the harsh language."

"I've heard worse," Lady Agnes said. "From my sister."

They shared a laugh, but Jack knew he needed to

say more. He needed to share himself. How could that be so hard? "A baby. A few years old, toddling, using the privy."

Lady Agnes let out a sad *oh*.

"Exactly as you think. Child fell in. I was nearby, playing with my mates. I didn't know what to think. I ran towards the mother, screaming her bloody head off. My mates lowered me down by my ankles and I snatched that baby right out of the offal."

"Did it survive?"

"It did." Jack nodded. It was that day that Roland couldn't forgive him for. That day, when Jack was the hero and Roland was forgotten as one of the boys who held fast to Jack's ankles, lowering him into the stench of the neighborhood's refuse. Jack got the praise, got a write-up in a local rag. Received gifts. Made his name from it.

"How fortunate you were there. The mother must have been beside herself with relief."

"She was. Got around the neighborhood that I was someone who helped. From that came finding things. Went from accepting gifts after the fact from neighbors to charging up front for strangers."

Lady Agnes fiddled with her gloves and shivered. It was time. Fact: Better to leave them wanting than wishing they'd left ages ago.

"Let me take you home, Lady Agnes. I've stolen you away for far too long."

"It isn't stealing if it's freely given." Her eyes bored into him, and he wanted so badly to kiss her. To lean in, taste the sweet cherries from her lips. Instead, he raised her hand, turned it slowly to face palm up, and planted a kiss in the same sweet cradle of her palm, as he'd done the first day they'd spoken. Her shaky intake of breath assured him that she felt the same.

"Then I thank you for the gift. Consider it the

payment for my services. Let me take you home so that I can start finding someone for your sister." Jack helped Lady Agnes to her feet, wishing the day could last forever but knowing better than to indulge himself.

"I can take a hack home if you wouldn't mind escorting me closer to a thoroughfare." She looked shy in the lowered sun.

He offered his elbow. "I will take you anywhere you wish to go."

10

"**Y**ou look like shite." Miss Persephone crossed
her arms, causing her biceps to bulge, which
was both intimidating and impressive. She
loved flexing at him. "Happy shite, but shite
nonetheless."

Jack had gotten a few hours of sleep that day and
was back on the door that evening at the Inn. It
didn't matter. He'd spent the entire day with Lady
Agnes. She'd laughed at his jokes, blushed in a way
that did unnerving things to his insides, and told him
silly intimacies that made him feel proud to know
her. "Haven't slept much. It's fine."

And, sweeping his eye across the evening's limited
patrons, his lack of sleep didn't really matter. There
shouldn't be much to worry about. They'd close up
early, and he could fall into bed when the time came.

"Really. Do tell." Miss Persephone perched near
him, her skirts not allowing a comfortable slouch like
his. "Is it *her*?"

"Her?" Had he mentioned Lady Agnes to Miss
Persephone before? He couldn't remember.

"Yes her. The *her* that you moped about for those
weeks. You were such a bore."

Jack tried to have the energy to bristle, but he

didn't. Bliss couldn't come close to the word he felt at that moment, and Miss Persephone goading him about his behavior wasn't enough to pop this bubble of happiness. "Fine, yes, the same her." His mouth wanted to shape her name, but he didn't. He couldn't utter her name here, at the Inn. She wasn't for this world, with its satire and unflinching mockery. The backbiting, both literal and figurative. There was freedom here in his world, but it came at a price. He wouldn't ask her to pay it.

"I'm waiting here, Jack. At this rate, I'll have to pluck my chin hairs before you'll tell me."

Jack swigged at his watered-down small beer. "I'll not tell you here. Later. After everyone's gone home."

"Everyone's gone home? I hope not," boomed a voice from the door. "I've a mind to have a drink or four at least!"

The flash of distaste that flitted across Miss Persephone's face was enough to tell Jack who the voice belonged to. Turning, he confirmed that it was Lord Haverformore himself. The bubble of happiness didn't so much burst as it evaporated. "Delighted to see you, my lord."

"Delighted to see you as well, my boy." The man swung a dandy's walking stick, flourishing it with absolutely no grace at all. Someone would lose an eye at this rate. "I do hope we get a chance to chat this evening. But first, a drink!"

The man marched off towards the refreshment table for a very middling claret.

"Oh, damn it all," Miss Persephone said, standing. "I'm on drink duty tonight. I don't truly dislike many things. But—"

"You can't say it out loud here," Jack reminded her.

She canted her hip. "But I truly dislike an unpoured drink."

Jack held up his rustic mug. "Cheers, then."

As Miss Persephone followed Lord Haverformore over to the drink table, wiggling fingers hello to various patrons and giving saucy looks to others, Jack leaned his head back against the wall. This was not good. Involuntarily, his eyes closed.

The door creaked again, and Jack's eyes snapped open. He didn't think he'd fallen asleep, and after glancing at the patrons' whereabouts, he found that mere seconds had passed.

"You." It was a dark voice. An accented voice. Jack feared who had found him. Worse than Lord Haverformore, it was Lady Agnes's Russian chaperone. The man was the size of a small elephant and far more irate.

"Good evening, sir," Jack said amiably. Shaking himself awake, he knew he had to be his most charming. "What brings you to the Inn?"

"You," the beast repeated. Up close, the man was more frightening. His dark hair was graying in a few places, running silver threads through a raven black beard. His dark eyes, barely visible under the brim of his hat, were full of violence, and Jack didn't doubt for a moment that the person looking at him had killed someone with his bare hands.

"Jolly good. What may I do for you? Would you like a drink? A small repast?" Jack offered his most winning grin to the list.

"No. Step outside." The fists balled at the man's sides sported dark hair at the knuckles. How terrifying to have hair in your eyes as he punched your face into plaster dust.

"Sounds lovely, truly does. However, you see, I am working at the moment. The door, as a matter of fact, and I cannot abandon my post."

"Step outside so I may beat you." The man didn't so much as blink.

"Would love to, absolutely cannot do it."

"I will call the magistrate instead," Vasily said with no more or less threat in his voice than before. Did he know what the Inn was?

But that was a bluff Jack could not call. Not that he wanted to get the shite kicked out of him, but perhaps he could continue to talk his way into Vasily's good graces. "No need, no need," Jack said. "Let me pop over to let them know where I've gone then." The magistrate could absolutely *not* be called. In the past, the dogberries had meant a death sentence for someone inside. A sacrifice for the good people of London. Likely not, but still, why risk it? Best to hum along, if they could.

"I will be outside." Vasily turned, flinging the door open with one of his great meat hooks.

"Of course." Whatever this was, it wasn't good. Jack made his way to Miss Persephone, timing it right to slip by Lord Haverformore as he turned away with his glass of claret. "I have some exciting and terrifying news."

"Ever thus," Miss Persephone rejoined, not taking her eyes off the dancefloor.

"The, ah, *chaperone* of my amore is outside."

"Delightful. Invite her in and we'll get her sauced. What's the trouble?" Miss Persephone helped herself to more claret, offering Jack a glass as well.

Jack waved her off. "Sadly, this chaperone is a Russian ex-soldier who is roughly the size of last year's Royal Ascot winner."

Miss Persephone tittered. "Do introduce me."

"Perhaps if my face still functions after he's done with me." Jack wasn't absolutely sure that the man was an ex-soldier, but he'd put the whole purse hidden under his bed on the idea. Something in his posture, the even cadence of his stride, even the blankness of his expression while he waited for Lady

Agnes to finish whatever occupied her. It all screamed military.

Her eyes widened. "What did you *do?* Or rather, what didn't you do?"

"Stop. He's outside now waiting for me to go to the slaughter. Tell my mother I love her."

Miss Persephone put her glass on the table and her muscles went slack for a minute, releasing all her pretense. "Do you need me to go see to 'im?"

That Miss Persephone would drop her façade at the drink table touched him. She was ready to battle for him, the butcher's apprentice who had moved to the Inn because being Miss Persephone was more fun. But the butcher's apprentice would never fade, always there, ready to be used when needed. As Miss Persephone, she was not a person who fought with fists—she was a person who teased and flirted and battled with veiled insults and fan positions.

"My transgressions, my responsibility," Jack said.

"You are a gem, Jack. Truly."

"Hopefully one that isn't about to get recut into a new shape." Jack steadied himself, touching one finger to his eyebrow as a goodbye. He tried to remember his training from Bess Abbott. All of her advice was how to duck and run. Especially if one was outmatched—and there was no greater understatement for what was happening here.

But run—where? This was his home, and Jack was in the wrong. A gentleman did not abscond with a lady. It had been a lark to Jack, and maybe even to Lady Agnes, but not to her family. If Lady Agnes were watching, what she would think? If he wanted to be worthy of her, then he would face the giant who protected her.

Jack swung open the heavy exterior door.

"Did you think I wouldn't find you?" The Russian growled at him from the shadows.

"I sincerely apologize, truly I do," Jack said, trying to maintain distance from the large man's fists.

"I've seen you in the kitchens. Your costumes do not fool me." His meat hooks clenched and his stance changed.

Ah. A cold dread spread in Jack's chest.

"What is your purpose? Why do you ask such questions? What do you want? And why do you lust after my Lady Agnes?" Fury burned through the man's face.

Another possessive. Was the man a father figure to her? Was he in love with her? "I had a job, but it's done now. Mr. Worley, you see, he needed to find his mother. Well, she is found now. You're welcome." Jack dodged out of the way as Vasily stepped closer, his manner dropping pretense and starting to look like fighting. Jack's heart pounded in real fear. It had been a long time since he really thought he might die.

"Then what is it you want with Lady Agnes?"

"I—I—" He stammered, watching his opponent's feet. Blood pounded in his ears. He couldn't think. There was no talking his way out of this. The range of the man's arms was too great—it was hard to escape his swing. A fist whizzed by his ear as he ducked and rolled away.

Fact: Chimney sweeps were short-lived, but they were nimble. The five minutes he'd been one definitely helped.

The giant advanced on him once again, not even short of breath. "What do you want with her?" Another swing.

Jack was only slightly faster than those meaty fists, dodging and retreating until the giant backed him into a corner. There was nowhere to go and nothing to climb. He loomed over Jack, and the impending pain of death caused him to blurt out the only thing he could think: "I love her!"

The Russian's fists stopped their ascent and inspected Jack's face in the shadows.

Did he love her? A bit of an overstatement, wasn't it? His opponent seemed to be thinking the same thing. Could he love her, having barely spent time with her?

"She is not for you." The giant dropped his fists.

"I wouldn't rightly assume—"

"She is a *lady*," he said. "And you—you are no one."

That burned. Jack's chest still thumped hard and fast, but he was able to catch his breath. "Perhaps you don't know, but—"

"You are no one," he repeated. "Stay away from my Lady Agnes. And if you take her again, no one else will know you either."

The phrase was clearly a threat by the way it was intoned, but Jack sat and parsed it while he watched Vasily walk away. He was someone. Absolutely was. He was the best finder in all of London, that much was clear. Everyone who needed something ended up coming to him eventually, including Lady Agnes.

Jack didn't care if Vasily thought he was someone, only that Lady Agnes thought he was someone. And if Lady Agnes thought he was someone, Vasily would know. A conundrum, clearly, because it showed that Lady Agnes didn't think he was someone, either. But he could show Lady Agnes that he wasn't some invisible nobody. In his own world, he garnered respect and friends. He stalked back into the Inn.

"You're alive," Miss Persephone said, sitting at the doorman's table. She held up her cup to toast him.

"You know I have a gift for conversation." His heart still pounded in his throat, and his hands still shook.

"If I didn't know better, I'd say that you put on

too much powder." She pulled a small flask out of her skirt pocket.

"Pardon?" Jack couldn't follow anything. His mind wouldn't work—still blank and scared and focused on the one thing he wanted: for Lady Agnes to see him. To want him. To love him. No, too far.

"I'm saying you're bleached out like old bones. Congratulations on convincing the chaperone not to throw a fist." She unscrewed the small flask cap. "Here. A gift from one of my admirers. I don't usually drink whisky, but this one is good."

Jack took the flask with shaking hands. The whisky burned going down, but it did the job. They sat there in silence as he recovered his wits. How could he prove to Lady Agnes that he was worth the risk? That they could be more than these hidden acquaintances, furtive and always in shadow?

Prove he was good at his job, clearly. She needed a midwife for her sister, and he would find the best midwife in town.

☙❧

THE NOTE WAS DELIVERED WHILE SHE BREAKFASTED at the table with her father. Agnes let it sit for a moment or two while she finished her chocolate. She didn't want to seem too eager in front of others, but also, she wanted to revel in it. That Jack was thinking about her. That he would help her.

In all her assignations—and there weren't many— she'd never been chased. Agnes had always been the pursuer, creating opportunities for her and her interest to be alone together, to meet up, to go for walks or visit. But Jack made things happen so effortlessly. All she had to do was say *I want...* and Jack filled in the blanks, making her whims happen.

A blush crept up her cheeks as she thought about

their day together. The two of them dashing through alleyways and the markets. Eating oysters by the Thames. Betting and cheering on beetles, spitting cherry pits into the mud. The way he spoke to her, the way he listened to her—actually listened, his head cocked to the side, nodding thoughtfully as he chewed through everything she said.

His cleverness dazzled her. She said something once and he filed it away, only to bring it around hours later at the most perfect and surprising time. And what was more, he thought *she* was intelligent.

There was so much more to him that was reserved, secrets stacked neatly like bricks, but she dared not ask and he didn't volunteer. She could wait. In fact, she hoped the note was asking for another meet, somehow. Vasily had been most unhappy with her running off and had told her father.

It was not a pleasant discussion.

Papa had sat her down in the drawing room and lectured her about the risks of a young woman alone. How her station in life was not to be disrespected. That in exchange for the pretty dresses and the food and the security, she gave up the ability to run amok in the streets with strange boys. Especially with strange boys.

Agnes had attempted to defend Jack—that he was not strange. Papa's even, droning tone kept her from getting in a word. She'd rather he yelled at her in a rage, but that wasn't Papa's way. Instead, Vasily had growled at her for the past few days and made oblique metaphors that didn't make any sense.

Finishing her chocolate, she pulled the note into her lap. Her impulse was to smell it, to see if it had any hint of Jack's distinctive soap. But she couldn't without giving herself away. Instead, she slid her fingers into the folds to open the artfully constructed letter.

My dear lady,

I have found one Mrs. Caldwell, a renowned healer and herbwoman, who is willing to aid wherever needed. Please let me know the time and place for the appointment. Reach me by letter at the Cock and Prance Inn.

Ever your servant,

Jack

MUST SHE REACH HIM BY LETTER? COULD SHE GO to him herself? Agnes glanced up at her dear, thoughtful, levelheaded papa. No. A letter would do. And they should meet at Lydia's house, of course.

Her stomach dropped. She didn't know if Lydia would scream at her or accept the help. A groan escaped her.

"Something the matter?" her father asked over his ironed newspaper.

"Not at all. The chocolate is sometimes so delightful one cannot help but appreciate it vocally." Agnes was not a good liar and never had been.

"Ah." He went back to his reading.

"I'll be visiting Lydia again this afternoon, if you would like me to convey a message."

He made a noncommittal sound but then folded the paper and put it down. "I'm glad that you are visiting your sister so much lately. I know you two have had your ups and downs, but family is important."

Leave it to her dear papa to pierce her with words this early in the morning. "I wouldn't say that *we* have had our ups and downs. More like Lydia has ups and downs and the rest of us follow in the wake of the tempest."

A small smile escaped from behind the newspaper. "Your sister is a force of nature. We are but insects to bask in her sunshine or suffer her storm."

"What if I don't want to be an insect?" Agnes hadn't meant to pout, but it came out of her mouth before she could stop it. "I only mean that I'm tired of being ruled by someone else's moods."

Her papa glanced to the doorway, folded the newspaper, and put his hand over hers. "Never breathe a word of this to another soul or I will disown you."

Agnes laughed. "I promise."

Papa sighed. "The first time we had Mr. Arthur over for dinner, I saw the lightning between them and I hoped—nay, prayed—that despite his low birth, he could bring your sister to heel. The dear Lord knows that no one else has ever had that power."

"Really? You approved of him, despite being a prizefighter?" This was news. This was...important news.

"Had I wanted your sister to marry a nobleman? Of course. Had I wanted a match that would benefit our family both politically and socially? Naturally. But your sister..." His eyes wandered the room as he searched for the words. "Your sister was hellbent on destruction. Pardon my phrasing, Agnes, but it's true. Lydia couldn't stop herself, and if we'd forced a match with someone more suitable, we would have only assured losing her forever in ways I don't wish to contemplate."

Agnes nodded, surprised that she and her father agreed. Surprised that he was so observant. "I'm ashamed to say that it's easier here in the house without her."

Her father barked out a sharp laugh and then sighed. "I'll deny it to my dying breath, but yes. Yes, it is."

"What about me?" Agnes asked.

Papa's eyes softened. "What about you?"

"What would you want for me?" the words came out small and meek, which is not how she wanted to feel about her future, but in the face of her father's approval, it seemed inconsequential.

"I want you to find happiness most of all. With Lydia's marriage, it will be hard to find you an advantageous match." He withdrew his hand and sat back. "But I don't think that's what you are hoping for. I honestly don't know what you are hoping for, and I'm not sure you know either."

It was true. Agnes had never wanted marriage or babies. But neither did she need to avenge herself like her sister had, or even explore the world like Rose Dorchester, now Lady Kinsley. Or be left in quiet to further scientific pursuits like her cousin Margaret, now Lady Elshire. "I only want happiness."

"We all do, pet. But think about what that looks like for you. What will fulfill you, make you a whole person? It's different for everyone, but you can't start finding it if you don't know what it looks like."

The clock struck the hour. Her father stood. "Must dash. But when you know what your happiness is, tell me, and I will do everything in my power to help. I promise."

Agnes smiled at him and couldn't help but think she wanted a partner in life who would say what her father did. No judgements or heavy-handed guidance. The exact opposite of her mother and sister.

Waiting until the proper hour to call, Agnes made her way over to Lydia's in stony silence, driven by Vasily. As they approached Lydia's street in Marylebone, he finally spoke. "He is no good."

"I beg your pardon?" Agnes asked, snapped from a reverie filled with Jack caressing the skin between her gloves and her sleeve.

"The boy. Man. Jack."

"I haven't the faintest idea what you are talking about."

This only elicited a harrumph from Vasily. "I saw him. His intentions are...honorable. But he is not for you."

For the first time in her life, Agnes felt her hackles rise. She drew herself up ramrod straight. "I beg. Your. Pardon. That is not for you to decide."

Vasily glowered back at her, his dark eyes filled with steel and certainty she knew had always been there but had never been directed at her before. "I know the world. You do not. That is no place for a lady."

Her breath came fast, but she dared not sputter in front of him. She matched his steel with her own. "I am the mistress of my own destiny. I choose."

"You are the mistress of nothing. You know nothing. You see nothing. You are like this horse." He gestured to the one pulling the phaeton. "Blinders so that it will not startle. That is how you have been raised."

"I know far more than other women of my station."

"Means very little."

"You do not choose my fate, Vasily. You are merely my father's man, employed at his behest. Your opinion is of no consequence to me nor to him. I choose. I cannot imagine what possessed you to choose this life for yourself, but you also chose. It's my turn."

Vasily stared at her, neither in awe nor in shock, but closely, as if seeing her for the first time. "There is much you do not know."

It was the echo of what he'd already said, but Agnes got the distinct feeling that he was referring to something specific. Something she most certainly did not want to know.

Their arrival precluded any more bickering. Agnes descended artlessly, almost twisting her ankle as she landed. But she collected herself enough to be led to the drawing room.

Pearl was darning socks when Agnes entered. She put aside her work and sprang to her feet, clearly relieved for the company. "Agnes, what a delight to have you here today."

The letter burned in Agnes's pocket. She could feel it as surely as she could feel Jack's hand.

"Let me ring for refreshments. Lydia has not yet come down." A shadow darkened Pearl's face as she mentioned Lydia.

Perhaps Agnes's efforts would be welcome. They waited for the tea tray to appear before settling in. Pearl poured and handed Agnes her cup.

"There now." Pearl's luminous face wavered between satisfied hostess and concerned sister-in-law. "Unless you'd prefer to wait for Lydia, but I don't know when she will be down."

Agnes accepted the cup, turning the handle to properly manage it. "To get straight to it, I have found someone to help Lydia with her troubles. Her maternal troubles, as you mentioned."

Pearl raised her fine ginger eyebrows. "That's wonderful. May I ask who?"

"A Mrs. Caldwell? I don't know her, but apparently she comes highly recommended."

Shock was apparent in Pearl's expression. "Mrs. Caldwell has agreed to see Lydia? That is more than I could hope for."

Now Agnes did feel a bit put out. She'd never heard of Caldwell. "You know her then?"

"I know of her," Pearl said, her voice breathy with admiration. "She's the best. Truly. If a woman was in trouble and the midwife on hand couldn't help, they would rush to find her. I remember her. That woman has performed miracles."

Agnes felt herself swell with a bit of pride, not only for herself but for Jack as well. Nothing but the best for Lydia. If Lydia could accept the help. "Do you think Lydia would consent—"

"Consent to what?" Lydia asked, sweeping into the room. She still looked pale and somehow similar to porridge. Still a shadow of her former self. Is this what motherhood was supposed to beget? A child at the expense of one's person?

"No room for manners today, I see." Agnes couldn't help but throw a few verbal jabs, hoping Lydia would rise to return them.

"As if you would appreciate them. What are your shoes today? Men's boots, or have you found something even more absurd to wear?"

Agnes tucked her feet, clad in a very serviceable men's work boot, the kind worn by the men who unloaded cargo from the ships. They were very comfortable and made Agnes feel at home no matter where she happened to be. "I'm not here to talk about myself."

"Of course not. We would all fall asleep."

Agnes let any harsh feelings leave her. Her prickly sister. At least she was able to banter again. "Then let's turn to your favorite topic: yourself."

"Of course. I am naturally compelling."

"Now you sound like my brother," Pearl said, watching the exchange with amusement.

"We must have something in common to sustain us," Lydia said, her eyes glancing toward the door as if she hoped her husband might appear any moment.

Pearl looked at Agnes, urging her to broach the subject she had come to share. But Agnes's tongue thickened. What if Lydia yelled at her for it? Agnes shook her head to strengthen her resolve. "Lydia. I. That is. I."

Lydia's eyebrow, the one that she used to cool effect in ballrooms throughout London, raised to its perfect arch.

Agnes hated it. She hated the eyebrow and the cool disdain. It was all part of Lydia's fakery—her show. "I found an herbwoman to help you, if only you'll accept the appointment."

"Pardon?" The eyebrow returned to its normal place, confusion marring her sister's face.

"Anyone can see you haven't been yourself since the babe. Pearl agrees. I have found an excellent herbwoman who may be able to help you feel more yourself."

"Is this about my weight?" Lydia asked, reflexively covering her stomach.

"No, no—" Pearl rushed in, but Agnes cut her off.

"Don't be ridiculous. It's about how you resemble a bowl of half-eaten porridge."

Lydia smoothed her flowing round gown, the exact style of which Agnes favored.

"I see."

"The rags, Lydia," Pearl said, wringing her hands. "You use so many."

For the first time in her life, Agnes watched Lydia blush. Not a pretty one, but one from shame, flaming and hot. Her heart went out to her sister.

"Please let me help," Agnes whispered, an ache blooming inside of her.

Lydia stared at her lap for a long time. Slowly, she began to nod. "The woman may come whenever is convenient for her. I have," she waved her hand around. "Nothing to occupy me since we have a nurse."

"I can be in the room, if you wish," Pearl said.

"No." The word came fast and sharp, a rebuke of

the worst kind. But then Lydia looked up at Agnes. "But you may."

"Of course." Agnes tamped down a smile, thrilled that Lydia wanted her, not Pearl.

❦

JACK RECEIVED LADY AGNES'S MISSIVE THE SAME day he'd sent his, which made him smile. He sat by the door of the Inn like a fat, broody hen.

Guests came through the door, cheered by his self-satisfied smile, and that made Jack all the happier. He'd already checked with Mrs. Caldwell, who was miraculously available the next day, and all was sliding into place nicely.

Miss Persephone came over and dropped into a chair next to him during a lull in company. She was sweating slightly from the dancing and huffed to catch her breath. The musicians were on a break, filing down to the kitchen to get their dinner and drinks. The next round of guests would likely show in another three-quarters of an hour, coinciding with the ending of dinner parties and the closing of the theatre.

She clinked her goblet of watered wine to his watered beer. "Have you worked out your plan to show yourself worth the trouble?"

Tomorrow he would escort Mrs. Caldwell to the Arthurs' estate in Marylebone, where he would see Lady Agnes and give a short, sugary speech—he couldn't think of what it might be, but something, and it would show her that his intentions were pure. That he...well, he...ah, bloody hell. Even in his mind, he choked on the words. He cared about her. Deeply.

"I have a plan—"

"Glad to hear it!" A voice boomed from the door. Lord Haverformore.

"What a prat," muttered Miss Persephone.

"Good evening, my lord," Jack said, hoping to not let this arse ruin his mood. And, honestly, for a day, he had forgotten about that other bit. The bit about the art portfolio of a dead man. The bit that would make him able to take care of Lady Agnes in style for at least a little while.

"I take it everything is in motion, as they say?" Lord Haverformore pulled up a chair and joined them. As soon as he sat, Miss Persephone stood.

"If you'll excuse me," she said, bobbing down in a genteel curtsy.

Lord Haverformore waved her away, his lusty gaze aimed at Jack. "Enlighten me to your details, please. I want to know my substantial investment isn't going to waste."

Jack pasted on a confident smile. "I wouldn't want to ruin the surprise."

"I don't like surprises," the other man countered, his expression turning to stone.

"I've had important conversations with important men. That's all I am willing to say at the moment. These things are delicate negotiations."

Lord Haverformore shook a finger in Jack's face. "I don't care about conversations or negotiations. I paid you to find something and produce it. So where is it? How close are you to retrieving it?"

"You paid me *half*," Jack corrected him. "*Half* to find an object that has gone unseen for fifteen years, whose owner has been dead at least that long. Requiring time is not unseemly. What has made it suddenly worth finding?"

The finger dropped. "I want it. That's all you need know."

"You needn't worry."

Lord Haverformore harrumphed and twisted in his chair to gaze at the drink table. "I'll worry until I hear something more solid about your progress." He turned back to face Jack. "None of this *conversations* business. I want steps. I want proof. I don't want you taking on other jobs while you string me along."

It was all Jack could do to keep his composure. "I keep my own counsel, *sir*. Our business will conclude soon." He wanted to remind this man that he was lord only in costumed name.

"See to it." He hefted himself up, not bothering to bid farewell as he went in search of the evening's first drink.

Jack collapsed against the back of his chair. If Lady Agnes found out that he was trying to steal from her kinsman, would she understand it was a separate endeavor? One had no bearing on the other? Well, it didn't matter. Lady Agnes wasn't on his arm, not yet anyway, and the portfolio was still in some unknown quarter, waiting to be retrieved. Or already destroyed.

What he wouldn't give for a night to poke around Andrepont's study. It didn't take too much digging to find out that this viscount didn't take his aristocratic duties seriously. He hadn't taken his seat in the House of Lords, and unentailed landholdings were being sold off. The man had decided to hie himself off on six months' worth of pleasure sailing. Well, word was that he accompanied a married couple and that there was more going on than regular companionship.

If Jack were a betting man, he'd say that the ancestral study was likely untouched. He finished his watered beer. If only the night would pass quickly so that morning could come all the sooner.

Mrs. Caldwell was as wide as she was tall, with freckled forearms bigger than Miss Persephone's well-muscled thighs. She was ruddy, with a round face and thin lips. Her stride was so brisk that Jack practically had to run to keep up.

Jack had offered to hire a hack to take her to Marylebone, but Mrs. Caldwell scoffed.

"I like to take my morning exercise when I can." There was a hint of an Irish brogue, long diminished. She kept up the brisk rhythm of her heavy wood-bottomed shoes, pat-pat-pat on the streets. Jack dodged the people and animals that instinctively parted when faced with the oncoming traffic of Mrs. Caldwell.

They entered the Arthur household through the kitchen. Everyone from the scullery maid to Cook murmured a warm greeting and thanks for her work on their behalf, whether it had been for a mother or a sister, or perhaps, discreetly, even themselves. The woman was a busy one, that much was clear. The butler, Robards, waited for them, escorting them first to Mr. Arthur's study.

Jack knew Corinthian John had blunt. Lots of it. He was touted by many as having a Midas touch, able to turn anyone's meager annuity into something grand. Seeing this all through Mrs. Caldwell's eyes changed his perspective.

Downstairs, she'd been a queen, accepting praise and thanks, laying her hands on top of Cook's to accept her gratitude. But upstairs, treading along the luxurious hall carpet, passing oiled landscapes in gilded frames, she became smaller. No longer the charging locomotive, but merely an old medicine woman, no longer an authority.

"They're good folk, don't you worry," Jack whispered to her.

Mrs. Caldwell gave him a worried glance and nodded. She straightened herself and regained a fraction of her previous confidence.

Robards announced them, and when they followed him into the study, Jack was rewarded for his efforts. Lady Agnes stood in the corner, wearing a soft green dress with a fitted bodice and a green ribbon banded below her breasts. The gown was soft and diaphanous, and she looked a wonder. She appeared welcoming and warm, embodying the softness of a gentle spring glade.

Not to say she hadn't been beautiful at the Cuttingsworth ball, but this was more fitting, clean and simple. The ball gown had worn her, but this dress was an adornment of what she already was: a warm sigh of contentment on a summer day.

"Mrs. Caldwell, thank you so much for coming to see us," Mr. Arthur said, coming forward to grasp her hands. Mrs. Arthur stood next to him, and Miss Arthur was not far from Lady Agnes.

For her part, Mrs. Caldwell seemed surprised at his warmth, but she took his hands anyway.

"I always help those in need." Mrs. Caldwell looked pointedly at Mrs. Arthur. "Are you the one, madam?"

Mrs. Arthur nodded. Once again, because of Mrs. Caldwell's gaze, Jack could suddenly see how Mrs. Arthur's pallor was off. How unnaturally puffy she was, even in her face. With Mrs. Arthur's assent, Mrs. Caldwell transformed back into her locomotive self.

"Then let's get you upstairs into a room so that we may begin. No need for an audience for this part." Mrs. Caldwell shot Mr. Arthur a mildly menacing look.

It lightened the mood in the study, and Mrs. Arthur even seemed grateful. "This way," the lady of the house said, leading Mrs. Caldwell out of the room.

As they left, Jack waited for Lady Agnes to drift over, but instead it was Mr. Arthur.

"Mr. Townsend, thank you so much for your aid in this endeavor. I was paralyzed in my ignorance, but apparently my sister knew what to do."

Jack frowned. "If I may, it wasn't Miss Arthur's request. It was Lady Agnes who came to me."

A mischievous spark lit in Mr. Arthur's eyes. "Is that a fact?"

Lady Agnes stepped forward. "A joint effort. Miss Arthur was kind enough to suggest the need, and I knew Jack could help us. Help Lydia."

"Either way, I'm happy to compensate you. I don't wish to deplete Lady Agnes's pin money."

Jack held up his hand. "No payment necessary."

Mr. Arthur stopped mid-stride.

Lady Agnes blushed, while Miss Arthur hid a smile.

Jack himself wondered what he was doing turning down immediate blunt.

Fact: Favors from gentlemen could inspire suspicion of improper behavior. *If only*. Had the Arthurs gotten wind about their day roaming the streets? Oh Lord help them both.

"I consider Lady Agnes a friend. Requests like this one, to help a loved one, should not require payment. It is a matter of compassion." Jack hoped his speech alleviated any suspicion of impropriety on Lady Agnes's part.

"Well said. Compassion is an underrated virtue." Mr. Arthur gave a tight smile. "Still, I hope I may at least make your time waiting for Mrs. Caldwell pleasant by offering hospitality."

"I never turn down a cup of tea," Jack said. "I can find my way back to the kitchen."

"No!" Lady Agnes said too forcefully.

"You should have tea with us in the drawing room. Don't you think, John?" Miss Arthur said, her hand stealing onto Lady Agnes's bare forearm.

Suddenly, jealousy tore through Jack. The elfin girl's bare hand touching Lady Agnes's flesh. Her warm skin. Desire pooled inside of him until he had to shake himself free of it by thinking of despicable things. And there was plenty in his mind to choose from.

Mr. Arthur let out a sigh. "I cannot join you. I have work that needs to be done, but by all means, keep Jack stuffed with whatever delights Cook allows, and be free with the tea."

Jack bowed. "Thank you, sir."

Mr. Arthur glanced between Jack and Lady Agnes, whose gaze was bordering on excitement. "And keep the door open."

PEARL LED THEM UPSTAIRS TO THE DRAWING ROOM. Jack followed her, and Agnes was a step behind him. His soap lingered in the air: a scent of orange and something else. She could feel her mind bubble away with inappropriate thoughts.

Jack wore trousers fitted well enough that Agnes could imagine his bare thighs—which she immediately pushed out of her mind. Very unseemly. But his hips were rounded—the sort she'd imagined gripping, allowing her fingers to sink in and take hold. Goodness. She was worse than a dog in heat.

Jack had called her a friend, procured Mrs. Caldwell without payment, and talked about compassion. She felt like a silly, trilling bluebird in spring. But it was fun to think this way, to imagine Jack was in love with her, and she gave herself permission to wallow in it, if for only a moment. Always so serious and pragmatic, when had she been head-over-heels like this? And what would Mary Franklin say if she could see her now? She let a single giggle escape her lips, and Jack glanced back over his shoulder.

In the drawing room, Pearl rang for tea and Jack sat on one end of the dark blue cushioned loveseat. Agnes arranged herself on the other side. There was space in the middle, but the magnetic pull of his presence made it feel as if he were far closer. Agnes couldn't even bring herself to look in his direction.

Pearl took a seat across from them. "What has you two grinning like a pair of jackals?"

"I'm so glad that Lydia is getting the help she deserves," Agnes said, her only attempt at explaining why she felt so happy.

Pearl made a gracious assent but clearly didn't believe anything Agnes was saying. Pearl excused herself to speak to the footman at the door.

Suddenly with some minor amount of privacy, Agnes took the opportunity to be bold. She laid her hand down in the space between her and Jack.

He looked at her in surprise, but his hand crept out. The back of his hand brushed hers. Surprisingly, given their height difference, their hands were the same size. Agnes's hands were small, pinkish, and soft, while his were wide-palmed with short fingers, the back of his hand tanned, roughened by work. Mesmerized by the sight of their distinct hues meeting, her head was full of indistinct thoughts as Jack's fingers curled around hers. There was no room for pragmatism or cleverness when he touched her.

She watched their hands twirl softly and gently on the cushion. Heat pooled involuntarily between her legs. His eyes were on her face, and she could feel the weight of his gaze. Without thinking, she licked her lips. He exhaled sharply.

Looking up at him, fingers still intertwined, she could see the lust in his eyes, mirroring her own. How did this happen? The air between them was thick. Agnes felt herself drawing closer to him, wanting to close the distance. The nap of the cushion felt almost rough in comparison to the idea of their skin against each other.

Abruptly, he jerked his hand back and shook himself. She felt the loss keenly. But then she realized that her sister-in-law was returning to her seat, loudly clearing her throat as she crossed the room. Agnes did her best to shake herself free of her daze as well.

"I've instructed them to bring up the best treats Cook can whip up. We shall see the heights of her imagination." Pearl looked between the two of them, amusement dancing across her features. "Goodness me, we need some refreshment, don't we?"

Pearl took control of the conversation, asking some pointed questions of Jack about how he had found Mrs. Caldwell. Unlike Agnes, Jack was able to recover and be a brilliant conversationalist in the face of the blinding chemistry between them. Agnes could barely follow the conversation.

"Anything for Lady Agnes, of course." Jack looked at her, pointedly.

"Naturally," Pearl echoed.

A footman brought up the tea tray, a few biscuits next to the teapot. "Cook will send up more when ready, miss."

"Tell her many thanks. When we know more about how Mrs. Caldwell fares, we will want a separate tray for her as well, with a fresh pot of tea."

Agnes realized that Pearl had a knack for running the household. Far more than Lydia did. Pearl was gracious and decisive without being abrasive or demanding. The womanly arts, which somehow seemed to escape both Lydia and Agnes.

No sooner had that footman departed than another came in. "My lady, Mrs. Arthur has asked for you."

Agnes felt disappointed that she would not be treated to Jack's first sip of tea. The softness in his face as he closed his eyes and inhaled the first scent. Her sister came first, of course, but there was natural trepidation in entering a room where they would be talking about babies and childbirth and goodness knows—the trauma that had shaped their childhood.

She slipped into Lydia's bedroom with a light tap on the door. Lydia was lying in bed in her shift, the covers up to her waist. Mrs. Caldwell sat on top of the covers, chattering about babes. The herbwoman seemed personable, at least.

"Good. You've come. Back to it, then. Aside from this babe, have you been with child afore?"

Lydia nodded, but her silence caused the woman to look at her sharply. Agnes looked down. It had been hard when Lydia had miscarried. They had all assumed it was because of what had happened to her as a child, but when hope came again, they had put those thoughts to the back of their collective mind.

"It didn't last long." Lydia shrank against her

pillows for a moment. "When I was a child, there was an incident. I was exposed to the pox."

"No shame, child. None to be had."

Lydia recovered quickly. "I was told I couldn't have children. We thought perhaps that was why I miscarried."

Mrs. Caldwell nodded as if she were lost in thought. "Those physicians are useless when they don't inspect their patients."

"But he did inspect me, often, it seemed."

"Did he touch you? Feel your abdomen? Any of the things that I have done?" Mrs. Caldwell challenged.

"Well, no, it would be unseemly. He merely looked."

Mrs. Caldwell clicked her tongue. "Fat lot of good that did them. They were wrong." She said the last word with a healthy dose of disdain.

"Pardon me?" Agnes blurted out.

"But—" Lydia protested in the same moment.

Mrs. Caldwell held her hand up for silence. "I do not doubt your story, not for a single minute. But many a dockside disease is called the pox. Some bad, some worse, and the idea of bedding a virgin to cure any one of them is an old idea. An excuse, to my mind, to take advantage of the innocent. I don't truck with any of it, of course. Despicable creatures who do this to children."

Lydia seemed to relax, but Agnes was paralyzed.

"Had it been the pox believed—syphilis —your physician would have been correct," Mrs. Caldwell continued. "You would not be able to have children. But you also would have had painful episodes throughout your life, and as I'm sure you've seen, it would have eaten more than your lady parts."

Agnes felt sick. She had seen those poor creatures

in the alleyways near the Women's Home, the flesh of their noses being eaten away.

"But there's another they call the pox. Bumps that come and go. Have you ever had bumps?"

Lydia shook her head. Mrs. Caldwell frowned. Clearly, her theory was not panning out as planned. "Is it possible, dearie, that you have been lied to?"

A cold, sick lump materialized in Agnes's stomach. She searched Lydia's face, but her sister had shut down completely.

"Not my business then," Mrs. Caldwell said briskly. She thumped her hands on her thighs and continued giving instructions about what to eat and how often. Lydia grimaced and bargained, which only irritated Mrs. Caldwell further.

"My lady. Mrs. Arthur. Those men wouldn't know the needs of a woman if she cut open her own self in front of them. It's all games and ideas in their heads. I've delivered hundreds of babes. I know how to help. If you question me again, God help me." Her hands settled on her wide hips.

"Lydia, Pearl was most impressed when I told her Mrs. Caldwell was coming." Agnes hoped Pearl's endorsement would help.

"If Jack About Town asked me to walk to the moon, I would," Mrs. Caldwell volunteered. "It weren't on your account that I'm here."

"What does that mean, I wonder," Lydia snapped.

Agnes didn't think it was an indictment of the Arthurs, but rather praise of Jack. Still, it wasn't surprising that Lydia took it personally. "I think it means that Mr. Townsend is worthy of praise."

"Praise is putting it lightly," Mrs. Caldwell said. "You don't rightly know Jack About Town?"

Lydia shook her head but still looked annoyed. But then, that was Lydia's natural resting state.

Perhaps Mrs. Caldwell's brand of care was already working.

"Started when he was mite more than a child. Saved a baby from drowning in nightsoil. When a child wandered, Jack could find them. When folk needed food, Jack would make sure they had some. Always able to give what was needed. None of us knew where it came from, and we all knew not to ask. But Jack About Town has saved more lives than you might think, given that tidy little package he's wrapped up in."

"But it's business, isn't it? He gets his due." Lydia folded her arms, clearly fed up with the conversation, but Agnes held her breath. She already knew this answer, hoped for this answer.

"He asks for nothing of the sort. We all give what we can. If Jack comes asking, it's for a good cause and a good reason. That's why when he came asking after the best midwife in London, I made sure to step myself quick. If a woman was in need, and a friend of Jack's, I'd be the first to answer."

"Please have the decency to look ashamed," Agnes told her sister. Her heart was bursting with pride. Of course Jack didn't ask for payment.

"Fine. A veritable Robin Hood. Now. Back to the matter at hand." Lydia picked at her blankets as if she were not feeling embarrassed at her own assumptions. Agnes knew that her sister was impressed now, with both Jack and Mrs. Caldwell. Perhaps she would follow the woman's advice and take care of herself for once. "What kind of exercise, Mrs. Caldwell?" Lydia folded her hands across her abdomen.

"Start slow with walks around your garden and build up from there. I think you did too much too soon. Your body can't do what it did before the baby."

"I haven't the faintest idea of what you're talking about." Lydia put on a pleasant smile.

"I know who you are, dearie. I know your husband, too. Can't fool an old woman like me. I've seen it all."

Lydia preened, lying back in bed.

"Admire your pluck, even if it ain't why I came."

"Thank you, Mrs. Caldwell. I appreciate your kind words."

"I'll drop by the ointment as promised. Use it until the jar is empty. Mild exercise can start today with your sister here. Take a turn about the gardens, and do it again tomorrow and the day after. On Sunday, walk to church if you can. Keep on like that. You'll be having another babe in no time."

"Oh no," Lydia said. "I don't think that's wise. This experience has been more than enough."

Agnes couldn't agree more. If anything could put one off having a baby, it would be having one.

Mrs. Caldwell nodded. "Entirely your choice. I'll send along two teas that should help as well. One for the morning that will have you feeling glad to go outside, and the other for night, that will help you sleep. Are you having the dreams?"

"Which dreams?"

"Dreams that you've lost the baby? It's somewhere in the sheets and you can't find her? Very common. You'd be surprised."

"Why does no one speak of this?" Agnes asked. The other two women looked at her, and then at each other. "Unless Mama told you something on your wedding day?"

Lydia shook her head. "She told me nothing."

Mrs. Caldwell gave a sad laugh. "You lot should come live in closer quarters. You'd be surprised what you learn by living surrounded by thin walls. It's supposed to be learned by watching, by helping. Were you there, in the room, to help your mother birth this one?"

Lydia looked appropriately shocked. "Absolutely not. I was a child."

"None of my business how children get raised," Mrs. Caldwell said, cutting Lydia off. She patted Lydia's knee. Agnes couldn't discern whether the gesture was maternal or a reminder of authority. "I'll come back next week to check on you. Go on and get dressed, dearie."

"Thank you, Mrs. Caldwell," Agnes said as Lydia slid out of bed in nothing but her chemise. "Let me take you to the drawing room. Cook has sent up her best."

❦

FACT: A BODY SHOULDN'T JUDGE ANOTHER ON looks alone. Miss Pearl Arthur was an excellent conversationalist. Jack was having a ripping good time waiting for Mrs. Caldwell and Lady Agnes.

Miss Arthur had an internal ease that relaxed others. She had the training of well-bred gentry, despite her origins, which made her seem genteel but also gave her practical wisdom that could only come from growing up surrounded by people of all types. Of course, her ease made him relax, which in turn made her relax as well.

Fact: Relaxed people trusted more easily. And that loosened tongues.

"I understand that Lady Agnes is also related to Lord Andrepont, but how exactly? I could consult a Debrett's, but I seemed to have misplaced my copy." Jack gave a winning smile.

"Cousins. Their mothers are sisters." Miss Arthur poured more tea for Jack and herself and subtly pushed the plate of biscuits towards him.

"Is there any interest there? Since there isn't a…" Jack trailed off. He didn't want to be impolite, and he knew the laws of consanguinity. Andrepont and Lady Agnes could marry, but it was clear from the dinner the other night that there was little interest. But that didn't mean it couldn't happen.

Miss Arthur's eyes widened. "Oh, no. I don't think that would happen."

"Andrepont is interested elsewhere?" Jack was interested in Andrepont for other reasons too—the art—but to couch it in terms of a competing suitor was helpful.

"I'm sure I don't know Andrepont's heart," Miss Arthur said firmly, though she was clearly keeping something to herself.

New tactic. "I had heard that Lady Andrepont is still quite a beautiful woman. Is she as lovely as they claim?"

"I've only seen her a few times, and we haven't spoken. She seems to be so, yes."

"So you've never had dinner with them?"

"Oh, they don't host dinners. I've never been to their house, as they don't entertain."

Jack filed away that knowledge for future use. Their skeleton staff was surprisingly tight-lipped, but Jack had heard insinuations that the house had remained virtually unchanged—word was that the study was untouched from the time of the former viscount.

"Seems strange to live in London and not enjoy the social aspects. Why do they not retire to the country? Surely, once Andrepont marries he will do so."

Miss Arthur shook her head. "He's made it clear that he has no intention of marrying."

Jack waited for her to look shocked and apologize

for talking out of turn, but she didn't. "I'll keep that to myself, then, Miss Arthur."

She gave a polite smile. "The viscount says all sorts of things in mixed company. None of it is a secret."

"How novel," Jack said. "A man without secrets."

"I wouldn't say that." Miss Arthur sipped at her tea, and then quite pointedly changed the subject. "You are quite taken with her."

Jack scrambled for the right answer, until finally landing on the truth. Being taken with Lady Agnes was an understatement. Bewitched, perhaps? "I am. I am doing my best to prove myself worthy of her, but I'm afraid I'm coming up short. If you have any advice, I would gladly take it."

"They—we, I suppose—are an unusual bunch," Miss Arthur admitted.

"So I've found."

Miss Arthur sipped her tea as she thought for a moment. "I think, perhaps, the best advice I can give to you in your suit is a small piece of knowledge. You are dealing with a family where nothing has ever happened the way it was supposed to."

Jack raised his eyebrows in hopes of encouraging her to say more. "Might you give me an example?"

"I know very little about the past, and I will say that everything I have gleaned is from conversations that weren't meant to include me. Where I have been forgotten."

Sounded familiar. Jack had built his whole livelihood on that talent.

"Lord Lorian was not meant to become the earl. And Lady Lorian was originally engaged to the former Viscount Andrepont. But then, somehow, Andrepont married his intended's younger sister instead. Nothing worked the way it was supposed to."

Excellent facts to file away, but best to act

uninterested. "A fascinating story, Miss Arthur, but may I ask how that helps?"

"That's precisely it, Mr. Townsend. Look at the children from their union. They had a boy and two girls. The boy, the heir, ends up dying before his twentieth birthday, and then the daughter takes up pugilism. What surprise does the second daughter have in store? They are quite cautious now."

Jack turned it over in his mind. "Or would they be more permissive, given what has happened to the other two?"

Miss Arthur stared him down. "Or would they want a more prescribed, predictable life for her?"

Ah. Jack saw her point now. They didn't get to live a quiet life, so they would want their children to have it. "You are suggesting that I seem more predictable?"

She smiled, apparently amused at the thought. "You could try?"

That was clearly impossible. There was no way to be himself and be predictable. He had enough earnings stashed away to be comfortable for a few years—he could rent a decent home here in Marylebone or in a lesser neighborhood. Certainly not a high society offering, but that wasn't what Lady Agnes seemed interested in. Her parents must see that.

In order to give Lady Agnes the predictable, expected life, he needed a respectable, predictable family. While he would go to his grave defending Miss Persephone and Mrs. Bettleton, they weren't the sort of family recognized by people like Lord and Lady Lorian.

His birth family was respectable, if not notable. Especially if he could get Roland to remember Jack existed at all. His mother had urged him to go to his nephew's christening. Perhaps that could mend a gap?

Enough to prove that he was a worthy suitor for Lady Agnes?

After that? Marriage. Easy enough, as it was what he wanted anyway. Jack didn't mind signing a parish register under his assumed name. That gave him no trouble, and they'd hardly be the first. Plenty of people lived and worked and loved as men. Why not Jack?

But Lady Agnes needed to know what she was getting into before things went too far. It was one thing to continue on as Mr. Townsend in front of Lady Lorian. It was another to ask for Lady Agnes's hand in marriage when she didn't even know the slightest thing about him.

Just as he had this thought, he heard Mrs. Caldwell's marching tattoo coming down the hallway. Mrs. Caldwell and Lady Agnes entered the drawing room. Jack scrambled to his feet and bowed, pushing back the thought that even if Lady Agnes's parents refused her dowry, they could still be quite comfortable between his skills and hers. First thing first: tell her everything. She had a right to know, even if it turned his bowels to liquid.

As Mrs. Caldwell answered Miss Arthur's questions and told her about a basket that would be arriving tomorrow full of ointment and teas, she explained she'd rather take her tray down in the kitchens. "Surely you understand, child. I'm not used to finery."

"I'll take you myself," Miss Arthur said, giving Jack a backwards glance that was full of mischief. The little elf.

❦

THE TWO WOMEN DISAPPEARED AND AGNES realized she was alone in the drawing room with Jack.

The door was open, and thus propriety preserved, but it didn't stop her heart from thumping hard in her chest. She wished she could loosen her stays. Jack stared at the empty doorway as well.

"I do believe we are alone," Jack said.

"Yes," was all Agnes could manage.

He closed the distance between them, seeking out her hand. He brought it to the center of his chest, and she wondered if he would kiss it again.

"Have you had a nice visit with Miss Arthur?" Agnes asked, hoping her voice didn't tremble.

"Lady Agnes, while we have this moment alone, I must entreat you." Jack kept his voice low, speaking swiftly. "Your man Vasily came to visit me the other night, threatening me to leave you alone. I cannot. But I know I must prove myself worthy of you. Court you properly as you deserve."

"To see if you're worthy?" It broke her heart to know that he didn't feel worthy. After all that Mrs. Caldwell had said. What he'd told her himself. He was good in his heart, down to his very bones. Of course he was worthy.

"Would you allow me to call on you? Perhaps tomorrow?"

"Yes," she said again, this time with a smile.

Jack smiled in return. "May I show you something?"

Agnes nodded, and still holding her hand, Jack led her to the window. It overlooked the gardens, but most importantly, they stood in a small alcove behind the door. Anyone who entered the room would have a hard time seeing them right away. "Lovely gardens."

Jack glanced at the back of the open door, as if to make sure she understood. "It's a lovely place to observe them from."

Agnes breathed her answer. She couldn't possibly make conversation while he stood this close to her.

How was her very skin on fire? He still held her hand, pulled against the soft wool of his waistcoat.

"Are you a fan of gardens then?" The smell of orange was everywhere. It was heady. He was looking at her, and she at him. It didn't feel like there was any force in the world that could keep them apart.

"Lady Agnes, I can't stop thinking of you."

"Nor I you."

"I've never felt this way about another person. Not in my life." Jack reached up his other hand and cupped her face, running the broad of his palm along her jaw.

"I don't understand what it is between us," Agnes confessed.

"But isn't it something?" Jack breathed, their faces closer, his breath smelling like her sister's blend of tea. He pulled a small wooden token out of his pocket and presented it to her. There was a shiny dark blue ribbon tied to it. "I'd like you to take this."

"What is it?" His lips were so close and she was aching for him. She was tired of being alone, and he was so clever and kind.

"It's a key, of sorts." His eyes sought hers.

He was telling her so much in this moment, but she wasn't able to understand it.

"If you go to the address printed on the token and present this, you'll get admitted immediately. Someone will find me if I'm not already by the door."

"To where?"

Jack looked around again. "I'd rather not say. It's preferable to go there after nine o'clock, when it's dark. This is not the sort of place you want anyone to know you are going to."

Cold thumped in her chest. Dozens of questions flew through her mind. "I couldn't possibly without Vasily. It wouldn't be safe—"

"Vasily won't allow you to go at all. Trust me on that."

She did trust him, she realized. He would never let her come to harm. She rubbed the wooden token between her fingers. It was smooth, except for the address etched into one side. "When shall I come?"

"I'm there every night, with the exception of your invitations."

She blushed again. "Like the Cuttingsworth ball."

"Yes."

She tucked the token in her dress pocket. "I can make no promises, but I'll try."

"I want you to know all sides of me. I want you to see who I am. All of who I am."

Agnes swallowed hard. His lips were so close. "I want to know. I want to see." Instead of waiting for him to move closer, Agnes pressed against him, stealing a kiss. His lips were soft and pliant. He breathed in and pushed his hands up into her hair. It was a sweet thrill and agony all at once. Like being a child and wanting to eat all the cake, not caring if a stomachache might be in the offing. She needed Jack and no one else.

Her hands clung to the lapels of his coat, as though she might drown if she let go of him. He pulled her by the nape of her neck closer and closer, their bodies pressed tighter, until she let go of his lapels and wrapped her arms around his shoulders. Her fingers brushed against a ripple of fabric across his back.

Jack nipped at her lips before diving back in. Agnes was lost to it all, craving to have the sensation deeper. There was nothing she could articulate, only that she wanted *more*. She whimpered against him, which elicited a moan from him. His hands dropped from her head to her neckline. He plucked at the fabric of her bodice, as if frustrated that he couldn't remove it.

"Agnes?" Lydia called. "Are you in here?"

They flew apart. Agnes practically dove into the curtains. Jack managed a casual-seeming lean against the back of the piano. He subtly touched his mouth and straightened his coat. Agnes, for her part, could barely breathe. If she could disappear into the curtain, she would. She checked her hair—it had been a bit of a to-do this morning. All seemed in place. She cleared her throat.

"Over here," Agnes called. "Admiring the gardens, as we will be walking in them later."

Lydia came over to join them, her gaze swinging from Jack to Agnes. "Oh pooh," she said, looking out. "It's beginning to rain."

"I rather enjoy the rain," Jack said. "Hence, looking at it here. Now. With Lady Agnes."

"Of course," Lydia said slowly. "If one couldn't enjoy the rain, England would hardly be the place then, would it? Excuse me, I should like to take some tea."

With that, Lydia walked away. Jack and Agnes looked at each other, both bordering on feral. Perhaps it was good that Lydia had interrupted them. Agnes couldn't guarantee her own behavior. She'd never had to check herself before. All her dalliances had been with other young misses. There hadn't been any thought to consequences. Something pricked her mind. Something not quite right. Well. She'd think about it later when not in company.

12

J ack slid into the last pew. The service had long
since ended, and the regular parishioners had
left to go about their Sunday business. The hard
wooden bench was cold, and the air even colder.

At the altar, the vicar stood with Roland and a
pale-skinned woman holding a baby. The baby was, at
this distance, an indistinct bundle of white blanket,
and one could only assume it was his nephew. Jack's
mother and father sat in the front row. His father
must have recently returned from sea. He looked
heavier, older if only because his jowls were more
pronounced, but he looked happy. Business must have
been going well, and Jack couldn't help but wonder if
his father had made it to his own children's
christenings. Already giving more to Roland's child
than he'd ever given them.

The woman at the fount was a pretty English
rose. She was plump from having been with child, and
her honey-colored hair and rosy cheeks gave her the
quintessential English quality that Roland had
searched for his entire life. The legitimacy he seemed
to have needed.

Jack wondered whose daughter she was. Had
Roland managed to reach as high as a bank president?

Or perhaps only a senior supervisor. Oh, it was hard not to let in poisonous thoughts. Roland had scoffed at Jack's individualistic needs, but it didn't mean that Jack ought to scoff at Roland's conformity. If this were to mend, Jack had to give his brother the benefit of the doubt.

Eventually, his presence would be noticed. Perhaps. The baby cried out, the sound echoing through the emptied building. Roland would likely never introduce his child to Jack voluntarily. Old wounds split raw in the wooden pew, and before he could be seen, he escaped. He paced the square outside the church and then wandered through the cemetery behind the building.

Jack took off his hat and ran his hand through his hair. *Jack* was improper and didn't belong in a church. His whole life was impropriety. He stank of impropriety.

Fact: These thoughts were not helping.

The church bells rang out, startling him. Shit on toast. He had to *try*, so he might as well do it now that Roland had a child. It changed things, somehow, didn't it? Perhaps a child would soften Roland. Or soften Jack.

He put his hat back on and ambled to the front, but before he could make it all the way up the steps, Roland's wife pushed open the doors. She came up short when she saw him.

Jack doffed his hat, unsure of what to do.

"You look like him. Oh, you must be." Her hand went to her chest, as if she were in shock. "Roland's long-lost brother."

There went any possibility of finessing an introduction. Long-lost brother, indeed. "Begging your pardon, Mrs. Townsend. My mother told me about the christening, and I wanted to see the babe. I mean no ill will."

"Of course you don't, you poor dear. Rolly will be so excited that you are here! I can't believe it! He thought you'd been lost at sea!" Her hands flapped in the excitement of it all.

Lost at sea? Is that the story he told? It was better than being dead, but not by much.

She grabbed his hand and dragged him back into the church. "They'll be overjoyed to see you. What luck! And on baby Matthew's christening day! God is surely shining his good fortune upon us."

Matthew? Not the fantastical glamour of the names their mother had bestowed upon her children, an ode to a fantastical time of honorable knights and chivalry. But then, his mother didn't read the Old Testament. She read novels.

And *Rolly?* Jack couldn't believe this woman called his staid brother Rolly. Positively ridiculous and didn't fit him at all. When Roland caught sight of Jack being led by the hand of his ruddy round wife, his brother's eyes fair popped out of his head. He shoved the bundled blanket he was holding to their mother, who remained with the family cluster at the fount.

"Look who is here!" *Rolly's* wife's eyes were full of tears. "The sheer fortune that God is blessing us with!"

While Jack's presence had usually been welcomed wherever he went, surely this was the first time his appearance had been called a blessing from God.

"I didn't want to spoil the surprise," his mother said, arranging the baby's blankets, snugging the child next to her body.

Rolly greeted Jack with open arms, a surprising turn of events. Without thinking, Jack stepped into his brother's embrace. His middle had gone soft, but his embrace didn't seem false—it was stronger than he remembered.

"I was lost at sea, presumably?" Jack whispered,

crushed in his brother's arms. "Feed me the story so that I am better able to play along."

Roland grunted and let him go. "Mother, you knew about this?"

"He came home a few days ago, worse for wear," his mother lied. His father lifted an eyebrow, which his mother interpreted for the crowd. "My husband found him, of course. Being such a consummate captain who would never give up hope that his youngest boy was lost overboard."

The chorus of Roland's in-laws' blue eyes all turned to him. "You must come to breakfast," Roland's mother-in-law said. "It will be no trouble to set another plate. And such stories to tell! Baby Matthew will not mind sharing the spotlight."

Baby Matthew, for his part, had fallen asleep and was not privy to Jack stealing the attention.

"Certainly," Jack said. "I shall do my best to entertain you."

"You could write it up in a paper, like one of those serials!" The father-in-law was a stout man, though slimmer than Jack's own papa.

"Those are very popular," Roland's mother-in-law said, her ridiculously feathered hat waving with her.

The brother-in-law, the one that had stood up at the fount as a godparent, gave Roland a skeptical look. "I thought you had a sister."

Roland shook his head, not denying it but not explaining. Jack wondered if this was the man who was supposed to court him all those years ago.

"Well." The father-in-law looked around at their small crowd. "I'm starving. Shall we?"

The baby returned to its mother and they tromped out of the church as a herd. Jack's mother gripped his arm as if he might be lost at sea again. "What are we doing?" Jack hissed at her. Lying in a church is what they'd done.

"A light luncheon to celebrate. You'll tell your story. It'll be lovely."

"I don't even know these people's names. Why did you not introduce me? And how did I get lost at sea?" Jack did not feel good about this, but if this was what he must do to be worthy of Lady Agnes, to patch things with his brother, then this is what he would do. Be the idiot who got washed off a boat.

Fact: This was lying. Jack was supposed to lie to these nice people for his brother's benefit. No, for Jack's own benefit. To get his family repaired, to present them to the Lorians, to properly court Lady Agnes. Lies were always convoluted, which was one of the reasons Jack hated them.

The in-laws' home wasn't far, and in no time, Jack and his family sat in the modest but extremely well-appointed dining room of the people that turned out to be the Woodson family.

Martha, the cherub Roland had married, was beaming in a way that surely couldn't be healthy. Her father, Mr. Woodson, was the same. Mrs. Woodson appeared less effusive, given her patter of vocal fretting about the succession of dishes and the quality of her serving implements. The younger Mr. Woodson still eyed Jack with suspicion, and his wife seemed most intent on tucking into her meal and not participating in any conversation that might seem at odds with her husband's unsettled temper.

Jack's mother, whom he suspected was the orchestrator of the lost-at-sea narrative, was calm as could be. Roland was unreadable, as always.

"To family," Jack's father said, raising a glass. "All of us together, celebrating the newest member, and the lost member. May we find comfort in each other."

"Very poetic, Captain Townsend," Mrs. Woodson said, raising her glass as well.

They all toasted, and Jack choked back the sweet white wine.

"So. Mr. Townsend, what is your story, if I may pry? We should get it before the papers do. Your mother assures me it is quite the tale." Martha smiled across the table at each and every one of them, as if to gather their support.

Jack wiped his mouth with his napkin and cleared his throat. How long could he put them off? He glanced at Roland, who returned a cold stare. Perhaps it wasn't as happy of a return as he'd initially thought. Shit on toast, he wanted to stop lying before he started. Jack cleared his throat. "As you know, with my father being at sea, it was only natural for me to want to enter the same trade."

"A boy always looks up to his father," Mr. Woodson said, pointedly looking at Roland.

Roland flinched, and Mr. Woodson had no idea what a dig he had taken at his son-in-law. Roland had been miserable with knots. Even worse with sea legs. There was no chance he could have been a sailor. He'd tried. To give Jack the narrative of the son who followed their father's footsteps must have galled Roland.

"With his help, I was able to secure a position as a cabin boy aboard a ship at a very young age. Naturally, I didn't want any favors, so I didn't take the offering aboard my father's ship."

"Independence is an admirable trait," Jack's father said. "Rather proud, I was."

For the love of all that was unholy, now his father was getting into this? Was he senile, or was he trying to smooth over the relations of his children? It suddenly made Jack wonder who they were telling this story for—would an invented life make Roland forgive Jack for being Jack?

Fact: People wanted entertainment more than

they wanted truth. All the bizarre stories he'd heard told at the Inn over the years, some true, most not, would help him make this a tale the Woodson clan would never forget.

"I've always been small for my age, through no fault of my parents, of course," Jack continued, gathering energy. "I'd hoped that I was late to gathering the height my brother enjoys, but while I was out at sea, it became clear that my size wouldn't help me becoming a midshipman." Jack paused for effect. "But it would help in the cramped conditions living below deck."

His father gave a quiet chortle. Glad he found that funny. "Small but nimble, I was able to be a lookout, aloft the highest mast." What were those boys called? Monkey somethings? No matter, the Woodsons didn't know either. Like Roland, Jack knew nothing about boats, got seasick easily, and had no interest in sailors other than the creative cursing he'd learned from them as a child.

"One dark day, a storm came upon us unexpectedly. These things happen." Jack looked to his father to nod and give his story credence. "We were blown far off course. For days we struggled in the midst of this storm. When it cleared, the captain asked me to climb up to the eagle's nest to peer out into the ocean to find our bearings."

"Could you not use the stars? I thought that's what sailors did." The younger Mr. Woodson was not held as rapt as the rest of the company.

"Not during the day."

"Why did you not wait until night?"

"We were afraid we were sailing in the wrong direction. We needed to adjust our heading as soon as possible." Jack took a sip of wine to stall for time. The entire table, minus Roland and the younger Mr. Woodson, leaned forward. "I climbed up to my perch, quick as I could, but another storm rolled in so fast that I was still scrambling back down the mast when the wind swept me overboard, depositing me into the ocean."

Martha gasped, the sweet gullible thing. The elder Mr. Woodson chewed his meat at a surprising pace. Jack's father drank another glass of wine.

"Then what happened?" Mrs. Woodson asked.

"I was fortunate enough to find a bit of the mast—"

Jack's father shook his head.

"I mean, the rigging—"

His father shook his head again.

"To be perfectly honest, I'm not precisely sure what it was. Driftwood, surely, and clung to it for several days. Finally, I found a small island, hot and dry, inhabited with crabs. I was able to sustain myself for months on these small island delights—"

"Enough." Roland dropped his utensils on his plate.

Here it was, the threshold of Roland's patience. He never could stand for Jack to be the center of attention for very long. Though truthfully, where was he going with the crabs?

"Oh yes, we shouldn't pry," Mrs. Woodson piped in.

"No, enough stories. Enough lies." Roland's jaw worked in every direction, his anger growing at a rate Jack remembered vividly. The kind of anger that had led to Roland trying his hand at beating the differences out of Jack.

"This is my family, Gwen. My *family*. Not that I expect you to respect such a thing," he spat.

The Woodsons all sat frozen in place. Finally Mrs. Woodson squeaked, "Who is Gwen?"

"Roland," their mother said quietly.

"No. No, I won't let you feed this charade. Not

this ridiculous lost-at-sea story, and not that ridiculous haircut."

"I think my haircut is quite dashing," Jack said, running his hands through the thick, dark locks.

"I've done everything I could to give us distance. To let you be. And you can't manage it, can you? Everything is about you and your...your...your..." Roland's face got redder as he stumbled over his words. "Your abomination!"

"Who is Gwen?" Mrs. Woodson whispered to her husband.

"She is!" Roland roared, jumping to his feet and pointing. His chair fell over backwards and the crash woke the baby, who had been slumbering peacefully in the corner next to his mother. The wail did nothing to calm Roland's heaving chest.

"I don't understand," Mr. Woodson said slowly.

Jack calmly put down his utensils and wiped his mouth. "Mama, Papa, so good to see you today. I'm glad you are well." He turned and addressed the Woodsons. "Thank you for a lovely meal. Mrs. Woodson, you have an excellent eye for both dishes and décor. I thank you for inviting me into your home." He stood slowly, staring down his brother. His heart beat cold. It felt like ice in his veins, and he wondered if this was what battle felt like. Not that either he or Roland would ever know. "What will you do now, brother? Strip me naked as proof? What is it to you?"

"You think you can do whatever you want? That you snap your fingers and the world doesn't work as it's always worked?" Roland's face was red, an accomplishment, given his even coloring. For an Englishman to turn that color was a matter of words. For Roland, it took more work, and Jack had always been able to goad him into it.

"That's a broad statement. I didn't know that

you've added *world scholar* to your titles at Drummonds."

"Oh, don't give me that shite. You know what I mean."

Martha gasped at Roland's cursing. Baby Matthew began to cry in earnest.

"Do I? I don't think I do. I think you are as small-minded and reductive as always. That you are so uncomfortable being who you truly are—and not who you think you ought to be—that you must lash out at me to prove you're right. Isn't that what this is about, *Rolly*? How right you are? How you must marry an Englishwoman to beget English babies? How you must rise in the ranks to prove your worth? For how could it be possible that merely being alive makes you worthy?"

Roland scoffed. "Worthy of what? Making a mockery of honest people?"

"Of love, Roland. You don't have to be English to be loved. You don't have to be anything to be loved."

Now his brother began to shake. "That's the kind of utter fucking nonsense I expected from you. You have no idea what you're talking about."

"Now, Roland—" Mr. Woodson tried his hand at managing the argument.

"How fast you dismiss me, brother." Jack needed to speak. He needed this fight. How the blood flowed faster than when faced with the massive fists of a Russian ex-soldier. "How fast you pretended I was dead. Because you can't stand the idea that I don't need to conform to be happy. That I can be different and still be welcomed."

"You are an eyesore!"

Jack raised an eyebrow, put his thumbs in his coat pockets to flare it out, and did a slow jaunty circle. "I have many a lady who begs to differ."

"And there is the abomination. You are a mere

woman! You are meant to be mounted! To bear children! To be under the protection of a man!"

To Jack's utter delight, Martha chose that moment to gather up the babe and leave the room, throwing the ugliest look at her husband that Jack had ever seen. He hid the laugh of triumph that sat in his belly.

"As usual, your interpretation of the facts remains faulty. Your logic is faulty. Face it, *Rolly*, you are not the brains in this family." Jack gave his parents and Roland's in-laws a flawless courtesy bow.

He left the room, and as he gathered his hat and gloves, he marveled at the utter silence that was left in his wake. The cold lump that he'd hoped to squeeze into a diamond persisted. His hands shook as he tucked them into his gloves. What a fucking waste of a day.

৩৯৪৪

LYDIA AND AGNES WALKED BACK TO THE ARTHURS' house from church. Lydia was walking faster than she had before, clear signs of her healing as Mrs. Caldwell promised.

"You seem to be improving," Agnes commented, hoping to elicit a smile from her sister.

Lydia tried to give a pleasant expression, but it didn't work. Church always made her grumpy. "Walking helps."

"I'm glad." They fell into another companionable silence. Up ahead of them, some of Lydia's servants cavorted, laughing and chatting, gossiping amongst themselves. That's how other people lived, Agnes mused. Unbothered. Uncluttered with the weights of family. She was envious. It made her want to trade her titled existence for one that felt freer.

But then, no matter whose roof you slept under, it

was still you doing the sleeping. "They seem to be having fun."

Lydia looked at them, the people in her employ, carefree in their half-day off, spent at church. "They're good people."

"Are you implying that we don't have fun because we aren't good people?" Agnes asked it to tease her sister, but as the words came out of her mouth, she wondered if Lydia did indeed think exactly that.

"What if there are no good people, Agnes? What if there are merely people?"

"Of course there are good and bad people. There are criminals and those who live righteously. I'm sure the vicar would have some words with you about it." Agnes felt unsettled. Lydia was poking at heady things.

"What if people are only people and we judge them by the worst action they've committed? If the worst isn't that bad, then they are good, even if they've never committed a good act. And what if a person did good acts, but then committed one very bad act? Are they then a bad person?"

Agnes stumbled. "Are you a good person, then?"

"I've done good, but I've also done very bad," Lydia said quietly. "I'd like to think I'm not a bad person. I've only done what I thought was right. Even if the vicar might not agree."

"You are a good person, Lydia. I know it."

"How about you, Agnes? Are you good?"

She opened her mouth to say *of course*, but then she thought of running away from Vasily, kissing Jack even though her father wouldn't approve of him. Then she countered with the weight of mended dresses. But were those any actions that should be made into a case for her morality? "I don't know."

Lydia looked at her with surprise and, Agnes suspected, pride. Lydia shifted her basket to the other hand and took Agnes's elbow, walking together on the sidewalk, snugged up as they had when they were little.

"I don't think anyone knows," Lydia said, and this time she did smile.

13

Miss Persephone cheered Jack on as he dressed. She helped him brush his coat and straighten his collar. She even tied a very creative knot in his cravat. He hadn't seen Lady Agnes in almost a week. Did she still mean what she'd said in the drawing room? Did she still want him to court her? Would she try coming to the Inn to see who Jack really was? It was Roland who had made him feel like he was on a leaking ship.

"Do you think her parents will even let you in the door? Lord and Lady Poop-and-Nonesuch?"

Jack rolled his eyes and snatched his hat from her. "Lorian. Very respectable types."

"So respectable their eldest daughter married a prizefighter?" Miss Persephone taunted. She was dressed more like the butcher's apprentice—no wig, no powder, just trousers and a banyan.

"It gives me an opening. And that's all I need. A crack in the door." Jack poured her a cup of tea from the tray she'd brought up.

"Oh," she said, sounding surprised. "You do that rather well."

Jack finished the pour, dropping in one lump of sugar before handing Miss Persephone the cup and saucer. "I was a good student, even if I didn't appreciate the subjects." His mother and governess had been adamant about pouring tea properly. The cant of one's head, the delicacy of hands, and of course, no spilling. Easier to attract the attention of a potential husband since speaking was not desired.

It wasn't that he didn't enjoy feminine pursuits, it's that he also enjoyed the masculine—mending by the fire and chopping wood were both enjoyable. How on earth was he going to explain this to Lady Agnes? He hoped she'd understand. Those work boots she wore made him think she might. Still, a risk.

Miss Persephone eyed him, accepting the tea. "Why don't you dress as a woman then, and you can cavort off together as two old spinsters, like the Mrs. Laceys. It's far easier than what you are proposing."

"And why don't you go back to being a butcher? Far easier way to make a living than off the goodwill of admirers."

Miss Persephone gave him a prim nod. "I see your point."

By all the rules, he ought to be charming Lady Lorian today, which was enough to make him quake in his boots. Not to mention there was a good chance Vasily would meet him at the door and chuck him out before he had the opportunity to make it to the drawing room. He leaned his head side to side, hearing the satisfying pop as he tried to right himself.

He had to show he was worth something. His jaw set. He'd spent years ignoring, conquering, vanquishing that old gnawing uncertainty. One afternoon with Roland, and it returned with his brother's voice.

"Not to be a nag, but last night Lord Haverformore..." Miss Persephone paused, shuddering for the theatrics of it all, nearly spilling her tea. "Made me promise to ask you about the job. Whatever that is. Please don't tell me because I sincerely do not wish to know."

Jack set his shoulders back again. That man wouldn't leave it be. For fifteen years, the art had sat in its hiding place. Why the hurry now? He'd avoided Lord Haverformore all week and thought he'd gotten away with it. Of course he would press others to pressure Jack.

But today was not about that cheeser. Today, he was focused on wooing Lady Agnes properly. Like a gentleman might. It had crossed his mind that if he were Roland, he might actually get approval to court Lady Agnes. Their family was a respectable merchant family, with his father owning two ships. All those years with the East India Company had to count for something. As the youngest daughter of a scandalized family, Agnes might be allowed to marry a man like Jack's brother.

So why not Jack?

He knew his mother would agree to meet Lady Lorian—she'd be over the moon about it. His father? Well, if he was in port. And Roland? Well. Roland would never change. His brother had been quite clear in their last row that Jack was a sickness, an illness.

Miss Persephone cut in on Jack's reverie. "Don't let those other thoughts bother you, pet. I can see it on your face. Lady Agnes is smitten. She'll be lifting her skirts in no time."

Jack blushed, and Miss Persephone laughed. "I know, I know. Don't be so coarse. But I know you've thought about it. Those long legs, and so on and so forth."

"How do you know she's got long legs?" Jack demanded, giving his hat a thump for good measure and turning from the looking glass. Watching Lady Agnes walk on a windy day was a gift from God. Her flimsy muslin dress battering against her, showing in intimate detail the length of her stride.

Miss Persephone smirked. "You've got a type."

His previous infatuations were nothing compared to the sheer force of his attraction to Lady Agnes. Their pawing at each other in the drawing room was evidence of that. "Wish me luck."

"You don't need it. Have fun instead."

Jack left the Inn, his heels practically kicking as he ambled along the streets to Mayfair, keeping well away from things that might impart a speck of dirt on his pressed trousers. He wore his best waistcoat since the wine stain had yet to be successfully removed—a dark cobalt blue silk that Miss Persephone had found left at the Inn—dressed down with brown trousers and a brown coat, accessorized with a beaver skin hat that cost a fortune.

When he rang at the Lorian household, he realized he was sweating. Not from the weather, for it was cool, but from nerves. It had been a long time since he'd felt this way. Since knocking on the door to the Women's Home over ten years ago, unsure if they would let him in.

Fortunately, the butler opened the door and not the giant Vasily.

Escorted, Jack entered the drawing room and was met with the sight of Lady Agnes in another beautiful, fitted gown, this one the color of sage and spring. Lady Lorian also sat in the corner, a cool but pleasant expression on her face. There was a tea tray on the table. An embroidery basket sat on the sofa next to Lady Agnes, barring any opportunity to sit next to her.

Jack performed an exquisite bow, if he did say so himself, and when Lady Lorian welcomed him to sit in a chair, he felt as if he'd somehow won a race. "Thank you, my lady."

The clock on the mantel ticked and Lady Agnes stole looks at him through lowered lashes. Fact: It was damned uncomfortable.

"Tell me, Mr. Townsend, what is it that you do? I've heard some conflicting reports." Lady Lorian was working on some kind of sewing as well, but nothing as ornate as what Lady Agnes was creating in her hoop.

No offer of tea, which was right there on the tray. It was either an oversight or a pointed withholding. He'd go with the latter. Straight for the jugular, then. "I find things."

"Things," Lady Lorian repeated in a tone of voice that was clearly not approving.

"Precious things, lost things, unusual things. It depends on the circumstance."

"Would you be willing to give me an example?" Lady Lorian asked, putting down her mending.

At least Jack had her attention. Made him nervous as all hell, but devil take him, this was the payment for courting Lady Agnes. He thought through his last few jobs, all of which had the whiff of pornography or unseemliness. "I generally don't take jobs where people are involved, because you don't know why they're being looked for, but I was right—er—rightfully proud of locating a man's mother recently."

"Oh." Lady Lorian looked to her daughter for confirmation. "Is this Mr. Worley and Mrs. Franklin?"

"Yes, my lady," Jack supplied before Lady Agnes could confirm.

"Yes, I have heard of this. Well done you. A happy ending for all." Lady Lorian suddenly seemed a mite bit perkier.

Perhaps Jack could win this fight. Best not to get ahead of himself. "Thank you. You are too kind."

"Ja—I mean, Mr. Townsend, procured the best

herbwoman in London for Lydia." Lady Agnes surely said this to be helpful, but Jack couldn't help but wince.

Lady Lorian picked up her mending. "Hardly an appropriate topic for conversation."

"I merely mean to point out that Ja—Mr. Townsend—is an extremely good person to know."

"That remains to be seen," Lady Lorian said, her voice suddenly light as air.

"If you have any needs at all, my lady, please alert me. I'm happy to procure anything you might desire."

She looked at him then, as if she was thinking about sending him on a wild goose chase. "I will let you know."

There was a silence as Lady Agnes looked across the table at him with luminous eyes. How much easier it was when it was the two of them. How perfect it was when they were left alone.

"May I—" Lady Agnes gestured to the tea tray.

"Before we get to tea..." Lady Lorian gave her daughter a look that could have killed the heartiest of rats. "Mr. Townsend, I need to be honest with you. I don't understand why you are here. Your family is not known. You have no fortune, no prospects. You can't possibly believe that I would allow my daughter to throw her life away on you."

Sharp words were supposed to hurt, but Jack was ready for them. "I do, in fact, have a family. And I was raised well, with an education. My father is a sea captain, engaged in trade. My mother was born in India to an English father and an Indian mother. She had the best governess available and maintains correspondences across all continents."

Lady Agnes looked at him with pleasant surprise that gave him not a small amount of satisfaction. Knowing he had to prove himself, Jack continued. "I have facility with several languages, including French,

German, and Russian. I have a smattering of other languages that I have picked up from the esteemed guests my father has brought home to our table. At times, when needed, I am known to aid merchants when their buyers fall through after cargo has been unloaded at the docks."

Fact: All this was technically true. Although *esteemed* might not be the most accurate word for the sailors that he'd met, and definitely not at his mother's dinner table, but the languages part was definitely true.

Lady Lorian held his gaze for a moment. Then, with a wave of her hand, Lady Agnes was finally allowed to offer refreshment. Lady Lorian studied Jack, and under her gaze, he found his own wandering all over the room. Then he saw it: his token on the tray, next to an empty cup. Lady Agnes was brandishing his token. She looked him square in the eye as she handed him his cup, making her meaning clear: *I'm coming.*

"Thank you, my lady." Jack bowed his head to both women, acknowledging that he was but a bug before them. His complete lack of social standing was not respectable. His lack of career was not respectable. And worst of all, Jack knew this better than either of them. He couldn't be a husband to Lady Agnes, but he was willing to try her world. How else to be with her?

Perhaps if he got the final payment for the art portfolio, he could afford the trappings of a fancier gentleman. A boarding house for a more ambitious sort. Put a down payment on a lease on a pretty townhome in Marylebone.

The rest of the visit they spoke of nothing of consequence: the weather, the markets, Lady Agnes's embroidery, the Women's Home. Jack took his leave at fifteen minutes precisely, gulping down his meager cup of tea. When the butler shut the door on him, he was exhausted.

He went back to the Inn, where all was quiet, and flopped onto his bed. He managed to shuck his shoes and hat before he fell into a dreamless sleep.

⚜

AGNES CLATTERED ACROSS THE SLATE TILES OF HER house's rooftop. This was not exactly the escape she'd planned, or rather, not as quiet as what she had planned. In retrospect, women's dancing slippers might have been a better choice than her favored boots, but that was neither here nor there when staring down two stories to the garden.

Fortunately, the path down was simple. A large tree to the side of the house made it easy to transition off the roof, then down the tree, over the stone wall, and into the mews behind the house. The transition from the stone wall to the ground...well. Her stays were hearty enough that they withstood the scraping.

She was not a graceful person. But, well. Everyone had their strengths. It wasn't much past nine o'clock, and the servants were still bustling through the house. Fortunately, with their curtailed social calendar, her parents didn't need the carriage for anything, and thus the mews were safer than one might expect.

She'd worn her plainest brown round gown and the simplest straw bonnet with the widest brim so that her face might remain covered. If she'd been able to walk the docks with Jack and go unnoticed there, perhaps she may be able to hire a hack to take her to the address on Jack's token.

From her own meager knowledge, she didn't know the neighborhood of the street printed on the token, otherwise she would walk. Her boots were comfortable, and her pockets were well-sewn and difficult for a thief to access. As she rounded the corner to the main thoroughfare, there was little indication that the night was getting on. Carriages clattered past at full speed and the sidewalks were busy. Agnes was jostled as several parties tried to move around her at once.

Finally she was able to obtain a hack. She handed the token to the driver, fully expecting to get it back. "To this address, please."

The driver turned over the token in surprise and glanced at her. "Now, where did you get this?"

Agnes tamped down the urge to blush. She put on her most imperious impression of Lydia and told him, "It doesn't matter where I got it. I wish to go to this address. Now go, good sir."

The driver shrugged, handing back the token, which she promptly stored in her pocket as the hack lurched into motion. She was going. Agnes had snuck out of the house and was free. As the vehicle bumped along, she felt a giggle escape. What a ridiculous thing to do. Take that, Mary Franklin. Agnes was no longer small. She was adventuring far more than marrying some moldering gentleman in the countryside.

And then they stopped. They arrived.

The Inn was not what she expected, but then, she hadn't known what to expect. In the distance, the church chimed half past nine. Gas lamps were lit along the main thoroughfare, and one flickered next to the door. The building was merely a building. Red brick with wood trim, no sign declaring itself. The door was wide and solid wood, crossed with iron for durability.

"If you're sure, miss," the driver said, looking very skeptical.

"This is the address?" Agnes asked, straightening her rough woolen skirt.

"'Tis. How abouts I wait for you? I wouldn't mind. Just to make sure you're safe."

Agnes looked around for the first time. It wasn't the worst place, certainly, but it didn't have the wide sidewalks and well-lit streets of Mayfair. This was certainly more than she'd anticipated, but Jack had asked her to come. If this is where he lived, then she would be safe. "No need. I'm perfectly fine. Have a good evening."

The driver accepted her payment but still looked dubious as she made her way to the heavy door. There was something about this door that felt like once she passed through, she could never go back. Life would never be the same. Was it because she was running from her parents' life? Or was it because Jack was not the man he claimed to be? Perhaps she should ask the driver to wait.

No. No, opening this door was trusting Jack. And if she truly wanted him, then she must soldier on. The door sat large and unmovable.

Should she knock?

"Go on then, miss!" The driver shouted. "I'll not leave 'til you make it inside!"

She could hear a violin playing. Music couldn't be all bad, could it? Using all her might, she pushed open the door to the Inn, hopeful yet dreading a transformation.

The sound of the music came unmuffled first. As her ears feasted, so did her eyes. There were diaphanous skirts of all shades swirling around smartly dressed men in fine coats and surprisingly tight breeches and trousers. The simple iron chandeliers dripped with tallow candles, but the large vases of lavender and herbs along the wall allowed a scent less of animal fat and more of a heady garden.

Fabric was hung on the walls to hide the brick and what looked to be a few amorous couples. Laughter came from every direction. Very tall women held glasses of wine aloft, and very short men carried mugs of beer. There were people of all shapes and sizes, some in bright colors, others in muted shades. But what struck Agnes was that they all seemed *happy*. There was none of the discomfort she saw in crowded ballrooms—public or private. Wallflowers were there by choice, drinking and gossiping. Dancers crowded the floor, some without a partner but dancing despite it all. The musicians seemed to have fun as well. The violinist stamped his foot to keep time for them all, creating a pulsing sound that thrilled her.

Agnes heard a sharp intake of breath and turned to see a heavily powdered woman sitting at a table, drinking wine.

"Hello. I have a token," Agnes said, pulling it from her skirt pocket.

"I'm sure you do," said the woman, looking her up and down.

Suddenly Agnes wished she were wearing one of her ballgowns. The dancefloor was like Margaret's beetle collections, satins of blues and greens, even yellows and reds swirling and exchanging places. The hues were surprising and brilliant. Why were the balls she attended not so bright and jewel-like? Her dowdy gown was serviceable and plain, and the dresses here were anything but. She should have known to wear full dress. Why did Jack not warn her?

Suddenly, he was there, at her side, taking her hand. "You came."

He looked different here, happier. There was something in his face that made it clear how comfortable he was. Then it dawned on her: he wasn't trying so hard. This was his domain. Instead, she was the outsider, the one of lower status. More than one patron eyed her with a knowing glance.

"Do I return this to you?" Agnes asked, feeling very awkward as so many people were looking at her with a mixture of curiosity and hope. She held the token out to Jack. How many other women had shown up here with his token?

"Drop it here," he said, pointing to a glass bowl sitting on the table next to the very powdered woman. She stood, towering over Agnes.

As Agnes dropped the token, she had a sudden realization. She looked through the crowd with new eyes. Men danced with men. Women danced with women. The very tall women and the very short men all stood out as very different from her standard ballrooms because very tall women were uncommon. She should know. She was one.

Jack watched her face as the realization dawned. "Are you well?" he asked gently.

Agnes nodded, her mind racing to keep up with her surroundings. Women dancing with women. Her breath came shallow. "This is—"

"Might you introduce me, Jack? It's rude to keep a lady waiting." The powdered woman shifted and stamped her feet.

Agnes would have gotten her ears boxed at any age if she'd ever done such a thing, but then, this woman didn't have to adhere to the rules Agnes was given. It was a different order here entirely.

"Give her a moment," Jack said, taking Agnes's elbow. "Would you like to sit down?"

"No." She shook her head. The light-headedness faded, excitement and hope taking its place. "I'd like to see more."

Both Jack and the woman grinned. "Let me introduce you to some friends. Lady of My Heart, this is Miss Persephone."

Miss Persephone performed a deep curtsy, one that Agnes wished she could have managed when she'd debuted. "Honored to meet you, my lady."

"And you, thank you," Agnes answered, still mentally foundering. Why had Jack not used her name? Was he ashamed of her?

"We'll return to chat with Miss Persephone. She and I both board here, so we shan't miss her." Jack steered Agnes away, but she looked back at the powdered woman. She was a wonder, with powdered platinum hair done up and a single ringlet curl that trailed down the side of her face.

"You live here?" Agnes asked. Where did he sleep?

Jack smiled. "I do. It's important to me that you know who I am. And a large part of who I am is taking care of the Inn." He steered her through a small crowd, all of them nodding and smiling at her as they parted. They ended up at a table with wine bottles and a beer cask. "You might need something to fortify you. There is a bit of a crowd wanting your acquaintance."

"Why?" Agnes asked, taking the glass of claret he poured for her.

Jack winced as he ran his fingers through his hair. "I may have mentioned you."

She shook her head again. None of what he said made sense. "But why?"

This time he chuckled. "Because, my lady. They ask me what I'm thinking of to have such a smile on my face. I cannot lie."

Finally she understood. The daze of the Inn lifted and she realized that there was more to everyone. Not only Jack, not only her, not only Lydia. Everyone had their secrets, and knowing a person's secrets was like love. It painted targets on the places where you might hurt them, handing you the arrow and begging you not to take the shot. Here was Jack's weakness, his target, his softness. Her heart felt full knowing how much he had to trust her to share this. "Then who else must I meet on this grand tour of the room?"

"Over here," Jack said, gesturing to a corner. As he led her there, she once again became self-conscious of her dress but pushed it out of her mind. Too late now. "We don't use real names here, as you may have realized. It's a modicum of respect, and a way to allow your true self to show."

"And I am the Lady of Your Heart?" Agnes teased.

Jack lifted her hand aloft and kissed the inside of her wrist. "Did you doubt it?"

She shook her head. "Not anymore."

"Good." He steered her toward two plump ladies who sported the same hairstyle and same gown. As the women stood, it was obvious they were not related, but their identical dress made it a dizzying introduction. "Lady of My Heart, the Missus Laceys."

"It's a pleasure to finally see your face," one of them said. The other gave a lascivious smile that made it clear it wasn't her face they were worried about.

"It's an honor to be here," Agnes said, meaning every word of it.

"We've had our own delights, but we're happy to watch as the younger people get their turn. It's a joy to watch. And Jack here has earned his!" The more lascivious Mrs. Lacey said.

"If I'd known I was to be meeting such a crowd, I would have worn a finer gown," Agnes said in an attempt at humor that might draw the women onto her side.

Jack frowned. "If that's the case, we have plenty of clothes upstairs."

"Oh, going to take her upstairs so early, Jack? But then, a lady can stay up all night." One of the Mrs.

Laceys cackled and the other gave a reproachful thump with her fan.

"Manners, May! My goodness. What will she think of us?"

"That we love each other and wish her the same," Mrs. Lacey replied, giving the other a peck on the cheek.

Again, realization dawned on Agnes. These women weren't sisters or spinster relations. These women were lovers! And by both being Mrs. Lacey, it was their way of declaring an unsanctioned marriage. Her pulse quickened. She'd had no idea that women did this. She'd had no idea anyone did any of these things. How could she have been so ignorant? Had Mary Franklin known all this and cast her aside anyway? Or had she been as naïve as Agnes?

"Oh, look. She understands now." The lewder of the Mrs. Laceys chuckled. "Need any more hints?"

Jack pulled at her elbow, steering her away. "No need, Mrs. Laceys, thank you," he said over his shoulder.

"Lovely meeting you," Agnes called behind her, feeling very rude and loud and deliciously like herself.

"Would you like to change clothes? We have quite the wardrobe upstairs. It is available to any of our guests who need a bit of a costume."

Agnes blinked. "Why that's..." she trailed off, looking around the room at the gowns. Some of them looked familiar, but Agnes assumed it was because she had seen so many of them while doing the mending for the Woman's Home. A woman drifted past them.

"Go on, ask," Jack said.

She nodded. "Pardon me. May I see the inside of your sleeve?"

The woman stopped and gave a slight smile, checking in with Jack.

"If you don't mind," Jack added.

"For you, Jack, anything," the woman flirted. She stood eye to eye with Agnes, and as Agnes tenderly reached for the woman's arm, she realized the wrist was large to be a woman's. Another example of someone dressing in a fashion not commonly their own. And sure enough, on the inside of the smart blue striped fabric, a yellow X. Her X.

"This is mine," Agnes gasped.

"I beg your pardon," the woman said, ripping her arm away.

"Oh, no, not like that. I'm terribly sorry." Agnes glanced over at Jack. "I mended this. This is a dress I did."

"Thank you, Mrs. Cockwell," Jack said.

"My pleasure, Jack," she said, giving an uncertain nod to Agnes.

"How does she have that?"

"I take certain ones from the Women's Home. In exchange, we give them a good sum of money. Besides, the dresses we take are the flashier ones, the ones that wouldn't be as suitable for the young women there. The Inn gets a regular supply of fashionable clothes, and the Women's Home gets much-needed cash donations. Our patrons give what they can when they use the clothes, and we give them a wash after wearing."

"That's quite a service." Agnes stared after Mrs. Cockwell. She lowered her voice. "Do all the men dress up?"

Jack laughed. "No. And not all are effeminate. Some nights they are, and some nights they aren't. It's different here. You don't have to play a role you don't want to play. May I show you upstairs?"

"Unhand that lady, you scurrilous rogue!" From behind them, Miss Persephone whacked Jack on the shoulder with her feathered fan. "You can *not* be escorting her up the stairs with no chaperone. I forbid it!"

Agnes giggled. "I welcome a chaperone. This one is obviously not to be trusted."

Jack gave a sly grin that spun her heart in circles. "So, you've been warned."

Miss Persephone cut through both of them and pushed Agnes up the stairs first. They came to a landing in what looked like a guest house. It really was an Inn. Was this where Jack slept?

"First door on the right," Miss Persephone instructed. Agnes opened the door to a bedroom with no bed. There were several chaise lounges and couches and several armoires whose doors refused to fully close. A dressing screen was placed in the corner of the room. It looked a mess, with dresses strewn about the lounges and the screen.

Miss Persephone harrumphed as she gathered dresses. "Honestly. There is so very little we require here, and they cannot manage it."

"I think Polly had a stomachache today," Jack said, aiding in picking up excess gowns.

"Stomachache or not, that child needs to earn her keep! And these dresses need to be shown some respect." Miss Persephone huffed as she stowed the gowns.

"My dear lady." Jack handed off his gowns and returned to Agnes to take her hands. "Would you mind if I picked something out for you?"

"Not at all," she said. "But if I do recall, this is the second time you've tried to convince me to undress in your vicinity."

"But the first time you might agree to do so."

"Start undressing, my lady. I'll come help you in a moment and bring you whatever Jack chooses," Miss Persephone called from the largest armoire.

Agnes went behind the screen, sat on the dressing

stool, and removed her boots. Was this an entirely ridiculous place? Well, yes, yes it was. But why shouldn't it be? The Cuttingsworth ball was ridiculous, and she hadn't an ounce of fun at it. Almack's assemblies were tedious *and* ridiculous and utterly devoid of fun. Was it merely that her whole life had prepared her to never have fun?

She pulled at the ribbon behind the nape of her neck. No going back now. She stepped out of the heavy woolen round gown and draped it over the stool. She waited in her chemise, her stays, and her stockings. Not even pretty silk ones with embroidered designs. Why couldn't she have thought to wear those?

Miss Persephone delivered a stack of clothing. She pursed her lips at Agnes, which made Agnes doubt herself.

"What is it?"

Miss Persephone shook her head. "Nothing. We can keep the chemise on. It'll be fine."

"Why would I not be wearing a chemise?" Agnes asked.

The other woman's mouth opened and closed. She shook her head.

Agnes pulled the first article of clothing from the stack. It was a pair of trousers. That surprised her. Jack wanted her in trousers? That was strange. But this was a place where everything could be any which way. She certainly didn't want to seem ungrateful or stiff. Standing on one leg, she slid the other into the trousers, but it caught in the fabric. She tipped over, hitting the floor with her shoulder, her hands still clutching the trousers.

"Oh no!" Miss Persephone shouted, but she didn't do anything.

"Are you hurt? What's happened?" Jack demanded.

Agnes sat up from the floor, one leg in and one leg out. She looked at Miss Persephone for help, but the woman nodded encouragingly. "I'm perfectly fine."

She managed to put the trousers on while on the floor, which seemed safer. When she stood, at Miss Persephone's instruction, she gathered the fabric of her chemise and stuffed it down the front of her and then between her legs, as if she were riding the smallest horse in the world. "This can't possibly be how it's done."

"How else do you think men keep their arse clean?" Miss Persephone asked.

"You cannot be serious."

"Waistcoat?" she said instead.

Agnes took it and slid it on, allowing Miss Persephone to tie it to her proper sizing in the back. It was a brilliant red color with gold embroidering. Agnes hadn't mended any waistcoats, so she knew it wasn't one of hers. The embroidery design, while elegant, was amateurish close up. Some of the stitching was irregularly spaced, but when covered with a proper coat, no one would notice.

She fumbled with the fabric buttons. Buttoning a waistcoat wasn't a normal occurrence for her, and it didn't feel right. The fit of it was fine, it was that wearing *trousers* felt strange. All the fabric between her legs. And nothing covering her bum felt indecent. She glanced over at Miss Persephone, who smiled with an air of odd encouragement. Agnes finished the buttons and reached for the coat. Instead, she was handed a watch fob.

"Drape it so that it is visible beneath the hem of the waistcoat," Miss Persephone instructed.

Carefully following orders, Agnes draped the watch fob with no actual watch attached, and was rewarded with a coat. She pulled it on, feeling not at all comfortable.

"And your shoes, my lady," Miss Persephone urged.

Agnes donned her work boots again, which, looking down, seemed overly large and quite assuredly silly. "Do all men feel this ridiculous while dressing?" Agnes asked Miss Persephone.

For her part, Miss Persephone barked out a laugh. "Yes. Men, by and large, always feel ridiculous. It's why we try so hard at other things."

"Pardon me?"

Miss Persephone raised her eyebrows to Agnes's challenge.

Agnes stumbled over her words. "You referred to yourself as a man, yet you powder your face and wear dresses."

"Well, yes, but I'm built as a man. Why wouldn't I count myself as one? My favorite parts belong to men."

Agnes blushed when she realized which parts Miss Persephone was referring to.

"Being a man or a woman is overly complicated, don't you think?" Miss Persephone asked, stepping forward to help Agnes with her cravat. "So many rules for behavior and profession and styles and speech."

"I've often been frustrated by my lack of choices in those," Agnes admitted.

"I dress as a woman in public, but whether alone or with a lover, I am a man. The satire I put forth as Miss Persephone is freeing, somehow. I enjoy the performance. It's funny, it's fun."

"But don't you get tired of acting?"

"Don't you?" Miss Persephone challenged.

Agnes smiled. "I feel ridiculous, but how do I look?" She held her arms aloft so Miss Persephone could see.

"Not for me to judge, my lady. Walk out from

behind the screen. You know Jack is impatient. Get to it, now." She stood aside.

Agnes yanked at the bottom of the jacket. If only it were longer. And walking in trousers was even stranger than standing in them. The fabric between her legs felt indecent as it rubbed. There was no reassurance of a skirt swishing backwards as one stepped forward. Jack sat on a well-worn couch of indeterminate brown color. He looked up as she appeared.

His jaw quite literally dropped, which was imminently gratifying. After a moment Jack collected himself and hopped to his feet. "You," he started, but then didn't finish. He guided her to a full-length mirror. Agnes didn't really care what she looked like as long as she made Jack's face do that.

Until she saw herself. It was akin to being naked. Her long legs were accented by the trousers, and her bum flared out for all to see. The shape of her was so obvious and on display. The waistcoat didn't hide her bosom either, as she thought it would. Instead, it hugged the curves of her waist and flared open, drawing the eye.

Agnes burst into tears.

"Oh!" Jack was clearly not expecting this reaction and clucked and shushed at her, but she couldn't stop crying.

She looked awful. It disappointed Jack and distressed Miss Persephone, who had helped her. Even Agnes understood that this was supposed to be a revelatory event, somehow freeing as Miss Persephone said, but Agnes wanted back in a dress —*any* dress. "I'm sorry," she sobbed.

"No, no, no. I'm sorry. I didn't think this was how you would feel," Jack said, pulling her onto another nearby sofa. He petted her hair and wiped the tears from her cheeks. "I thought you would enjoy wearing trousers."

"I'm sorry," Agnes repeated, wiping her eyes and suddenly feeling the well of inadequacies surging to the surface. She couldn't be the worldly partner for Mary Franklin or the proper debutante young miss for her parents. She couldn't even be the supportive sister for Lydia. And now, now she was in a molly-house in God knew where, unable to wear *trousers* for Jack. She was a miserable failure, and even Jack would leave her to be alone with her silly embroidery for the rest of her life.

"There now, it's not life or death here," Jack whispered.

His kind words made her sob harder. She tipped from sitting upright to laying across his lap. There was enough fabric bunched around his knees to get a proper grip, and she continued to cry.

"I'll be..." Miss Persephone said as she tiptoed out of the room.

This was so pitiful and ridiculous and *small*, as Mary Franklin had said.

14

"Tch, tch, tch," Jack clucked, desperately wanting to stroke Lady Agnes's hair, or even worse, her trouser-clad thigh. "Do you want to talk about it? I'm here. I've been told I'm a fairly decent listener."

That made Agnes smile through her tears, which were wetting Jack's trouser legs. "Eavesdropper, you mean."

He handed her a handkerchief, but he did not mind a bit her head staying right where it was, in his lap. She dried her eyes and her nose before sitting upright. The chill from where she'd been was noticeable, and he couldn't help but feel the loss. "There, now. Progress."

Agnes nodded. "Thank you."

"I don't need you to wear these clothes. I think you look positively devastating, of course, but I always think that."

Agnes gave her best withering look, but with red eyes and a red nose, she looked like an adorable mouse.

"I am deadly serious. Agnes, you try so hard to be what other people need you to be. I wanted to give you space to express the person *you* are, without being beholden to others. I misjudged you, which, I'm learning is a constant state of affairs."

Agnes continued to sniff, as if she were trying to hide how much she wanted to blow her nose. That's what ladylike behavior got you—a stuffy nose and a clean handkerchief. "What do you mean?"

"The 'misjudging you' part? You keep me guessing. I never know what you'll say or do next. For some that might not be ideal, but to me, it shows me how incredibly clever you are. How thoughtful you are."

"I meant about trying to be what other people need me to be, but thank you. I will take all the compliments you are willing to give at this particular moment."

Jack pushed an errant wisp of hair away from her face. "I see you, Agnes. I really do. You try so very hard, and because you are not satisfied with anything but total and complete success, you feel like a failure when you are anything but."

"How would you know?" Tears were coming again, and the tip of her nose reddened in anticipation.

"That you spend your days desperately trying to make the world a better place?"

Tears spilled over again, and she looked abjectly miserable.

Fact: Commiseration sometimes made misery more acute.

"So this next bit is something I swore to myself I would take to my grave." Jack wanted to erase those tears. He would do anything—say anything—to make her happy. As long as it was the truth.

"Sounds like a juicy bit of gossip."

"Oh, it is," Jack assured her. He took her hands in his and sighed. "This is a long story. Have you your wine?"

They both looked around for her glass and found

it on the table next to the door. Jack retrieved it for her.

"Thank you," Agnes sipped at the claret, feeling the dry red wine calm her before she even swallowed. "I feel as if I could really use it about now."

"I ran away from home when I was sixteen." Jack watched her face, looking for disapproval. Finding none, he continued. "When I left my parents' home, I arrived at the Women's Home and was given shelter."

"How?" Agnes frowned.

Mrs. McKenzie was very strict about her rules. No men, no boys over the age of five. No exceptions. Jack set his jaw. "Agnes."

He wanted her to figure it out without him saying it because he felt like a coward. He wanted her to *know*, even though it was a ridiculous thing to expect of another person. But there were so many other things tied up in these secrets—so much shame and discomfort and betrayal.

Lady Agnes pulled herself up straight, as if she were trying to concentrate very hard. Her eyebrows were knitted together and she stared at him, but understanding refused to dawn. "I'm sorry," she said, shaking her head. "You'll have to tell me using words."

"Remember at the Cuttingsworth ball when you asked me if I was Miss or Mister Townsend?"

"Of course. And you assured me you were Mr. Townsend. The brother. A brother? Her brother?"

"I did not lie to you." Suddenly, it panicked him to think she might believe otherwise. "I told you the truth but did not entirely illuminate its meaning."

"What do you mean, entirely? I asked and that is what you said. I remember it quite distinctly."

"As do I. Because what I actually told you was that I was neither. And both." The complicated part of his insides never made sense to anyone, including himself. There weren't words for this in-between space. The place where Jack wanted to be that was neither and both and completely beside the point.

"Of course. A nom de plume. Many do it, and with your profession, entirely understandable." Color came into her cheeks and she huffed out an irritated breath. "I assumed you must be quite young, given your smooth cheek."

Jack winced. "No. I'm twenty-five, well out of the range of childhood."

"Then what—" Agnes's eyes widened. And that's when he saw her understand.

"Yes, there now, you're getting it," Jack said. "But it's more and less than that."

"This is quite a lot to think about."

"I was raised a girl. But I don't feel like one. I don't really feel like a man either. I'm neither. I'm both. I'm a person that lives in the middle."

"Which is why you were comfortable being a flower girl in the market."

Jack nodded, watching her expressions change, afraid of detecting disgust or repulsion, but so far, he could find none. "I left home because being a young woman had more responsibilities than I could manage. My brother had begun clerking at a bank— Drummonds of all places—and wanted to marry me off to one of his more senior colleagues as a way to help him ascend through the ranks. I was young, and I refused."

There was more than that. It was Roland's anger at him, the horrible words, the tantrums. But being asked to submit to courtship to further his brother's career was a step too far. It had assured Jack of Roland's belief that a woman was chattel and nothing more. No brains, no life behind the eyes.

"Drummonds is where my father banks." Agnes looked like her mind was still churning.

"My brother, Roland, pressured harder and harder. My father was back at the time, and he agreed that I should at least allow the gentleman to call on me."

Agnes shivered. She could sympathize, clearly. It was Jack's turn to feel the surge of emotion to share a memory with a person who understood him so completely.

"I'd been wearing my brother's old clothes for years, running around with neighborhood boys. I wasn't terribly convincing, but convincing enough. When the time came for the gentleman to call, I put on my favorite trousers and ran off. My family shouted for me all over the neighborhood, but as a slouching boy in the alleyways, no one paid me any mind. I was invisible because of the clothes I wore."

"I understand that." Her gaze turned to the brown round gown that was lying on the stool behind the dressing screen.

"And I liked being a boy. I liked being able to run and jump and climb anything I wanted. Far easier than in my skirts. It wasn't that my insides needed to be a boy, it was that they couldn't be a girl. I was neither. Both."

"And being a boy was far easier?"

"Far easier, but it took time. After I ran away, I was scared. I didn't have any skills worth a damn. The only thing I could really do was listen."

"And help people," Agnes said.

"I see Mrs. Caldwell has been telling stories." Jack flushed a bit with pride, but he needed to tell her the rest. She needed to know. "I needed food and a jingle in my pocket. I took boxing from Miss Abbott for the free pasties and discovered I would never make it as a pugilist."

"Really? How come?" Agnes appeared surprised.

He shrugged. "I'm willing to fight to defend myself, but I'm far better at talking my way out of a situation than I am taking a punch."

"I tried once to take exercise with Miss Abbott," Agnes confessed. "I couldn't bring myself to hit her even though she assured me I wouldn't hurt her."

Jack squeezed her hand as a reflex, to say he understood, but it felt like far more than simple communication. It felt like energy being transferred from him to her and back again.

"Then how did you come to this? Finding things, I mean."

"People that I knew needed things, and I wanted to help. Easy enough. Depending on what it was, it was easier to be a girl or a boy, and I dressed accordingly." He did not want to get into the nightsoil story. Not exactly something a person wanted to brag about—jumping into a pool of excrement. Then he'd have to explain that he needed to take at least four baths after that to feel clean.

"You still do dress the part as a flower girl at the market."

Jack chuckled and looked down. A lock of dark hair dangled in front of his face. The fashion was to have long hair, the elegantly coiffed dishevelment. Miss Persephone assured him it was appropriate, but he wasn't sure. He should ask Agnes if she liked it. When he looked up and found her staring at him, he realized that she did like it—his hair, his past, him. The real him. He could feel her affection and he wanted it, wanted to be worthy of it, and he wanted to fall into her like curling into sleep as it came for him after a long night.

"THE MOST AMAZING THING TO ME WAS THAT YOU saw me. You recognized me, even in a dress." Jack gazed at her in a way that should have scared her. Instead, for the first time in Agnes's life, she felt brave. Braver than Lydia.

"Well, you are rather obvious." Agnes looked back down at her hands.

"I'm rather not," Jack protested. "My own mother didn't recognize me when I started climbing in through the windows. She beat me with a broom the first time."

Suddenly, the Mrs. Laceys downstairs came to mind, as if they were an unbidden thought that had waited patiently for her to pay attention to them. She gripped Jack's hand with an intensity that surprised herself. Jack would be hers. All hers and no one else's. Agnes got to come first for someone. Finally.

"I'm glad you've come to court me." She tried to sound firm, clear. This was the best she could do when saying what she wanted. That she wanted him and no other.

"Even though you understand who I am?" Jack asked.

She'd been able to see the subtle shifts in mood across his face from the start, but she was very much looking forward to becoming an expert on Jack's expressions. "Yes. Of course."

"That's something, then." Jack rubbed his thumb along her cheek. "I-I-I can't tell you how much you mean to me."

"If I could think of other words than merely parroting yours, I would say them."

Jack leaned forward and brushed her lips with his. She answered back, but then pulled away. "I should change into something I can bear."

"Our closet is yours," he said, opening his arms wide. "Quite literally."

Agnes stood and wandered the armoires, finding garments categorized and organized. There was a men's wardrobe, and then a costume wardrobe. Finally, she came to a women's dinner gown collection. She'd sewn a particularly lovely emerald green dress once. Searching through the selection, she found it.

Behind the screen, she shed the masculine clothing, still marveling at how comfortable Jack seemed in it. She pulled her chemise from the trousers and shook it out. After those were doffed, she pulled on the gown. "Are you still out there, Jack?"

"Of course. Do you need help finishing up?" He appeared behind the screen and quickly did up the eyelets in the back. "I do this for Miss Persephone as well. I have a second career waiting for me as a lady's maid."

"How is your hairstyling?" Agnes teased, turning around and fluffing the skirt.

"Dashing is the word I'd use. As in, the lady is dashing away from me so I can't tug on her hair any longer."

"What a superb reference."

"I'm highly employable."

Agnes kissed Jack on the cheek before sitting down to tug on her boots again. She liked his flirtations, and she liked being able to kiss his cheek without preamble or reason. A kiss could happen for no other reason than she desired to do so. What a lovely, easy thing that could be.

❦

JACK KNEW AS HE ESCORTED THE NOW JEWEL-TONED Lady Agnes down the steps and back to the Inn's main guest area that his chest was puffed out like a rooster. There was no mistaking it—this was the best night of his life.

He felt like he could do absolutely anything, anywhere, anytime. They strutted in as the musicians were in the middle of a particularly raucous reel. Guests skipped along in two lines, laughing and clapping along. It seemed to put Lady Agnes at ease and she laughed along with them.

They refilled their claret and then went in search of the Mrs. Laceys again, only to have Miss Persephone inform them that they'd departed for the evening, but with a message of love and encouragement for both Jack and the Lady of his Heart.

As they perused the room, Lady Agnes came to a sudden halt.

"What is it?" Jack asked, scanning the room for anything that she might find obscene or immoral. Nothing seemed out of sorts. Not tonight, anyway.

"What is the protocol for when you know someone from your social circle and meet them here?" Her voice wavered.

"Ah. Well, here you may acknowledge each other, depending on if you wish to greet them. It wouldn't be considered a snub if you don't choose to engage. However, out there, never engage with someone you only know from the Inn, unless it has been agreed upon." Finally, the crowd split open, and Jack knew who it was that caused Agnes such distress.

Bill headed toward them, a nervous frown on his overly chiseled brow. As an infrequent guest, Bill's appearance was always a pleasant surprise, but he was typically relaxed when here.

"Bill, what a pleasure to see you tonight," Jack greeted, glancing back to Agnes to see if this was the issue. He was very well aware of Bill's status, but no one else was. Lady Agnes's presence must have been quite a shock if they knew each other. Lady Agnes started to sink into a curtsy, but Jack held her firmly up.

"Your gr—"

"Not here," Jack whispered.

Bill bowed, a shallow and curt greeting, barely perfunctory. "Yes, hello. Good evening."

"Bill, may I please introduce you to someone extremely valuable to me. This is the Lady of My Heart."

His face relaxed. "My lady. What a pleasure."

"My lady, this is...Bill."

Confusion wafted across her face. "That's it? Bill?"

"I'm afraid my imagination is quite lacking when I'm under pressure," Bill said.

"It's lovely to see you here, then, your g—sir." Agnes blinked to cover her blunder. It would take her some time to get used to these kinds of rules, but Jack had no doubt that it would become second nature to her in no time.

"I am equally pleased and surprised to see you here, my lady. At your leisure, I am happy to escort you home." Bill offered it, glancing to Jack, which Jack understood that he didn't wish to cause offense.

"Thank you, but I have squired myself this evening, and I can return the same way." Her eyes sparkled. She was so proud of herself, and the emerald green gown set her off so that she was a precious jewel. Jack couldn't have been prouder of her himself.

"I see. Well. Should the need arise that you need my assistance, do not be afraid to ask. There are some benefits to my friendship, I should like to think."

Jack frowned. There was an intimacy here that he had not known about. Lady Agnes had never called at his home to visit Bill's wife. Nor had they ever come for dinner at the Lorian or Arthur homes that Jack had heard about.

Even knowing Lady Agnes's penchant for women, Bill's extraordinary handsomeness made Jack peevish. Beauty caused people to do strange things.

"Bill and my cousin are fast friends," Agnes explained.

Jack thought through the cousins that he had memorized from the copy of Debrett's. The only two he could recall were Lord Andrepont and Miss Margaret Miller, the bastard daughter, now Lady Elshire. Bill must be friends with Andrepont. Interesting.

"Any friend of yours is a friend of mine," Jack said.

"Mine or hers?" Bill asked. "I'm afraid you get top billing, my lady."

"As it should be," Jack said. Both aristocrats seemed to relax now that they'd found each other. Jack escorted them over to a table to set their drinks down, and they chatted amiably for hours. Time passed, and occasionally Jack was pulled up to dance by different guests, and then Bill and Agnes took to the floor. By the time the wee hours came for them all and the Inn's clientele was dwindling, Agnes's hairstyle showed some wear, but she herself did not.

She'd made jokes with surprising quickness and laughed as freely. They drank more claret, but not to the point of drunkenness. Finally, Bill stood.

"My lady, truly, the hour is quite late. Please allow me to take you home." Bill's eyes were hooded with fatigue, and Jack could tell that he'd stayed far longer than he'd intended out of sheer politeness and courtesy to Lady Agnes.

"Good sir." She giggled. It must be hilarious to someone like Lady Agnes to address a marquis as *sir*. "Thank you for the kind offer. However, I have every intention of transporting myself under my own powers."

There was hardly anyone left. The musicians had packed up and gone down to the kitchens for their final repast. Miss Persephone was making the rounds, checking the rooms in the back and upstairs for amorous couples that needed to be told to find another place for assignations. Was Lady Agnes angling for his bed?

Desire coursed through him as the thought evolved. He could barely imagine it.

Fact: He had, in fact, imagined it many times. It didn't seem real. The entire evening felt like a fantasy.

"Jack, please help me to show her reason." Bill looked defeated with barely a fight.

"Not to worry, Bill. Take yourself home. My lady is in good hands."

"Jack, this isn't a good idea. She's an unmarried miss of the *ton*. If anyone finds out—" Bill whispered.

"If anyone finds out," Lady Agnes broke in coolly, "I will be forced to marry. And my parents can have no objections over the kind of man I've ruined myself with."

Shit on toast, his lady was a clever one.

"Of course, who would find that out, *Bill?*" Lady Agnes gave him a sweet smile, one that dimpled in the corner. Oh, she had to have practiced in a mirror to know how devastating of an effect that dimple could be! "How would they know where I was since I will be waking up in my own bed tomorrow morning, having had a terrible megrim. Sleeping powders, while effective for such a malady, can leave one so drowsy."

Bill harrumphed. "You're far more devious than anyone gives you credit for, my lady."

"Thank you, your grace," Lady Agnes returned in kind.

"Good night then, Jack, Lady Agnes. I'll see you at the next dinner party, I'm sure."

"Good night, *Bill*. I promise to never call you that in public," Agnes said with a sly smile.

"And I shan't answer to it in any case," he said in good humor. He gathered his hat, gloves, and coat and left the Inn.

Mrs. Bettleton came upstairs for the first time that evening, gathering a load of glasses on a large tray. Jack excused himself from Lady Agnes and trotted over.

"Mrs. Bettleton, would you mind terribly much if I did my chores tomorrow before opening? I've got a guest that I need to see home."

Mrs. Bettleton squinted over at Lady Agnes then snorted. "Is she going home? I doubt that. Well, off with the both of you then. It isn't like Miss Persephone hasn't done her share of shirking end-of-night duties herself."

"You are a dream, Mrs. Bettleton." Jack could have kissed her. He started back to Lady Agnes when Mrs. Bettleton called him back.

"Mind yourself, son. The rich ain't like the rest of us. They can go back to their protection. But if we get exposed, there's nothing to keep us safe but our wits. Keep us safe. I know you're clever, but please be smart." The lines on her face seemed deeper at this hour, when fatigue caught up with them all.

Jack understood Mrs. Bettleton's hesitation. But the inn owner didn't know Lady Agnes or their situation.

Fact: There was the theoretical, and then there was the specific. Theoretically, Jack could find any object in London and Jack was a Finder of Lost Things. Specifically, he was a finder of Lady Agnes and himself. He grabbed a single candle from the table to light his way.

Lady Agnes was sitting primly at their table, looking about the room with her usual wide-eyed innocence. She looked so perfect right there. So much like a woman that could be his. The things he would find for her. He held out his hand. "Come, my lady. Our last stop of the evening."

She stood, taking his hand, and he led her through the doors and up through the back servants' stair. "Where are we going?"

They arrived on the landing and walked past Miss Persephone's room to Jack's. "I'm showing you where I live. If you'd like, you are welcome to stay with me. If not, then I will escort you home in a hackney. Whatever you prefer."

"Let me see it," Agnes whispered. "I want to see where you sleep. Where you are only you."

His hands shook as he opened the door to his bedroom. It wasn't much, but it was his. And she was right: it was where Jack was himself and not anything more.

Lady Agnes walked into the room, and he felt as if the whole world might go sideways at any moment. Nothing felt real. But also, nothing had ever felt *more* real than this. The brown round gown she'd worn to the Inn was folded neatly on the chair in the corner. Miss Persephone had been feeling either sly or thoughtful when she took it from the dressing room and brought it here.

"Show me," Lady Agnes said, turning a full circle in the room, noting each and every piece of furniture.

Did she think there was more than this? "What else can I show you? This is all that I have. All my meager possessions."

She hid a smile. "I don't mean your things. Show me who you are. Show me you."

His heart sped up and his breath went shallow.

She couldn't have asked for something more difficult than this.

"Unless you don't wish to," she said, no doubt sensing his nerves.

"I—I do wish to," he managed. "But that is a big request. I've never done that before."

Lady Agnes went to his bed and sat. Part of his brain was exploding with the sheer idea of it. *Lady Agnes was sitting on his bed.* "Patience happens to be one of my virtues," she said.

Jack nodded and went to his bureau, where the ewer and basin were. Glancing over at her, he slowly began unwrapping his cravat. He first laid it out flat across the bureau and then rolled it up before stowing it in the drawer. Next he took off his waistcoat. Then the buckles on his shoes, and then the shoes themselves. Off came the trousers. Then the stockings. With each article, he glanced over at the incredible woman perched on his bed, but she said nothing.

Finally, in nothing but his shirt and his breast binding, he stood before her. "Anything more is to go past a point of no return."

"Do you wish to stop?"

"No," he answered immediately. "But you might."

She shook her head. "I am not a reckless person. But you may have noticed that once I take a risk, I enter it as fully as possible. I'm choosing you, Jack. All of you. And I hope that you choose me."

He wanted to sink to his knees and assure her that he chose her. But this was about showing her, unfettered, who he was. So he took the rag, dipped it in the basin, and washed off his face and neck, erasing the last vestiges of Jack. The dark-colored powder that he used to create the fiction of Jack. The stronger jawline, the false cording in his neck, the impression that stubble might appear at any moment.

He didn't need the makeup, or even need to be Jack. It was that other people needed it to treat him with respect.

For her part, Lady Agnes did not gasp, but she did let out a compelling "oh."

At last, Jack removed his long linen shirt, standing in nothing but a breast binding, which he now unwound. He let these last garments fall to the floor. This was it. This was the person beneath all the fast words and amiable conversation. The person that didn't have a name.

A part of him expected her to leave. To express her disgust or say something like, *such a waste to dress like a boy.*

But instead, Agnes sighed. "You're beautiful."

He thought he would be embarrassed. But he felt humbled. The cold air prickled his skin, only calling his mind to the heat gathering between his legs.

Agnes stood. At first he thought she was going to touch him, but instead, eyes locked on his, she began to undress. When she struggled with the eyelets in the back of the gown, Jack stepped forward. Those long legs under her gown made him want things that he couldn't name.

"Let me help you," he whispered. While she stood in front of his bed, he went to his knees and lifted the hem of her dress. His hands skated underneath her chemise, feeling the fullness of her calves and the dimple of her knees, to the ties of her garters around her thighs. He untied them and rolled her woolen stockings down, one leg at a time.

Agnes pointed her toe as he removed one and then the other. She pulled up the hem of her skirt and he allowed himself the indulgence of kissing the inside of her ankle. "God, I love your legs."

"You've never seen them," she said, her voice hoarse with desire.

"There, my love, you are mistaken. I've seen them encased in skirts, and I've seen them now in sturdy trousers. But mostly, I've seen them in my dreams. And they are better than anything I could have imagined." He kissed the insides of her knees and pushed her skirts higher. Her holding them, accommodating him, inviting him, made him even wetter.

"I, I—" Agnes began, but as Jack's kisses reached her thighs, her skin softer than kid leather, her words dissolved to sharp, panting exhales.

He let his thumb brush over the seam in the thatch of her crux. Even slight pressure and it yielded, swollen and damp.

"God, Jack," Agnes breathed.

The smell of both of them filled the room. He nuzzled his face up to her, extending a kiss, and then his tongue. She shuddered.

"I can't, please."

Jack stilled. "Can't what? Do you need me to stop?"

"God no. I don't think I can stand much longer with you doing that. My legs are shaking."

Jack slid his tongue into her crease and licked hard and firm. His arms wrapped around her thighs and her arse, and her knees buckled in response. "Sit down," he growled, not moving an inch.

She obeyed, falling back to his bed, pulling up her skirts and propping up on her elbows. "If you don't want to—"

"There is literally no place I'd rather be on God's green earth," Jack said in between nips at her labia. Each movement created a mewl from Agnes, which was gratifying. "This is perfect. Your pussy is perfect. Your words are perfect. You are perfect."

Jack slid two fingers inside her as he pushed harder on the firm bud of her pleasure. She cried out and arched her back, rising away from the mattress. He sat back on his heels, still stroking her with his fingers. "Shh, my love. Miss Persephone is very cranky about her beauty sleep."

◈

"LET'S GET YOU OUT OF THAT GOWN," JACK SAID, standing and holding out his hands to her. Agnes struggled to her feet, wondering if she'd ever experienced a climax so blinding in her life.

The low light of the single candle lit his skin like a painting, smooth and perfect. His small breasts were hard and pebbled, and it was hard for Agnes to concentrate on the mechanics of getting her dress removed. Jack was good with his mouth—but then again, she'd not ever had anyone do that to her. It had never been something Mary Franklin—or anyone else —had desired to do, despite Agnes's own ministrations. To have someone give her that gift was more than she'd ever expected. It made her feel wanted, desired, as she had desired others, and it felt so good to be on the receiving end of that want.

Jack turned her away from him so he could finally undo the eyelet closure of her borrowed clothing; a task he'd foregone earlier in favor of doing other wicked things. It made Agnes ache to touch him. She wanted to feel the curve of his back, the musculature of his thighs and his bum. The softness of those teacup breasts and the dampness in the dark thatch hidden between his legs.

Finally his fingers had done their work and Agnes peeled off the heavy dress, stepping out into only her chemise and stays. Jack made quick work of the stays, and soon those were off as well. All that was left was her sheer linen chemise. With her back to him, Jack wrapped his arms around her, cradling her breasts, now heavy and hot. "I need you," Agnes whined.

One of Jack's hands slid down her belly to her crux and cupped her there. "How badly?"

"Don't tease me," she begged. "I need to touch you. Please let me."

"Come for me again and you'll get your turn," he promised. "I know you can do it." He pulled up the thin chemise and slid his fingers into her slit. He worked there, kissing her back, kneading her breast until finally she came so hard she bent over to brace herself on the bed. Jack pushed his other hand between her legs from behind and slid into her. "There you go, pet. Keep coming. Feel it. Feel me."

Her body spasmed again in response, and again. Desperate, she climbed onto the bed, out of his reach. She caught her breath, steadying herself. No one had ever been so adamant about her pleasure, not even herself. Jack's eyes glittered at her. But turnabout was fair play. "Lay down, Jack."

"Are you sure? After all that?" Jack asked, but still, he climbed onto the bed next to her.

"You're always moving, always running. I'm going to make you stop." Agnes ran her hand from his lips, down his chin, between his breasts, past the sweet dip of his navel, to the dark hair between his legs. The slickness of the path down gratified her. Let her know that Jack's efforts had filled him with lust.

"With you, this won't take long," he said. Agnes slipped her finger between the folds and started dancing her fingertips over the hard nub. Jack grabbed her head between his hands, locked eyes with her. "Harder."

She obeyed, and with their eyes locked, their breath coming fast, Jack kissed her lips as he came, hard and with such desperation. "I see you," he whispered as he laid his head back, spasming once more, then grabbing her wrist to stop her.

The air was thick with them, the light of a single candle cocooning them in the attic room, a place to call their own.

Agnes laid her head on his shoulder, curling herself around him. "I see you, too." She kissed his neck, having never felt so right in her life.

15

The room was light, which in and of itself seemed strange. The maid must have come in and opened the windows earlier than normal, Agnes thought. But then one eye opened.

"Fuck me running!" Jack yelled.

That brought both eyes open. Her body felt sore and wonderful and tired in the best of ways. The night had been more than she'd ever dreamed. Jack was more than she could have ever wished for, and he'd chosen her. And she was in his bed.

In his bed and it was morning. This was not as she had intended. The throat-clearing in the corner of the room caught her attention, and to her horror, she saw her sister sitting in the chair.

"Good morning, Agnes. How are you feeling? Still have a bit of a megrim?" Lydia asked. The cool tone of her voice chilled Agnes to the core. Lydia wore her pelisse, and her dark hair was perfectly coifed, which means she'd gotten up early. Or that it was late. Either way, this was not what Agnes had intended when she followed Jack up to his room.

"What are you doing here?" Agnes demanded. The heat from Jack's body was a draw, and all she wanted to do was wrap herself around him and pull curtains and close out the world forever. Close out her family at least.

"You honestly don't think that Vasily would let you sneak out alone, do you?" Lydia picked off her kid gloves and held them in her hand. "Agnes. Use your head."

"But he didn't—"

"Of course he did. He knew exactly when you left, and knew exactly where you'd go. You aren't that clever."

"My lady, there is no reason—" Jack was interrupted.

"Yes, good morning, *Mr. Townsend.*" Lydia's eyes glittered. "We all look different when we wake up in the morning, but you dress up more than most, don't you? Were you surprised, Agnes, when you arrived to this room?"

"Lydia, there's no need to be coarse." Agnes wished she could die of embarrassment.

"That remains to be seen since I'm the only clothed person here. I'd say we're past politeness. This isn't good for either of you." Lydia glanced at Agnes but glared at Jack.

"It isn't as if you didn't do your fair share of doing things you weren't supposed to do," Agnes said, wrapping the flimsy blanket around herself tighter, as if it would give her some kind of strength.

"Ah, yes. I knew this would come up," Lydia said, standing up. "But you forget, Vasily took me everywhere I needed to go. I was never in danger of being abducted off the streets."

"You engaged in public brawling, Lydia. Not exactly the paragon of womanhood." She may have feigned a megrim the night before, but her argument with her sister was absolutely giving her a headache now.

"You little fool. Don't be so naïve. Get dressed. As

for you, Mr. Townsend. You'll be sent for by my father when he is ready. At the moment, he's more likely to call for pistols at dawn, so be thankful for his forbearance."

"This isn't Lady Agnes's fault," Jack protested, holding the blankets to his chin.

Agnes appreciated his willingness to defend her, but at the moment, she wanted only to quiet him. He had no idea what fury he was up against.

Lydia rounded on him. "I don't care whose fault it is. The issue is that I'm dragging my unmarried younger sister naked from someone's bed. My younger sister who was put to her own bed early last night lamenting an illness. While she may claim she came here of her own free will, it is a perfectly reasonable expectation that my parents believe she was abducted from her quiet bed chamber." She narrowed her eyes at Jack, fists balling. "You may not know this, sir, but my sister has a reputation for modesty and cautious optimism. She is absolutely not the type of young miss who would lose her wits and abscond to a Drury Lane molly-house to conduct a clandestine affair with a thief."

"Lydia—" That was more than Agnes could bear.

"Don't, Agnes. Enough. Get dressed. The carriage is waiting out back." Lydia yanked open the door and then slammed it shut.

They lay there, listening to Lydia stomp down the hallway.

"I'm sorry," Jack whispered. "She's right. I shouldn't have let you do this. I should have never asked you to come. I'm so, so sorry."

"Last night was the best night of my life," Agnes said, hoping her tone would tell him how sincere she was. "To be here, to meet people like Miss Persephone and the Mrs. Laceys, have a real conversation with Lord—I mean, Bill. It was like a dream. I didn't know a place like this existed, let alone would welcome me."

He turned up on his side. "Is that really the best part of last night?"

Agnes felt the blush heating her from her toes to her hair. "Of course not." They stared at each other, and she felt like she could get lost in his eyes for days at a time. "I love you."

Jack took her hand and intertwined his fingers with hers. "And I love you, adore you, desire you."

They didn't have time for another round of bedsport, despite how Jack's gaze made her body respond. "I'll tell my father. I want us to be together. That is—if you want."

"It is my wildest dream," Jack said, kissing her hand.

It was a promise that she could make, but not one she could not guarantee her father would allow. They both knew how unlikely it would be for her father— or anyone—to sanction a marriage like this.

"Let me help you dress."

They scooted out of bed. Jack helped tie her round gown and dress her hair. He slipped on his clothes and they went downstairs together. Miss Persephone was in the kitchen, dressed in trousers, a banyan, and no wig, sipping a cup of chocolate with a tired, thousand-mile stare. It was strange to see her outside of her persona, with no powder or ribbons. The sharp jawline and muscular shoulders made her seem masculine and at odds with the person Agnes had met the night before.

"I'm sorry to wake you," Agnes said, her cheeks coloring. She hated the idea that Miss Persephone would witness her retrieval. Her humiliation seemed endless.

Miss Persephone put down her cup and gave a wistful smile. "At least you have family that will come for you when they think you're in trouble." She held out her hand, and Agnes instinctively went to squeeze it. A connection of sorts. Unspoken support. It did give her strength.

Mrs. Bettleton poured a pot of tea that smelled malty and earthy and delicious. The innkeeper looked up at her with a discerning look. Not much got past this woman. "Go on, girl. I told Jack to be careful with you, but I guess yer more important than I thought. And if I may beg you to be careful with your words about us, too, my lady."

"I am sorry if this affects you adversely," Agnes said. "I had no intention of hurting anyone."

"Come on." Jack urged her to the door with a hand to the small of her back.

This wasn't her family, and this wasn't her world, but it felt so easy and wonderful and right. It wasn't that her family was wrong, or that her room in Mayfair was bad—it was that her life was barren and small. Oh God, what Mary Franklin had said about her. When she was with Jack, she wasn't small anymore. Her world had expanded overnight.

"I'll let you know what's happening as soon as I can," she promised.

Jack shook his head, his dark hair still mussed from sleeping. How handsome he was. How perfect he was. "Appease your family. Be safe. I couldn't bear it if I brought harm to you. When your father sends for me, I'll do whatever it takes."

A lump formed in her throat as they walked through the kitchen garden to the mews. She gripped his hand. "I love you," she whispered.

"And I you," he whispered back.

Then the back gate was open and her family's carriage sat there, Vasily glowering at her from the driver's seat. His unhappiness was heavy and loud like a thunderstorm. It was awful. At least she didn't have to sit next to him in the carriage. No, she had to sit in an enclosed space with her cold, caustic sister.

"Good luck," Jack said, and handed her up. He closed the door, lifted the step, and thumped the side to signal that the carriage was ready.

The vehicle lurched into motion and she stared out the window at him as he watched her drive away.

࿔

JACK KICKED HIS WAY BACK THROUGH THE KITCHEN garden. He should have known better than to let her stay all night. Bill said as much as he'd left the Inn, but both Jack and Agnes were too caught up in the moment to listen. Not that Jack regretted a single second of their time together. Well. The night had been long in all the best ways.

He had expected a shy, virginal experience with fumbling and smiles and sweetness. Instead, he got a woman so accustomed to giving that her receiving was more potent than any apothecary's powder.

When he entered back into the kitchen, he was doing his best not to whistle. Neither Mrs. Bettleton nor Miss Persephone would meet his eye. Jack decided to sidestep the whole situation and go back to bed.

"You stupid boy," Mrs. Bettleton grumbled. The dough she was kneading took a hard pound from her fist. "Leading yerself around by yer britches, you'll be the ruin of us."

Jack turned on the stairs and returned to the kitchen out of respect. "We don't know what's going to happen. This might be worry for naught."

"Worry? Jack, that was an earl's daughter." Miss Persephone ran her hand around her chin. "If he decides to, he can void our lease, evict us, and throw us to the wolves."

"Or the hangman," grumbled Mrs. Bettleton.

"Oh, come now. No one has been hung for these sorts of things in years."

"Seven years," Miss Persephone corrected him. "1811. They hung the pretty one."

"You can't possibly believe that will happen to us." Jack looked at both of them, Miss Persephone staring at her cup, Mrs. Bettleton pounding the bread dough into submission.

"Jack." Miss Persephone sighed.

"I thought you liked her. I thought you wanted me to find love. You were excited to meet a real earl's daughter!" Jack felt like he was reeling drunk from one side where he got nothing but kindness and encouragement to this morning where he faced nothing but shame and recrimination.

"I didn't think you'd let her spend the whole night."

"I had to wake up to that woman pounding on the kitchen door. That was a fright," muttered Mrs. Bettleton. "She looks all class and elegance, but it's plain as day that she'd rather knock your teeth in than look at you."

"I apologize. I wasn't thinking." Jack felt terrible for scaring them, but he honestly didn't think they would get raided and shut down, let alone executed for running a molly-house in Drury Lane.

"Well, now's the time to start charging more money from our patrons. We've got to put together some blunt just in case. Miss Persephone, you spoke once of doing a piece of entertainment. What's the cost on that?" Mrs. Bettleton looked up, blowing a loose piece of her graying hair out of her face.

"I don't remember," she said. "Honestly, it's Jack's fault, he should be the one to come up with blunt."

"Blunt for what? Nothing will happen," Jack insisted.

"Bribes," Mrs. Bettleton said. "The magistrates I know are easily swayed if the number's right. So we need the right number several times. All I know is that a pile can save us from the worst of it."

"If money is what you're worried about, then we'll be fine. I have plenty," Jack said.

"That tiny wrinkled sack you have hanging underneath your bed? It's less impressive than the sack between your legs," Miss Persephone said. "It isn't enough. Not for this."

"You don't have to be an arsehole, *Bryan*," Jack said, throwing Miss Persephone's apprentice name back.

Miss Persephone finished her chocolate instead of answering.

"Fine. I'll finish the job for Lord Haverformore. It's a hefty sum."

"Get it done fast, then." Mrs. Bettleton tossed the dough back into a bowl to rise, dusted her hands on her apron, and turned away.

He climbed back up the stairs and went to lie in bed. It wasn't as bad as all that. He nestled back down under the blankets, smelling Agnes. This is the only place he wanted to be. Why couldn't he forget the world for one night and be selfish? He'd handle it, they'd see. There wasn't a fight yet that he hadn't been able to talk his way out of. Why would that change now?

AGNES STOOD IN THE DOORWAY OF HER FATHER'S study. She'd at least been able to wash up and change clothes and stuff a bit of bread and tea down her throat as she did so. Her maid gave her worried looks, but when Agnes asked what the trouble was, the maid merely shook her head.

It wasn't cowardice if one stood at the precipice for a long period of time. It was only cowardice to never jump. Delay was merely strategy. Agnes waited for her father to finish his task and notice her. Which he had yet to do. She had expected this kind of discipline to come from her mother, but her father's interference had a much more sinister implication.

She wondered how much Lydia had told them of the scene when she arrived. For that matter, why Lydia had gone to fetch her and not her mother.

Her father finally looked up from his task. "Agnes." His normally smooth brow and pleasant grin were replaced by lines and a haggard expression. This is what it took for her handsome father to finally look his age. It only compounded her feelings of guilt. He shuffled some papers and closed the accounting book. "Come in."

She crossed the threshold, wincing with every step.

"Close the door, please," he said, making her retrace her steps and walk the dreaded journey all over again.

She stood in the middle of the rug in front of his desk. It wasn't an intimidating desk, though it was large. He had been fond of carving objects when he was in the army, and some of those talismans sat on his desk now, on display. When she was little and Lydia refused to play with her or was having yet another exam, Agnes would creep down here and her father would let her play with the wooden carvings underneath his desk as he worked.

"You may sit. This will likely be a long conversation." He steepled his fingers, only to drop them and run them through his hair. "I have half a mind to scream myself hoarse at you."

"Yes Papa," she murmured.

"You cannot leave the house without informing someone of your whereabouts."

"Yes Papa."

"This was inconsiderate, selfish, and foolhardy. Not to mention dangerous."

"Yes Papa."

"And your mother and I are very angry with you. Very, very angry."

"Yes Papa."

Her father sat forward in his chair. "You aren't the daughter that is prone to rash action."

Agnes couldn't bring herself to look at him. Her shame was piling on top of her head so heavy that she felt as if she would drop through the floor.

"You are my practical miss. The one I can count on to have a cool head and an even temper. I'm not supposed to worry about you."

The weight of his stare was unbearable. Her skin flushed and sweat prickled under her arms. Tears blurred her vision.

"Agnes. My darling girl. What happened? Where did you go? Why did you go?" His voice went quiet, which only made her skin prickle in fear.

She couldn't answer any of these questions. There was nothing to say and also everything to say. It all led back to one thing: she loved Jack and Jack loved her. Tears began falling, heavy and full. She let them dampen her hands and did her best not to sniff.

"I know you left early, around nine. I know you went to Drury Lane in a hired hack. You stayed all night inside the Inn you went to. And I know that your sister roused you out of a bed this morning."

She didn't believe for a minute that was all he knew. Between him and Vasily and Lord knew what other resources he had, Agnes believed he knew the name of every single person who had been at the Inn last night. *Bill.* Lord Kinsley would not appreciate his activities being found out. He had specifically asked her to not speak of his presence, and now not only did she know, but so did her father and Vasily.

This was only getting worse. She wanted to crawl into a ball and hide forever.

"Agnes. Whose bed were you in?" His voice was low and dangerous. This was not the caring father who was asking. This was the vengeful, wrathful soldier that had been locked away for decades. "Look. At. Me."

Raising her head proved easy. Training her eyes to meet his was the difficult part. But she managed. And there was a fire in his eyes that she recognized in herself. It wasn't the long rage of her mother and Lydia. It was the cool, calculating anger that could be appeased but not forgotten. Her whole mouth felt dry and stuffed with cotton. She licked her lips. "Mr. Jack Townsend."

Her father nodded his head. "And your mother informs me that she warned you about him some time ago."

"Yes. At the Cuttingsworth ball."

"Have you been sneaking out to see him all this time?" The spark in his eyes burned furious.

"No. It wasn't until Mr. Arthur invited him to stay for dinner at his home on an evening I was visiting Lydia."

"And how does Mr. Arthur know him?"

"I don't know."

"Agnes."

"I don't know," she blurted. Had he decided that she was a liar? That nothing she said could be trusted? She had wiped out her good deeds with a single night? Surely that wasn't right.

"I'll be asking Mr. Arthur about his connections." Her father shook his head. "I'm angry, Agnes. Very angry."

"And you have every right to be." Could the deviousness that Lord Kinsley accused her of actually work to her favor here? It was worth trying, she had promised Jack that. "I have spent the night in the company of another. I am ruined. Should I not now wed him?"

His face turned bright red. "*That* was your end game? You wish to marry this rogue, so you spend the night with him in order to force my hand?" He exploded out of his chair and paced the room. He was shaking with rage. "I might have heard your entreaties before. I might have humored you and allowed him to continue to court you. I might have done many things, Agnes, but now all I wish is to have him in Newgate and you in a walled-up convent on the Canadian frontier."

She'd never heard of such a convent existing on the Canadian frontier but had enough sense to realize this was not the time to point it out. "He asked me to go home, Papa, he really did. I refused. This is my doing."

"You are damned right this is your doing." His pacing quickened. In his path, he swept up one of the wooden carvings—a horse she had particularly liked —and threw it hard against the built-in bookcase. "I can't believe you would do this, Agnes. And your mother asked me to handle this because I would be less angry."

"Which is understandable, and I—"

"Think, Agnes. Think. Use your head."

Her mind could do nothing but cringe in shame, interrupted only by her father's yelling.

"A man. Who works in a molly-house. What on God's green earth is he doing pursuing you?" He whirled back on her, as if he was mystified as to how stupid she was. "You know what a molly-house is, don't you? You spent the evening carousing at one."

"I didn't *carouse*," Agnes sniffed.

"Men prefer men in a molly-house. Why would Mr. Townsend waste his time on you if it weren't for your money or your connections?"

Her father had a fair point, although not all the facts. Was this something that she could reveal? It wasn't her secret to share. "That is something you will have to take up with Mr. Townsend."

"Go to your room. You'll take dinner there until further notice. No visitors. I'm so disappointed in you, Agnes."

The last sentence hit like a dagger. Taking meals in her room was no surprise. Nor was a restriction on visitors. But his disappointment loomed larger than any specter she'd ever faced. "May I be excused?"

"Go." He waved her away with his hand and then threw himself back down behind his desk. He picked up another of his wooden animals and flung it hard against the bookcase. This time, she heard it crack.

◈

LORD LORIAN DID NOT SEND FOR JACK THAT DAY. When Jack awoke from his morning nap, restless energy flooded him. What was he supposed to do? When would the man want to see him?

He worked the door that night, hoping that Bill would come in with some news. Anything. Had Agnes's father shipped her off to a faraway land as punishment? He wouldn't be surprised. Well, if he did, Jack would go after her.

By the end of the night, he realized his family would be the only way out of this. Lorian wouldn't respect his family here at the Inn, Mrs. Bettleton and Miss Persephone, but he would respect Jack's birth family. They weren't noble, nor would they ever be, but a firmly respectable trade family was something to be proud of. True, his father was not a rich sea captain, but he was worldly and educated in his own way. His mother was intelligent and charming and could easily hold her own in a drawing room with Lady Lorian. His brother. Well.

The Lorian name was plagued by scandal. A youngest daughter needed a respectable family to marry into, didn't she? Jack could supply that.

A shroud fell over the evening, and the last guest left at the ungodly early hour of midnight. They cleaned up and finished before one, none of them speaking.

"I'm going to bed," Jack said and the women nodded, as if they, too, thought it was a good idea.

He slept fitfully and woke early. Knowing this might be the only way to get in front of the bullet speeding towards him, he dressed and went to see his mother.

Ever the habitual early morning riser, his mother was in her dressing gown and at her desk, busy scribbling away when Jack opened the window and slipped in. Her pen clattered and ink splashed across the page.

"Jack, you scared me." One hand was on her chest and the other was grabbing blotting paper.

"How did I scare you? You're never scared when I visit." He eased himself in and then closed the window behind him.

"It's a good deal later than you usually come. I've already prepared my tea and everything." The tea tray sat on the small table, the steam rising up from the pot. Catching her breath, she looked him over as only a mother would. "I'll ring for another cup. You look like you need to talk."

He wished he could say *don't bother*, but it was true. His stomach was twisted in knots and he felt the long road of regret stretching out in front of him.

He'd made a hash of everything, and he needed to start repairing things fast.

Jack settled into the chair next to the fire as his mother returned to her seat at the desk. She finished blotting the letter and stowed her implements, as if she preternaturally understood that this would be a long discussion. "Now. Tell me everything."

"It's more than one thing," Jack said.

"Then tell me that, too. I have all day, and a fresh delivery of tea." She smiled and flicked her thick braid over her shoulder, as if she truly had no other plans.

So he did. He told her about Agnes—all about her. From her yellow stitch to the heartbreak in front of the Franklins' house to her rejection at the Cuttingsworth ball. Then the dinner at the Arthurs house and getting the herbwoman for her sister. Finally, about giving her his token and asking her to come to the Inn.

"And she came." His mother said it as a statement when Jack stopped to take a sip of tea.

"She did." He tried to feel regret that he'd asked her, but still, he didn't. Agnes's eyes when she realized what the Inn was, and who frequented it, were enough to keep him going until the end of his days. It wasn't only her in his bed—though it was spectacular. It was also introducing her to a world she needed to see, and the pride he took in being the one to show it to her.

So he told his mother about Mrs. Arthur dragging them out of bed the next morning.

"Oh, Jack. Hm." She took a sip of tea, something she did when she needed to think. "How is her family reacting?"

"I don't know yet. Mrs. Arthur told me their father would send for me when he was ready."

"And who is the father?"

Jack had purposely not told his mother exactly who these people were, not out of shame but out of habitual protection. That need for deniability ran deep at the Inn, but it was a double-edged sword. No identifiable names was good for secrecy, but it also fed the need to forget who they were on the other side of that door. No last names, no family, only the person standing there. It felt like freedom, until it felt like abandonment.

"Her father is Lord Lorian."

His mother's eyes went wide with recognition. "Jack," she sputtered, and in her one incredulous word, Jack heard her implication.

Lord and Lady Lorian were not names known for excessive spending or wild parties. They were a family known for philanthropy. Lorian had introduced bills in the House of Lords from advocating the end of slavery to lessening of the Bloody Code and establishing protections for orphaned children. He was a man known for fairness and compassion.

And Jack had just sullied his daughter.

His mother's hand crept over her mouth and she stared out the window, deep in thought. He knew that her mind ran fast, constantly calculating possibilities and games and outcomes. She couldn't help it—her mind did it of its own volition. Sometimes he was disappointed that she wasted her intellect on endless letters, but then, what should she turn herself to? Who would take her seriously, this wife of a sea captain?

"I have an idea. I don't know if it will work," Jack offered, even though he hated to interrupt her reverie.

"Let's hear it." She smiled brightly, as if they were discussing the possibilities for colors in a flower arrangement.

"They are a respectable family and thus they

would expect a respectable match. I've told them about you, and I was wondering if you would be willing to meet them?"

"As whom?"

"My mother." Jack didn't understand what she meant.

"And what exactly kind of mother am I to play?"

"No, Mama. No games, no playacting. You and Papa. I want my family."

"Only us?"

"Only you. I need you. I need you on my side." It was the first time he'd ever said such a thing. The first time he'd been willing to put a voice to it, but it was true. He wanted them. Needed them, especially now.

His mother sprang from her chair and flung her arms around him. She murmured endearments in his ear, and the smell of her, spices from her tea and the scent of her soap, surrounded him. He gripped her back, hanging on as if he were on a sinking ship. This morning, she smelled like peace.

Gradually, she disentangled herself, wiped her eyes, and returned to her chair. "I have one more question."

"I assumed you would have more. But what is it?" He sipped some tea, gone cool. The flavor was still exactly what he needed. Strong and dark and spicy and perfect.

"Does this invitation extend to Roland?"

Jack grimaced. He played with the handle of the teacup.

His mother contemplated him once more. "It's an open wound. Of course it will hurt. I can give my advice, but that's all I can do. And my advice is that you make up with him. He'll be dazzled by an acquaintance so lofty as an earl, and his position at Drummonds will make you seem more respectable.

He is so in love with his new baby that he cannot see straight. He's not the same man as he was."

She meant that he was not the same as the man who screamed at them both, wanting his mother to punish Jack until she'd beaten the deviant out of him. Wanting him to be publicly shamed in front of the house so that the whole neighborhood could witness Jack's humiliation. How angry he was when their parents refused. When his parents protected Jack instead of acquiescing to Roland's demands. And then, at the christening luncheon, to humiliate Jack in front of his in-laws, where he knew he could force Jack to slink away.

Jealous Roland. Seeing love and thinking it couldn't extend in an infinite way. That love for Jack didn't mean there was no love for Roland. Jack had always understood that a person loves in different ways. He loved both his parents, but his father received a love more distant and respectful, while the close love he felt for his mother was colored with camaraderie and friendship because they were so similar.

Is that what his mother meant? That having a child had opened a door in Roland's hard chest, and he finally realized that opportunities for Jack didn't automatically mean no opportunities for Roland? Then he shouldn't have humiliated Jack.

"I should go soon. I don't want to miss my summons from Lord Lorian."

"Of course."

"May I ask one more favor? Would you be willing to write a note to Lord or Lady Lorian, introducing yourself and us? I mean, as a family?"

His mother's face changed to one of joy. This was her specialty. "Do you have time to sit while I do so?"

"Can we ring for more tea?"

His mother waved him toward the bell next to the door, and she pulled out fresh paper.

She was done before Jack had finished a second cup of the new pot. "Already?" Jack asked as she waved the paper in the air to finish drying the ink. She blotted and sanded, though she hated sanding. Messy business and she didn't care for it.

"They are individualized for each, a subtle plea for you, and of course, announcing our respectability. Would you care to read them?"

Jack shook his head no. "I need to have plausible deniability of what's inside. That you wrote them and I didn't dictate them to you."

She murmured her understanding and folded them, labeling each in her careful, beautiful hand. "Let me know if I can help more."

Jack kissed her on the cheek. "Thank you, Mama. I'll let you know." He went to the window.

"It's a decent hour now. You can leave through the front door, if you like. I always worry about you and that tree."

He pulled a face and strutted to the door. "Thank you." Leaving by the front door meant the neighborhood could see him. He wanted to claim his family, and he wondered how long his mother had been trying to claim him but he hadn't let her.

16

Agnes was trying to read her book. She sat next to the window in her room. There was no sound to be found anywhere since her room faced the back of the house, overlooking the gardens. It should have been a perfectly suitable place to read. In fact, she'd read an inordinate number of books from this exact spot.

But there was no way to concentrate today. Not a single sentence stuck in her brain. All she could think about was Jack speaking with her father. And giant Vasily bodily hauling Jack out onto the street, Jack dangling from Vasily's massive paws.

A quiet knock on the door made Agnes jump out of her skin. "Come in," she called, expecting a tea tray or some such. Perhaps a copy of a contract from her father, revoking her dowry.

Instead, Lydia entered, holding a tea tray.

"I'm not supposed to have visitors," Agnes said, happy to see anyone at all.

"Of course you aren't. But I'm not a visitor. I'm a *spy*." Lydia set the tea tray down at the table in the sitting area. "Come now, I had my cook smuggle in some treats."

Lydia's cook was a far better pastry chef than her

parents', but not as good of a cook. Trade-offs were everywhere. Agnes snapped her book closed and hurried over.

"What kind of spy are you?" Agnes asked as Lydia poured two cups of steaming black tea.

"For our parents, of course. I'm to get you talking about your horrible mistakes, how you were coerced, etcetera, and then report back so that they may make their decisions in an informed manner."

"Sounds very underhanded."

Lydia dropped a lump of sugar in her tea and stirred. "It is dreadfully devious."

"What should I tell you?" Agnes asked, her eyes trained on her cup. Her heart thumped painfully hard against her chest. She loved that her sister was being *sisterly*, which was rare enough, but her shame felt like a powder that covered her head to toe. This was a different Lydia than the one who had fetched her the other morning.

"Whatever you like. I've already decided what to tell them. We could talk of the weather, if you prefer." Lydia uncovered a plate loaded with scones and biscuits.

"You seem like yourself again." It had been a bit slow coming on, and admittedly, Agnes had not been paying attention, but she realized that her sister's pallor was normal again. She no longer seemed puffy and swollen. Her personality was back—caustic, but not without cause. She had humor beneath it all, and that was the Lydia Agnes had missed.

"Yes, Mrs. Caldwell was worth her weight in gold. The teas are working beautifully, and while the moving about was difficult at first, now it invigorates me. Although, I still must eat liver every other evening for dinner, which is perfectly ghastly to choke down."

Agnes hid a smile. "I'm glad you are getting

better. I missed you. But only a bit."

"Bored, were you? And this is the kind of trouble you get into when I'm otherwise occupied, I see."

"Oh, no, I was only filling the role you left when you decided to become the invisible sister."

Lydia snorted and picked apart a scone. Agnes selected one of them herself, but while her stomach was empty, she couldn't quite bring herself to eat.

"Tell me about it," Lydia said.

"It?"

"Yes, *it*."

"What, precisely, are you referring to?" Agnes asked, the scone crumbling beneath her fingertips as she picked it apart, ostensibly to take a bite.

"Playing coy this early in the morning? I know you, Agnes, and you are devious as they come. This was obviously to force father's hand into letting you marry Mr. Townsend, who, by the way, may not be accepted at the altar."

It was Lydia's way of mentioning that she'd noticed Jack's body—that Jack was not legally a man. Although confusing at first, Agnes thought she understood Jack's point about wanting to be neither sex. Did it matter what was underneath his clothes? Why couldn't Jack be himself and flow as he required between proper tea-pouring and manning the door at the Inn? Did one really have to choose to be a man or a woman when finding items for London's lost?

"Only if the vicar doesn't know what is none of his business," Agnes said. Honestly, did a vicar demand every groom drop his breeches before marrying a couple? "It was a gamble," she continued. "But I want to be with Jack, and I needed to play as heavy a card as I could."

Lydia murmured her assent. "But perhaps a garden tryst, rather than creating a festival of pain for the entire family?"

"I never take half-measures." Agnes smiled, glad that her sister might be on her side.

"Of course not. That's not how we are made." Lydia took a sip of tea, as if the comment were a mere aside.

Agnes felt the words reverberate in her chest. They were the same, these two sisters. There was a common ground, and they could feel it. "He loves me, you know."

"Of course he does. During that dinner party, it was almost laughable the eyes he was making at you. We could barely maintain conversation."

"Was it that obvious?" Agnes asked, though very pleased by the whole idea that Jack could barely speak because of how much he longed for her. Something very romantic and satisfying about remembering the evening.

"You were encouraging him the entire time with your own version of it. John suggested we make a betting pool, but Pearl felt it would cheapen it."

"Did you ever expect me to run away with him?"

"To Gretna Green, yes. That was John's bet. Pearl thought he might court you properly and charm Mama in the process."

"What did you think?" Agnes was curious.

"Honestly?"

"Brutally honestly."

Lydia toyed with her teacup. "I thought you would sabotage yourself. Somehow, you would find something wanting, or something in yourself. I wasn't convinced you knew how to allow yourself to be happy."

Her speech caused Agnes to sit back in her chair. The comments didn't sting, but they had the ring of truth. The old Agnes, the one that carried on in secret with Mary Franklin, content to hide from the world forever—she would have sabotaged herself.

That is, if Mary Franklin hadn't already left because she wasn't enough. "I think the right person helps you become more than what you are, or at least, more than what you were before."

Lydia's smile was genuine and soft. "I couldn't agree more."

Agnes hesitated. "But you have the right person. What happened to you? Was it not enough?"

Her sister's expression changed. "A baby is bigger than anyone leads you to believe. It's an entangled mess of all things, including the babies that never come to be. Some women seem to bear the burden better than I could."

"Yes, but you'd had this baby. It was over."

"Oh, Agnes, it doesn't end after the birth. I don't want to detail the physical for you—it's much too gruesome—but even the rest of it. I knew there was a possibility of trouble afterwards. Mama warned me of that much, at least. But it was more than melancholia. Every time I closed my eyes, the nightmares returned. I couldn't sleep, and I'd wander to the nursery, terrified that our nurse accidentally smothered her or wrapped her too tightly. I didn't trust her or me or John. The turmoil was unbearable. I wanted to close my eyes forever and wink out of existence."

The thought of Lydia's pain anguished Agnes. She hadn't known, hadn't even a clue.

"My body was not my own, my mind was not my own. It brought back memories that I thought were left behind."

Agnes winced. "And now?"

"The tea for sleeping keeps me from the nightmares. The tea in the morning gives me energy to move my body. And the liver," Lydia shuddered, "has helped make me feel strong again. I'm not who I once was, but how could I be? I've been through the storm and come out the other side."

"I'm glad."

"I owe Mr. Townsend for finding Mrs. Caldwell." Lydia looked at her.

This was the reason for Lydia's change of heart. Mrs. Caldwell's stories and Jack's aid. Lydia owed him.

"And you as well, for asking. I didn't know how much I needed her. And you. I didn't know what to ask for, and you did."

"I only wanted to be useful."

"You were." Lydia sniffed and blinked rapidly. "Enough about me. Tell me about Jack. And the Inn. I'm very intrigued."

It was Agnes's turn to snort. "I'm sure you are." But instead of telling her sister about the Inn, she told her about Jack. About seeing him at the market and Miss Perry and the Women's Home. About how Jack knew her yellow stitch. She even told her sister about how Jack had kissed her hand at the Women's Home. She thought it would embarrass them both, but Lydia murmured her understanding of such a touch.

They talked until they reached the bottom of the teapot and the plate of scones and biscuits became crumbs. It was the closest Agnes had ever felt to her sister: the first time they had been equals in need and emotion.

⚜

AFTER LEAVING HIS MOTHER THAT MORNING, THE day had passed in agonizing fashion. Unable to return to sleep, Jack busied himself with light repairs at the Inn. He tossed on his old skirts and pinafore to clean. He fixed wobbly chairs and uneven tables. The worn-looking silk flowers were shuffled to the back of the vases and all the arrangements were dusted and fluffed. He found a pair of wine-soiled gloves stashed in one vase, a wine goblet in another, and a leather dildo in yet another.

He brought them all down to the kitchen to Mrs. Bettleton. "Put them in that box over there. I'll take care of them later."

A knock at the back door had them staring at each other. Mrs. Bettleton wore an expression of fear, which melted into apprehension. "I'll answer it," Jack said.

As he'd both anticipated and dreaded, it was an errand boy with his summons to see Lord Lorian. "I'll be there directly," he said to the boy. Jack looked down at his skirts and pinafore. "I mean, Mr. Townsend will be there directly."

Mrs. Bettleton maintained a cool expression.

"My lord has directed me to inform Mr. Townsend that there is a carriage waiting for him in the mews."

Ah. His lordship didn't want him dillydallying or making an escape. "I'll fetch him. Come in for a bite while you wait." He glanced over at Mrs. Bettleton, who nodded her permission, and Jack opened the kitchen door wider.

"Won't be a meal, mind you. But we can offer you some refreshment," Mrs. Bettleton grouched.

The boy entered cautiously and sat at the table, perched as if he might bolt at any moment. Jack went upstairs to clean up, changing into a waistcoat and trousers. He washed his face and neck and reapplied the darkening powder that accented his jaw and the cording in his neck. Lord Lorian needed to see him as reliable and strong, and there was nothing like a manly chin to convey that. He changed his shoes into the slightly raised heels he'd polished to a high shine.

Taller would help as well. He retied his cravat three times, something simple but elegant. Finally, he slid into his coat and grabbed the beaver skin hat.

Once he reached the bottom of the kitchen stairs, he found the boy elbow deep in scones and bread and butter. A large glass of milk, half drunk, was beside him. Mrs. Bettleton chattered away, making him feel welcome. They were speaking of gardens when Jack arrived. The boy looked positively disappointed.

"Oh, take it with you, child. I'll wrap it up for you." Mrs. Bettleton placed the half-eaten scone in a cloth along with another thick slice of bread. The boy shoved the rest of the biscuit in his mouth and gulped down the milk. He wiped his mouth with the back of his sleeve, accepting the package from Mrs. Bettleton.

"You should sell those biscuits, missus. They're better than most," the boy said, his voice sincere.

"Just you bring back my cloth."

"Come on, now. I'm ready to go." Jack ushered the boy out the back door, feeling a kind of kinship with him. He'd been an errand boy. Sometimes still was. A treat like this was rare and welcome.

The boy clambered out past Jack and opened the gate first, revealing the carriage. The menacing Vasily sat on the driver's perch, staring Jack down as he opened the door. The boy took a seat up front with Vasily.

A carriage. It was a power play from Lord Lorian. A reminder of the earl's wealth and status and Jack's lack thereof. Not to mention it kept him concealed from the public.

When they arrived at the Lorian house in Mayfair, Jack was escorted to his lordship's study. The room itself was lush in hardwood, polished to show the fine grains. It smelled of books, ink, and beeswax. Lord Lorian stood near the empty hearth, his hands behind his back, in deep discussion with Mr. Arthur and Lord Andrepont.

Jack was surprised to see the other men here. He'd assumed his verbal whipping would be a private affair. The butler bowed slightly, announcing Jack's presence. For his part, he bowed as well, figuring as much scraping as he could do would be beneficial.

"Mr. Townsend," Lord Lorian greeted him. Deep lines were beginning to etch his forehead, and a wrinkle between his brows seemed to threaten permanence. Gray touched the sides of his hair, but it lent him a distinguished air that made him all the more imposing.

"My lord." Jack bowed again.

"You remember these gentlemen," he said, gesturing to Andrepont and Arthur.

"Indeed, my lord, sir." Jack acknowledged them both. They inclined their heads back at him.

There was stony silence as Lorian moved across the room to his desk. "They are here not only because they are family but because they both believe we should place confidence in your good intentions."

Involuntarily, Jack's eyes skated back over to them.

"Which is helpful for you as my inclination was to use every power that I possess to punish you ruthlessly." Lorian sat down at the chair behind his desk, extending a hand to invite Jack to sit in one of the chairs opposite the desk. Jack did so, but not entirely willingly. His instinct was to flee, but he knew he could not.

"You've bewitched my daughter. Beguiled her. No one has ever done so, and that alone should single you out. But you have gone about it in the most vile way possible."

Vile? What happened between Agnes and him had never once been vile. It made it sound as if Jack had forced himself on her. Or kidnapped her. "Pardon, my lord, but you speak as if Agnes had no agency of her own."

"She's a child," Lorian spat.

"She's twenty."

The fact stilled in the air between them. Surely Lorian knew the age of his own daughter?

"She was an innocent," he whispered.

"And she still is," Jack said, meaning it in a metaphorical sense. But Lorian gave him a look of disdain.

"My other daughter assures me that she pulled Agnes from your bed."

Jack winced.

"My lord," Mr. Arthur said, crossing from the sitting area by the hearth to the desk. "Agnes has been happier in the last few weeks than I've ever seen her. I know that Mr. Townsend has been the reason for this. Both my sister and Lydia have witnessed their interactions in our drawing room and assure me that nothing is untoward. In fact, Mr. Townsend is responsible for finding aid for Lydia's illness after the baby."

"Of course, as his job. His finding of things, as it were." Disdain was clear in Lorian's voice.

"He did not charge us, my lord. And the woman he brought has wrought a miracle on my wife." Mr. Arthur spoke with familiarity, despite the distance his polite words maintained.

"And you, James? Do you also have bolstering of his character? Have you witnessed him running out of a burning fire with a puppy?"

Andrepont shrugged, moving across the floor like a cat. His nonchalance was practiced and fluid. It prickled the hair on the back of Jack's neck. All he could think of was the stories of the father. How charming he must have been to have a face like that.

"In truth, I barely know this man. But I have heard from several different and separate quarters that he is someone to be trusted with discretion and valor." Andrepont flicked his gaze over to Jack, his green eyes fairly piercing Jack's skin.

Lorian stared at Jack, which he took to mean it was his turn to speak.

"My lord, what happened was not how I intended to woo Lady Agnes. True, I invited her to the Inn so that she might see where I worked and understand the world in which I have lived the past decade. I did not do so with the intent to steal her away from you. And certainly I did not intend, when I made the invitation, that she would, ah..." Jack cleared his throat. "Spend the night. What occurred was not a manifestation of disrespect but the blindness of love."

There was silence in the room so deep that Jack could discern each man's breathing.

"I am a man of wealth, Mr. Townsend. I've been aware of fortune-hunters of both sexes as I've looked to favorable matches for my children."

"My lord, I assure you that I am not—"

"I am not done, Mr. Townsend. Do not interrupt." Lorian stared him down. All Jack could do was nod. "I have not always possessed wealth. I was a young man without means for many years. I had enough to buy a commission, and that is what I did. When I returned to London, I sold my commission, and I thought about trying to marry a wealthy heiress in order to solve my problems. I was a third son, far enough down the line that I never had a moment's thought I would inherit this title and wealth. I have sympathy for your status."

There was silence, so Jack looked up. "I've been in love with Lady Agnes for years. Since I saw her donating gowns at the Women's Home."

Mr. Arthur gave a small, supportive chuckle.

"My wife says you are from a respectable family."

"Yes, my lord." Jack scooted forward in his chair, pulling his mother's letters from his internal breast pocket. "These are from my mother."

"Not your father?" Lord Lorian took the letters, setting aside the one addressed to Lady Lorian. Then he pulled reading glasses from his breast pocket.

"My father is a sea captain and is not due back until next week. However, I'm sure he would welcome anyone looking into his reputation. He's a decent man." Hope flourished in Jack's heart. If Lorian was looking into Jack's family, there was a possibility that he might allow Agnes to marry Jack.

Lorian nodded, unfolding the letter. "I assume you know its contents?"

"I do not."

Lorian nodded as he read. "Your mother is a poetic writer."

"It is what she loves." Jack hoped his mother's charm and wit came through.

"One last question, Mr. Townsend, and then I will tell you what will happen."

A lump the size of St. Paul's Cathedral formed in his throat. "Of course."

"Is there a possibility that my daughter could be with child?" Lorian glared hard enough to turn Jack to stone.

It took a lot to make Jack blush, but this question did the job. "No, my lord. Not a chance."

Lorian stared at him harder. Relenting only to refold the letter. "At the suggestion of my nephew, we will have a dinner. You will invite your parents. It will be held at Andrepont's house in order to give us neutral ground. If, and I cannot stress this enough, *if* you succeed in impressing me and my wife, I will allow you to continue to court my daughter. In four months' time—and I say four months because it is convenient for me—if she still feels this way about you, and you have not shown yourself to be a fortune hunter or otherwise undesirable, I will consent to *discussing* a marriage contract. Is this understood?"

"Yes. my lord. Thank you, my lord." Jack's hands were shaking. This was better than he could have hoped for. This was big. This was bigger than big. He would have to tell Mrs. Bettleton and Miss Persephone not to worry about money for bribes to keep them safe. Jack would keep them safe.

"Don't make me regret this."

"I won't, my lord."

Lorian let out a sigh like this had been some sort of tough negotiation and not a thorough set-down for Jack. "You may go. But you'll have to see yourself home. I have other plans for my carriage."

"Of course, my lord. Thank you again."

"And you're not to see my daughter in any unsupervised manner ever again. You may call on her tomorrow afternoon during normal visiting hours."

"Yes, my lord." Jack stood, wanting to cast up his accounts and jump in the air all at once.

"I'll show him out," Andrepont said, following Jack out of the room.

As they reached the dim hallway, Andrepont put his arm around Jack's shoulders. Their size difference was notable. "You have friends in the oddest places."

"Do I?" Jack asked. Andrepont smelled of clean sweat. Only athletes smelled that way. Jack knew the man boxed, and it made him seem all the more menacing.

"If I didn't trust those people with my life, I wouldn't have stood for you. But on their insistence, I did. Something is strange about you, and I can't put my finger on it. I don't like puzzles I can't solve."

"Who does?" Jack asked. They arrived at the

foyer, where a footman retrieved Jack's hat and gloves.

"Let's hope your strangeness is something we can all live with. If we are to become family, after all." Andrepont's smile should have been encouraging, but instead, Jack had to suppress a shiver. "Good day, Mr. Townsend. I'll send round an invitation to dinner with specifics later on."

Jack gave a bow to show respect. "Thank you. For both your support and for being willing to have a dinner to give me a chance."

"Yes. Well. My mother hates playing hostess. Thank her when you get the opportunity." Andrepont turned and ambled away.

Jack popped his hat on and slid on his gloves, and the footman opened the door. He knew it was courtesy, but he couldn't help but feel like he'd gotten the boot.

AGNES HAD ALREADY PUT ON HER DRESSING GOWN. It was late—the tray that held her dinner had long since been cleared. Her sister's visit had invigorated her, made her feel like they were on the same side for once. And Lydia had come to Agnes's aid, not the other way around!

She heard a soft scratching at her door.

"Are you up?" Her mother asked through the door.

Agnes flung the door open, anxious for any kind of news regarding her imprisonment.

"Oh, good." Her mother was still fully dressed for dinner. But instead of a warm, welcoming expression, she was all polite and cold. Agnes's heart sank. Her parents were still angry. This wouldn't give her the happy ending she'd hoped for. "Join us in the drawing room."

"I'm not dressed," Agnes said, holding out her arms.

Her mother didn't wait for her. "It'll do. It's only your father and me."

Agnes grabbed a candle and drifted down the dark hallway after her. The servants had all gone to bed, and the candles that would light their hallway had already been snuffed. She felt exposed in her dressing gown, and she pulled her wrap tighter around her shoulders.

Her father was in the drawing room, hair mussed and a drink in hand, which was unlike him. He was a man of moderation in all things, including good wine or even a dram of spirits. She glanced to the side table where a second glass sat. Even her mother had been drinking in the drawing room. It was as if the entire world was collapsing in on itself. What had she driven them to?

"Good evening, Agnes," her father greeted, running his hand through his hair, showing Agnes how it had become mussed in the first place.

"Good evening, Papa." She sat in the chair opposite the sofa. Her mother sat down next to her father, grabbing her glass as she sat down.

Dear Lord, her mother was drinking in front of her. What would the rest of the *ton* think?

"We would like to speak with you regarding your, your..." Her father stumbled on the words.

"Antics," her mother supplied.

"With Mr. Townsend."

Agnes folded her hands in her lap, preparing herself for another tongue-lashing.

"We are not happy with your behavior. Rather than continuing to rehash our unhappiness and disappointment, we've decided that it's much more prudent to make a plan for the future, with your actions born in mind."

Agnes looked up. There was hope that she might one day be allowed to have sunshine on her face once again.

"Mr. Townsend assures me that there is no way you might be *enceinte*. Is that true?" Her father looked as if he might toss up his accounts.

Agnes blushed beet red from her feet to her hair and looked to her mother for help. But she only raised her eyebrow, as cool as could be, and suddenly Agnes realized where Lydia had inherited it. Sweat prickled at her scalp. "There is no possible way for me to be with child."

"You can't trust that. She couldn't possibly know the treachery that men may employ, the things they might say," her mother said, taking a gulp of claret, or possibly port.

"I'm not a child, Mama," Agnes said sharply. If only she could assure them that there truly was no possible way that Jack could sire a child ever. But that stance would surely backfire. "And I assure you, no possible way. None."

"We must trust her at some point," her father murmured.

"Why? She's certainly not proving to be trustworthy. She lied about a megrim and then crept off into the night alone."

"And before that, I did everything anyone ever asked of me. I performed endless hours of charity work, went to countless thoroughly unenjoyable balls for Lydia's sake. All I've ever done has been for other people, and the one time I take the initiative that Lydia has had her entire life, I'm suddenly not trustworthy? How low an opinion you must have of me."

"Can you be so ungrateful?" her mother

thundered. "The countless gowns, new gloves, new dancing slippers—not that you ever appreciated those efforts. I've done all I could to entice you to live a full life, and every time, you've turned away, preferring your needlework to polite conversation."

"With men who were courting my fortune, not me. They should have delivered those flowers to Papa themselves."

Her father barked out a laugh, but her mother shot him a look of disdain. "Do not encourage her."

"Our dear girl has a point. If she were not our daughter, and instead a man at trial, would they not take the man's prior good deeds and character into consideration?"

Agnes was both honored that her father might be so gracious as to allow her good deeds into consideration and insulted that he thought of her as a criminal.

"But this isn't a court—this is my house." Her mother threw back the last drops of the contents of her glass with the expertise of an inveterate gambler.

Papa shook his head. "We've already come to a decision, so we needn't torture the poor girl any longer."

Agnes's heart reacted to the words first, skipping faster and making her feel light-headed.

"I've met with Mr. Townsend. He delivered letters of introduction from his mother to both of us. I've looked into his father, who is, in fact, a respected sea captain. And, both James and John have come forward to vouch for his good character."

While she was glad to hear all of this, grateful that Jack was coming up to scratch, she was put out that *her* belief in his good character seemed to count for naught.

"I've never believed that money was the measure of a man, and I can't very well hold Jack to a standard that I myself would have failed when I was his age. While I'm still extremely angry about how you handled this courtship, I will allow it to continue."

She let out a breath she didn't know she'd been holding. For the first time that day, tears threatened to fall, this time of happiness.

"Supervised by your mother, of course. He may continue to visit here, but you are not to go anywhere with him, supervised or not."

"Vasily told us about your day at the market," her mother said. "I don't trust who you are with him, Agnes. You are normally such a cautious, practical girl. With him you are reckless. Wild even." Her mother frowned, and wrinkles that Agnes had never seen before appeared between her eyebrows.

"It isn't recklessness," Agnes said. "It's that I've never wanted anything more in my life."

"I'm giving it four months," her father said, ignoring her comment. "In four months' time, if you still feel the same way, and if we are suitably impressed by him and his family, then I am willing to entertain the idea of a marriage contract. But I can't guarantee it will be favorable."

"Why four months?" Agnes asked.

"Because it is convenient for me, and I had to come up with some time frame. Would you rather I make it six?"

"No," Agnes answered quickly.

"We will be having dinner at James's house at the end of the week with our family and Mr. Townsend's."

"But she hates having dinner parties," Agnes said.

Papa threw his hands up in the air as if he were sick of answering that particular question. "James suggested it. I don't know why. But it seemed a good idea, so we shall do it. I'm giving you what you want, Agnes, even when I don't want to. Be grateful."

"Yes, Papa. Thank you."

"I still think this is a terrible idea," her mother said.

Agnes stared at her hands, hoping that if she didn't move, her father's plan would stand and her mother's objections wouldn't sway him.

"We've made a plan, announced it to all parties. As far as I'm concerned, the boy has four months to prove himself worthy while I turn over every stone to prove him otherwise. If you like, Agnes, you may tell him that."

Hope was a seed in her belly, though nothing her parents had said nourished it. She couldn't be happier that they would give Jack a chance. However, it seemed more like they were setting him up to fail. But she could help him, coach him through what would impress them. If, in the end, they were able to be together.

Before her fantasies swept her away, she asked to be excused.

"Of course," her father said, all good humor, as if all things were right in the world.

"Good night, Agnes. You may be free of your room tomorrow. Come to the drawing room after you break your fast. We'll welcome your sister and the babe for a visit in the afternoon, and you may continue on with mending dresses for the Women's Home. It isn't the fault of those poor women that you have behaved in a reckless manner."

"Yes, Mama." Agnes stood, and given the fraught nature of the conversation, gave a formal curtsy as was their due as earl and countess. "Good night."

She retreated, wondering what a marriage to Jack might look like, but also wondering if she had ruined her relationship with her parents forever.

17

The ride to James's estate was stony at best. Agnes was dressed in her very best gown, actual slippers and not her boots, and a new pair of gloves. She would be meeting Jack's parents for the first time, and it had her nerves all ajangle. Jack had called on her a number of times, but each visit was the requisite fifteen minutes or less and had absolutely no moment for private conversation. It felt more like Jack was calling on her mother than on her.

She wasn't sure if she'd be able to eat tonight. Since Lady Andrepont disliked throwing dinner parties, Agnes hoped the menu would be light so she could pick at her meal and escape notice. But they were now one week closer to being together. One week closer to a life together, whatever that might be.

Her father gazed out the carriage window. Looking every inch the earl he was, his lordship would require nothing but the most formal address this evening. Papa was hoping to make Jack run scared. Her mother looked equally foreboding. She'd even retrieved the jewels from the safe. A fat ruby sat smugly around her neck, surrounded by pearls. It was an inherited family piece, the sort of finery that would inspire envy in most Peers, let alone the untitled.

They pulled up to the Andrepont home, and already there were two carriages there. The guest list included Lady and Lord Kinsley, whom Jack knew as Bill. Agnes was relieved that someone there might be on their side since James didn't seem to be very enthusiastic. Of course, the Arthurs would also attend.

A liveried footman ushered them upstairs to the drawing room, where Lady Andrepont was holding court. She was the younger sister of Agnes's mother, and beautiful in a harder sort of way. She had the same dark hair and high, angled cheekbones, but her dark eyes were hooded and assessing. Though James looked so much like his father, his mannerisms were very much like his mother's. His parentage could never be in doubt.

Jack was already there with his parents. He looked resplendent in an emerald green waistcoat embroidered with gold thread. He wore old-fashioned breeches, which were clearly an acknowledgement of the event's formality and importance. Trousers at a dinner like this would have been fashionable, but breeches were respectful of their parents' set. Jack's father wore formal dress as well, but he looked most uncomfortable. It wasn't surprising since he was likely far more comfortable in wool. Still, his blue eyes were insightful and hawkish, as if nothing could escape his notice. The lines in his face were etched deep and his jowls were beginning to see the weight of time's passage. Even in breeches, he looked a capable and reliable captain. Exactly the person Agnes would want to see guiding a ship.

Jack's mother was surprisingly beautiful. Not that Agnes had expected her to be plain, but her dark hair was thick and plaited and pinned in an exquisite manner. The pins were gold, or perhaps gold-plated, but they winked this way and that as she turned her head. Her skin was darker than the rest of theirs, and the richness of her emerald green gown made her seem to glow. In the company of her mother, her aunt, and this woman, Agnes felt the familiar sensations of envy and plainness.

"James is showing the Arthurs his lair. They shall rejoin us in a moment," Lady Andrepont said before entering into formal introductions.

Jack's parents acquitted themselves well, and Agnes was desperate to tell Jack how beautiful his mother was. It was strange to have an urge to say it, but she wanted to somehow reassure him that while her parents had the wealth and finery of generations behind them, his parents were dazzling in their own way.

James arrived with Lydia and John in tow.

"There you are, darling," Lady Andrepont said, bringing them into the conversation. Another round of introductions was made, and Agnes noticed that Jack's father was much more relaxed dealing with John than with anyone else.

Lydia was looking well—her shine had returned. Agnes couldn't help but look at John, remembering what Lydia had said about having one's person. John gave something to Lydia that no one else could. Made her feel special and safe and loved. Was that what Jack did for her?

Yes. And she hoped she gave that in return.

"I think we are waiting on Kinsley, then," James announced.

A footman came around with aperitifs for everyone to enjoy. Agnes took a glass even though she had no intention of drinking it. Her hand trembled as she lifted it from the tray, a stray drop falling to the carpet below. When she looked up, she saw Jack watching her. He gave her an encouraging smile, as if to say, *this agony was worth it.*

If the ordeal ended with them being married, having a place of their own, a life to forge out of nothingness, it would be worth the crucible. The weight of her ancestors, of titles and wealth and expectation, would be lifted from her shoulders. Such a prize was worth fighting for.

❧

THIS COULD VERY WELL BE THE WORST EVENING OF Jack's entire life. On the surface, it might appear delightful. Dinner at a fancy residence, company of powerful people, the woman he loved.

But it was torture.

First: Agnes's parents. Thunderous in their expressions and god-like in their full dress, Jack was surprised his eyes didn't burn out of his skull while looking at them. Mere mortals weren't allowed to gaze upon those so lofty. The ruby at Lady Lorian's throat was obscene: half the size of his fist and red like blood. She wore a muslin gown that was gossamer thin over a sheath of red so it looked as if she had somehow birthed that ruby herself.

Then the cool gaze of Lord Andrepont, assessing Jack, examining him. Jack wasn't sure what the man was looking for, but he didn't like the scrutiny.

But above all that, he was finally in the house where the art portfolio likely sat. It was here, he could bloody well feel it. If he retrieved it, he would have enough money to either protect Miss Persephone and Mrs. Bettleton if the Lorians disdained him or set up himself and Lady Agnes at a respectable address if they did not. If he didn't retrieve it, Mr. Wycliff would turn Jack in to the magistrate, which would possibly land not only Jack but also Miss Persephone and Mrs. Bettleton in jail. There was no way Agnes's parents would allow her to associate with him after that. There was no winning the day.

When else would he be in this house? When else could he get his hands on a dead man's sketches? And was it really stealing if the family didn't want them anyway?

Kinsley arrived with his wife. As Jack suspected, Bill acted as if they'd never met, which was fine by him. The wife, however, surprised him. She was a pleasant-looking woman, younger than Jack imagined. Her hair was dark blonde, perhaps brown, with honey-colored streaks evident in the strands that were pulled up in an elaborate chignon. But she wore spectacles.

Spectacles!

The tone shifted once again in the drawing room as introductions were made. Jack swiftly realized that Lady Kinsley took up Andrepont's attentions. No longer the subject of the green-eyed scrutiny, Jack relaxed. Interesting. Perhaps this is why Bill spent some evenings at the Inn instead of at home.

Lady Kinsley immediately sought out Agnes, while Mrs. Arthur dramatically hid her annoyance. This was clearly a group of people who knew one another well, and Jack and his parents were interlopers. This dinner was not the even playing field Lord Lorian had assured him of.

Fact: Lorian didn't play fair.

Not that Jack did either. This was a company where half believed him to be Jack, a man, and the other half believed him to be a woman. Which, in a strange sort of way, was exactly what he'd been hoping for his whole life. To be seen as both, or rather, neither. Someplace in between skirts and stays and breeches and cravats. But it was enough to make him sweat and hope that no one addressed this directly. Fortunately, the English were not known for direct dinner party conversations.

Dinner was announced, and the company hushed, silently making their order of precedence in their head. It grated to see their nobility in practice. Kinsley, being a marquis—a bleeding marquis!— escorted the hostess, Lady Andrepont, into the dining room. It was all so fucking predictable, but at least Jack was allowed to escort Lady Agnes into the dining room, with his parents processing behind them.

The dining room was predictably gorgeous. Another room that was meant to intimidate, and judging by the looks of awe on his parents' faces, it was working. A chandelier filled with beeswax tapers dominated the room. The aroma of roasted meat, fine wine, and the faint mix of vinegar polish reverberated, occupying Jack's senses as he sat down. A footman pushed in his chair behind him.

The table was set with silver and a bone china place setting so fine Jack could have picked up the plate and seen Mrs. Arthur across from him. Instead of a centerpiece for décor, a massive roast sat there, its juices collecting into the tray. His mouth watered at the sight of it. How polite would it be to ask to forgo all the other food and go straight to this massive beef roast? Jack didn't eat much on the regular, far too busy, but he loved roast beef. Loved it to distraction, and rarely ate it. Of course, here in Hell, where conversation could expose him at the drop of a hat, where he must concentrate on Agnes and not fall victim to the calling of the art portfolio he'd promised to steal, he must wait and drool over a beef roast. Holy hell, this was agony.

A light broth was served first, refreshing and pungent, not the usual fare of a dinner party, judging by the pleased looks on the faces of all the dinner guests. It had a hint of ginger and saltiness that one might find in more Eastern fare, but light and lemony.

"Oh, thank God it isn't turtle soup," Mr. Arthur said.

"Language," Mrs. Arthur said, even though she seemed to actually giggle.

Talk was sparse, even though that was why they all sat around this table. Wasn't Kinsley here to grease the wheels? Jack gave the man a hard stare as the bowls were cleared and the next course was brought. Finally, the marquis, the highest-ranking man at the table, and probably in at least several square miles, cleared his throat and smiled.

"Captain Townsend, then? What sort of trade do you do? You must be a busy man."

Jack winced and prayed his father wouldn't answer the question. If Mr. Arthur couldn't blaspheme in peace at this table, then his father's business was not polite dinner conversation. Not here. Not with these people.

"Dung. Excrement." His father dug into the fish that had been placed in front of him.

"Pardon?" The marquis fairly choked.

"Which kind?" Lady Kinsley asked, leaning forward.

Dear Lord, the woman may have saved his neck. And indeed, she did. While his father documented the various excrement that he bought and sold across the world, some for fertilizer, some for munitions, Lady Kinsley forewent her fish course and asked questions about the chemical composition of different animal excrement and its uses.

The rest of the party flew through the fish course in an effort to ignore the fact that dung was discussed in detail for a quarter of an hour to great aplomb by a marchioness and a sea captain. Jack could barely contain a smug grin.

"We are extremely pleased to meet your parents, Mr. Townsend, but I believe you also said you had a brother and a sister. Yet no one had an address to which I could have sent an invitation." Lady Andrepont was as cool and collected as her sister. She was like this room, beautiful and glittering, designed to intimidate.

Jack cleared his throat, but his mother jumped in first. "Yes, we have an older child, Roland Townsend. Recently a father, you know." Her face beamed at her own good fortune. "Busy as a bee, that one. He works at Drummonds. Charmed his supervisor so much he married his daughter! Lovely girl. We couldn't be more pleased."

"Sounds like charming company. And your sister, Mr. Townsend?" Lady Andrepont cocked an eyebrow so high Jack thought it might fly off her perfectly sculpted face.

"I met her myself," Lady Lorian said, her eyes boring into Jack.

Jack's parents exchanged a worried glance.

"We don't often discuss Guinevere," Jack said. Silence blanketed the room.

"As a working man myself, there is honor in finding an occupation that fills not only a need but also fulfills a personal calling," Mr. Arthur said, glancing about. Jack could have kissed the prizefighter for trying to save them.

More throats were cleared, and finally the beef roast was hoisted off the table to be cut on the sideboard and delivered by the white-gloved footmen. Wine was once again switched out and refreshed. Lady Andrepont and Lady Lorian did their best to stimulate conversation, but given the awkwardness of the company, it did not go well.

Finally the cheese and nuts appeared on the table. No one so much as picked at them, eager as they were to relieve the agony. Lady Andrepont excused herself and the ladies to tea in the drawing room. Remaining with the men at the dinner table, Jack picked at the walnuts on the serving dish. The butler appeared to offer port, and in an effort to seem congenial under the now watchful eye of Andrepont, Jack accepted a glass.

"I swear, Andrepont, you serve enough wine to drown a horse." Mr. Arthur stood, ambled over to the long credenza, and took out a chamber pot. He undid the fall of his breeches, and with his back to the company, began to piss.

Jack knew this was common practice at even this kind of dinner party, but it still unnerved him. Would he also be expected to do this? The sound of it hitting the pot made Jack squirm, but everyone else ignored it.

"You aren't forced to drink everything that is poured for you," Andrepont said.

"Can't not, you know that. Growing up like I did, I'll eat every scrap presented to me and guzzle every cup." Mr. Arthur finished his business and buttoned up his fall. "You know what I mean, don't you Jack?"

Jack's father turned to him, his eyes wide. Knowing that a famous prizefighter addressed him by his first name. Lord Lorian said nothing during all this time, his eyes cool and watchful.

"Is that why you're developing such a paunch?" Andrepont challenged before Jack could answer.

Mr. Arthur put his hands over his stomach. "It isn't a paunch."

"You're getting slow," Andrepont said.

"I'd say let's go down to your gym and settle this right now, but fortunately for you, there are guests."

Mr. Arthur sat back down in his chair and gazed at his half-full cup.

"I don't think our guests would mind. In fact, I think they would love to participate, wouldn't you, my lord?" Andrepont turned to Lord Lorian, purposefully not looking at Jack.

Jack suddenly realized that Andrepont was orchestrating this conversation, right down to baiting Mr. Arthur. Jack wasn't sure he could talk his way out of this one.

"Let's not. After so much wine, it isn't as if anyone will make a good showing," Kinsley said, shooting a perplexed glance at Jack.

"If Kinsley is out, then we're uneven with only five men. I'll call Vasily up and we can partner off." Lorian finished his port, set down the glass, and looked at Jack.

Oh. The whole evening was a setup. Of course it was. These people didn't like him and wanted to show him his place. Well, Jack had managed to calm Vasily's fists once. He could certainly do it again.

"What say you, Captain Townsend?" Andrepont asked.

Jack's father looked chuffed. "I'd be honored to see the great Corinthian John spar close up. I don't get to the mills much, being at sea so often."

"See?" Mr. Arthur said. "I'm great. Captain Townsend said as much."

"Jack?" Andrepont asked him, ignoring Mr. Arthur's boast.

Jack shrugged. What was he going to say? "Lead the way."

"Splendid." Andrepont didn't sound as enthusiastic, he sounded like a predator catching its prey.

AGNES LOVED JACK'S MOTHER. EVERYTHING ABOUT
her. The luscious, thick hair coiled and pinned with
gold, her scent of jasmine and something unfamiliar
that Jack also carried. Her eyes, large and dark,
darting to follow every speaker, taking in every bit of
their surroundings. Agnes even loved her habit of
nodding and giving a quiet, melodic *mm* in response
to others' comments at more frequent intervals than
any of them were accustomed to.

They all nestled in the drawing room, thankfully
away from the men, who had made the entire dinner
far more awkward than was necessary. Agnes could
practically hear her father and James rubbing their
hands together in anticipation of making Jack
uncomfortable.

She felt guilty leaving Jack there with them, but
she figured that Jack had his father, and Mr. Arthur
was always a champion for the common man, and
that was certainly what Jack was, wasn't he? Of a sort.

The tea was good, served in delicate bone china
edged in an elegant gold band. With all the women in
their finery, it felt even more sophisticated to be
sitting here with her mother and aunt. It was the first
time Agnes felt like an equal. Somehow, having a
potential mother-in-law elevated her. She liked the
sensation but resented that it took having Jack in her
life to achieve it.

"How lonely that must have been to raise children
alone with your husband at sea all the time," Lady
Andrepont said.

Mrs. Townsend shook her head. "It may sound
that way, yet it wasn't. I am a fortunate soul who
doesn't experience the sensation." Her smile slid into
view and her confidence grew once more. "I must
admit my infatuation with correspondence. My
family is scattered across the globe. I daresay I think
the need to travel may be a familial shortcoming,

though it skipped me. But corresponding with my family from all corners brings comfort."

"I would imagine so. How fortunate you are," Agnes said. "You have traveled then?"

"Some," Mrs. Townsend said. "I was born and raised in India, which is how I met Captain Townsend. After we married, we settled here, in London."

"Away from your family," Agnes said.

"Yes, in a way. But London is the hub of the world. I had a better chance of seeing family by moving here than by staying where I was. Trade takes you nearly everywhere, and a letter can follow."

"That's a very lovely sentiment." Lady Andrepont smiled. "I wish we were all such prolific letter writers."

❦

ANDREPONT LED THEM DOWN THE HALL, PAST THE drawing room where Lady Agnes sat with Jack's mother, down the stairs, and into what anyone else would use as a ballroom. It clearly had once been a ballroom, with glass-paned doors and a sweeping veranda where all sorts of couples could stand and talk in full view of approving chaperones. Chandeliers held a handful of tallow candles, none to capacity. The scent of sweat and animal fat lingered in the room.

This was a room to intimidate on an entirely different level. A straw-filled dummy sat in one corner, and there were weights on pulleys in another. Garish black tar paint marred the floor, outlining a ring of sorts. Vasily and a footman entered behind them. The footman carried a basin and a large ewer of water.

"How shall we pair off?" Andrepont asked.

"This is dreadfully unnecessary," Kinsley said, still holding his glass of port, having carried it down from the dining room.

"Let the old men spar. Vasily and I have a long history together." Lorian had already crooked his finger at the Russian, and they went to a far end.

Mr. Arthur locked eyes with Kinsley and seemed to suddenly realize there was a game afoot. "Captain Townsend, I would be happy to go a round with you."

Jack's father seemed in heaven at the idea of it. "You'll be gentle, won't you? I can keep my crew in line, but I'm not one for fancy footwork."

"We can work on that, if you like. I'm not a bad instructor, if I do say so myself."

"I'd be honored, sir."

Andrepont turned his sharp gaze on Jack. "Well, then, it looks like we'll be squaring off."

"How convenient," Kinsley said flatly from behind them.

Jack steadied his expression. His whole body wanted to run. The other men began shucking their dinner jackets and waistcoats.

"Quite." Andrepont took off his coat without losing eye contact with Jack.

Ah, it was a simple game of domination, was it? Fine. Jack kept the man within his sights as well, letting his heavy coat fall from his shoulders. He unbuttoned his waistcoat as well. The blunt he'd parted with for this gold thread was ridiculous. But he wanted—no, needed—to show Lady Agnes that he was worthy, that he could not be intimidated by her family. Even though they wanted to bury him in the garden and never speak of him again.

"Have you learned the sweet science?" Andrepont asked.

"Some," Jack said. "I've not fought in the ring, like you or Mr. Arthur." Jack rolled up his sleeves. To his horror, Andrepont removed his shirt entirely. He must not have been able to hide his discomfort.

"Come now," Andrepont said. "If we are to engage, then let us be honest about it. This is the most noble of sports, after all."

"Even if Mr. Egan writes it, doesn't make it true." Jack began to back up. There was no rhyme or reason as to why, but the urge to flee was becoming harder to tamp. There was a glitter in Andrepont's green eyes that was most disconcerting.

"Come now, I can move faster than that," his father said, not looking away from Mr. Arthur. They kept their shirts on, though Lorian and Vasily were still in the act of peeling.

"So let's make it fair. Peel," Andrepont demanded.

"No," Jack blurted immediately.

"Why not?"

"Because I don't care to. I'm not a pugilist, and this isn't a set mill. I won't be disrobing, thank you very much." Jack backed away as Andrepont advanced on him. The man was faster than Jack expected. He got a hold of Jack's shirt and tugged, managing to pull it free of Jack's breeches before Jack wriggled out of his grasp.

"James, leave it!" Kinsley shouted.

By now, the other men had stopped their own activities and turned to watch. Jack skittered backwards, Andrepont advanced. Time and again they danced around the ballroom, the expression on Andrepont's face morphing into a mask of rage as Jack twisted away.

"Oi, Andrepont!" Mr. Arthur yelled.

"James, enough," Lorian called.

Still Andrepont advanced. Finally Jack twisted, turning to run full force, but Andrepont got a hold of his shirt and pulled. Jack was able to keep the shirt on before letting the fabric tear as he separated himself.

"James!" Kinsley yelled.

"Get a hold of yourself, man," Lorian said.

Andrepont stopped, panting and glaring.

Jack shrugged his ripped shirt back over his shoulders. His hands shook, but he couldn't take his eyes off the man in front of him who looked at him with disdain.

The other men crowded Andrepont, but Jack put distance between them. "If you'll excuse me," he said, trying to keep the tremors out of his voice.

"Let him go," Kinsley intoned.

Lorian nodded his dismissal and Jack backed out of the room, into the hallway. Once in the darker recess, around the corner from the ballroom, Jack caught his breath. It should have felt like a schoolboy joke. Some kind of manly bonding moment, but it didn't. It felt far more sinister and personal.

His heart still pounded, and Jack realized his body was in that moment of fear where none of his senses worked quite right. Jittery energy coursed through his body, and he had no choice but to move. Wandering the darkened hallway without a candle was not a smart idea, so he grabbed one from a sconce and took a walk, hot wax spilling on his hand. Andrepont owed him at least that. In all his wanderings, everyone had said how horrible the father was and how this Andrepont was nothing like him. But was that completely true? The menace on the man's face had sent chills down Jack's spine.

There wasn't much to see in the long hallway, but no servants seemed to be about, so Jack started opening doors. It wasn't polite, but then again, neither was chasing your guest around trying to tear his clothes off. Unless, of course, there was an agreement to the effect.

He found a music room that resembled a rumpled study, complete with a desk, sherry cart, and piano.

There were books stacked high against an armchair near the hearth and music stacked high on the piano. It smelled of stale alcohol, and Jack could guess this was Andrepont's broody lair. Clearly, the maids didn't visit this room.

At the end of the hallway, Jack found two locked doors. Fortunately, Jack had once made an acquaintance who happened to be excellent with locks. It didn't speak well that Jack had thought to bring his lockpick set to a dinner party, but old habits die hard.

He picked the first door, and it swung open to reveal a study. A very dusty one. The maids hadn't entered this room in ages, either. It smelled of must and mildew. Tentatively, Jack entered the room, closing the door behind him. This must have been the study of the elder Andrepont.

So hated that his son didn't even enter the room. That must have been something. He edged in, letting the meager light of the candle guide his way. No doubt there were awful things hidden in here. If half of the things Jack had learned about the man were true, he'd want to set fire to the whole damn house.

The carpet was still lush, and his feet sank into the thick nap. No expense had been spared here. He got to the large desk. No papers were out. It had been cleaned after his death, then. Every surface was covered in a layer of dust, which meant anything Jack disturbed would be obvious. He slid open the first drawer to find an inkpot and an assortment of quill pens. Creamy high-quality paper sat at the ready in the next drawer, waiting for a powerful man's signature.

The one after that held a knife and pencils, whittled to fine points. More papers, these covered in unfinished studies of hands, feet, and even a bird.

The man had moved fast when he sketched, light lines hastily capturing what he saw.

Jack opened the last drawer. This must be the portfolio he'd been hired to find. It was bound by a dark red ribbon. Footsteps came down the hallway. A door opened and closed. Jack shoved the portfolio down the back of his breeches, letting his shirt spill over it. He hadn't had the time to tuck it in, and after that episode perhaps he wouldn't be expected. As he pulled his shirt back, the door swung open.

The flame from the candle made it impossible to hide his presence.

"What. Are You. Doing. In Here." Andrepont's voice was unmistakable.

"It isn't what it looks like," Jack said, holding up both hands. The candle flickered on the desk.

"It looks like you picked a lock and helped yourself to my father's desk." Andrepont called something unintelligible down the hallway. More feet thundered down the passage. "Don't make me come in after you."

There was a moment when Jack considered jumping out the window behind him. But, given that the window hadn't been opened in who knew how long, not to mention that his parents were here and it would give a terrible impression to Lady Agnes, Jack complied. As he approached the threshold, he heard Lady Agnes's voice.

"No, I don't believe you. He wouldn't." She gasped when Jack showed himself.

"See? There was something else he wanted. A man who works at a molly-house isn't interested in marriage." Lorian sounded smug.

Jack watched as Agnes crumpled inwards. He knew that she was returning to her invisible self, the one that didn't want to take up room, the one that had been sat upon when no one noticed her presence.

"That isn't true," Jack said. "Agnes, you must believe that everything I've said to you—"

"Dear God, stop talking. You gave up the right to defend yourself when you picked this lock." Andrepont looked murderous.

Kinsley closed his eyes, struggling to control his regret.

"Do we check his pockets?" Mr. Arthur asked.

"No need," Jack said, his heart ticking faster, the urge to run pushing him. "I left them all in the ballroom."

"Why is his shirt ripped?" Agnes asked, but no one answered.

His father stood at the edge of the crowd, slack-jawed. His disappointment was evident. Jack had never told his father that he stole outright. Sometimes. Not always. And never for things that would harm anyone.

The rest of the ladies came up behind them, chattering until they saw the men's faces and Jack's guilty mug. His mother's face shuttered in almost the same way Lady Agnes's had. It hit him square in the chest, as if Andrepont had managed to lay a punch on him.

"Get out," Andrepont said. "Vasily, please make sure he leaves without stealing the silver."

"James. What did you do to his clothes?" Everyone ignored Lady Agnes. His beautiful love, made invisible by her family. This was the cost of their protection. To keep her a child.

The big man handed Jack his waistcoat and coat. The rest dispersed up the stairs, with the exception of his parents, who were also escorted to the front hall. A carriage was waiting to take them home, but Vasily kept a grip on Jack's shoulder. "You'll not be going with them," he rumbled.

As his parents fled in the carriage, Jack felt the

weight of all he'd attempted—and failed—come down on him. "So this is where you beat me to death? Won't it look suspicious, out here in front of the house where anyone might see?"

"In the boxing gym. I saw who you were," the Russian said, his voice pitched low. "I understand now why my Lady Agnes liked you."

The use of *liked* instead of *likes* didn't escape Jack. He squirmed under the massive palm on his shoulder.

"I even understand why you live at a molly-house. These things I overlook. No problems. But why steal? Nothing of value is in that room."

"Nothing of value to *you*." Jack hated this night. He hated the dinner, the clothes, his parents, this man, Agnes's parents. He hated boxing and wine and most of all, himself. Why did he do this? He could have told Mr. Wycliff to sod off and damn the consequences. But no, Andrepont got the best of him, goaded him, made Jack *want* to take from him.

The Russian worked his massive jaw. "I have never seen Lady Agnes happier than with you. She deserves happiness. I am sorry you are not worthy."

Jack would have preferred the beating. Vasily let go of his shoulder, gently pushing him away. Jack stumbled down the steps. There were miles to go before he would arrive back at the Inn. How far he was from where he had woken up this morning. This morning he'd had a lady love, parents excited to meet future family, a life in front of him. Now, he had sketches shoved down the back of his breeches and nothing else. It was tempting to go straight to Mr. Wycliff to get paid for his loss, should Lorian send the magistrates.

But no, he needed to find a carafe of wine and find out exactly what had cost happiness. He kicked his way home, and by the time he had arrived, he wanted nothing more than to go to bed. Coming through the kitchen door, he was greeted by a laughing Mrs. Bettleton.

Mrs. Bettleton did not laugh. Not as far as Jack had ever experienced. But sitting at her elbow, grinning like a jackass, was the errand boy who had delivered his summons two weeks prior.

"You look terrible," Mrs. Bettleton said, giving her signature sour glare.

"Thanks. I feel like it, too. How is it upstairs?" Jack slumped on a stool—or at least tried to. The portfolio kept him sitting up straight.

"Slow night," Mrs. Bettleton shrugged. "Like it usually is when everyone leaves town."

The rich escaped town and their servants went with them. Only the lonely and the poor stayed put. Then why weren't the Lorians gone? They certainly owned a gaggle of country houses.

Not that it was any concern of his. "Then you won't mind if I nick this claret." Jack lifted the carafe over the small trays of food and left the kitchen with a single glass before Mrs. Bettleton could say one way or another.

He trudged up to his room, pouring a glass as he went. Epic bleeding disaster of an evening. Although he had to admit that he didn't bollocks up the evening entirely on his own. He did the large portion of bollocking, yes. However, it had been clear that Andrepont had been hoping to make his case for the permanent severing of ties with Lady Agnes.

In his room, he slid off his coat and waistcoat. Unknotting his cravat proved another crucible, and he was tempted to find a knife and slice it clean through. Fortunately, the knot yielded before drastic measures were required. He shucked his shoes, not bothering to take off and store the buckles. Yanking out the voluminous shirt, he pulled out the portfolio and threw it on the bed. He took down his breeches and stockings and garters and pissed and poured another glass of claret.

"You," Jack said, pointing at the portfolio with its red ribbon. "Let's see why you are so damned expensive." He sat on the bed and untied the ribbon, now creased into its tied configuration. He opened the heavy folder and stared in disbelief at the top sketch.

"Shit. On. Toast." It was hard to turn such a shit night worse, but it was possible.

❧ 18 ❧

Her father knocked on the door again. "Agnes, be reasonable."

"I'm exceedingly reasonable. Ask anyone." She sat in her shift next to the door. Sleep had not come for likely two days. Plenty of tears had. Her eyes were dry and itchy, and she hadn't exactly noted the time when her life fell apart.

"Requesting your dowry in order to move into a house alone is not reasonable. Open the door so we can discuss this."

"No." Agnes was not interested in opening the door. Or standing. Or dressing. She wanted a small life. A tiny, tiny one consisting of herself and a cook. Her dowry would be enough to sustain that—at least, with John's help it would.

"I'm told you haven't eaten today either."

Hadn't she? It was hard to tell. She felt like her mind was floating near her body, not precisely in her body.

"I have a tea tray here. Some lovely treats, including a pot de crème that I assure you is delectable." Her father was trying to bribe her.

Well. It wasn't as if pots de crème were growing on trees. Agnes staggered to her feet, somewhat dismayed that she did indeed stagger. She'd lost her suitor, her dignity, her pride, and her balance. She threw on a dressing gown and opened the door.

Her father stood there with a maid holding the tray in question. Agnes waved the tray in but left the door open so her father could make his own decisions. She wasn't good company, and he had been made aware of the fact.

"Agnes, you don't look yourself."

The maid placed the tray on the table in the sitting area, and Agnes followed like a moth to a flame. "Who do I look like, then?" She poured a fresh cup of steaming tea. It did look more appetizing than she'd thought it would. Two slabs of cheese, a thick piece of bread slathered in butter and honey, a scone with jam, and apricot halves accompanied the famous pot de crème. They were clearly trying to lure her out with food. At least they were being smart about it.

He sighed and sat across from her. She didn't want to look at him. What he'd said—that it had made sense Jack was there to steal something, that he couldn't have possibly liked Agnes for herself—it hurt. Her father would never intentionally say something so insulting, but his insistence made it sound as if there was nothing anyone would want Agnes for. That she was not worth the trouble in and of herself.

But she knew, *knew*, Jack thought she was special. He'd been so clear that her embroidery work, her charity work, her odd bits were endearing and loveable. That it didn't matter that she preferred to remain quiet, or wear men's work boots, or support a charity by creatively darning clothing. Jack said these were admirable traits. Desirable, even. He'd shown her a world where women could love women openly, live freely. There was more to that evening than her family was telling her. Jack's torn shirt had made that evident.

But then, as her family said, he'd prowled James's house, finding his way into a locked room. They said she was a means to an end for Jack. But James had checked the room, found the handprints on the desk, yet admitted that nothing appeared to be missing. So what happened?

The scone turned to ash in her mouth, but she dutifully kept chewing as her father watched her. She wanted to speak with Jack, but her family would never let her out of their sight.

"How about a new frock?" Her father suggested.

She looked at him as if he had asked her to go for a swim in the Thames. "Papa."

He looked baffled. The ache that had taken up residence in her chest shook her from the ribcage out. She put down the teacup with a clatter. "You've made it abundantly clear that I am but the passage of dowry to another person. Since you promised not to pressure me into marriage and that I might have my dowry for my own, then I want it. Since love is my requirement for marriage, and it is clear that I am not the kind of person that will be loved, then I see no reason to delay."

"Agnes, surely you know that I don't think you are unlovable." He put his hand out, hoping that she would reach out and grasp his, but she didn't. His hand wavered in the air before he gave up.

"You were suspicious of Jack from the instant you knew of him."

"Of course I was, and it bore fruit, did it not? One doesn't simply pick locked doors and rummage around in desks of dead viscounts."

There wasn't a retort to counter his logic. No savvy quip or tart return to make the situation change. Jack had disappeared from her life in a puff of air. Their great love affair extinguished. What she'd thought of as a raging inferno was nothing more than a single wick on a tallow candle, snuffed by a cold draft.

❦

THE ASSEMBLED BASKET WAS THE BEST HE COULD DO. Ink, beeswax candles, a length of ribbon, and the gold thread leftover from his waistcoat for his mother. A choice cut of beef, a dram of smuggled Irish whisky, and peppermint lozenges for his father. Jack knocked at the door given that it was a normal visiting hour and not the hour before the cock crowed.

The maid opened the door and ushered him in, giving him an odd look as she did so. Jack waited in the parlor for his mother, a strange and new development in their relationship. Perhaps that was how strained they were.

The parlor was not well used. The rug seemed threadbare compared to the luxury he had encountered at the Andrepont estate. It was almost obscene, the difference in wealth. The revelation of the portfolio had him reeling, and he'd spent a few days holed up in his room, not wanting to confront the conundrum before him. So he solved the simple problems first: apologizing to his mother.

His mother came down, hastily tapping at the pins in her hair. "This is unexpected."

Jack held out the basket.

She pawed through it, looking up at him with a genuine smile. "You didn't have to do this."

"But I did." The memory of the evening at the Andrepont household made his ears burn with shame hourly. "What I did was inexcusable, and it reflected poorly upon both you and Papa."

"He is already back out at sea, so he'll enjoy these

in a fortnight when he returns." His mother gestured for him to sit as she did the same. "I'm glad you came."

"I wasn't sure you would want to see me." A pit burned inside of him, both of flame and ice together.

She shook her head, opened her mouth to speak, and then shut it again. "I have so many things to say, and not one of them is advice you've ever asked for. And I don't think it's my place."

"I've done an excellent job mucking it all up, so at this point, any advice is welcome."

His mother sighed and rearranged her skirts. "Lady Agnes seemed like a very lovely girl."

The words made him well up with tears. Had he loved her? Yes, he really had. He would have given anything to be with her. But clearly, he couldn't. He couldn't help but be who he was.

"What exactly was your plan?"

The question set him back on his heels. "What do you mean?"

"Were you hoping to live as man and wife here in London? Were you going to falsify records and move to the Italian peninsula? Were you planning on running off to America?"

Jack blinked. He hadn't thought it through. Not really. He had wanted to wake up next to her. Bring her flowers. Chat with her over tea. Smell her. Tease her. Kiss her. To his mother, he shook his head.

"Does she know your secret?"

Jack nodded. "She does."

"You trusted her with that," his mother said.

"Of course."

"So did you think to live with her as a man or as a woman?"

"I don't know. You know how I feel. You know that—"

His mother held up a hand. "I know. And I've

respected that feeling inside of you. I understood that you couldn't live the life that an English girl should lead. But I also want to point out to you that you *have* made a choice."

"Pardon?" Jack felt it coming—a hammer blow that he wasn't ready to receive.

"You told me, many years ago, that you were both or perhaps neither. That you weren't a girl or a boy. Or perhaps a girl *and* a boy. And then you left. You didn't allow me to show you your options here at home."

The anger came rolling in like a tidal wave. "Roland threatened to—"

Another hand to quiet him. "I know what Roland said. But I am saying you chose to live as a man, to be known as a man, to work as a man. If you truly are neither, or perhaps both, you are still not living the life you told me you wanted."

It felt as if she'd stripped him bare and shoved him in the middle of the road. At that moment, the maid came in with a tray of tea. Jack looked away.

After the maid left, his mother poured them both tea. She sipped and waited as Jack struggled, his blood pounding so hard in his ears that he wouldn't be able to hear church bells ring the hour.

"You went to dinner as a man. You presented yourself to her family as a man."

Jack was on his feet, feeling once again like running. "How else am I supposed to present to those people? Do you think they would allow Lady Agnes to go traipsing off with some unknown young miss?"

"Like they would with some unknown young mister?" His mother sipped at her cup, watching him.

She was like that—pressuring only a little at a time, keeping the pot roiling but not boiling over. "I know you already have an opinion, so out with it.

What is it? What am I really? What have you figured out?"

She gave him a look that said that he was being overdramatic. And perhaps he was. But it felt good to be this angry. To be safe and be angry.

"I've known you all your life. I've watched you learn and grow and play. I think you present to the world as a man not because you are one, or feel like one. I believe you when you say that you feel like neither, or perhaps both. But I also know that you received praise when you looked like a man. When you rescued that baby from the soil pit, you were a boy hero. And later, when people needed food, you donned those breeches and dashed food all around the neighborhood."

The reminder of those incidents grated. Roland had accused him of trying to be heroic, of needing the praise to live. But he hadn't done it for the attention. He'd done it because it needed doing.

"The praise came when you were a boy. And I think this was the same feeling. That you would feel more accepted if you approached her family as a man, even if you wanted Lady Agnes to know you as you truly are."

All of this hurt in a way that he couldn't put words to. Tears formed in his eyes. Living wasn't supposed to be this hard. "Being a man is so much easier when I'm on my own. There are fewer dangers when you don trousers. That isn't my fault. And it shouldn't matter what I'm wearing. It shouldn't be so complicated."

"Isn't it?"

"No, it isn't. I love Lady Agnes. I want to be with Lady Agnes. That's it. The end."

"You love Lady Agnes, but you go snooping in her cousin's house in a very mysterious manner."

Jack crashed back down onto the stiff settee. He

hung his head in his hands. She didn't know the worst of it. "That. That part is complicated."

"It seems that all of it is complicated, then. I don't want to ask questions to which I don't wish to know the answers. But figure out what you want to happen with Lady Agnes. Figure out who you want to be with her. You can't merely hope for the best."

"Shouldn't love be enough?" Jack asked.

His mother gave him a smile that looked sad. "Love is never enough."

"It has to be enough." Jack stood and paced the room. "It has to be enough," he repeated. "Otherwise, why move across the world for it? Why fight for it? Why sacrifice for it?"

His mother bloomed right there in front of his eyes. It was a sight he had never seen before, didn't know that it was a feat that humans could perform. Her warmth and her wisdom and her love for him filled the room. "Indeed. And why tell the truth, if not for love?"

"ARE YOU OFFERING ME SHERRY?" AGNES ASKED John. Lydia already reclined with a glass of whisky.

"Whatever you'd like. If your tastes run to the exotic, I'll have a runner go out and fetch it." John put his hands on his hips. His mention of a runner made her think of Jack, and that made her sad.

"Agnes, for the love of all that is holy, have a drink. When else will you get to do this? Would you care for a cigar while we're here?" Lydia looked at Agnes like she was full of disdain, but Agnes could see her eyebrow arched low instead of high, and there was a dimple in her cheek, letting Agnes know that Lydia was in fact amused by the whole exchange.

"Don't offer up my cigars," John protested. "But, if

you wanted, I would give you one. Or a pipe for that matter."

"Thank you, no." Agnes wasn't about to add tobacco to a list of vices. She already had women, molly-houses, and men's work boots.

"Ugh," Lydia groaned. "Please do something wrong for once."

"Oh, was spending the night at a molly-house not enough for you?" Agnes asked.

There was a moment of silence. And then John started laughing.

"Don't you laugh at my sister's moment of shame," Lydia admonished her husband.

Lydia began to laugh as well. Was she that absurd? Were her dreams so very laughable? She drifted over to the sitting area in front of the hearth.

"I hear laughter. What a welcome sound." Pearl entered her brother's study. She'd opted to go up to the drawing room after dinner, no doubt hoping Agnes would join her and not carouse with John and Lydia. As Pearl came to sit, her expression changed as she saw Agnes.

"My trampled hopes are the cause of such laughter. And why wouldn't they be? Absurdity induces a veritable chuckle at the very least."

"Oh, Agnes, that's not why I'm laughing," Lydia managed, wiping her eyes. "I'm laughing because of all people—all people! Who would have guessed that I would have to retrieve you from a bender at a *molly-house*."

Her speech sent her into renewed peals of laughter.

"I do apologize," John said, sweeping into a half bow, but his formidable shoulders still shook with laughter.

Robards, the butler, knocked and entered. "Pardon the interruption, sir."

John straightened himself. "Yes, Robards. What is it?"

"You have visitors."

"At this hour?" Lydia sat up.

"Miss Abbott—"

"Who can be shown in no matter the hour," John interrupted.

"And a Mr. Townsend."

"Jack?" Agnes gasped. Her stomach plummeted. The dinner, which had been a light and flavorful fare, suddenly felt leaden and heavy.

"Would you prefer to leave?" John asked Agnes.

She shook her head. Whatever it was, she wanted to be near. Even for a moment. To catch a glimpse. Perhaps would she be able to see love in his face? Did he hurt like she hurt?

John gestured for Robards to fetch the guests. Pearl looked at Agnes, searching, no doubt, for some kind of resolve. But Agnes didn't have any resolve. All of it had leaked out with her tears over the past week.

Bess Abbott entered first, her face drawn and tight. She looked determined, as if she were going to square off with an opponent. Jack looked—well, Jack looked marvelous. He wore all black, as if to blend in with the night. His face was also all straight lines, tight and shuttered. He carried a beribboned portfolio under his arm. When they reached the middle of the room, they both stopped and waited. Jack lifted his head, searching her out.

The naked longing on his face when Agnes met his gaze was enough to fuel years of fantasies. Her family would never allow them to be together, but she could dream.

"I apologize for the intrusion, sir." Jack cleared his throat. It wasn't that he stammered, but it was that his voice was pitched low and solemn. Goodness knew that Agnes's blood suddenly felt cold and hot all at the same time.

"I trust this is important," John said, walking over to meet them on the thick carpet near his desk.

"Jack asked me along to make certain you'd grant an interview." Miss Abbott and John had a long and trusted friendship. Her word was truth, no matter what. Her folded arms and canted hip implied that John was the unreasonable one. Which Agnes would wholeheartedly agree—her family was wrong about Jack. She could feel it to the marrow. "Jack says he needs to see the family, that there is a misunderstanding, though he won't tell me what. But I believe him. Jack About Town is a good bloke."

"It's a matter of privacy," Jack said, shifting the portfolio under his arm. "Highly sensitive."

"And it's in there?" John pointed at the portfolio.

"Yes, but it isn't for you." Jack took a small step back. "It's for Mrs. Arthur. And her mother. And Lady Agnes. And perhaps a few others I do not recognize." Jack averted his gaze, as if he was ashamed to even speak the words.

Lydia rose from her seat. "Then perhaps Agnes and I may have a look in private. Mr. Townsend, would you mind leaving the portfolio on the desk? Pearl, why don't you escort everyone up to the drawing room. I'm sure between John's stash of liquors and Cook's pastries, we can offer something to our guests."

Agnes's throat went dry. She couldn't even stand. All she could do was watch Jack as he placed the portfolio on the desk. The length of a leg, the smoothness of his neck. He had a relatively low collar for the fashion of the day, and his cravat was tied in a simple low knot. This was a solemn affair, and he had dressed to match.

Pearl escorted everyone upstairs. John held Lydia's arm.

"Do you want me to stay?" he asked her, his eyes searching hers. Agnes ached to see their intimacy. The kind she could have with Jack if only her family would believe in her ability to know her own mind.

Lydia stretched her arm out behind her, reaching. Agnes rose to take her sister's hand. "I have Agnes."

"Ring for us when you are finished. I'd like to know the contents so that I may negotiate appropriately." John turned to leave.

"Negotiate?" Agnes asked.

John turned around. "For the blackmail. What else would it be?"

"Jack wouldn't ask for—" For what exactly? Is this what he'd found in James's house?

"Let's find out what it is, first." Lydia guided her to the desk. They waited for John to close the study door before she untied the dark red ribbon.

Her heart began to pound. She did not want to know what was inside this folio. She didn't want to see, for fear she would never unsee it. And for fear of knowing what was worth throwing away a future.

"Ready?" Lydia asked, but Agnes couldn't answer. Lydia exhaled slowly, a steadying breath that Agnes recognized as one Bess Abbott taught her boxing students. Agnes did her best to approximate it as well. Lydia opened the cover.

It was a collection of loose papers, pencil sketches, some redrawn carefully, others clearly studies. The first page was a portrait of Lydia as a child.

She was laughing, in her little girl dress, her face free and happy. On the same page, lower, was a closer sketch of her face, terrified. Though the sketch ended at the shoulders, it was clear that she was wearing a night rail.

Lydia flipped to the next page. The next one was a cleaned-up, redrawn pencil sketch. It was Lydia again, a grown man's hand around her throat. In the image, her night rail was bunched up, but the sketch made clear what was happening.

They turned the page. Another page of quick studies, this time of Agnes. She was even younger, hardly more than five years old. The artist had captured her babylike transition, her joy. The next page was her a few years older.

The next page was Lady Andrepont. The sketches showed her coldness, her aloof demeanor, but also a touch of sadness. On the first page, the sketches looked almost fae-like, otherworldly, as if her beauty was impossible to render in this world. The next page was her without clothes. Flesh splayed, her expression still detached, as if she weren't even in the room.

"I can't," Agnes said. "Stop."

Lydia was in a trance. She kept flipping the pages, seeing sketch after sketch of women, some they knew, some they didn't. Until finally, sketches of their mother. None of them nude. None of them in the violations depicted on earlier pages. But there were pages of her, and judging from the hairstyles, it went back years. Decades.

When Lydia reached the end of the sheaf, she turned it over, her child's face on top. She closed the portfolio and tied the ribbon. Only then did Agnes notice that her hands were shaking. Agnes felt sick.

Lydia gripped her hand again. This time, it was Agnes that led her over to the fireplace. They sat there, together, holding hands for a while. Her mind was all at once blank and whizzing with thoughts. What did this mean?

"Should we call for John?" Agnes finally asked, her voice trembling.

"Yes. We need to make a plan." Lydia's voice sounded distant and cold. "We need Margaret and James and Sebastian."

Agnes shook her head. "Margaret is married and lives in the country. Sebastian has made it clear he doesn't want to be involved. And James?" Her father had finally confessed their plan to scare Jack off with a boxing session that went awry. "I'm not sure James can behave."

Lydia shook her head, her eyes distant. Agnes knew she was reliving those feelings she'd had since childhood. A chill ran down Agnes's spine. The same moment had been waiting for her, had the viscount not died.

"Perhaps we should go join them in the drawing room," Agnes suggested, her teeth starting to chatter. This is what it was for Lydia, the need to control the fear in her body.

"No. Drawing rooms are for politeness and euphemisms. Studies are for business. Call them down," Lydia commanded.

Agnes rang for a footman who appeared instantly. Lydia said nothing as they waited. The other guests filed in. John's curiosity was obvious, as he pulled towards his desk until he saw his wife distraught.

Lydia lifted her head and stood. "Mr. Townsend. What is your price?"

Black eyebrows went up in surprise. "My price?"

"You've presented this as blackmail, have you not?" John said.

Agnes waited for the answer, knowing already Jack's heart. What happened to Lydia had not happened to her. And Jack would keep them safe.

"Of course not. I was paid to find this portfolio, and I knew nothing of its contents. When I discovered what it was, my immediate thought was to return it not to its original, deceased owner, but rather, to the victims of it." Jack sketched a nervous bow.

"Why." Lydia didn't ask, she demanded.

"Because it is depictions of predation. It is not for others to find, but for the victims to dispose of how they please. I would not dictate terms to anyone."

"But what of the person who paid you to find this? I assume someone alerted you to its existence." John's even-temperedness was extraordinary. He was negotiating, without emotion or pride. Agnes was impressed. She could see why Lydia relied on him.

"I have investigated the man again to see how he knew of such a thing and why it might surface now. I would be happy to share this with you or with Lord Lorian."

"My father?" Lydia asked. "Why him?"

Jack ducked his head. "Pardon me, my lady. While the sketches are all of women, and they should be in charge of their disposal, your father is the most powerful man in this circle. He has not only wealth but political power and connections that may aid in keeping such men in check."

"Very practical," John answered.

"So you ask for nothing in return?" Lydia asked.

Jack shook his head, though he looked miserable.

"Even asking for a boon at a later date is not a bad thing," Bess Abbott said, nudging Jack.

"If I were to ask a favor, it would be a moment to speak to Lady Agnes," Jack said. "But only if she were willing. And if she said no, I certainly would not renege." He gazed at her with such longing that she couldn't say no, even if she wanted to.

"With a chaperone," Lydia said sharply.

"Why not here, by the fire?" Agnes twisted her hands together. "Surely we can have a quiet chat while you make plans." Though she knew it wasn't possible, it felt as if her heart had stopped altogether.

Her body ceased to breathe or pump blood as Jack crossed the room, ever so slowly, to reach her. She sat in the settee and gestured to the chair next to her.

"My lady," he breathed.

"Jack." She'd never call him Mr. Townsend again.

"I can never apologize enough for my behavior at your cousin's house, though I do not regret discovering that vile portfolio so that I could deliver it to you and your family."

His words were far more formal than she'd hoped. He must have rehearsed this speech in the event that he might see her.

"My father told me of the boxing match. I'm so sorry."

Jack hung his head. "Andrepont—your cousin—he knew how to goad me."

Agnes missed his laughing cadence, his easy and congenial speech. The discussions that made her feel like there was a world where only two of them existed.

"Can you ever forgive me for not protecting you?" Agnes asked, hating that her voice was so small. She looked back over her shoulder at the crowd of people around John's desk. None of them so much as looked in her direction. "My family, they only want to protect me."

Jack's head snapped up. "I hate what your father said to you that night. The only reason I want to be with you is because I love you. There isn't a moment of the day where I do not think of how to make you sigh with contentment."

Agnes felt a hot lump form in her throat. Jack took her ungloved hand. He turned it over so that her hand was facing palm up. Slowly, reverently, he kissed the fleshy mound where her palm met her wrist.

"I've never lied to you, my lady."

"Jack," she whispered. "Why can't—" she didn't even know what she meant.

"Every bone in my body hurts when I think you might hate me. Every muscle strains against the idea that I might never see you again. I've never needed anyone before, Agnes. But I need you." Jack's eyes were shining, filled with unshed tears.

A wave of fierce need and protection came over Agnes. "I don't know how to be with you. How do we do this? I don't even know what a future could look like."

The slow, familiar grin that she had longed to see spread over Jack's face. "Does it matter? We make our own." He turned her hand over and kissed her knuckles. "I want to wake up in the morning curled around you. My hand will be the one that brushes your hair out of your eyes. I'll read to you while you embroider. We'll visit the Women's Home together, dropping off your donations. We'll live together, quietly or loudly, it does not matter. If you want me to live as a man, I will be a man. If you would be more comfortable if I were to appear a woman, I will. Whatever it takes so long as it means that I'll be with you."

Her hand dropped. "Jack, no."

His eyes shuttered and he dropped her hand. He looked as if she had hit him.

"Only, I can't tell you who to be. I want those things, but only if it is with you. I don't care what clothes you put on as long as it is you underneath."

"Even if it's both?" Jack asked.

"As long as you are you." Agnes picked up his hand. "Do you not understand? I love you—the you that helps other people in need. The clever one, the trickster one, the one who tells a joke instead of throwing a punch. And if that person wears a skirt, I love them. If that person wears a waistcoat, I love them."

"You would have me then?" Jack asked, his eyes wide and searching. Agnes had never seen him so vulnerable, so open, so needy.

"If you would have me."

Jack cradled her cheek, rubbing his rough thumb along her jaw. It felt like heaven. "Then how do we navigate your family? For I only know how to navigate the world."

"I don't think this is a good idea," Miss Persephone said, stifling a yawn. Wearing her red banyan, she stretched out on Jack's bed.

"Oh, I agree," Jack said, buttoning his waistcoat. "This is the worst idea."

"The public is not welcoming on this sort of thing. Take it from me." Miss Persephone sat up and stretched.

"At least it'll be easier to take a piss," Jack said.

"Fair point to you." Miss Persephone rearranged her banyan. "Dear Lord, is it early!"

"It's normal calling hours. A very reasonable time to request my presence." Jack brushed the beaver pelt hat. "Besides, they've sent a carriage for me. I can't exactly say no."

"But you don't have to—"

"I love her, Pers. I do."

Miss Persephone came fully awake, beaming. "*That's* why you're going in this hare-brained getup." She clapped her hands. "I love it. I *love* that you love her."

"And I have a plan." Jack carefully arranged his hat on his head, making sure that tendrils of hair emerged just so.

"I *love* that you have a plan." Miss Persephone squealed. "Don't even tell me. I don't want to know. But you must invite me to tea when it's all settled."

"That I can promise." Jack surveyed himself in the misty glass. He thought he'd be nervous. But he wasn't. He was calm. Ready. Prepared. "Wish me luck."

Miss Persephone enveloped him into a hug. "You don't need luck."

Jack went down to the kitchen, gave a nod to Mrs. Bettleton, and left through the kitchen garden. The carriage waited for him in the mews. This time, it was an unknown chauffeur driving—Vasily must have been busy.

Surely, if he were to get nervous, it would have been in the carriage on the way to face Lord Lorian.

When Jack arrived at the Lorian residence, the butler took his beaver skin hat and gloves. Trained to be stoic in service, the butler didn't even raise an eyebrow at Jack. He guided him upstairs to the drawing room. Once the butler announced him, Jack took a deep breath and stepped into the room.

This time he entered the presence of Lady Agnes exactly as he was. The way he'd always wished he could be. He could practically hear Agnes's smile split along her face. Lorian frowned at him for a moment and then shook his head. Lady Lorian looked as if she hadn't slept at all, and thus didn't register Jack's unusual appearance.

Mrs. Arthur raised an eyebrow but hid a smile behind her teacup. Mr. Arthur didn't look surprised at all. Vasily sat in the corner looking smug. It was Andrepont who spoke.

"Of all the strange things, I did not expect this." Andrepont put his hands on his slim hips.

Jack performed a bow. "My lady." He greeted Lady Lorian first, and then, in turn, the other ladies and then Lord Lorian and Andrepont, and lastly, Mr. Arthur and Vasily.

Agnes gestured to the chair near hers. He took it, arranging the long, plain gray skirt around himself.

"You wanted to see me be happy as myself. Well, this is what I would choose to wear if no one would look askance." Jack smoothed the embroidered waistcoat that hugged his body. He still banded his breasts, as he preferred that flat silhouette. The cravat was tied simply, in a male style. He'd had his coat tailored in the fashion of the times, nipped in at the waist and then flaring, and it worked very well with the skirt. It was unusual yes, but not daring, not really. It was comfortable and felt right.

"Ah," Lord Lorian stared at Jack. Leaning against the mantle as if he were in a position of relaxation, the earl ruffled his own hair, as if it might stimulate his mind.

"You may still call me Jack. Or Townsend."

Andrepont grunted. "Things are beginning to make more sense to me now."

"I knew you'd come around eventually," Lydia teased.

"But—" Lorian squinted. "You were courting my daughter."

"I still am," Jack said, maintaining clear and level eye contact with the out-of-sorts lord.

"But..."

There was a pause as everyone waited and thought through all scenarios.

"I love Lady Agnes, and I will do whatever it takes to be with her. If I needed to falsify church documents to marry her, I would have. If I must be her secretary for the rest of my life, I will do that."

"Congratulations, Papa," Agnes said. "I'll remain untouched by a man forever."

Lorian turned bright red, but Andrepont laughed.

"Agnes, don't be vulgar," Lady Lorian chastised.

Lorian cut his hand through the air. "Be that as it may, let's discuss the business at hand first."

Lady Lorian took notes in her florid hand as Jack detailed what he knew of Mr. Wycliff. Conveniently, he did leave out the persona of Lord Haverformore at the Inn and added that he would prefer the Inn to remain untouchable. They had nothing to do with sketches nor knowledge of them. Lorian agreed to the terms.

"It appears that Hackett hoped these sketches were in Lord Denby's possession. When they weren't, he began to ask around, which gave Mr. Wycliff the idea. No doubt Hackett would blackmail you, but Wycliff decided he would try to find them first." Jack had a contact in almost every kitchen, including Hackett's. The rest he found out through his contacts at the clubs.

Jack handed over a copy of Wycliff's address and business contacts, the bank he kept his meager funds in, the gentleman's club memberships. It was enough to quietly ruin him without being involved in a legal suit, which was better for all involved.

"Is that enough, Lydia?" Lorian asked.

She nodded. "We've taken care of our..." She hesitated. "Artwork. I'll ride out to Mrs. Miller later in the week to give her the remainder of the portraits. She'll recognize the other women."

"Mister...ah...er. Jack, this is most generous of you. You've saved us not only from a costly scheme but also a tremendous amount of turmoil." Lorian looked as if he didn't know whether to shake Jack's hand or kiss it.

"Papa?" Agnes asked. "Jack and I would very much like to ask for your blessing."

His face grew dark. "This is not how it works, Agnes."

Jack's heart sank. He had come wearing his truth on his sleeve, hoping it was enough for a future with Agnes. Hoping that Lorian might be different than Roland.

"There can be no marriage contract. Why can it not work like this?" Agnes pleaded.

"Contracts are there for legal protection, for permanence. I'm sorry to offend your sensibilities, but there is no guarantee that Jack will stay."

Lydia snorted. "There's no guarantee that any man will stay, contract or no."

"But the legal precedence for a widow is far greater than an unmarried woman." Lorian shot his elder daughter a look. Jack liked that Lydia seemed to be on his side.

"And why shouldn't Agnes be a widow?" Andrepont asked. He leaned against the bookcase and smiled a jackal's grin at Jack. "She deserves it."

⚭

THE FAMILY HAD NEVER EXPERIENCED THIS KIND OF intimacy. The evenings following the demise of the sketches had been ones for family gatherings. They did not speak of the past or the future. They ate and drank and reclined in each other's presence for the comfort of shared secrets, shared pain. At the Arthur's home, the babe's heavy exhale filled the study as she nuzzled further into the side of Lydia's neck. Lydia slid further down in the chair, letting the babe sleep to her content. Lydia's face radiated a happiness Agnes had never seen on her sister's face. Pearl practiced her stitching on a handkerchief near the fire, and Agnes's mother stared into the fire, holding a glass of sherry aloft.

John Arthur reclined against his desk next to James, both of them sipping whisky. Agnes sat near her father, in the chairs near the bookcases. Her father pretended to read through the day's newspaper. Lady Andrepont scanned the bookshelves, occasionally pulling out a tome and flipping pages. They were all sated with dinner and the triumph of Lydia's cook's patisserie skills. The taste of chocolate lingered, making the unusual, sleepy contentment they found in John Arthur's study, of all places, all the sweeter.

"You owe him, my lord," James said, his voice ringing in the quiet room. "And Agnes."

Lydia didn't even open her eyes, though Agnes was surprised enough to look at James. He'd been up late again. It could have been his worry over Lady Kinsley, or just his usual insomnia. He'd never confided in Agnes the way he had in Lydia or even Margaret.

"You haven't a clue what we owe," Lady Andrepont said without turning around.

That comment brought Lydia's gaze to bear and caused Pearl to stop stitching. "Then the first atonement you could make is to Agnes and her love."

"What atonement is there?" Their mama asked, her eyes still on the fire. She took a slow sip of her sherry.

"Let them marry," Pearl said quietly, as if she knew it wasn't her place to speak up. And it wasn't. But also, it was. Why shouldn't it be?

"Thank you, Pearl," Agnes murmured. Even if nothing could be done, to at least have some support made all the difference. She hadn't seen Jack in days. It was as if futility had taken over both of them. Being apart hurt, but being together hurt as well.

"Say the word and we all get what we want," James said. "Well, Agnes, Jack, and their parents, anyway. Not the rest of us sorry lots."

"Speak for yourself," John said, going to his wife

and sleeping child. "Some of us already have all we could ever hope for." He planted a kiss on Lydia's head.

Next to her, Lorian grumbled, turning newspaper pages. "And how do I get what I want?"

"You want assurances for Agnes, do you not?" Lydia asked. The challenge glittering in her eyes was matched only by James's.

Agnes felt the coalescing of something in the room, something woven by Lydia and James, and she had a feeling it might be for her benefit.

"Of course."

"The least I can do to make up for trying to beat her beloved is to make Agnes a proper widow." James pushed off John's desk and walked over to Agnes's papa. This time, his grin was wiped of all grim sarcasm. "Lydia and I already have it all worked out. We just need to send some letters tomorrow."

Lorian stared at James and then swung his gaze to Agnes, a question there.

She nodded. "Yes," she whispered.

"And Jack?" he asked.

She nodded again.

Finally, Lorian nodded an assent. "Do it. We all deserve happiness."

MISS PEARL ARTHUR'S AFTERNOON TEA WAS THE talk of the ambitious merchant class set. It even made a Society page announcement. Lydia rolled her eyes every time it was mentioned.

"Hold your tongue," Agnes told her sister.

The target was Miss Mathilda Perry. At the crowded tea, filled with respectable young misses, eager to climb the social ladder as the Arthurs had done, Agnes took Miss Perry aside.

"I've met someone," Agnes whispered over a teacup. Lydia had purposefully watered down the tea in the hopes that the event wouldn't last very long.

Miss Perry's eyes shone with delight at the gossip, just as Agnes had predicted. It wasn't hard to act excited and in love. She was both of those things.

"He's very mysterious."

"Tell me more!" Miss Perry was practically shaking.

With the idea planted of a mysterious Russian count who had come to town to explore London—related to their dear friend Vasily—Agnes swooned and left the tea. Her acting skills on swooning left much to be desired, but within minutes, Miss Perry told everyone in whispers that no doubt Lady Agnes was faking in order to meet up with a mysterious suitor.

Thus, the following week, when Vasily drove an elopement carriage to Gretna Green, it wasn't a great surprise in certain circles. Sources close to the family spoke of Lady Lorian's disappointment of her youngest daughter eloping with a man who would force Lady Agnes to relocate to a distant and forbidding land. Other than that, the unknown Russian count—he had been a baron the week before—was not only morally upright but devastatingly handsome.

Gossip papers distributed as far as the border detailed Lady Agnes's unexpected flight but wished her well.

By the time Agnes arrived at Gretna Green, she never wanted to see the inside of a carriage again. "Is this why we stopped going to the country?"

"No, but I can understand why you'd say that," her mother answered, stretching. "Let's find our rooms."

Jack had gone ahead days ago to book rooms. She

disliked not seeing him for so long, but she supposed it was how other couples experienced their upcoming nuptials.

Vasily stabled the horses while they found the inn. Jack was waiting in the public area and shot to his feet as soon as he saw them.

"My lady." Jack bowed, and the innkeeper was immediately alert.

Before long, they were hustled upstairs and assured refreshments. But it also meant she wasn't able to see Jack.

The next morning, after a terrible night's sleep, thrashing in a bed with her mother, Agnes prepared to be married. As Jack requested, she wore her sage-colored dress, on which she'd embroidered several different-hued green leaves draping down the bodice and skirt. Her mother surprised her with peridot hair combs to match her dress. For the first time in her life, Agnes felt beautiful. Not because others told her that her dress was beautiful, or because of her hair, but because she herself knew it.

Jack was already at the blacksmith's when they arrived. It was dark and dusty inside, and already the forge was hot.

"Such a crowd," the blacksmith muttered in his thick brogue. "It's a wonder you dinna want banns read."

৩৯৫

JACK HAD ALREADY SPOKEN TO THE BLACKSMITH, paid the exorbitant price, and sweated inside the forge with Lorian and Andrepont. He resisted the urge to triple-check with the earl that he still had the man's approval to marry his daughter, but even still, that wasn't quite right.

Because the man who was about to marry Lady Agnes was already scheduled to die.

"I bet there was a moment when you thought to yourself, 'I'd die for this woman,'" Andrepont said, leaning close enough to Jack that he could smell his sweat. "Bet you didn't think you would."

"You've an uncanny ability to read my mind," Jack said.

After Jack had apologized for invading the man's privacy and stealing from the desk of his long-hated and long-dead father, Andrepont became surprisingly friendly. It turned out that Andrepont had a cutting sense of humor, though had yet to apologize in so many words for trying to tear Jack's shirt from his body. Though Jack considered the wedding plot must be Andrepont's way of making amends.

Jack's parents entered the forge, his father sweating and red within seconds, but his mother beaming with pride.

When Lady Agnes entered the forge, wearing the green dress covered in leaves, Jack caught his breath. She held a nosegay of white flowers, and her skin practically glowed. He loved her, and the swelling he felt inside his chest made him feel like he would burst.

Once everyone was inside, dark and hot as it was, the blacksmith stared at the lot of them. Admittedly, having Jack's parents, Agnes's parents, Andrepont, and Vasily was an unusual number of people for an anvil wedding.

"Please," Jack nudged along the blacksmith.

"Fine," he brayed. The blacksmith was a strapping man, as one might expect of a blacksmith, with the red-tinged hair that one might expect from a Scot. "This is Lady Agnes Somerset? And you are, ach, surely, you canna expect me to say that ridiculous name."

"Count Vladimir Sergei Alexandrovich Nikita Odeyevsky? I assure you, it isn't ridiculous." Jack pulled himself up to full height, which still only got to the blacksmith's aromatic armpit.

"Fine," the blacksmith. "And yer him, are you now?"

"Yes," Jack said, taking Agnes's hands, hoping that the blacksmith wouldn't spot the absurdity that Jack couldn't resist.

"You don't look like a count," the blacksmith said.

Lorian flipped a coin over and it landed on the anvil. "It's hot in here man. Hurry it up."

The blacksmith shook his head, pocketed the coin, and began the ceremony.

◌⁂◌

AGNES FELT DRUNK. THEY'D TAKEN THE ENTIRE private dining hall at the inn and her father had provided sparkling wine. John had brought gin that he said was the best, and James had procured whisky from a very tall Scotsman.

But finally, they'd been allowed to leave as the rest caroused.

"It's our wedding night, my lady." Jack locked the door.

"You don't need to be so formal." She wondered how this would go. Should she be her pragmatic self and strip down to her shift?

"I don't say it to be formal. I say it because I like calling you mine." Jack approached her, almost dancing to her as he swayed closer. He kissed her knuckles. "My lady." He turned over her hand and kissed the fleshy part of her palm. The part that made her melt. "Mine."

"But Count Vladimir Sergei Alexandrovich—oh, I

forgot the rest." Agnes giggled. She actually giggled! She sounded ridiculous, but she didn't care.

Jack pulled her down to sit on the bed next to him. "That's fine," he whispered in her ear as he nipped at it. "If you shout 'oh God,' I'll know you mean me."

Agnes's brain didn't understand quite what he meant until he'd nestled himself on the floor between her thighs. He folded up her skirts, running his hands up the inner lengths of her legs to untie the green ribbons that held her silk stockings in place.

He rolled down her stockings, kissing the bare flesh as he went. "I missed you," he whispered. "I missed your taste."

"I missed yours," she said, already short of breath.

"I thought I wanted to go slow," he said, his breath coming fast, so close to her crux. "But now I find that I'm not sure I can bear it."

"We have all the time in the world." Agnes scrabbled at Jack's shoulders, wishing his clothes were already off, that she could expose him as he had exposed her.

"But there's only one wedding night," Jack said, nuzzling closer to the dark, wet heat of her.

Agnes squirmed, wanting him to touch her, lick her—something, not talk. "Then let's make it count."

She hauled him up to her and stripped off the waistcoat he wore. The trousers were discarded, and the linen shirt. Agnes tore the bandage from Jack's breasts. "Mine," she said, looking at the now-nude form of her beloved.

Agnes laid Jack down on the bed, lifted his knee to part him before her. She started rubbing slowly along Jack's slit, finding him already wet.

"Agnes, this is your wedding night," he panted.

"And it isn't yours?" she challenged.

Agnes lowered her face, licking so delicately at

Jack's hard nub that it wasn't long before Jack arched, his firm thighs clamping around Agnes's head.

When he relaxed, he flipped their positions, pushing Agnes to the bed. "That was very sneaky, my lady. Playing my desire against your own."

"I have my ways."

"But I brought a surprise. Every bride needs to be deflowered on her wedding night." Jack hopped up and rummaged through his luggage. He produced a leather case and brought it over to the bed.

Agnes propped herself up on her elbows to look, and as she did so, Jack pulled up her skirts again. His hand found her clitoris and started in lazy circles. It wasn't enough to make her cry out, but it was enough to make it hard to think.

"I brought this for you, my bride."

"Why thank you, Count Sergei—" When she got his name wrong, he pressed harder against her, enough to make her buck against his hand.

"Who am I?" he whispered.

"Count Alexander—" her mind was a fog of lust. He pressed harder, this time circling longer, and her desire surged.

"Try again."

"Count Vladimir," she panted.

"Good girl," he encouraged, but he didn't press harder.

"Do I not get a reward for getting it correct?" She whimpered, pressing up into his hand.

"Only if you finish."

"Finish what?" Agnes asked, feeling quite proud of herself for managing a double entendre under the circumstances.

"Exactly. Go on now. What's my name?" He pressed harder and she bucked. With the other hand, he opened the leather case to reveal a glass rod that was shaped unmistakably like the male member.

"What is that?" she asked.

"It is the count's magnificent member, which will deflower you so that under no circumstance could this marriage ever prove invalidated." Jack pushed his finger inside of her, letting the palm of his hand continue to work against her tender nub.

She groaned. "Oh God."

Jack leaned close and whispered in her ear. "Good girl. I told you that I would know when you meant me."

He glided the glass rod along his own slit, wetting it before placing it along hers. "Do you want this?"

She had never contemplated this kind of intimacy, but it was Jack. "If it's you, then yes."

He pushed in slowly, watching her closely as he did so, rubbing against her in hard circles until she bucked and arched and fell apart.

"My love," he whispered. "My only love."

❦

THE SAME GOSSIP SHEETS THAT HERALDED LADY Agnes's daring elopement were also the first to break the tragedy. After their hasty marriage in Gretna Green, the mysterious Russian count sailed for his homeland to prepare a house for his new bride, and whilst traveling, he was swept overboard. His body was never found.

Fortunately, the earl and countess, the lady's own parents, had followed the fleeing couple and were able to comfort their daughter during her fraught time. Society understood nothing quite so well as mourning.

They engaged a companion for their daughter, a Miss Jack Townsend, whose own family history of sea travel made her an ideal confidante for the now widowed lady. Rather than take the name of her foreign husband, the widow chose to remain styled as her lineage allowed, the Lady Agnes.

While it took time for a widow to procure the funds from a foreign land, she would at least have the comfort of her substantial dowry.

THE WORLD WORKED EXACTLY AS THEY'D HOPED. The years together, no one questioned them. They held hands in public, declared their love openly, and not one person thought anything extraordinary about it. Because women were incapable of not expressing emotion. It was, after all, only natural.

Jack continued to find, when called upon. With Lady Agnes's dowry, they were set well enough that Jack could help those in need, and not those in need of trinkets. The rich social life was not unusual in certain circles of Marylebone, and Lady Agnes became known as a connoisseur of artists. She could spot potential in an instant and guided others to aid investment in their efforts. Jack, of course, could spot fakery just as quickly.

Lady Agnes became known as a Grande Dame of the neighborhood, hosting the best luncheons and salons, organized by her personal live-in secretary, Miss Jack Townsend. Their arrangement was unusual, yes, but as a widow who had lost her beloved so soon after marrying, her tragedy would make her very attached to the person who came to her aid after such a trauma. Everyone said how lucky it was that Lady Agnes and Miss Townsend were to have found one another, and who were they to disagree with the world?

HISTORICAL NOTE

There have always been people, in every culture, that don't quite fit into the prescribed gender roles dictated by their culture. There are many, many examples of queer communities in and around the Regency era, and too many to go into any depth here. If you are interested in the topic, please refer to any number of resources, including Rictor Norton's research, easily found on the internet.

The things I have taken whole cloth from history include:

The Women's Home on Hog Lane was actually a workhouse for pregnant and "fallen" women, but it did exist on Hog Lane.

Mrs. Tyler's Boarding School was a real business, and I took the name as found in one of my research books when I was writing *A Lady's Revenge*. I have, however, made up the personality of Mrs. Tyler in this book.

Children falling into nightsoil and drowning in excrement was a real thing that did happen. Small children who were potty-trained to use outhouses would sometimes fall through the hole and drown in the vast nightsoil pits. Jack's initial foray into heroic works is absolutely founded in history, however, the vast majority of these efforts did not end so happily.

Molly-houses were popular and varied. Many of them had names that played at the double entendre, and many were catering to homosexual men and drag queens. Many, including the London club Bunch of Grapes, christened every man that entered with a female name. As mentioned by Jack in this book, different clubs had different levels of scandalous behavior. Some were very close to brothels, with a "marriage room" in the back rooms where couples could consummate a relationship. But others were coffeehouses, and in some instances, were private clubs held in personal homes. What makes The Cock and Prance different in this book is that it caters to all genders. I needed a place that showed the full gamut of acceptance. I don't know that these places did NOT exist, but I have also not found substantial proof that they did.

Women, given their stature in Society, did not have to hide their homosexual behavior as much as men did. As I wrote at the end, women were expected to be more "emotional" in that time period, and that their ardent love and affection for each other was seen as natural. Also, as the Regency time period had a dearth of young men, given so many decades of war, it was not unusual for women to become spinsters. There are many, many instances of women living together in this time period, in arrangements that may seem like very cozy roommates to past historians.

To read about people who have lived interesting and varied gendered lives, I recommend the book Female Husbands by Jen Manion. You can also follow my social media, as I sometimes post about my research. Another person with a fascinating social media presence who does mini book reports concerning gender expression, particularly in regards to fashion, is Alok Vaid-Menon. Another non-binary activist who promotes self-acceptance is Jeffrey Marsh, whose posts on self-love can sometime hit hard, in the way a good hug can.

ACKNOWLEDGMENTS

This is the third book, and at the risk of sounding completely repetitive in my thank yous, I'm going to say it all again.

Thank you to Fiona Jayde for the beautiful cover. Lady Agnes is on point. Thank you to Anya Kagan at Touchstone Editing for the developmental edit and wise advice. Thank you to Sarah Clark for the sensitivity read. And thank you to Signe Jorgenson for the copy editing. Writing and producing a book is a big job, and I appreciate you all working with me to make these people in my head come to life for others.

Thank you to my Street Team! I love hearing from you all, and I love the enthusiasm of you. Particularly, thank you to Kellie Dunn who will listen to me yammer on about thread color and webs of kinships of imaginary folk. Thank you to Stephanie MacDonald for after-bedtime walks. Thank you to my husband for taking bedtimes and cooking dinner so I can have zoom meetings and writing time on those busy days.

Thank you to my parents, for loving my kiddo. It's an easy job, but somebody has to do it.

And thank you to my kiddo, should you ever (learn to read) see this, you have taught me so much, and I have experienced so much joy in seeing you grow and learn. It is a humbling experience to be your mother, and I could not love you more.

ABOUT THE AUTHOR

Edie Cay writes feminist Regency Romance. Her debut, A Lady's Revenge, won the 2020 Golden Leaf Best First Book, Indie Next Generation Book Award, and was a finalist for the HOLT Medallion. The next in her series, The Boxer and the Blacksmith won the 2021 Best Indie Book Award, and is short-listed for the Chatelaine Book Award. Her award-winning series continues with A Lady's Finder. She obtained dual BAs in Creative Writing and in Music from Cal State East Bay, and her MFA in Creative Writing from University of Alaska Anchorage. She is a member of The Regency Fiction Writers, the Historical Novel Society, ALLi, and a founding member of Paper Lantern Writers. You can keep track of new releases by signing up for her newsletter, or following her on Instagram or Facebook, @authorediecay.

A Lady's Revenge (First in When the Blood is Up series)

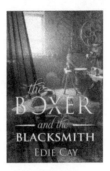

The Boxer and the Blacksmith (Second in When the Blood is Up series)

A Lady's Finder (Third in When the Blood is Up series)

CPSIA information can be obtained
at www.ICGtesting.com
Printed in the USA
BVHW072355090322
630953BV00001BA/8

9 781734 439755